This Real Night

By Rebecca West

Fiction

The Return of the Soldier
The Judge
Harriet Hume: A London Fantasy
War Nurse: The True Story of a Woman Who Lived,
Loved and Suffered on the Western Front
The Harsh Voice: Four Short Novels
The Thinking Reed
The Fountain Overflows
The Birds Fall Down

Non-fiction

Henry James
The Strange Necessity: Essays and Reviews
Ending in Earnest: A Literary Log
St. Augustine
Black Lamb and Grey Falcon: A Journey
through Yugoslavia
The Meaning of Treason
The Meaning of Treason, revised edition
A Train of Powder
The Court and the Castle: some treatments of a
recurrent theme

Books with David Low

Lions and Lambs
The Modern 'Rake's' Progress'

Rebecca West

This Real Night

VIKING

FIC

VIKING
Viking Penguin Inc.,
40 West 23rd Street,
New York, New York 10010, U.S.A.

First American edition
Published in 1985

LIBRARY OF CONGRESS CATALOGING IN PUBLICATION DATA
West, Rebecca, Dame, 1892–1983.
This real night.
I. Title.
PR6045.E8T5   1985   823'.912   84-40467
ISBN 0-670-80432-0

Printed in the United States of America
by R. R. Donnelley & Sons Company, Harrisonburg, Virginia
Set in Palatino

Publisher's Note

This Real Night is the second volume, complete in itself, of a trilogy of novels to which the author gave the overall working title of *Cousin Rosamund: A Saga of the Century*.

When Rebecca West published the first volume, *The Fountain Overflows*, in 1956, she had already written a further nine draft chapters of the saga. In the years that followed she worked on and expanded some of those chapters and they now form Part One of *This Real Night*. (An abridged version of the first chapter was published in *A Celebration* in 1977.) Part Two is taken from further original chapters and the book finishes at a dramatic point which, in terms of structure and narrative, falls naturally. Nothing has been added to Rebecca West's typescript but it has been necessary to make minor cuts to ensure continuity.

There remain additional chapters and it is planned to publish this unfinished volume in due course, together with the eight-page original synopsis of the whole saga.

Part One

I

THE DAY was so delightful that I wished one could live slowly as one can play music slowly. I was sitting with my two sisters, Cordelia and Mary, my twin, and our cousin, Rosamund, in the drawing-room of our house in Lovegrove, which is a suburb of South London, on a warm Saturday afternoon in late May, nearly fifty years ago. It was warm as high summer, and bars of sunshine lay honey-coloured across the floor, the air above them shimmering with motes; and bees droned about a purple branch of viburnum in a vase on the mantelpiece. We four girls were bathed in a sense of leisure we had never enjoyed before and were never to enjoy again, for we were going to leave school at the end of term, and we had passed all the examinations which were to give us the run of the adult world. We were as happy as escaped prisoners, for we had all hated being children. A pretence already existed in those days, and has grown stronger every year since then, that children do not belong to the same species as adults and have different kinds of perception and intelligence, which enable them to live a separate and satisfying life. This seemed to me then, and seems to me now, great nonsense. A child is an adult temporarily enduring conditions which exclude the possibility of happiness. When one is quite little one labours under just such physical and mental disabilities as might be inflicted by some dreadful accident or disease; but while the maimed and paralysed are pitied because they cannot walk and have to be carried about and cannot explain their needs or think clearly, nobody is sorry for babies, though they are always crying aloud their frustration and hurt pride. It is true that every year betters one's position and gives one more command over oneself, but

3

that only leads to a trap. One has to live in the adult world at a disadvantage, as member of a subject race who has to admit that there is some reason for his subjection. For grown-ups do know more than children, that cannot be denied; but that is not due to any real superiority, they simply know the lie of the land better, for no other reason than that they have lived longer. It is as if a number of people were set down in a desert, and some had compasses and some had not; and those who had compasses treated those who had not as their inferiors, scolding and mocking them with no regard for the injustice of the conditions, and at the same time guiding them, often kindly, to safety. I still believe childhood to be a horrible state of disequilibrium, and I think we four girls were not foolish in feeling a vast relief because we had reached the edge of the desert.

We sat in the sunlit room as much at ease as if we had been flowers instead of girls. Our teachers still set us homework, but our books lay unopened on the table. We might look at them while we were dressing on Monday morning, just to avoid unpleasantness. I was lying back in an armchair with my feet on another chair, because I never tired of contemplating the narrow tube of my new long skirt. Mary had put up her hair for the first time that afternoon; for the last few months she had had, like me, a cadogan, as it was called in those days, a plait doubled up and tied at the nape with a bow of broad moire ribbon, but now we were venturing on proper grown-up buns, which were far more difficult to tether. So she was sitting with a lapful of hairpins, a comb in one hand and a looking-glass in the other, every now and then shaking her head and bending her long white neck over her reflection to see if her black hair had stayed sleek. One sees swans shake their heads like this, and then glide on above their images on the smooth waters. Rosamund was sewing a flounced petticoat for the Bond Street shop which bought the fine underclothes she and her mother made; but even for her, who did everything slowly, even to speaking with a stammer, she was taking her time. Once in a while she laid down her needle and put out her arm to the tea-table, which in our laziness we had not cleared, and took a lump of sugar. While she crunched it she lay back and chose one of the heavy golden curls which flowed over her shoulders, and twisted it round her forefinger, perhaps to tighten the rich spiral, perhaps just to admire it. Cordelia was mending her stockings, bowing her red-gold head with the pious and unselfish air she brought to everything she did: a stranger would have thought the stockings belonged to someone else. But she was not really as bad as she seemed. Had she been asked she would have owned that they were hers. She was a humbug, but it was a physical rather than a mental quality. Whatever she was doing her body put up a claim that it was of great moral importance.

Today we four girls would seem so insipid as to be disgusting. Rosamund and Mary were beautiful, beautiful beyond argument, like women in Tennyson, with eyes larger and more liquid than the ordinary, and all colours extreme. Rosamund's hair the richest gold, Mary's skin quite white; and Cordelia, with her short red-gold curls and her skin flushed as by reflection from a rosy lamp, was as pretty as could be. And I myself was not too bad. I was nothing like so good as the others, but the behaviour of male strangers was now constantly giving me assurances that I was nice-looking enough. If I went to the bank for Mamma with a cheque to cash the clerks seemed to wish that the business of giving me the money had been more of an effort than it could be made to appear, more of a testimony of their good will towards me. We liked this, and did not like it. We wished we were growing up into something other than women. It was true that the development of our figures made us look like some of the best statues, but that could do us no good, as there was nowhere we could live where we could go about without anything on or in Greek dress, and as it was it simply meant that our blouses and our bodices were more difficult to fit. As for the other consequences of our sex, fatuous was the word we most often used. We were all of us infuriated except Rosamund, who could accept any physical fact. Our robust health prevented them from being anything worse than an inconvenience to us, but it was fatuous, yes, fatuous, that we were to be so greatly and constantly inconvenienced because some time, years ahead, we might have children, which was indeed most unlikely. We grimly supposed we knew what marriage was. My father had recently left us; he had not died, he had deserted us, not from cruelty, we were sure, but because he could not do us any good by staying with us. He was a gambler, and my mother had had to fight continuously, like an infantry soldier in the kind of battles waged in those days, to keep a roof over

5

our heads and food in our mouths. Rosamund's father was a malevolent eccentric, a successful business man who was so averse to spending money except in the investigation of spiritualist mediums that she and her mother, Mamma's Cousin Constance, had had to seek refuge with us. We realised that our experience was not typical, for certainly some people seemed to have reliable fathers. The homes of our school-fellows often startled and pleased us by their air of stability, which plainly proceeded not only from their mothers but from the kind and sensible men who came in just after we had finished tea. But we doubted if these good Papas were not so by default. Our father had gambled, Rosamund's father wasted his time and money sitting in the dark accosting the dead who were not there, because both of them disliked this world and were leaning out into that other world, the existence of which we are told to believe may exist by the half-hints dropped by chance and the supernatural; and they both knew a great deal about the world, for my father was a genius among writers and Cousin Jock was a considerable musician. It appeared possible that these other men were good fathers only because they knew too little of the world to grow frenzied against it. Also, though we despised Rosamund's Papa, we deeply loved our own, and we knew that Mamma had bought with her misery an unhappy happiness which was greater than the ordinary kind. But this made us still more determined not to marry. She had committed herself to this marriage without knowing what it was going to cost her. If we who had seen her pay the price condemned ourselves to such misery, even for the same reward, there would be something suicidal about it, and that would be contrary to the desire to go on living which was her chief characteristic.

Indeed, marriage was to us a descent into a crypt where, by the tremulous light of smoking torches, there was celebrated a glorious rite of a sacrificial nature. Of course it was beautiful, we saw that. But we meant to stay in the sunlight, and we knew no end which we could serve by offering ourselves up as a sacrifice. We therefore wanted to go along the straight lines which seemed to run from our bodies to the horizon, keeping above ground all the way. Mary and I were all right. Throughout our childhood we had said we would be, and we were. We had been brought up to be concert pianists, like our mother, and now Mary had got a scholarship at the Prince

Albert College in South Kensington and I had one at the Athenaeum in the Marylebone Road. Rosamund was all right, too. After the holidays she was going as a probationer to a children's hospital in an eastern suburb of London; and she wanted to be a nurse as much as we wanted to be pianists. She sat and thought of wards and out-patient departments and bandages and uniforms with quiet, reflective greed, just as she crunched lumps of sugar. We were not sure exactly how Cordelia was going to be all right, though we knew she would be. Ever since she was quite little she had wanted to be a violinist, but she had played as people do in tea-shops; she really did not understand anything about music at all. Not long before it had been brutally revealed to her that she had no talent; but she had stood the shock so well that obviously she could not be defeated. Mary and I were astonished, all our lives we had been sickened by the glycerine flow of her playing, and now we found her behaving as she should have played, and showing as much vigour as any of us; and vigour was what we esteemed. The world was full of opportunities, and one required vigour to seize them, and if one seized them, one would be all right, one would be quite all right. Our reactions to life were so natural that, as I look back on us, we do not seem natural at all. We might have been four brightly painted robots.

Then something very agreeable happened. Richard Quin, our schoolboy brother, ran in from the garden to say that the tulips we had planted had come out at last, and he was going to fetch Mamma to see them. Cordelia, who never believed that anything our family did could succeed, exclaimed, 'What, have they really come up?', and Mary and I answered fiercely, as if more than tulips were involved, that most certainly they had done that, we had been watching the green buds for days. Rosamund followed us down the iron steps into the garden, rather clumsily, because she was so very tall. Then Mamma and Richard Quin came out and we all stood by the round flower-bed on the lawn, looking down on the twenty-four tulips, twelve red and twelve yellow, and the thirty-six wallflower plants which surrounded them, and we felt deep emotion. They were a sign that we had broken a long enchantment. For the first time we were quite sure that we were able to do the things that other people could do as a matter of course. Our garden had always been pretty, for its many lilacs and syringas, and the chestnut-grove at the end of the lawn, had been planted by some dead owner as if he were setting a scene in a play; but there had never been any flowers in the beds except some old rose-bushes and irises which were no more than clumps of leaves. It had had to be like that so long as Papa was at home and was gambling everything away. Plants and bulbs were very cheap in those days, but while he was with us we could not bring ourselves to buy anything not strictly necessary. In our worst times Mamma had been down to our last shilling, and our better times never lasted so long that we forgot our fear of going over the edge of the cliff. Any spare money we ever collected we spent on going to concerts and theatres and the places which we ranked with these, like Kew Gardens and Hampton Court. There was therefore a very simple reason why we had no flowers in our garden: we had not the money to pay for them. But the poor hate to admit that they are slaves to their poverty, and invent mystical explanations for their lack of freedom. So we said to ourselves that it was a queer thing, flowers would not grow in our garden.

Then, the previous autumn Papa left us, and Mamma sold some pictures which she had known were valuable but had pretended were not, so that she could provide for us in just such an emergency as this, which she had, of course, always foreseen. Suddenly we were, so far as money was concerned, all right, or nearly so. And one day Cordelia and Mary and Richard Quin and I had gone to a nursery garden on the edge of Lovegrove, and had ordered some bedding-plants to be delivered in the New Year and had taken away some hyacinths and tulip bulbs to be planted at once. We had kept the enterprise a secret from Mamma, and that had been just as well, for the hyacinths had never come up. We had hated that, for it was fuel to Cordelia's flame. But there the other flowers were, a small but complete victory. The scarlet and gold tulips rose from a circle of wallflowers far better than their descendants are today, for the growers had not then injected them with reds and yellows, and they were then a deep and tender brown, the brown of brown eyes; and we stood there lapped in satisfaction.

'Oh, the scent, the scent of those wallflowers,' said Mamma, her voice girlish, though she was so old and thin and worn. She was not our mother but our sister, as she always was when she felt great pleasure.

8

I put my arm round her waist, and marvelled again over what we all felt to be oddity in our relationship with her. We were now all taller than she was, and we could look down on her protectively, as she had looked down on us only a short time before. We were as amused at this as if it had never happened in any other family. I would have been very happy, had not happiness always brought me its opposite at that time. Mamma had now enough money, all of us girls were sure of our futures, and Richard Quin would always be able to look after himself. We could now grow flowers like other people, and do anything they could. But it had not been so until Papa went away, and it was as if we had got these things in exchange for him. I wished I could make it clear to God that I was ready to do without them for ever if only Papa would come back to us. But my grief at the loss of him was already not as acute as it had been. But that was another grief, for it proved me callous. Yet I took advantage of my callousness, I looked at the tulips and listened to what the others were saying, knowing that I would soon forget to think of Papa; and so I did.

'We must give each other bulbs and plants for Christmas and birthday presents,' Mary was saying, 'and then we can fill up the other beds.'

Cordelia said, 'We will be quite old before we have enough Christmases and birthdays for that,' but she was happy, too, she spoke her bitter words without bitterness.

'No, dears,' said Mamma, 'you need not charge yourselves with that; of course we must be careful until you are all settled, but even as it is I can afford to set aside something for the garden.'

She had been poor for so long that even when she said she had money for something it sounded as though she were afraid that she had not. We faintly felt Richard Quin to be a little brutal when he said, 'Then make it enough to run to a jobbing gardener once a month, instead of waiting to call him in until the tradesmen have to hack their way in with axes – with machetes—'

'With franciscs,' I said.

'What nonsense you children talk,' said Mamma. 'What are franciscs, in Heaven's name?'

'Think, Mamma, think,' I said, 'you do not come to school to have your heads crammed with facts, you come to school to learn how to think—'

'How I hate that one,' said Richard Quin.

'What, do they say that in boys' schools, too?' asked Mary.

'Of course, there is a sort of very low thieves' slang, do not use it in the house, common to both men and women teachers,' said Richard Quin.

'A francisc is a battle-axe used by the Franks,' I explained. 'If you had only thought for a moment, dear Mamma. . . .'

'Barongs,' said Mary, 'I hope the tradesmen use barongs. They make such a nice sound as they cut through the weeds, barongg, baronggg.'

'The tradesmen use machetes, I tell you,' said Richard Quin. 'They bring "a dozen machetes to minch the whale".' That was in a book of Elizabethan travels we had liked. He went on, 'Yes, Mamma, I know you think it is a good thing to get your pallid children into the open air—'

'All grown-ups feel that children ought to be brought up as merry peasants,' said Mary.

'I wonder if Weber invented that expression,' said Mamma. 'I always like to see it in the cast of *Der Freischütz*.'

'Mamma,' said Richard Quin, 'let us stick to the point. I cannot mow the lawn regularly, if I am to play all the cricket and tennis I should, as well as pass my Matric at more or less the proper time, and Cordelia is not strong enough since her illness, and when Mary and Rose do it nothing is gained except that one sees how a lawn looks when it has been mowed by two gifted young pianists who think of nothing but their art. You really should try to look at it from the lawn's point of view.'

'The poor lawn,' said Mamma, 'like a woman who goes to an incompetent hairdresser.'

Our laughter was more than the little joke was worth. But we were very happy. I was standing between Mary and Rosamund now, our arms were enlaced, we swayed as though we were light as branches and the wind could move us.

'Dear me,' sighed Mamma, 'it is so many years since I went to a hairdresser.'

'Well, go,' we all incited her, very assured about this matter, because we had just begun to go to hairdressers instead of washing our hair at home. 'There is no reason why you should not. Silly Mamma, of course you should have your hair done like other Mammas.'

'No, no, children,' she objected, poverty claiming her again.

10

'It would be a waste of money. I am old now, and it does not matter how I look, and it is so easy to twist it up myself. . . .'

'Not half so easy as you suppose, Mamma,' said Richard Quin.

'I am having my hair cut tomorrow morning,' said Cordelia. 'I will make an appointment for you.'

'Why did we never think of this before?' marvelled Mary.

'You and the lawn,' I said, 'the proper people will attend to you and you will both be beautiful.'

'No, lawns renew themselves,' she said, 'and Mammas do not.'

'Never mind, other Mammas believe they renew themselves by going to the hairdresser, and you can too if you try,' said Richard. 'And anyway you are perfect.'

'Ponce de Leon, court hairdresser,' said Mamma. 'Oh, how sweet these wallflowers smell, it is a wonderful scent, so heavy and yet so fresh.'

'Such a pity the hyacinths did not come up,' I said, 'they have an even richer scent.'

'Why do you speak of it? We planted them the wrong way, of course,' said Cordelia. But again she spoke without bitterness, it was simply that she could not break her habit of depreciating everything we did. Her head was thrown back and she was smiling at the sunshine. 'Sand. I read somewhere that one should always put sand under bulbs.'

'The man at the market garden said nothing about sand,' said Mary, but without passion. Today we would not quarrel.

'It was so small a purchase he would not bother to tell us,' said Cordelia, but she was still smiling.

'I know why the hyacinths did not come up and the tulips did,' said Richard Quin. 'We planted the hyacinths, and Rosamund planted the tulips.'

'Of course,' we exclaimed, 'that would be it.'

'No, no,' stammered Rosamund. 'It cannot have been that. Planting a bulb is quite simple. You just put it in the ground, and it comes up.'

'Nothing is quite as simple as that,' said Mamma. 'Oh, the scent, the scent, it comes in waves.'

It was then, I remember, that my happiness became ecstatic, that I felt again impatience because one cannot live slowly as one can play music slowly. Yet what was happening was the vaguest possible event, a matter of faint smiles and semi-tones

11

of tenderness. A woman in late middle-age, four young girls and a schoolboy were looking at two common sorts of flowers and were not so much talking as handing amiable words from one to another, like children passing round a box of chocolates. I could not imagine why the blood should sing in my ears and I should feel that this was the sort of thing that music was about. But the moment passed before I could explain its importance to myself, for someone called from the house, and we looked round irritably, angry because our closed circle was broken.

But it was Mr Morpurgo, and of course we never minded him. He was Papa's old friend, who had always looked after him, even when Papa had behaved to him so strangely that they could not meet again, who had made him editor of the local newspaper in Lovegrove. We had never seen Mr Morpurgo till Papa went away, but since then he had often visited Mamma and had given her great help in restoring her affairs to order; and our impoverished childhood had given us a certain connoisseurship which appreciated the care he took to intimate that he was kind, not because he was sorry for us but because he liked us, particularly Mamma. He came across the lawn with the hesitation we had learned to expect of him. First he sent us a bright smile across the distance, then his face darkened and his step wavered, as if he could hardly bear to present his body to people whom his mind found attractive. He was indeed a very ugly man. His mournful face was sallow, his immense black eye-balls rolled too loosely in their bluish whites, and the pouches under his eyes drooped down to his cheeks, which drooped down towards his drooping chins; and under his beautiful neat clothes his little body was sagging confusion, as if an umbrella with all its ribs broken had been tied up to make a bundle. But we no longer thought of his appearance as a departure from the normal, rather we took it as a sign that he belonged to a species sweeter and more subtle than ordinary humanity: that he was not Mr Morpurgo but a morpurgo, as he might have been a moose or an ant-eater, and that that was a good thing to be.

Mamma exclaimed, 'How good that you have come back! Your secretary frightened us by writing that he did not know how long you were going to stay on the Continent.' As he took her hand she gazed at him with concern, and indeed he was very yellow and mournful, even for him. 'But how ill you look!

12

I know what it is. You have been staying in some place where they cooked everything in oil!'

He repeated, 'Where they cooked everything in oil?' For an instant he kept an awestricken silence. 'How strange it is that you should have guessed that! Yes, they certainly cooked in oil. It was a harsh coast, and they were disobliging people. If they had had all the butter in the world, and all the lard too, they would have sent away for oil, and if it had been delivered to them fresh they would have kept it till it went rancid, just to have the right disgusting fumes pouring out of their disgusting kitchens into their disgusting alleys. But I am unfair. They were simple people and meant no harm. The fault lay in the business which took me among them. It gave me,' he said, looking piteously at Mamma, 'a horror of the place. But at least it was all over sooner than I had expected, and it is quite at an end. So now we will forget it. There is no point in not forgetting it,' he told himself peevishly. 'So I have tried to find some distraction in bringing the Aubrey family some flowers, and I find them looking at their own flowers, which are more beautiful than any I could bring you.'

'You are laughing at us,' said Cordelia.

'No, I am speaking the plain truth,' said Mr Morpurgo. 'You will not hear from me any humbug about crusts being better than caviare, in any department of life. Clare, your children will only be building up disappointments for themselves if they do not realise that as a general rule costly things are far, far nicer than cheap ones. This is true in a garden as in anywhere else. The superiority of orchids to Virginia stock is so great that you would have to degrade your minds not to perceive it. All the same, it is true that nobody can bring a friend flowers more beautiful than that friend has in his own garden, for the reason that a growing flower has an iridescence which a cut flower loses in an hour. Your tulips have a light on their petals which the ones I have brought you must have lost on the journey, and if you look inside you will see a powder on the anthers and the stamens' – we were afraid he was going to pick one to show us, but of course he did not – 'which started to drop off mine while the gardeners were carrying them up to the house. So I have brought you flowers that are not as good as those you have already, and I have done something else that is wrong. I have brought you too many. Look at my chauffeur, standing at your window, carrying twice his own weight in carnations and tulips and orchids, his controlled Gentile face taking care not to show his opinion of my excess. And there are more in the car. I always overdo things,' he complained, looking round for sympathy.

We had never heard him make so long a speech, and his querulousness sounded as if he were talking to prevent himself from doing whatever it was that men do instead of bursting into tears. We gathered closer to him, and Mary said, 'But we like that. You can't bear the idea of there being only one of anything nice, and the further you get from that stingy number the better you are pleased.'

'But this time it is going to be inconvenient,' grumbled Mr Morpurgo. 'Your poor Kate will be looking everywhere for flower vases. I will go and buy some.'

'No, no,' begged Mamma. 'You will buy far too many'.

'You see!' said Mr Morpurgo. 'You know what I am.'

'Come indoors and sit down quietly and have some tea while the children put the flowers in what they can find,' said Mamma. 'Really, Edgar, I am worried about you. To be troubled because you think you have brought too many flowers – too many flowers! – it is quite absurd. You must be ill. I tell you, it is all that cooking in oil. But we will find you some plain biscuits for tea.'

So Mr Morpurgo huddled in the biggest armchair, looking as if he were much in the wrong, while we fetched vases and jugs and ewers, and filled them with his prodigious flowers until Mamma said, 'Now it looks like fairyland,' and he sighed, 'No, it does not, it looks like a flower-show.' Then he took an envelope from his pocket. 'Please read this letter from my wife,' he said, and when she had taken it from him he smiled, as if glad to remember that in one respect the world was going his way.

But my mother soon laid down the letter and said, 'It is very kind of your wife to say she wishes to know me. It is really extraordinarily kind of her, particularly at such a time as this, when she has just come back from Pau, and must have so much to do. But I would never think of intruding on her. She must have so many friends, and it must be pure kindness which makes her invite me. She cannot possibly have any real desire to meet anybody as uninteresting as myself.'

'Nonsense,' said Mr Morpurgo, 'you were a celebrated pianist, and you are a remarkable woman. Also,' he added,

14

'you are the wife of an old and dear friend of mine. Of course my wife wants to know you. If she did not she would be stupid, and very distant from me, and she is not that. She is very intelligent, and very handsome, and very impulsive and warm-hearted.'

'It is natural that your wife should be all those things,' said Mamma. 'Still, she is being far too kind. Why, she says she wants all of us. But we are such a troop! And Richard Quin is only a schoolboy, he is far too young to go out yet.'

'No, no,' said Mr Morpurgo, 'you must all come. For one thing, it is absurd that you should none of you have ever been to my house.'

'But we have,' said Mamma.

'No, never,' said Mr Morpurgo. 'Oh, I see what you mean. But that house in Eaton Place is not mine. It belonged to an uncle of mine who died some years ago, and my uncles and my cousins and I thought it saved trouble to keep it on. It is very handy when one or other of us want to close his town house, as it happened to me this winter, or if any of our relations from Paris or Berlin or Tangier turn up. Though as to that,' he said, with the stern yet self-gratulatory air of a man who has struck on a thrifty notion, 'the new Ritz Hotel is so pleasant that a suite there will really do them just as well. But my own house is quite a different matter. Look at the heading of the letter. I would like you all to see it, and never mind about Richard's age. I want the whole of your family to meet the whole of mine, and anyway I don't think he is more than a month or two younger than my Stephanie. If she is at luncheon there is no reason why he should not be there too. It may be a little dull for him but I hope Richard Quin will put up with that for once, to please me.'

Richard Quin sat back on his haunches, yellow tulips strewn all round him, and smiled brilliantly. 'I would do anything to please you.' It was not humbug. He liked pleasing people as much as he liked playing games.

'It is important that he should be there,' said Mr Morpurgo over his head to Mamma, with a mystical air. 'Have you thought of it, he is the only son in both our families? Oh, do not look so doubtful about the whole occasion. All things are in order, or I would not have brought you the invitation. My wife and I talked it over last night. She and my girls and their governess have been away at Pau for the last six months to be

15

with her mother, who has asthma, and lives there now. She came back for twenty-four hours to tell me that her mother was better and that she intended to bring the whole party home in ten days' time.' He laughed. 'I told you she was impulsive. She could not wait to tell me the news, she said that she felt suddenly that she must see me, and there she was. And now she is off again. How much I like it when she and my girls are back! To be with one's wife and children and to entertain one's friends, there can be nothing better. And you are the very first guests we will entertain. Well, I must go, and we will all see each other a fortnight from today. I chose a Saturday so that there could be no question of school for any of your young people.' He rose, smiling, as if he had something pleasant to think of and wanted to hurry off and enjoy it all by himself. His black eyes, bright with their secret, fell on a heap of red carnations which Mary had laid on a tray, and his plump fingers shuffled among them till he found one of the more splendid flowers, broke its juicy stalk, and put it in his buttonhole. But he looked down on the dark rosette and grew sad again. 'When things go well,' he said apologetically to Mamma, 'one cannot help feeling cheerful.'

'Why not?' said Mamma.

He hesitated. 'Surely it's a kind of treachery', he said, 'to all the things that haven't gone well.'

'Such a ridiculous idea would never have come into your head,' said Mamma, 'if it had not been for all that cooking in oil.'

Mary soon found an excuse for not going with us, I thought rather unscrupulously, by converting what had been a vague suggestion into a firm promise and then pressing on one of Mamma's most sensitive points. We all knew perfectly well which day we were going to Mr Morpurgo's house, but Mamma did not mention the exact date till some time had passed, and then Mary started and exclaimed, 'The tenth! Well, Mamma, you must tell Mrs Bates that I cannot play at the St Jude's Charity Concert that afternoon.' At once Mamma replied, as Mary had known she would, 'What! Is that the same day? Can you get back in time? No, I suppose you cannot. Well, you cannot break a promise to play just to keep a social engagement. You must never, never do that. What a pity! I will write at once to the Morpurgos.'

I kicked Mary under the table, quite viciously, for we carried

16

on a permanent quarrel over this issue of going out into the adult world. Mary thought that the people we would meet there would be just as tiresome as the girls and the teachers at school in Lovegrove, and that we should make up our minds to have nothing to do with them except play to them at concerts. There would be a few nice ones, just as at school there was Ida, who meant to be a doctor and had a mother who played Brahms quite well, but we would get to know these people anyway, they would be on the outside like us. And anyway, Mary said, we need not fear loneliness, for there were enough of us at home to give us all the companionship we needed. We were numerically quite strong. Now that Rosamund and her mother, Constance, were living with us for good, we were eight, including Kate our servant, who was completely one of us; and nine, if we counted Mr Morpurgo, and he seemed to have joined us; and if Papa came back we would be ten. What did we want with anybody else, Mary asked. But I held that it must be worth while exploring the territory outside Lovegrove because there must be people who were like the characters in books and plays. Authors could not just have made them up out of nothing at all.

This luncheon-party had raised this hope of mine in a most attractive form. It seemed certain that Mrs Morpurgo must be kind and noble, for her husband said she was beautiful, and no beautiful woman would have married such an ugly man, had she not valued goodness above everything. We were very fond of George du Maurier's novels, and of *Peter Ibbetson* specially, ~~Trilby~~ and I saw Mrs Morpurgo as the saintly and gigantic Duchess of Towers. She would be a little different; because she was a Jewess her hair would be black and not copper-brown, as du Maurier says that the Duchess's was. But like Mary Towers and all the great ladies du Maurier drew, she would be very tall, and would lean slightly forward, her brows clouded with a concern which was not irritable but tender, provoked by fear that since she was so tall she might have overlooked some opportunity for kindness. I thought Mary a fool for throwing away her chance of meeting this splendid person, and I told her so on the day of the party while she was doing up the buttons at the back of my best blouse. But when she had finished and I faced her I saw she was looking cold and fierce and this was a sign that she was afraid. She looked like that

17

when any of us were ill. So I simply called her a fool, to make her think I had not noticed anything, and went downstairs.

In the drawing-room Cordelia was sitting on the sofa, ready dressed, even to her gloves, which the rest of us put on only at the last moment, because we disapproved of them on principle; and she was watching Richard Quin and Rosamund play a game of chess. She was frowning, although Richard Quin was as ready to start as she was, and Rosamund was not coming with us. It worried Cordelia that Richard Quin was always playing games, and indeed as he and Rosamund sat at the chessboard they had a spendthrift and luxurious air, perhaps for no other reason than that they both were fair and the sunlight was pouring in on them. Nowadays Rosamund wore her hair up when she went out, but though she looked more grown-up than any of us she did not enjoy doing grown-up things as we did, and the minute she got home she used to raise her long hands and slowly draw out the pins from her hair and let it fall loose, slowly, curl by curl, over her shoulders. As I came in Richard Quin struck the board and set the red and white chessmen sprawling, and leaned across the table and tugged hard at one of these loose curls.

'You have beaten me three times running,' he said. 'That's against nature. The rule is that I beat you, you beat me, for ever and ever, amen.'

'It would be like that,' stammered Rosamund, 'if today you weren't thinking of something else.'

'You never concentrate on anything,' Cordelia told him.

'Rosamund, I shall never understand this business about chess,' I said. 'You always say you are not clever, and you never got any prizes at school except for needlework and that horrible domestic science, and they didn't think it worth while even putting you in for the Matric. Well, chess is a very difficult game, and Papa is a genius, and Richard Quin would be clever if he ever did any work, and yet you can beat them both. How can you do that if you're not clever?'

'It is quite simple,' said Richard Quin. He had kept her long barley-sugar curl to twist between his fingers. 'Rosamund hasn't got a mind. But she does quite well without it. She thinks with her skin. The people who examine for the Matric don't like that sort of thing, they don't hold with it, as Kate says, but chess is different. So long as you can make the moves, chess doesn't care if, like Rosamund, you just have something shining instead of a brain.'

Without resentment Rosamund asked him, 'Since I am like that, will I be able to be a good nurse?'

But Richard Quin looked past her at the opening door. Mamma came in and went silently to an armchair and sat down. Cordelia and I inspected her to see if she were properly dressed for the party, but Richard Quin asked sharply, 'What is the matter?' and we saw that her face was quite white and that she was twisting a piece of paper in her hands. It was as if Papa were still living with us.

'Children,' she said, 'a horrid thing has happened.'

'Oh, not today! Not today!' exclaimed Cordelia. 'Mr Morpurgo will be here at any moment.'

'There is a man who has come here from time to time to ask for money,' said Mamma. 'It is his trade, and of course such people must exist, and there would be no need for them to exist if everyone paid their debts. Oh, children, you must always pay your debts. This man came here first to ask for the rent, but you must not count that against Cousin Ralph, the house-agent did it without telling him. I wrote to your Cousin Ralph, asking him not to do it again, and explaining that it was useless, that when I had the money I paid the rent. He answered me quite nicely, saying that he had not known about the bailiff and would see to it that we were not bothered in this way again. Then another time this man came to ask for the rent for those offices your father and Mr Langham took for that company that never was started, something to do with ostrich feathers. And there were other times, but I forget them.'

'Well, if he's here now, it can't be for the same reason,' said Richard Quin, who had gone to sit on the arm of Mamma's chair. 'The solicitor has had all the bills.'

'He is in the dining-room now,' said Mamma, 'and he says we owe a printer ten pounds.'

'Well, let us pay him off,' said Cordelia, rising to her feet. 'Surely we have ten pounds? I will run to the bank if you will write a cheque. But perhaps we have not got ten pounds. I suppose we still have very little money.'

'Sit down again, dear, you give no help by standing, and it makes me nervous,' said Mamma. 'The trouble is that we do not owe him ten pounds, or even one pound. Or so I should think. I am sure that everything is settled, and this man has

19

nothing to prove the debt but this piece of paper. Marchant & Ives, printers, Kingston, in October, to account rendered, ten pounds. I never heard of them, and I do not think that your father had had anything printed for a long time before he went away. That was one of the ways I knew he was ill, he was not writing any more.'

'And the date is October,' said Richard Quin. 'Papa had gone by then.'

'That means nothing, the months mentioned in connection with any of your father's debts might be in any year, past or to come; your father was debt itself,' said Mamma, quite without bitterness, simply as if she spoke of a storm. 'But this thing is absurd. When this man came before, he had official papers. He always showed them to me, though I did not look. But now he has nothing but this dirty piece of paper.'

'Then we'll go and tell him that we'll fetch the police if he does not leave at once,' I said, sitting down on the other arm of the chair and kissing her.

'You are all a great comfort to me,' said Mamma, 'but get up, dears, no furniture was built to stand such a strain, and you are missing the point. You see, he is just a poor old man. He has a grey beard, it used to be trim, now it is straggling, and his coat is dirty. I remembered him as quite neat when he came before. What can have happened to him? But what a foolish question, so many things may have happened to him. In any case I suppose the word has gone round among such people that we are paying all our debts, and he has thought of this way of raising money for himself.'

'Let us turn him out,' I said, 'and I wish we could kill him.'

'But why do you think Papa did not really owe this money?' asked Cordelia. 'When he owed money everywhere, why should he not owe money to this Kingston printer?'

'I am sure this is not a real debt,' said Mamma. 'When I first went into the room I saw that the old man had been crying. It is not only that he is much more unkempt than he used to be, he seems years older. Also he looked at me sideways after he had been rude to me, to see whether I was going to give in, and his eyes were like an old dog's. What can we do for the poor wretch? We cannot pretend that we really owe him ten pounds, that is too mad, and five pounds, too, is a lot of money.'

'But how do five pounds come in?' asked Richard Quin.

'Why, I do not see how we are to offer him less than five pounds without letting him see that we know him to be a fraud,' said Mamma. 'And I feel so guilty, for I never thought of such people as having a life of their own; I saw them as coming into existence in order to plague me and then vanishing. But this old man certainly has a life of his own, and I think it is sad.'

'Mamma, try to stick to the point,' Cordelia implored her. 'How do you know we do not owe him this money?'

'Oh, my dear,' said Mamma, impatiently, 'if it would not hurt his feelings, I would tell you to open the door and look at him. He is in utter misery. I wish there were something small in the room that was worth a little so that he could put it under his coat and take it away.'

'No, Mamma,' said Richard Quin. 'No. We cannot stock our rooms with objects which are just the right size for putting under a coat so that thieves can steal them and thus not have their feelings hurt by the knowledge that you know they are dishonest. That really is too mad.'

'Yes, but what are we to do?' asked Mamma. 'I tell you, he is suffering.'

'Aunt Clare,' stammered Rosamund. She had been setting the red and white chessmen back in their proper places on the board.

'But what does it matter whether he is suffering or not,' I said, 'if he has been rude and tried to cheat you?'

'The car will be here in a second,' said Cordelia. 'We must do something; will nobody be sensible?'

'Aunt Clare,' Rosamund repeated. With a clumsy gesture she upset the chessmen on the floor. 'Oh, dear,' she breathed.

'Papa's beloved chessmen!' exclaimed Cordelia. 'Rose, take care not to tread on them. Oh, I cannot kneel to pick them up, my skirt is too tight, it will get creased.'

'There is no reason why you should pick them up, Rosamund will do that,' said Mamma. 'And she so seldom drops or breaks anything that we can let her have an accident without drawing attention to it. I wish I could think what I should do about this poor old man.'

Richard Quin winked at me. We both understood that Rosamund had upset the chessboard in order to break up the argument and get us to listen to her, and that Mamma and

Cordelia, for quite different reasons, were incapable of divining this.

'Aunt Clare,' stammered Rosamund, 'you should not try to deal with this old man yourself. It is not for any of us to do that.'

'Well, who else is to do it?' asked Mamma.

'Why, there is K-K-Kate,' said Rosamund, opening her eyes in a wide, babyish stare. 'Give me some money and I will take it down to the kitchen and ask her to make a cup of tea for the old man, and she will carry it up and give him the money, and she will say something that will show him that we know he is a fraud. She will be able to put it in a way that will not hurt his feelings, at least not as much as anything we could say.'

She had risen, and now she was standing on one side of Mamma's chair, while Richard Quin stood on the other. 'Yes, Mamma,' he said, patting her thin shoulder, 'Rosamund is right, that is the way to do it.' She looked up at them fearfully, so much smaller than they were, and so pale. They bent down over her, strong and bright, and working in smooth confederation. 'If you give me the money it can all be settled before you go,' said Rosamund, and Richard Quin said, 'Your handbag, dear.'

Mamma's eye roved fiercely about her in search of a better solution. She was an eagle plagued by a conscience. 'I wonder if this is not too much to expect of Kate,' she said. 'She is very kind, otherwise she would have left us years ago to work in a place where she had less to do and would be paid more. But she might not see the necessity of sparing someone who has tried to harm us.'

'You are a fuss-box, Mamma,' said Richard Quin. 'When Cordelia fusses she is being your own daughter. Kate is all right. You need not be afraid of what she will do to the old man. If a dog attacked one of us she would beat it, but not cruelly. Here is your handbag.'

He gave it not to Mamma but to Rosamund, who opened it with her slow dexterity, and found at once the sovereign case which lay in its disorder. 'How much money shall I take, Aunt Clare?' she asked, in docile tones.

'He has asked for ten,' sighed Mamma, 'it would be insulting to offer him less than five – oh, I know that is absurd. Say three.'

'Not three sovereigns, but one,' said Richard Quin to Rosamund, 'and don't you be misled by the Prayer Book into thinking that this is the same as saying not one sovereign but three.'

'I have told you children again and again that you must not make fun of the Athanasian creed,' said Mamma. 'Do you listen to nothing else in church? And it is foolish to laugh at the Athanasian creed, you will understand it when you grow up. Or perhaps that is too much to say. But you will see that things can be like that, more or less. But yes, one sovereign to begin with. Oh, I must be honest, he smells of drink. And mercifully Kate will find out if there is some way of helping him later.'

'Yes, Aunt Clare,' said Rosamund. She took a coin and gave Mamma back her handbag, remarking that there were some stitches gone in the sovereign case and that she would take it to the saddler's next morning, and then she was gone. Mamma looked round at us and asked, as if we were her elders, whether it was going to be all right. Then she sighed, and said that she supposed her hat must now be crooked, and crossed the room to the looking-glass. But she struggled only feebly with her lack of interest in her own appearance, and I went to help her. Though her voice had been steady enough she was trembling; it was like having a bird under one's hand. But of course to have a dun in the house again had reminded us all of the offences Papa had committed against us, which we had been able to forget now he was not there. It was a blessing that Rosamund and Richard Quin had been clever enough to find a way by which Mamma could get rid of the old man without doing what was against her nature and refusing to help him. Yet I was not quite pleased by that. As the two had stood on each side of my mother's chair, they were not unprepared, like the rest of us in that room. They had moved in such perfect concert and had been so ready to pick up their cues that they might have been playing a scene which they had often rehearsed in secret; and their smooth and radiant colouring gave them the appearance of players made up for the stage. But the comparison was not apt, for the faith of actors is that they should speak and move so that the meaning of the play is made plain to their audience. Richard Quin and Rosamund were more like a conjuror and his assistant, who practise the false candour of rivers, which run open under the light but will not stop to be examined. I loved Richard Quin and Rosamund more than I loved anybody except Papa and Mamma, for I could not exactly love Mary, she was my twin and we were both pianists, we were nearly the same person. I was sure that Richard Quin and Rosamund loved me in return, but there was an understanding between them to which I was not admitted, and I found it hard to see how that was compatible with any love either might feel for me.

Cordelia said explosively, 'Oh, how foolish we shall all look when it turns out that the man really has a writ.'

Mamma wheeled about, saying irritably, 'Nonsense, men who have writs do not cry.' Then she saw that Cordelia was near to tears and she cried out tenderly, 'Oh, Cordelia, I have been stupid. I thought you were being silly about that man, but what is really the matter with you is that you are nervous about going out for the first time to a big house, to see people who are rich. Of course you are frightened, it is only natural. But you need not have the smallest alarm. There is no reason why I should not speak frankly to you, you are not conceited. You are a pretty girl, even an exceptionally pretty girl, and people like young girls who are pretty.'

'Yes, Cordy,' said Richard Quin. 'I will now tell you something which should prevent you getting the wind up, now or ever after. After you've been to a cricket-match it isn't only the other boys who ask me about you, it is the masters, too. They raise the subject in a roundabout way, particularly the older ones, but they get to it in the end. Well, you know, that's a test. If you can get schoolmasters interested you can get anybody.'

'You remember how your father used to say how like you were to his Aunt Lucy,' Mamma went on. 'Well, she was considered quite a beauty. When you go to any new place and you feel nervous, just stand there and let people look at you, and you will find that everybody wants to be friendly. I never had that advantage. When people first saw me, even when I was quite young, they felt that I was strange. But I have often seen pretty girls coming in and everybody liking them at once. It is a charming sight,' she said, smiling at some memory.

Cordelia laughed timidly. 'Am I really all right?' she asked us. She turned towards me and seemed to steel herself, and repeated, 'Am I really all right?'

I thought to myself, 'Why, it is as if she thought that I was always so hard on her that if I say she is pretty it really must be true,' and I wondered why she should feel like that about me.

24

Was I sometimes savage? I was under the impression that I was mild, though often people were savage to me. I thought too how odd it was that she needed reassurance about her looks, considering that when she had played the violin badly at concerts she had exploited her prettiness with what had looked to me like a complete understanding of its effects. Could it be that Cordelia had been so disconcerted by having it proved that she had no musical gift, that she now doubted the existence of the gifts she really possessed? I said, 'Of course, Cordelia, you are lovely,' but I do not know if she ever heard me, for at that moment our servant Kate came into the room, followed by Rosamund, and Kate wore her wooden look of consequence, which meant that she thought the family which employed her had gone too far in its path towards folly, and she was about to call them to a halt.

My mother cried, 'Kate, you must be gentle with that poor old man.' She had never learned to recognise the warning in that wooden look.

'What poor old man?' asked Kate. She held the pause as if some invisible conductor was giving her the beat. 'Tom Partridge is no poor old man. He is the laundryman's father-in-law and a great grief to all his family. But I have been gentle with him, to please you.'

'What, have you seen the old man already?' said Mamma.

'Yes, indeed. I did not wait to make tea for him. Tea is not his drink. I went up and gave him money as you had ordered, but not all you gave Miss Rosamund. Here is five shillings change.'

'What, you gave him fifteen shillings?' exclaimed Mamma. 'I am sure you were right, but it is an odd sum. One never says to oneself, "Poor man, I would like to give him fifteen shillings".'

'I did not give him fifteen shillings. Fifteen shillings for old Tom Partridge! I gave him five shillings,' said Kate, as much timber as an old sailing ship.

'It was a half-sovereign I took from your case, not a sovereign,' explained Rosamund. Her tone was bland. I had noticed before that she often spoke of her own actions as if she were reporting something of no interest to her, simply what she had chanced to perceive.

'Oh, Rosamund! That was mean, and not like you!' exclaimed Mamma. 'And, Kate, you have been hard! The old man may be a bad character, but he was in some sort of trouble. He was crying, Kate.'

'Yes, ma'm,' said Kate. 'He is in some sort of trouble. His trouble is that he is bad. If he was crying, it was most likely because he had drunk too much last night, and, ma'am, since you are so, so, so –' she wanted to say 'foolish', but that would have destroyed the system of relationships to which she was accustomed. 'So kind,' she said, 'he has gone away happy. What he wanted was to get some money out of somebody by a trick, so that he could spend it on drink, and feel how clever he was. If you had given him nothing, then that would have been hard on him, he would have slunk off like a dog, and felt that his day was over. But the smallest sum that he got by his tricks would send him out in good heart. To be sure, he begged for a little more, but I said something that brought our talk to an end without being disagreeable.'

'Oh, Kate, Kate, are you sure it was not disagreeable?' Mamma begged.

'No, no, it was nothing cruel,' Kate assured her. 'I simply said that if he went about pretending that he was collecting debts that nobody owed, it would be no time before he found himself inside again.'

'Inside what?' repeated Mamma.

'In prison,' explained Kate.

'Has the poor man been in prison?' asked Mamma.

'Six months in Wandsworth,' said Kate, 'and not a day too short.'

'But he must have been terribly hurt when you said that!' protested Mamma.

'No, he would not be hurt so long as I called it inside,' said Kate impatiently, as if Mamma might not understand quite a lot of things, but she should have understood that.

'Why was he sent to prison?' asked Cordelia, shivering with distaste.

'He got into trouble because he cannot leave well alone,' said Kate. 'He has this good job as a debt-collector, but the thought of a roof on an empty house is too much for him.'

'But what can he do with the roof of an empty house?' marvelled Mamma.

'He gets together with some like himself, who you would probably like to help as well,' Kate told her, just not altering her deferential tone, 'and they break into the house and climb on the roof and strip off the lead and take it away and sell it to dealers, who give them next to nothing for it because they know where it comes from, and that is what annoys the laundry-man most, his name dragged in the mud and all for a few shillings. And it is a cruel thing to do, too. When the lead is gone off a roof, the rain comes in, and think of the poor people who are the next to move in and find themselves soaked in their beds, and the poor landlord who has to replace the lead! And it is not like giving way to a strong temptation, like a poor man passing a shop and seeing something only the rich can enjoy and making away with it. To break in to a house and take the lead off the roof a man must carry tools and have his mind made up. And it was a mean thing to do, to come to you and blacken the poor master's name with a debt more than he owed, when there is no grown man in the house to give scoundrels what they deserve. I did not think the old wretch was as bad as that.'

'But he cannot help being what he is,' said Mamma.

'And if you had sent for the police you could not have helped that either,' said Kate.

'That is what I am saying,' said Mamma. 'We all act as we are made.'

'If we are all as we are made, why have you tried, year after year, sun and shine, to make the young ladies less wild and hasty and to get Master Richard Quin to work at his books?' asked Richard Quin.

'Oh, training is another thing,' said Mamma. 'But I do not suppose that old Tom Partridge had much training.'

'He had as much training as the laundry-man and his wife,' said Kate, 'and they are sick of his thieving, sneaking ways.'

'It is not only the question of whether people can help doing what they do,' said Mamma. 'One must be kind to them whatever they do, when things have gone wrong that is the only way of getting them right.'

'But it would be far better if you were kind to the laundry-man and his wife,' said Kate.

'I will be kind to them if they need it and if I can give them what they need,' said Mamma. 'But they probably do not require my help. It is the terrible thing about the other people, the ones like Tom Partridge who are gripped by this desire to do fatal things, that they get themselves into positions where they are lost if they are not helped.'

27

'But such people could stop doing all these foolish things the minute they wanted to,' said Kate. 'Old Tom Partridge chooses to steal lead off roofs, the laundry-man and his wife choose to be honest and decent, and that is what makes the difference between them, and nothing else.'

'Oh, Kate, do not believe it is as simple as that,' my mother begged.

'What is this argument about?' enquired Mr Morpurgo. He had been knocking at the front door for some time, but we had been too deeply interested in the discussion of Tom Partridge to hear him. In the end Mary had let him in, and they were standing together in the doorway. 'Who is old Tom Partridge, and what have the laundry-man and his wife been doing?' He had often the air, when he came to our house, of a child who wanted to be told a story.

'Mamma is saying that people are good and bad because they are born like that,' explained Richard Quin, 'and Kate is saying that they are good and bad because they choose to be, she thinks they only do it to annoy because they know it teases.'

'Oh, that is what they are arguing about, are they!' exclaimed Mr Morpurgo. 'I can myself make only one small contribution to that argument. I can tell you that it is most unlikely that you will settle it before luncheon. It has been going on elsewhere for some time now. Come, we must start.'

II

THE LARGE SQUARE ROOM of Mr Morpurgo's car trundled us across the Thames and past the Houses of Parliament into the part of London south of Hyde Park, where the squares are faced with stucco and the tall houses are white cliffs round the green gardens; and he grew very cheerful. 'Now we are near home,' he said, 'and I am quite looking forward to meeting my wife at luncheon. Though she has been back for two days I have hardly seen her. Unhappily her journey has given her one of those agonising headaches which are the curse of her life. They make it absolutely impossible for her to talk to anybody, and while they last she simply has to shut herself up in her bedroom and pull down the blinds, and that's what she has been doing ever since she came back. We had a long talk together on her arrival, and suddenly the old pain started. No, no, there was no question of putting you off. I would have been quite ruthless in asking you to come another day if it had been necessary. But I asked her yesterday evening, and she said that if she dined in bed and took a sleeping draught she would be quite fit for the party today.'

'Travel has been unlucky for you both lately,' said Mamma. 'You really looked quite ill when you came back from that Continental journey which you said you hadn't enjoyed.'

'Ah, yes,' he sighed, sobered by the memory. 'But that, as you realised, was because of all the cooking in oil. See, this is where I live, the big house, the very big house, lying crossways at the corner of the square, and not at all in keeping. There is nothing one can do about that. As the Almighty pointed out to Job, nothing can be done about behemoth and leviathan. No, do not get out yet, the footman will open the door.'

At those last words I was stricken with terror. Like all people brought up in households destitute of menservants, we regarded them as implacable enemies of the human kind, who could implement their ill-will by means of supernatural powers which enabled them to see through a guest's pretensions as soon as they let him into the house and to denounce him to the rest of the company without the use of speech. We hurried past the footman with our eyes on the ground and thus were unaware till we had entered the hall that this was not just a large house, such as we had expected Mr Morpurgo to possess, it was large like a theatre or a concert-hall. We stood washed by the strong light that poured from a glass dome far above us, on a shining floor set with a geometric pattern of black and white marble squares and triangles and crescents; a staircase swept down with the curve of a broad, slow waterfall; the walls were so wide that one took a tapestry where two armies fought it out on land round a disputed city in the foreground, and in the background two navies fought it out among an archipelago lying where a sea and estuary met; and on the facing wall a towering Renaissance chimneypiece rose into a stone forest honeycombed by several hunts. When Mr Morpurgo had had his hat and coat taken from him, he wheeled round and faced us, his little arms spread out, his little legs wide apart.

'Of course,' he said gravely, 'we have no need for a house as large as this, there are only five of us. But a man must have a house he can turn round in.' We remained silent, and he went to Mamma and took her hand and kissed it. 'Clare, you have brought up your children beautifully. Not one of them laughed. So I will tell you about this house, and why you must not laugh at it.'

The butler and the footman all suddenly looked as remote as if they had taken a drug, and shifted on their feet. They did not look like the devils I had expected; rather they recalled Shakespearean courtiers dealing with what must have been the chief problems of their lives, how to stand within earshot of their loquacious betters and seem not to be listening, and how to find a stance which would carry them comfortably through soliloquies. 'The truth is,' said Mr Morpurgo, 'I have too much house, as I am apt to have too much everything. But there is reason to be kind about the excess of this place. My father built it, because he was a Jew, one of a persecuted people, and he was entertained by King Edward the Seventh, on an occasion

30

which really deserves to be remembered. Nobody said anything about it the other day when he died, I suppose it was impossible because we want to keep the peace among the nations. But it may in the future be remembered as an example of a thing that only a king could do, and a thing that you would not expect to be within the range of a Hanoverian king, for it had wit. As you are sure to know, the Tsar of Russia hates his Jewish subjects. He has been furiously anti-Semitic ever since the time when he was a young man travelling in Japan and a waiter who had gone mad hit him on the head with a heavy tray; and it does not merely happen that there are pogroms in Russia, they are promoted by the government, that is to say, by the Tsar. Well, when the Tsar came to England in 1894 the Prince of Wales administered a rebuke to his niece's young husband. He invited him to spend a weekend at Sandringham, and when the Tsar got there he found that nearly all his fellow-guests were Jews. One of them was my father, and he was profoundly impressed. It is true that many people, on hearing this story, are less impressed, and point out that the Prince of Wales had borrowed a great deal of money from those Jews which he had never repaid. But such people are always Gentiles. We Jews know that there are many people who borrow money from us and do not repay it, and that it is not really very usual for such borrowers to make beautiful and courteous gestures in defence of our race. So my father, having been asked to Sandringham on this auspicious occasion, built this house, because he felt exalted and wanted to make a visible symbol that our race is honoured on earth as we have always been perhaps a little too certain that it is honoured in heaven. Therefore, children, think gently of this house, and forget, as I try to forget, that my father should really have understood that it is ridiculous to build in the Renaissance style with machine-cut stone—'

He suddenly came to a halt and his smile faded. 'Manning,' he said, and the butler came forward. Mr Morpurgo pointed to a Homburg hat that was lying on the hall-table, and asked, 'Does that mean that we have another guest for luncheon?'

'Yes, sir,' said the butler. 'Mr Weissbach is in the drawing-room.'

Mr Morpurgo repeated, 'Mr Weissbach? But why has he come? I did not ask him.' He passed his hand across his forehead. 'There must be some mistake. I must have asked him for another day. Yet I can't remember doing anything of the sort.'

The butler licked his lips. 'Mr Weissbach rang up this morning just after you left, sir, and said that he had just come back from abroad, and was very anxious to see you, and I put him through to Madam, who spoke to him and then told me there would be another guest for luncheon.'

He spoke with gloating discretion. Mr Morpurgo seemed stupefied by what he heard. There was the same atmosphere that there used to be at school when there was trouble between the teachers. Only Mamma did not realise that something had gone wrong. Her eyes were wandering among the handsome valour of the lances and pennants of the armies in the tapestries, the compressed churches and palaces in the city they disputed, she was softly humming some music that seemed to her appropriate.

Mr Morpurgo continued to stare at the Homburg hat. At last he said, in the voice of a reasonable and unperturbed man, 'It seems that my wife has arranged for you to meet Mr Mortimer Weissbach. An art dealer, a famous art dealer. Not one of the dealers I took you to see, Clare, when we had your pictures to sell. He specialises in Italian art. God has thought fit to take the Holy Land away from my people, but of late years He has done much to compensate for this by giving some of them the Quattrocento to cultivate instead. Come, let us go up my staircase, my enormous staircase.'

He halted us on the landing. A single picture hung between two doors, presented with pomp, set in a gilt panel carved with pilasters and adjoining arch; a Madonna and child painted in flat bright colours with much gold. 'My Simone Martini,' he said tenderly. As he gazed on it he might have been sucking toffee. Shyly he added, 'Hardly a painting, I've often thought, more a mosaic made of tiles taken up from the floor of heaven. New tiles. I've got another picture, my Gentile de Fabriano, who did the trick with some of the worn tiles from the same place. I don't know which I like better.'

'Beautiful, beautiful,' Mamma murmured and passed into a trance. She opened her mouth, and Mr Morpurgo drew nearer to hear what comment his treasure had drawn from her. She said, 'I wish Piers had been more interested in pictures. It would have given him such a nice rest from politics, and he would have enjoyed painting had he turned his mind to it, he had quite a feeling for painting.'

'Indeed he had,' said Richard Quin. 'We have lots of sketch-books of his, you know, with water-colours he did in Ireland and Ceylon and South Africa.'

'Where are those sketch-books now?' asked Cordelia in sudden panic. 'We must not lose them, we lose everything.'

'I have them, dear,' said Mamma meekly, and continued, 'He had no ear for music, and anyway music would not have been right for him. But painting is a calm art, and he needs calm.'

'Well, calm can come to a man in many ways,' said Mr Morpurgo. 'And what a family it is!' he groaned. 'You look at a picture, and you appreciate it, I can see by the way you keep your eyes on this one that you get its form and its colours, yet they all turn into thoughts of Piers. But for you everything, absolutely everything, turns into thoughts of Piers, doesn't it?'

'You must forgive us,' said Mamma, 'we cannot help it. And really —' she added impatiently, and then checked herself and smiled. For an instant she had supposed Mr Morpurgo was being silly, but of course he was so nice that it was wrong to admit that, even when it was true. 'And really it isn't a fault. Even if it wasn't Piers we're talking about, and of course he stands head and shoulders above anyone else, isn't it natural for a wife to think of her husband, for children to think of their father?'

'Yes,' agreed Mr Morpurgo, 'it is natural. One might go further and say it is nearly the whole of nature.' The idea seemed to please him. He warmed himself at it for a moment, then said gravely, 'And now, come and meet the people of whom I naturally think. Come and meet my wife and daughters.'

Now the butler, who had maintained his character as a Shakespearean courtier by moving a couple of paces away from us with an air of withdrawing to another part of the forest, came forward and opened a door at a blank verse pace. We found ourselves in a large room which seemed to us glittering and confused. The light that streamed in from high windows was given back by chandeliers, brocaded hangings, the glass on pictures and in display cabinets, and a number of crystal and silver objects; and among the buhl chairs and tables there stood several great screens of flowers, four or five feet high. At

33

the end of the room, dark against a window, stood a group of people, from which, after too long a pause, a tall and rounded figure detached itself. It was Mrs Morpurgo, and she was extremely surprised. She wore a hat; at that time all women of position wore hats when they entertained their friends to luncheon. Her hat was huge, and under it her thick ginger-gold hair was piled up in the shape of a Phrygian cap, and this gave her a preternaturally massive head, so it could clearly be seen that she had drawn it back, as people do when faced with something they simply cannot understand. Her body too was magnified by her puffed sleeves and her rich, self-supporting, flounced skirt, and so the questioning shrug of her shoulders, the hesitation of her gait, were magnified too. It was nothing about us which had startled her; her glance had not examined us. She seemed not to have expected anybody, anybody at all, to have come in by that particular door; and as there were two other doors in the room, and as the three young girls behind her were smiling as if they were witnessing a ridiculously familiar scene, I supposed that Mr Morpurgo obstinately entered this room by a door which for some reason should not be used, just as Papa always left the gas burning in his study when he went to bed. But it was odd of Mrs Morpurgo to make a fuss about so small a matter at this moment, for her husband was caught up in solemn exaltation. If his eyes had met mine I would not have dared to smile. He said, 'Herminie, this is my old friend, Clare Aubrey.' His voice wavered, and he cleared his throat. 'The wife,' he explained, 'of Piers Aubrey, whom I so much admire. And here are her Cordelia, and Rose and Richard Quin.' As he slowly spoke our names he spread out his arms around us in a patriarchal gesture which announced his hope that his family and ours should be welded together for ever in the shelter of his affection. But he immediately curbed his gesture. Had it been completed, it must have included within its scope Mr Weissbach, who at that moment stepped from behind a pyramid of gladioli and roses and took up a position beside the young girls. The manner in which Mr Morpurgo exclaimed, 'Ah, Weissbach!' conveyed too brutally just where the project of adoption he had declared left off. Though Mr Weissbach plainly did not need to be adopted since he was an elegantly dressed gentleman in middle life, silver-haired and neatly bearded and closely resembling King Edward the Seventh, he might well have felt hurt. Mr

Morpurgo began again, 'You remember, Herminie, I have so often talked of these young people,' but the remark broke against the hard surfaces of his wife's total bewilderment. His voice cracked, his hands made fluttering, coaxing movements, and then were still. He sighed something kind which could hardly be heard.

I had mistaken the cause of Mrs Morpurgo's surprise. We had not come into the room by the wrong door. But her husband had come into the room, and had brought us with him, and she was surprised by that, because everything her husband did struck her as inexplicable. This I realised very soon, for Mrs Morpurgo had no secrets. She controlled her words well enough, saying the same sort of things that the mothers of our school-fellows said when we went to tea with them, but as she spoke the truth was blared aloud by the intonations of her commanding voice, the expressions which passed over her face, legible as the words on a poster, and her vigorous movements. 'This is Marguerite,' she told my mother, 'and this is Marie Louise, nearly grown-up, just grown-up, which should I say? Just like your Cordelia and Rose. Oh, yes, terribly dignified, aren't you, my pets? And here's our baby, Stephanie. Is your boy as young?' But her clear, protruding, astonishingly bright grey-green eyes were saying, 'Well, I am doing what he wants, but why should he want me to do it? Who can these people be that he thrusts them on me?' She went on, 'Ah, then there are three months between them, but he is inches taller,' and her accents asked, 'What can possibly come of it if I am as nice to them as he insists? We have nothing in common with them, how am I to carry on a relationship even if I begin it?' In the midst of a pleasant remark about Cordelia and myself, she bit her lip in annoyance and shuddered, 'It is always the same,' she might as well have said aloud, 'he never stops doing this sort of thing, it is insupportable.'

Then her eyes flashed, she turned aside from us. 'Edgar, my dear,' she said, with the air of clearing up at least one tangle in this disordered world that was being created about her against her will, and seeing to it that he should not make one of his absurd accusations that she was the one who muddled things, 'you may be surprised to see Mr Weissbach here, but he rang up just after you went out, and specially wanted to see you, because he's just this minute come back from Italy, where he's been picking up all sorts of lovely things, and I thought that as we were having Mrs Aubrey and her family to lunch, we would be delighted to see Mr Weissbach, too.'

A coldness came into the genial smile that lived brilliantly and all the time between Mr Weissbach's neatly clipped moustache and pointed beard, and Mr Morpurgo put down his head as if his wife's speech had had an echo and he were listening to it with scientific interest. The extreme fatigue with which Mrs Morpurgo had uttered the last phrase could not have more clearly intimated that as her husband had insisted she should waste time to luncheon, Mr Weissbach, who also wanted to waste her time, might as well waste the same piece of time. Mamma regarded her with the pity she always extended to people under a special handicap, one of the daughters giggled, the tick of the ormolu clock on the mantelpiece sounded very loud. Mrs Morpurgo looked at her husband with the expression which could have been foretold. 'Again you are behaving incomprehensibly,' she wondered silently, running a firm finger over her lips in affected doubt. 'Why on earth could what I have just said have annoyed anybody?' Furiously she addressed my mother, 'Will you not sit down?' and drew her to a chair beside the fireplace, and remained standing beside her, sometimes rocking back on her heels, as if the strangeness of what was happening to her had actually thrown her off her balance, while she impatiently engaged her in light conversation. She was splendid under the light from the high windows. Her face was unlined. Her skin was smooth and radiant like the surface of fine porcelain. It seemed to have something to do with her difficulty in apprehension.

I was left with her two elder daughters, at whom I smiled, for they had aroused my respect. They had escaped the ugliness of their father but they had not achieved the handsomeness of their mother; for she was handsome. Though she made war on ease by every word she said, she promised ease by the cushioned firmness of her flesh, the brilliance of her flesh, her eyes, and skin and hair. But the girls were exquisitely neat in their blouses and belling skirts, even neater than Cordelia. It did not occur to me that this was because they were dressed by a lady's maid, so I imagined them to be deft and fastidious and precise. I saw them preparing for the day in miraculously tidy bedrooms cleaned by the cool morning light, standing in front of cheval glasses and stroking their blouses into the right flutings at their waists, their narrow beds smooth behind them, almost undisturbed by the night. I was disconcerted when they answered me with smiles which were certainly reserved and perhaps mocking. Cordelia was having better luck, for Mr Weissbach was talking to her as politely as if she were a grown-up; I had expected this in Mr Morpurgo's house, I had supposed that there people would take it for granted that they should make much of everybody they met. Richard Quin had asked Mr Morpurgo about a miniature on one of the tables, and Mr Morpurgo was answering, 'It is interesting that you should want to know who that is. My little Stephanie here is always fascinated by him. He was a Bavarian Marshal of Irish origin. Come here, Stephanie, and tell Richard Quin all you know about him.' That, too, I had expected here, his happy, harmless pedantry, his enjoyment of knowledge which was as purely ornamental as flowers, unlike my father's kind of knowledge, which was a stock of fuel for crusades. But Marguerite and Marie Louise, who continued to be silent and look as if I amused them, were not what I had expected. I had to own that Mary might be right. The world might have its resemblances to school.

Mrs Morpurgo suddenly broke off her conversation with Mamma to remark in the voice of desperation itself, 'Surely luncheon is very late!'

'No,' said Mr Morpurgo coldly. 'It is now three minutes before our usual hour.'

'I could not have believed it,' said Mrs Morpurgo. 'But it is strange, time seems to pass so quickly at times, and so slowly at others. Well, at luncheon,' she said, with an air of clinging to a plank, 'we will be able to listen to Mr Weissbach telling us of all the treasures he found in Italy. Treasures,' she explained to us with a light laugh, 'to Mr Weissbach and to my husband, not to me. Can you bear these stupid-looking stiff Madonnas and these ugly little Christs? And no perspective! What's a picture,' her upturned eyes asked not only her family and her guests but the gilded and painted ceilings, 'without perspective? I tell my husband that my Marie Louise can paint a better picture than all his Florentines and Siennese. But he won't believe me. He follows the fashion,' she told Mamma. 'I believe that some things are beautiful and other things are ugly, and that nothing can alter that. Nightingales and roses,' she said to her husband, in accents suddenly sharp with hatred, 'you'll be telling me next there's no beauty in them.'

'Here is Manning to tell us that luncheon is ready two minutes early,' said Mr Morpurgo softly and sadly.

When we left the room we were led across the landing to a room on the same floor, and he spoke from behind us, 'Are we not to have luncheon in the dining-room?'

We all paused. The butler again reminded me of a Shakespearean courtier. Mrs Morpurgo replied, exercising again her faculty for surprise, 'It never occurred to me that you would wish to lunch down there today.'

'I should have liked to show Mrs Aubrey and the children the room and the Claudes and the Poussin,' said Mr Morpurgo.

'The Claudes and the Poussin, perhaps, but why the room? Is there anything special about the room, except that it's very large?' asked Mrs Morpurgo, wrinkling her nose. 'But, oh, dear, oh, dear. Shall we all go back to the drawing-room and wait till they move luncheon down to the dining-room? It could,' she said, as if inviting the headsman to use his axe, 'be done. If, of course, you do not mind waiting.'

'Our company includes six people below the age of nineteen,' said Mr Morpurgo, pleasantly, 'and there must be something wrong with them if they are not so hungry that snatching luncheon from under their noses would be sheer cruelty.' Stephanie was hanging on his arm, and he suddenly drew her to him. He seemed to think she was the nicest of his daughters. Perhaps she was. She had been all right with Richard Quin. 'Even this skinny little thing eats like a wolf. And Mr Weissbach and I have come to an age when we are fussy about our food and would prefer not to eat luncheon that has been kept waiting for twenty minutes. But next time the Aubreys come we must have luncheon in the dining-room. Will you remember, Manning?'

The room where we lunched was not suitable for our party. Evidently the Morpurgos lunched there with their children when they had no guests, and it was pretty enough; and it interested Cordelia and Richard Quin and me to see that the walls were covered with photographs and pictures which were not only of people. There were many horses and bulls and cows and dogs as well. The table was too small, for we now numbered eleven, having been joined by the daughters'

French governess, a woman in a black dress, who had the same look of gloating discretion as the butler. She sat with her head bowed, and this might have been partly because it was weighed down by a large chignon of chestnut hair; but she had also the air of hoping to evade attention lest she be brought into the conversation and say too much. This was so little subtle a method of avoiding notice that it appeared possible that she was not very clever. But this was not a clever household. Mrs Morpurgo had certainly chosen to have luncheon in these cramped quarters to express her impatience at having to entertain Mr Weissbach and us; yet she was astonished at the inconvenience she had brought on herself. She looked about her in annoyance and said, 'How crowded we are! It is quite uncomfortable. Mrs Aubrey, I must apologise. Stephanie and your boy might have had luncheon together in the schoolroom, but I did not think.'

'No, indeed, that would not have done,' said Mr Morpurgo, 'see, I have put Richard Quin at my left instead of Cordelia, because I have put Stephanie on his other side, so that she can learn how clever someone of her own age can be, and every now and then I am going to lean across him and tell her how shocked I am at the difference.'

Mrs Morpurgo took no notice but continued, 'I must really apologise, everything went out of my head, I have had such migraine.' Abruptly she fell into a reverie and only answered in monosyllables when Mr Weissbach spoke to her, and she might have remained sealed in a surly dream had she not been aroused by the odd consequences of his interest in Cordelia. He was sitting on Mrs Morpurgo's right and faced Cordelia across the table; and he kept on speaking to Mrs Morpurgo of her possessions and her interests but shifting his gaze from her to Cordelia before the end of each remark, so that the possessions and interests seemed transferred to my sister. 'I was only one day in Padua,' he told Mrs Morpurgo, 'but I took the opportunity to call on your charming cousin, the Marchesa Allegrini.' His eyes had gone to Cordelia long before the Italian name was pronounced, so that it was as if my sister had suddenly acquired a Marchesa for a cousin. 'Are you still breeding those charming little French poodles?' Even in the course of so short a sentence the ownership of the dogs passed from Mrs Morpurgo to Cordelia. Mr Weissbach's absorption in my sister was so extreme that it was soon noticed by

Marguerite and Marie Louise, who raised eyebrows at each other across the table and giggled; and the French governess raised her head and hissed a rebuke. She was not a woman with a light hand. Mrs Morpurgo was drawn from her abstraction by the sound, and looked about her with an expression of fear lest something to her disadvantage might have happened while she had laid down her defences. She raised her head, confident that she had only to capture the attention of the room for all to be well. She said so loudly that everybody stopped talking, 'Well, let us hear what treasures Mr Weissbach found in Italy to delight my husband, and not me.'

'A Lorenzetti panel,' Mr Weissbach said to Mr Morpurgo.

'Which Lorenzetti?' asked Mr Morpurgo.

'Ambrogio,' answered Mr Weissbach. 'You are not a Pietro man.'

'You blackguard, you,' said Mr Morpurgo, 'you would have thought me one if you had found a Pietro.'

'Do you never think,' said Mr Weissbach, 'how painful it is for me to do business with someone who understands me as well as you do? But anyway, this is an Ambrogio, and the attribution is quite firm.'

'To the dickens with the attribution,' said Mr Morpurgo. 'Does it look like an Ambrogio? The two things should be the same, but with all you rascals getting so scholarly they often aren't. An Ambrogio Lorenzetti! Well, anyway, it will be too dear for me.'

'I would certainly think it too dear,' Mrs Morpurgo told the table. 'But my husband can have it his own way – the house,' she said with distaste, 'is his. All but my drawing-room. That drawing-room we were in,' she informed my mother, as if to indicate that differences of rank mattered nothing, one woman could understand the other, 'is mine, the pictures are mine. I might say that the century is mine, for everything in it is eighteenth century, and that was the age in which,' she said, lifting her glass with a gesture which made too broad an attempt at refinement, 'I should have been born. It was then that everything was perfect, and my pictures are nearly as perfect as pictures ought to be. You must look at them, Mrs Aubrey. A couple of Chardins. Three delightful Greuzes. An Oudry. A Largillière. A Fragonard. A too delicious Vigée le Brun, of my great-grandmother. And though, of course, that's

40

late, a Prudhomme. My husband and Mr Weissbach can fill the rest of the house with their wooden-faced saints and madonnas, their cardboard landscapes with the trees coming straight out of the ground like telegraph poles. They don't seem to care that anyway they are wrong in this house, which is, so far as it's anything, in the Renaissance style.'

'More or less,' agreed Mr Morpurgo, smiling.

'Oh, more,' said Mrs Morpurgo, 'there's nothing less in this house; everywhere there's more, and more, and more, and in fact too much. But why should I grumble? I can always go and shut myself up among the real pictures in my drawing-room, which I have known all my life. For I brought the whole room as it stands from my house in Frankfort when my father died.'

'From Frankfort!' exclaimed my mother happily. 'You are a Rhinelander! That explains why you and your daughters are called by charming French names. You are, of course, bilingual. That is what struck me when I was in Frankfort, it is a meeting-place for French and German culture.'

'You have been to Frankfort then?' asked Mrs Morpurgo.

'I have played there several times,' said Mamma.

'Played there? What did you play?' asked Mrs Morpurgo, in a tone of bewilderment, as if she suspected Mamma of being a footballer.

'I told you, my dear,' said Mr Morpurgo, 'Mrs Aubrey was Clare Keith, the pianist.'

'You must forgive me,' said Mrs Morpurgo. 'I never remember the names of musicians except the ones like Paderewski. But you were saying you knew Frankfort?'

'I had several very good concerts there,' said Mamma, quite at ease, supposing that Mrs Morpurgo would like to hear pleasant reports of her native town, 'and one most agreeable private engagement. I was engaged, secretly, to play a piano quintet at the golden wedding of a banker and his wife, and the composer was the banker himself, who had been a fine musician in his youth, and had given it up for banking. His sons and daughters had the charming thought of having his favourite composition played by professionals after the family banquet, and the old man was delighted. I have never forgotten the lovely room, yes, very like your drawing-room, and all lit by candles in great silver sconces, and everything reflected in great mirrors. And such nice people. I grew very friendly with one of the daughters and stayed with her once

41

when I had played in Bonn. Oh, I envy you coming from Frankfort! It was a world which was infinitely distinguished without being aristocratic.'

Looking back, I see that my mother was speaking with the utmost simplicity of a society as she had seen it; but it was not unnatural that the remark should fail to please Mrs Morpurgo. Mamma did not perceive this and continued happily, 'My children will tell you that I have often told them about Frankfort. There was such lovely eighteenth century everywhere, and not only in the houses, it seems to me that I remember a most beautiful bank, with a wonderful wrought iron staircase.'

'The Bethman bank,' said Mr Morpurgo. 'The first Rothschild started there, working as a runner. My wife's family bank was beautiful, too. she was a Krossmayer.'

'Oh, but I knew the Krossmayers well,' said Mamma. 'I visited them every time I was there; they lived in ————.'

'No,' said Mrs Morpurgo.

'Those were my wife's cousins,' said Mr Morpurgo. 'The house from which I abstracted my bride was in the ————.'

'Well, then I knew your parents, too,' said Mamma. 'The Krossmayers took me to their cousin's home for a party, to drink that lovely kind of punch called the *Maibowle*. How strange, I must have seen there all those beautiful things we have just seen in your drawing-room. Dear me, I played a duet among those pictures and that china with your cousin, Ella Krossmayer. She would be your cousin? She was older than you, she might have been an aunt.'

'My cousin,' said Mrs Morpurgo.

'I knew her best of the whole family,' Mamma said in a tone of tender reminiscence. 'We had a special sympathy because she loved music. Indeed, she hoped for quite a time that she might play professionally.'

'Oh, surely not professionally,' said Mrs Morpurgo, smiling.

'Yes, though that may surprise you,' said Mamma, missing the point. 'But it is very easy for an amateur to be deceived by the politeness of relatives and friends.' Cordelia moved her head sharply. 'But Ella was a charming girl, and as I say, I have always remembered Frankfort as one of the most civilised places in Europe.'

'It may have been so,' said Mrs Morpurgo. 'I left it,' she added, with discontent, 'so young. But at any rate we had pictures that looked like pictures. I am sure,' she said, turning to Mr Weissbach, 'that you know in your heart of hearts that pictures should look like mine and not like yours.' But he did not reply. His eyes were set on Cordelia's red-gold curls, her candid sea-coloured gaze, her small straight nose with the tiny flat triangle just under the point, her soft but dogged pink mouth, her round chin, pure in line as a cup. Mrs Morpurgo followed the line of his eye and was arrested. Till then she had turned on us only vague, unfocused, sweeping glances, but she stared at Cordelia intensely and then grew sad; she might have been spreading out cards to read her fortune and come on the ace of spades. Suddenly humble, she looked round the table, as if begging someone to say something that would distract her. The sight of her daughters recalled her usual exasperation, and she looked again at my flawless and collected sister, and muttered to the governess, 'Can you really do nothing to make the girls sit up straight?' The governess raised her head with an air of resignation which was not meant to go unperceived. A silence fell, and as it grew oppressive Mrs Morpurgo flung at Mamma the questions, 'So you have travelled? And your husband is a great traveller, too, isn't he? What was it that Edgar was telling me about him, that he's gone on a journey?'

Mamma's eyes grew large, she opened her mouth but no word came out of it. I could not say anything, because I so vehemently wanted to kill Mrs Morpurgo.

Cordelia spoke, her white brows creased with a gentle frown. 'Yes, Papa has gone away to write a book.'

'And where has he gone?' asked Mrs Morpurgo. 'Where does one go, to write a book?'

Cordelia could say no more. She made a movement of her little hand, and looked about as if for mercy. Richard Quin leaned forward from his place at the end of the table, and said, 'My father has gone to Tartary.'

Mr Morpurgo said, 'Yes, he has gone to Tartary,' and laid his hand for a second on my brother's wrist.

'To Tartary,' repeated Mrs Morpurgo, busy with her lamb cutlet. 'Is that,' she asked, as if she were saying something clever, 'a good place to write a book?'

Nobody answered her, and she looked up and saw that her husband was staring at her in open rage. She recoiled as if his hatred had a definite range and she wished to retreat beyond

43

it, and sat turning from side to side her large, blunt, handsome head. She had gone further than she had wished; she had meant to be nearly, but not quite, intolerable. Again we could see her telling herself that she had not the slightest idea how she had overstepped the mark. Had she said something so very tactless? And if she had, how could it matter, when there was only this obscure woman, this unknown Mrs Aubrey, these tiresome girls, this schoolboy, to be offended? All this was just more of her husband's nonsense. Her contempt for him re-established itself. She shook her head to disembarrass herself of all these absurdities, and went on eating. But her hands were trembling.

The silence that had fallen once more was broken by a peal of bells, and another, and another.

'Someone's getting married,' said Mr Weissbach, bravely jovial, 'and making no end of fuss about it.'

'I did not know we had a church so near,' said Mr Morpurgo.

'Did you never happen to notice,' asked Mrs Morpurgo, 'that St James was just round the corner?'

The bells rang on. A remark bubbled in laughter on Marguerite's lips. Finally, she had to say it. 'Why, these might be the bells at Captain Ware's wedding.'

She had said it. Her two sisters covered their smiling mouths. They looked just like the most horrid girls at school. 'Why should they be that?' said Mr Morpurgo, absently.

'Marguerite is talking nonsense,' said Mrs Morpurgo, 'she is talking about someone who is getting married in Pau, not in London.'

'Yes,' said Marguerite, 'but this is the very day, isn't it?'

'Who is Captain Ware?' asked Mr Morpurgo. He was like that. If he heard a name, any name, he liked to know all about the person who bore it.

Marguerite hesitated. Her sister's shining eyes dared her to go on. Her own answered, 'Oh, then, if you think I won't, I will!' She continued with the blandness of malice, 'Why, he's the handsome captain who's been teaching us riding all the time we've been at Pau. We made great friends with him,' she finished artlessly, 'we were so surprised a fortnight ago, when he told us he was going to marry the daughter of the rich old man who owned our hotel. He hadn't said a word about it, not till the invitations went out. We were asked,' she said, as if that had been the cream of the jest.

The governess jerked up her head. She had ceased to look a humbug; and she uttered a sound that was not, 'Hush,' but a noble and vulgar ejaculation of disgust, such as I had once heard from a woman in the street who saw a drunken man lurch against a frightened child. The three girls had been staring down at their plates, the corners of their mouths twitching, not merely enjoying their victim's pain, but acting their enjoyment so that she should feel a second pain. They were indeed very like the worst girls at school. But the governess's expression of contempt, which sounded as if she had just checked herself from spitting, frightened the girls into a second's rigidity. They turned to their father almost as if they were expecting him to protect them from her rage, but his eyes were set on Stephanie's face. I think he felt horror because she had not shown herself different from her sisters. Then he looked at Mrs Morpurgo, who had been in an instant changed from persecutor to persecuted. She was not terrible any longer. She tried to go on eating, but found it hard to swallow, and soon laid down her knife and fork and sat quite still, her chin high and her lids lowered as people do, when they are keeping themselves from shedding tears.

'I wish,' he said to my mother, 'that you could see my wife on horse-back. I have never seen a woman look better in a riding-habit. Not even the Empress of Austria. My dear Herminie, I am so very glad that you have come home, so that when I boast of you my friends can see that I am not exaggerating. Now, Weissbach, tell us about your Lorenzetti.'

After luncheon it seemed as if we were going to have a good time after all. We crossed the landing and went into a library, the first of a line of small rooms that ran along the side of the house. There Mr Morpurgo said to Richard Quin, 'You would like to stay here and look at the books, wouldn't you?' Richard Quin nodded. He was quite white, which was strange, for usually when anything disagreeable happened, he did a conjuring trick in his mind and it vanished. But of course it would have been hard to annul Mrs Morpurgo and her daughters. 'On that stand,' said Mr Morpurgo, 'there is a Book of the Hours with very lovely pictures in it. Sit on that stool and look at it. Or take anything you want from the shelves, and ring if it is too heavy for you to handle by yourself.' He laid his arm round my brother's shoulders and for a second I saw them as men together, men in over-womened families, who found comfort in each other. Then the rest of us went on through another room lined with cabinets full of porcelain figures, into a corner room, flooded with light from windows in the two outside walls, and hung with silk neither quite grey nor quite blue. There were some very comfortable chairs there, and we sat down and drank black coffee, which I did not think nice at all, out of little ruby red cups encrusted with gold which were very nice indeed. The three girls sat at the other side of the room in sallow and restless silence. Their governess was not with them. She had broken away on the landing, and we had seen her hurrying up the staircase to a higher floor, her elbows held well out from her body as she lifted her skirts to clear the steps, a kind of fish-wife vigour and freedom about her which she had not seemed to possess when she had first glided into the dining-room. Mrs Morpurgo took her coffee and drank it by the window, moving her head as if to see something in the street below.

Mr Morpurgo put down his cup and said to the footman, 'Please set up the easel, but first ask Mr Kessel to be kind enough to come here,' and told us with happy smugness: 'You may think this a dull room, but it is designed to fulfil a special purpose. There is a cold light from the north and from the east, and the walls and the carpet are of no particular colour, so that an object can be seen quite clearly, without any reflected colours spoiling its own. And I brought you here because I want you to see some things from the collections my father and mother started. But I will not be the showman for some of the things you might like best, for Herminie knows more about them than I do. My dear, you had better show them my mother's collection of Chelsea and Bow, you have far more feeling for that sort of thing than I have.'

Mrs Morpurgo whirled round. 'Alas, there's no question of that!' she exclaimed. To my astonishment she was no longer pitiful, she was once more a brass band, she had not been abandoned to grief as she stood hiding her face by the window, she had been recovering her faculty for insolent surprise. 'No, indeed! How I wish there were! But the girls and I have to go to a charity fête at Gunnersbury Park. The Rothschilds, you know,' she explained to Mamma, meaning that she was sure Mamma did not know. 'It's in aid of all those poor horses somewhere. The Rothschilds are very fond of horses. I said I'd go so long ago that I can't possibly not keep my promise.' It appeared then that she was no more able to keep her private thoughts when they were to her own disadvantage than when they assailed other people. Her expression now made it plain that what she had just said was not true, that she thought her husband would perceive this, and that now she was improvising. 'To tell the truth,' she said, 'I'm being punished for my dishonesty. I wrote from Pau saying I would be pleased to come to this wretched fête, thinking I hadn't a ghost of a chance of being back here for months, because of Mamma's illness, so that I'd seem good-natured, and have a perfect excuse when the time came, because I'd be out there in the Pyrenees, hundreds, or is it thousands, of miles away. But here I am, and Lady Rothschild's telephoned twice since she saw in *The Times* that I was back again. I can't, I really can't, disappoint her.' She paused, quite relaxed. But as Mr Morpurgo said nothing to break the silence, her handsome features broke their ranks again, she looked disturbed. 'I suppose you're not going to maintain,' she said bitterly, 'that we're in a position to snub the Rothschilds? And we have to start early, it takes hours and hours to get out to Gunnersbury.' She appealed to my mother for sympathy. 'Isn't it tiresome when one's friends live neither in town nor in the country? One has to set out in one's car for a journey one should go by train, but trains don't go to such suburban places. Well, we must go now. I know you will understand, Mrs Aubrey. And so should you, Edgar.' Again it was apparent that she was a little frightened by her husband's continued silence. 'I told you all this. Long ago. I really did. I told you that I had an engagement early this afternoon. Always, from the first, I said, "Luncheon, luncheon I can just manage, but I will have to leave immediately afterwards."'

'I do not remember that,' Mr Morpurgo answered pleasantly enough. 'But very well, go. We will get on very well by ourselves. I have sent for Mr Kessel and he will look after us, and Mr Weissbach,' he said smiling, 'can fill in the gaps. So you and the girls can say goodbye, and go off to give the poor horses what you might have given to us.'

'I need not go this minute,' said Mrs Morpurgo, suddenly timid.

'Oh, you had better not wait any longer,' her husband told her. 'Gunnersbury Park is certainly a long way off, as you say, and if you leave later you may disturb the Aubreys when they have settled down to looking at the things.'

When she and her daughters had left, the time and the place came to their own. We became aware of a fine day looking in at the windows, and of the great ugly, competently capacious house which pretended to be a palace, but was something better, a complex of store cupboards stocked with celestial sorts of jam. 'My father and mother collected all sorts of things, but hardly any pictures except what they brought back from the Continent when they'd been travelling; the rest I've found,' said Mr Morpurgo comfortably. 'But I keep up the original collections, I even add to them, I like to keep things going. One must,' he sighed, 'keep things going. There are the bronzes, I'm fond of the bronzes. They're all over the house. When you see a bronze about, Rose, go up and look at it, it's probably good. There's a copy of a classical Andromeda by a man called Bonacolsi Antico who worked at Mantua, and that's something more than the original. And I've got a room full of prints, but I don't believe you'd care for them, though probably that's because I don't care for them myself. My father loved them, but then he loved technicalities and I hate them. The first impression, the second impression, the third impression, it puts one in touch with the artist's troubles. I like objects which pretend to have been laid like an egg. Don't you agree, Weissbach?'

'I do indeed,' said Mr Weissbach. But he was in a state to agree to anything. As soon as he had been given his coffee-cup he had sat down next to Cordelia, and had minute by minute grown more rosy and contented, while she had assumed the character which had been hers on the concert platform, and became a remote and dreaming child, unaware of her own loveliness, and terrified lest someone should be unkind to her, since, so far as she knew, she had no claim on the world's kindness. He rose and said to Mamma, 'With your permission I am going to take Miss Cordelia – what a lovely name! – into the next room and show her the English porcelain.' Mamma assented without enthusiasm and indeed uttered a faint moan when he turned as he led Cordelia over the threshold and said richly, 'I feel I'm doing something most appropriate, there are at least two charming figures here which are quite in Miss Cordelia's style.'

Then the footman returned with Mr Kessel, who was a little old man in a black suit, who bowed obsequiously to Mr Morpurgo and then fixed him with a small tyrannical eye. No, he had not brought the Gentile de Fabriano, he had not been sure that that was really the picture which was wanted. He was sullen as a child asked to share his toys. As he turned to go back for it, the footman began to put up the easel and Mr Morpurgo asked if it could be set nearer Mamma so that she would not have to leave the sofa when the picture came. Mr Kessel paused on the threshold to say that the footman had been placing the easel on the very spot at which, as had been established by experiments he had carried on during the first five years after the house was built, a picture could be shown to best advantage, and if Mr Morpurgo had any reason to think that there was a better spot he would be glad to know it. Mr Morpurgo said quickly that it did not matter where the easel was, and Mamma said she could easily move, but the young footman was annoyed, he clicked his tongue before he could stop himself.

As soon as Mr Kessel had gone, Mr Morpurgo said in an undertone to the footman, 'Ah, Lawrence, you must remember that you will be old some day,' and when we were alone he sighed, 'What am I to do with Kessel? He is a pest about the house, and I do not know what to do with him. It is an odd story. He is a Russian of German descent, the great-great-grandson of a Dresden silversmith who went to Russia in a party of craftsmen imported by Peter the Great. But I cannot send him back to Russia, for it is forty years since he left it and nobody he knew will be alive. He worked at his hereditary craft at Fabergé's, and then was sent over here to bring the Russian Embassy a new set of table silver Fabergé had made for it, and to do some repairs to a famous silver table equipage they had, a glorious thing with elephants. He liked England so well that he decided to stay here, and worked for Spink's for a time, and got interested in all sorts of works of art outside his own line, and presently came to my father and mother to look after their collections. That was while we still had our old house in Portman Square. I wish we had never left it. I have told you why my father built this barrack, and it has to be respected, yet I have never felt life to be very lucky here. But what has amused me always about Kessel's story is that he decided to stay in England after a fortnight spent in Stoke Newington, where the Russian Embassy boarded him out so that he could be near some special workshop. I think this must be the sole occasion when the charms of Stoke Newington have detached a single soul from its allegiance to its native land. But what a fool I am! Kessel probably stayed here not because he liked London, but because something had happened to him which made him dislike St Petersburg. Clare, why are you tearing yourself in two by trying to listen to what I say and at the same time give the most frenzied attention to what you can see in the mirror?'

'Edgar, you must forgive me,' breathed Mamma, 'I am sorry for that poor old Russian and it is wonderful to hear how careful you are for all your people, but the door to the next room is open, and I can see the reflection of Cordelia and Mr Weissbach, and I feel I ought not to take my eyes off them; he may be very nice, I am sure he is very nice, but he is so remarkably like King Edward.'

'Clare, Clare,' laughed Mr Morpurgo, 'you don't understand your children. You know that Cordelia is a very proper little girl, but not I think that she is also a little prizefighter in disguise, who would knock Mr Weissbach into the ropes if he offended her sense of propriety, and would have done the same by King Edward if he had earned it. But Mr Weissbach won't do anything he shouldn't because he hopes to sell me a great many more pictures. Cordelia's virtue is being safe-guarded not only by her own ferocity, but by a number of long dead Florentines and Siennese, who might not have been on that side had they been still alive. But I'll sit beside you and watch them, just in case poor Weissbach should forget himself and have two ribs and a collar-bone broken.'

He poured himself out another cup of coffee and sat down on the sofa, still laughing. 'Clare, it is so pleasant to be with you, I forget all my troubles. This is just like the very first day I met your mother, Rose. She cheered me up then when I was feeling very sad. Has she ever told you about it?'

'No, please tell me now,' I answered with avidity, and Mamma leaned forward eagerly. He was constantly alluding to his first meeting with her, and she retained no recollection of it whatsoever. But we were never to be enlightened. Mrs Morpurgo was with us again.

'Sit down, my dear,' said her husband.

She remained standing. 'I wanted,' she said hesitantly, 'to explain something that may have puzzled you at luncheon.'

'I don't remember anything happening at luncheon which I didn't perfectly understand,' said Mr Morpurgo.

'The girls were giggling,' said Mrs Morpurgo sadly.

'Why, Herminie, you should not have bothered to come back to talk of this!' He looked up at her tenderly. He could not bear her to be sad. 'Yes, the girls were giggling, and I did not like it. They had some private joke, and I suspected it was an unkind one. But there was no reason for you to give it another thought.'

'But I wanted to explain what it was all about,' said his wife. 'I knew you would be annoyed, who wouldn't have been? But it was just a piece of schoolgirlish nonsense. Marguerite and Marie Louise have been teasing Stephanie for months because they said she had fallen in love with this Captain Ware. He was a handsome fellow. In his way. And they pretended that she was upset when he suddenly announced that he was getting married. But of course there was nothing in it at all. Nothing.'

Mr Morpurgo made no reply, and Mrs Morpurgo continued to stand beside us, swaying backwards and forwards on her high heels. 'I thought I had better tell you what was behind it all,' she said.

'Will you not sit down, Herminie, my dear?' said Mr Morpurgo at last. 'I am sorry you have vexed yourself about this business. You are wrong, quite wrong, in thinking that I had not grasped what had happened. Handsome riding masters have always existed and will always exist, and they have a right to existence, because they redress the balance of nature, which swings too much the other way. There are so many men like me who are not handsome, and do not become any better looking when they get on a horse. I assure you that I am not angry with Stephanie for her flight of fancy. It was most natural. I am only sorry that she should have suffered some distress. For I know quite well that you are not telling me the truth.'

Mrs Morpurgo stared at him with protruding eyes.

'I think Stephanie was in love with Captain Ware,' said Mr Morpurgo.

'There was nothing in it,' repeated Mrs Morpurgo.

'That is what I think, too,' said Mr Morpurgo, smiling. 'There was nothing in it. But my poor girl was in love with her riding master. And such things are nothing.'

She continued to look at him doubtfully, swaying backwards and forwards.

'Herminie,' said Mr Morpurgo, speaking slowly, with spaces between the words, in much the same manner that our

51

mathematics mistress used towards her most backward pupils, 'I assure you, there is no need to concern yourself with this business any longer, so far as I am concerned. There are some things so sad that when they happen to people one cares for one cannot be angry about them. I mean to forget that I ever heard Captain Ware's name, and I hope Stephanie will soon forget it too. My only sorrow is that she will take longer to forget him than I will. For I know that such disappointments take their own time to heal.'

His wife still said nothing, and he sighed and went on: 'Now come and sit down with us. I will send Manning to ask Mademoiselle to take the girls to Gunnersbury House without you, and I shall have the pleasure of your company, which I missed so much when you were at Pau.'

'I cannot do that,' said Mrs Morpurgo. She was perplexed. Surely there was a second meaning in what he was saying? She had better leave him as quickly as possible before she got caught up in his incomprehensibility. She bounced back into the part of a woman of the world. 'Lady Rothschild will be expecting me, what's the use of offending people, one's got to live with them.'

'People will eat strawberries and cream off glass plates in a marquee as well without you as with you,' said Mr Morpurgo. 'But Mrs Aubrey and Rose and I will not be nearly as happy sitting here unless you are with us.'

Mrs Morpurgo resorted again to her affectation of surprise. 'I'm charmed,' she told Mamma, 'that my husband should have this passion for my company. But I wonder why it should choose to burn so fiercely just this afternoon of all afternoons, when my friends are waiting for me miles away.'

'This point is,' said Mr Morpurgo drily, 'that this is indeed an afternoon of afternoons.'

She was the dull pupil again, staring at the blackboard.

'Not,' he said, more drily still, 'that anything has happened which has not happened before. But we are going to behave as if nothing had happened, and as if Stephanie had not been more foolish than I have a right to expect.'

'I have told you that there was nothing in it,' she said again, perplexed.

'Yes. Yes. I accept that,' he said. 'And now sit down, my dear. First I want to show the Aubreys some of our things, and then it would be kind of you to show them your pictures and your drawing-room, which I know they did not have the time to look at before luncheon. Then they will be going home to Lovegrove, and you and I can have the end of the afternoon to spend together.'

A look of fear passed over her face. 'I have told you,' she said, 'Lady Rothschild telephoned to me more than once. She wants me to do something special, at this wretched fête.'

'The end of the afternoon is always pleasant,' said Mr Morpurgo, 'and we will talk of nothing troublesome. We will be beautifully vacant, like two horses in a meadow.'

'Two horses!' said Mrs Morpurgo. 'That would be delightful, no doubt. And the Rothschilds would love us all the better for it. But we're not horses, my dear Edgar, and we have duties horses haven't got.'

'You will not stay with me though I particularly want you to?' asked her husband.

'If I may talk of my plans,' said Mamma, while Mrs Morpurgo shook her head, 'I think that, lovely as your house is, and much as we are enjoying being here, we will not take up so much of your husband's time as he proposes.' Her face lit up with amusement. 'I resemble Lady Rothschild in one respect, and in one respect only. I also live a long way off. I think we should be going home at once.'

'No, not at once,' said Mr Morpurgo. 'Your home is quite a distance away, but you have plenty of time, Clare. It is Herminie who is running short of that.'

'Yes, I spend my days hurrying from pillar to post,' said Mrs Morpurgo. 'That is what I am always complaining about, and I will not make things any better by breaking engagements.'

'You have less time at your disposal than you realise,' said Mr Morpurgo. 'Will you stay with me this afternoon or will you not?'

He had till then been speaking in quiet and even tones, but now his voice was thin and strained, an odd voice to come from so fat a little man. Now Mrs Morpurgo lost her perplexity, now she was sure of her ground. Requests coming from the bottom of the heart were things one refused. 'I've already made it clear, dear Edgar,' she said triumphantly, 'that Gunnersbury House is where I've promised I'll be this afternoon, and like all good women, I keep my promises.'

She turned away from us as if the pleasure she felt at denying her husband what he wanted were so strong that she herself recognised it as gross, and wished to hide it. She went towards the door, just as Mr Kessel shuffled back, faintly smiling, and holding a panel wrapped in a cloth, with an air of consequence. Mrs Morpurgo recoiled, crying archly, 'What's this? One of my husband's treasures brought out for your special delectation, Mrs Aubrey? I hope you'll find the right thing to say about it, or he won't continue to adore you.' As he so unaccountably does, her tone added. 'Now, which of them is it, I wonder?' she demanded. 'I can't wait to see!' But that she could not do at once. The old man halted and hugged the panel closer, like a child whose game has been interrupted by a stronger and rougher child, and fears for his toys.

'You've been very quick, Mr Kessel,' said Mr Morpurgo, and rose and took the panel from him, and put it on the easel and drew the cloth away. He was no taller than the easel, and as his little arms spread out and settled the panel on the ledge he looked comically like an up-ended tortoise. Mrs Morpurgo shuddered in sudden rage. 'Oh, your Florentines, your Siennese, your Umbrians!' she exclaimed. She had cast away her affectations. This was honest hatred, eager to destroy everything that was dear to the object of its loathing. But the moment passed. She stood raising and lowering her eyebrows while Mr Morpurgo spoke of his picture. 'Not a great masterpiece, I'll admit it, though Weissbach wouldn't. Not as great as the Simone Martini I showed you on the landing. Too much a piece of happy story-telling. But it's lovely. Isn't it, Clare? Look at that pale gilding I was speaking about. Those men in their gilded crowns, their horses champing beside them in their gilded harness, the woman and the child sitting in the broken house with gilded circles round their heads. And above the hills at the back there's the night sky, and beyond it another firmament, that's faintly gilded. It's an exquisite way of underlining what one knows to be really important in the story, the power, the trappings, the real thing above it all.'

But we were interrupted by a cry from Mrs Morpurgo. Her hands were fluttering in a gesture expressing violated refinement, so wide that it included in its complaint the picture, her husband, and the ornate house about us. 'I believe,' she told her husband, 'I really do believe that you only like these pictures because there is so much gold on them.'

'No, you must go,' said Mr Morpurgo. 'You really must go now. You must be off to Gunnersbury Park.'

'Why?' asked his wife. This time she was really surprised.

'In pursuit of holy poverty, I suppose,' he answered.

She could make nothing of that. 'How you change!' she said, in a teasing tone. 'A minute ago you seemed about to go on your knees to me in your anxiety that I should stay here.'

'But you have let your time run out,' he said. 'Now you must go.'

She repeated his words to herself several times; one saw her lips moving. True, he had not said that he was angry with her; but she could not help suspecting that he was not pleased. She made herself gentle for his benefit, compliance soft on her face like the bloom on a peach. But he had set his eyes on the picture. She shook her head and shrugged her shoulders, said a second and absent-minded goodbye to my mother and myself, and left us. The doors of the rooms were all open, and I watched her walking away through the room where the porcelains were, through the library where Richard Quin was reading, through the antechamber beyond. Before she went out to the landing she stopped and looked back, small at the end of a long strip of shining parquet. All that could be grasped of her at that distance was her huge hat, her bright hair beneath it, and her forthright womanly figure; but even so her appearance seemed to promise melting ease and the forgetfulness of care; it was hard to believe that spending an hour with her had not been as agreeable as sailing under a cloudless sky on a calm sea. But she made a slight but ugly and argumentative movement of her head and shoulders, and swung about, her full skirts turning more slowly than her hips, and was gone across the threshold. I was sure that I would never see her again. My mother and Mr Morpurgo and Mr Kessel were contemplating the Italian picture in silence. We could hear Mr Weissbach and Cordelia talking in the next room: his quick questioning murmurs and full-bodied chuckles, the crisp yesses and noes with which she began each of her answers. Outside in the street the horses' hooves clattered, the motor-horns hooted, the more distant traffic was a blur on the ear. I was sad as I had thought I would never be outside my own home.

Presently Mr Weissbach and Cordelia joined us. Bowing voluptuously from the waist he told Mamma that he thought her charming daughter possessed a real feeling for art, while Cordelia stood by and primly put on her gloves. 'And about that Lorenzetti?' he asked Mr Morpurgo. 'I've kept the gallery open, on the off chance you cared to look in this afternoon.'

'That was good of you,' said Mr Morpurgo. 'I hate to wait, once I've heard of a picture. But I can't look at it now.'

'Why not go, Edgar?' said Mamma. 'You might enjoy it, and you need not think of us. We are going home.'

'It isn't that,' said Mr Morpurgo. 'The fact is, I do not feel very well.'

'Quite so, quite so,' said Mr Weissbach, nodding. 'Next week, perhaps. I'll let nobody else look at it,' he added, obviously wanting to be specially nice.

'You always treat me well, Weissbach,' said Mr Morpurgo, 'and I'm very grateful for the wonderful things you bring me. But today I'm feeling ill, and I have a great many things to attend to.' They shook hands, and Mr Weissbach said something pleasant in German to Mr Kessel, and went away.

'Sit down and look at my Gentile a minute longer, Clare,' said Mr Morpurgo, and we all sat down again. But Mr Kessel said contentiously, 'He is civil, Mr Weissbach. Always he is civil. And it is not every art dealer who troubles to be civil to wretched old Kessel. Never a word from Mr Merkowitz, never a word from Mr Leyden.'

Mr Morpurgo groaned, and then said, 'I know, I know. But they are busy men, and they forget, they do not mean to be rude. I assure you they do not mean to be rude.'

'Maybe yes, maybe no,' grumbled the old man, and Mamma cried out in German, 'Oh, Mr Kessel, Mr Morpurgo has a dreadful headache.'

'*Ach, so*,' breathed the old man. 'Yes, they are busy men,' he said a moment later, and then was quiet. We all stared at the picture: at the people who were dead tired at the end of a journey but so excited at what they found there that their fatigue did not matter to them. An unnatural and ecstatic wakefulness was painted into the night itself. Then Mr Morpurgo told Mr Kessel to take the picture away, gently and affectionately, telling the old child that playtime was over and it was time he took away his toys. Mamma stood up and thanked them both and said that now we must really go. We went out into the room where the porcelain shepherds and shepherdesses, nymphs and fauns in leopard-skins, teapots and vases and tureens, stood in the white over-garment of their glaze on the lit shelves, and Mr Morpurgo said, 'Nobody will be looking at them again today,' and touched the switch, and the things lost their glory and were dull among the shadows. In the library we found that Richard Quin had tired of the Book of Hours, and had taken another great book over to the window-seat, but had tired of that too, and had laid it down and was staring out on the treetops in the square. He turned a sad face towards us and Mr Morpurgo said, 'Take the girls downstairs, Clare, Richard Quin and I will follow, we must close the cases.' Though it was the afternoon, it was as if he were shutting up the house for the night.

As we came to the head of the stairs we looked down on the butler and the footman in the hall below, whispering together in a knot. They dispersed and stood a little apart from each other on the black and white tiles, like chessmen on the board as the game comes to an end. While we sat on a Renaissance bench, rich but hard, waiting for the others, I could hear the quick and shallow breathing of the younger footman, who was standing nearest me. I wondered if he were still angry with old Mr Kessel or if the whole household knew that Mr Morpurgo was angry with Mrs Morpurgo. Of course the servants had been in the room during luncheon, and what had happened since she had probably conveyed to them by an expressive departure, by coming down the staircase with her huge hat bobbing on her large contemptuous head, by sweeping through the bronze doors as if they had not been opened widely enough to let pass her swelling indignation, her great sense of wrong. The menservants had some knowledge of the crisis, for they stirred sharply and then became rigid when Mr Morpurgo and my brother appeared on the landing. It was horrible that this poor little man should have to endure his sorrows before so many people; at least Mamma had not had to bear her troubles over Papa's gambling in front of a crowd. I looked up at him in pity, but immediately my heart closed in the spasm of jealousy. At the turn of the staircase Mr Morpurgo and my brother had paused and exchanged a few words and nodded, as if they were confirming an agreement, smiled as if they liked each other the better for it, and made their faces blank as they continued their way down. My heart contracted. I loved Richard Quin, and I loved Rosamund, and I was beginning to love Mr Morpurgo as I had not thought I would ever love anybody outside the family, and I was glad that these three should love each other. But at the thought that Richard

Quin had compacts with both Rosamund and Mr Morpurgo from which I was excluded I felt as if I were exiled to a distant place where love could not reach me.

My mother uttered an exclamation of surprise. 'Why, Richard Quin is taller than Mr Morpurgo,' she said. 'How strange it is that a boy shall be taller than a grown man. But of course,' she added, speaking quite stupidly, 'it often happens.' I thought this was an odd remark for her to make, since it was usually the fault of her conversations that it left the obvious too far behind. I put it down to her distress, which increased when Mr Morpurgo came towards us, and the butler, evidently thinking his master might be going back to Lovegrove with us, approached him and said to him in an undertone, 'Mademoiselle wishes to see you as soon as possible.' He looked up at the landing, and all our eyes followed his. There a figure had taken up its stand, with her head bowed and her hands clasped before her dark flowing skirts, and a threat in every line of pent-up emotion about to burst its dam. 'Oh, no!' groaned Mr Morpurgo, 'Oh, no!' Recovering himself, he told us, 'She is an excellent creature.'

As soon as the Daimler had rolled us out into the square Mamma cried out, 'Oh, children, and I thought this was going to be such a treat for you,' and took off her hat. This was an extraordinary act for a respectable woman to perform outside her own house in those days and I expected Cordelia to protest, but when she said, 'Mamma,' it was with the air of one who wants to make an important announcement on her own behalf. 'Not now, dear, not now,' said Mamma faintly, grasping the speaking-tube. She made such a poor business of using it that the chauffeur stopped the car and asked, smiling, what he could do for her. It was Brown, the younger of Mr Morpurgo's two chauffeurs. We preferred old McIver, who had been a coachman and used to click his tongue to encourage or check the Daimler, but Brown was nice too. He had thick brown curls and bright blue eyes and strong white teeth, and would have been handsome if he had not had a thick neck and a look of being full of blood.

'Please do not drive us home,' my mother begged. 'Put us down anywhere. Anywhere! St James's Park, that is near here, isn't it? Put us down in St James's Park.'

'Yes, madam,' said Brown. 'But whereabouts?'

'Near a flower-bed,' sighed Mamma.

He drove us down Birdcage Walk, but we stopped him before we got to the flower-beds because we saw the lake lying silver behind the trees, and cool waters seemed an answer to Mrs Morpurgo. We thanked Brown and bade him goodbye and walked along the path, Mamma uttering little cries of relief and appalled recollection, until we found some little green chairs near the edge of the lake, just as some people were rising from them. 'How lucky, when the place is crowded,' said Mamma, sinking down, 'and what peace, what calm! Oh, children, I would not have chosen to expose you to that! But I could not tell that such extraordinary things were going to happen, and perhaps it served a purpose. I suppose that sooner or later you had to learn that there are husbands and wives who do not get on together.'

She spoke with something of the smugness of a happily married woman considering the fate of her less fortunate sisters, and strangers might have been puzzled since she was a deserted wife. But I knew what she meant. My father had left her because he disliked not her but life; and though I was aware that sometimes they had long and aching arguments, for we had lain in bed and heard the tide of their low-toned words shift to and fro in the room underneath ours till late into the night, these were just disputes about the way to live. Neither had ever felt hatred against the other. My mother was right, she had not lost her fortune.

'Mamma,' Cordelia began again, but Richard Quin interrupted her. 'Let's forget this horrible visit,' he said. 'Don't let's talk or think of this hateful woman again, any more than we would talk or think of some drunkard we saw in the street.'

'Oh, Richard Quin,' said Mamma, 'you must not talk like that about her, you have eaten her salt.'

'No, that was Mr Morpurgo's salt,' said Richard Quin. I saw to my surprise that he was trembling, that there was a blue shadow round his mouth, that he was looking down on the ground as if he felt sick. I had not seen him angry since he was a baby and had hated being taken from his games to go to bed. 'What she did takes all her rights away from her. Mr Morpurgo had told her that you were unhappy because Papa had gone away, and asked her to do what she could to make you happier, and she was too brainless and too careless to remember, and worse, she was too drunk, drunk with stupidity and ill-will. Mamma, promise you will never go near her again.'

'I hope I never shall,' said Mamma. 'It was dreadful, sitting in that small room and having all that hatred played at one on the cornet. But you did not hear what poor, poor Mr Morpurgo said as we left. "I hope you will come again and bring Mary." How could he think we could go back and endure all that a second time? And bring Mary, the most sensitive of you all.' Cordelia jerked up her head and stuck out her stubborn little chin, angry at the idea that any of us were considered more sensitive than she was. 'Poor Mary would have taken weeks to get over this, while all of you will be no worse by the time you have got home,' Mamma went on, unconscious that she was giving any of us cause for offence, believing indeed that she was paying us a compliment. 'But I am sure poor Edgar meant it, and I know he will be hurt when I refuse the invitation, and perhaps he will guess at the reason, and that is the last thing one must ever do – to make a husband think badly of his wife, to make a wife think badly of her husband. But I really will not be able to go.'

'Well, stick to that,' said Richard Quin. He sat back and looked down at his hands, clenching and unclenching them. 'Anyway, we are probably worrying about nothing. She was not pleased that we had been invited, and she will be less pleased to have us in the house now she has seen you. Cordelia and Rose are much prettier than her daughters, and much younger than she is, and you have something that trumps her ace. Oh, ten to one we'll not be asked again.'

'Richard Quin,' exclaimed Mamma, 'how can you be so vulgar? I am sure that the woman, idiot as she is, would not have such petty thoughts. People are not like that in real life, only in *Punch* jokes.'

'Mamma,' I said, 'how can you say that? Richard Quin is perfectly right. Of course Mrs Morpurgo was as jealous as could be. Didn't you see how she was glaring at Cordelia?'

'That horrid common woman does not matter,' said Cordelia. 'But, Mamma—'

'Anyway, Mrs Morpurgo will not be in the house if we are asked again,' I said. 'I think Mr Morpurgo is going to divorce her.'

'Oh, Rose! Rose!' cried Mamma. 'What has come over all of you? Talking of divorce beside this beautiful lake? Divorce! You are too young to utter the word, and there is no reason why you should, for you know nothing about it. You have never known anybody who was divorced. I don't think I ever have, except of course Cosima Wagner, and I don't expect you ever will. And nothing happened today to make you say the dreadful thing you have just said. Mrs Morpurgo was rude to us, she was disagreeable to poor Edgar, and of course it is the worst condemnation of a woman that she should not appreciate a husband like that. It was so strange,' she said, going into a dream, 'that she would not do what he wanted. It is such a pleasure when people you are fond of want you to do something. Your father was so taken up with his writing that he rarely asked me to do anything in particular. But Edgar asked his wife today to stay at home instead of going out, you would have thought that would be a great pleasure for her. But beyond that, Rose, Mrs Morpurgo did nothing wrong. There was no hint of any of the awful things that have to happen before there could be a divorce.'

'But, Mamma,' I protested, 'there was the riding master.'

'Yes, Mamma,' said Richard Quin. 'Mamma, didn't you understand about the riding master?'

We eyed her innocence with something of the same amazement that she herself had felt at seeing a grown man shorter than a boy.

'Mamma, dear, there are lots of things we don't know about,' said Richard Quin. 'I wouldn't know how to go about getting mixed up in a divorce myself, and I don't think Cordelia and Rose have the slightest idea how to start. But everybody has made us read the Bible, and our house is always knee-deep in newspapers, and we have a general idea as to why people get divorced. It starts with flirting, and goes on to mug-smudging, which is what the boys at my school call kissing; and, Mamma, do you know about things called limericks?'

'Of course,' said Mamma. 'Edward Lear.'

'No, not at all,' said Richard Quin. 'But let's get on. Those beastly daughters, when they talked about the Captain Somebody-or-other at Pau who was getting married, they weren't just drivelling. They were doing what is called letting the cat out of the bag. They were telling their father that their mother had been flirting with this riding master. They were sneaking. They were sneaking on their own mother to their own father.'

My mother laughed, her voice rang out as if she were young. 'No,' she said, as if she were a girl who had scored a victory over a boy. 'You are wrong. I tried not to listen, but it was Stephanie who had been foolish about the riding master. Stephanie, the youngest girl, poor child.'

'Why, who said that?' wondered Richard Quin.

'Mrs Morpurgo!' I said scornfully. 'Oh, Mamma, really! You see,' I explained to him, 'while you were in the library she came and told Mr Morpurgo a silly story about how it had been Stephanie who was in love with the captain, and Mr Morpurgo as good as told her to shut up, and she would go on, and then he said that anyway it didn't matter, and she was so stupid that she didn't see that he was being nice to her. But you should have understood, Mamma, really you should.'

'No, surely not, dear,' said Mamma. 'Surely what upset him was that she insisted on going to that silly fête, and that she was so rude about his beautiful pictures. But perhaps . . . oh, yes, it must have been more than that. She did not suddenly start being disagreeable this afternoon, she was so good at it, she had evidently practised whatever are the scales and arpeggios of rudeness every day of her life, he must be used to her refusing anything he might admit he wants, and that silliness about the pictures was something she had often brought out before, like the way people play the same encore. But Edgar was as if he had been hit a great blow which he had not expected. Oh, perhaps it is as you say,' she said, her voice dying away.

'Poor, poor Mr Morpurgo,' said Richard Quin. 'He is so. . . .' The words choked in his throat, he passed his hand over his forehead.

Cordelia broke into the silence. 'Mamma,' she said.

'Yes, dear?'

'Mamma, I have found out what I want to be.'

'What?' asked Mamma incredulously. 'During that luncheon? In that house?'

'Yes, Mamma. Mr Weissbach gave me the idea. I am going to be an art dealer's secretary. Not just a typist. A sort of assistant. I know exactly what to do. I will find out everything tomorrow.'

'Why, Cordelia,' breathed my mother. 'How single-minded you are!' Then she grew wild and seemed to spread wide wings, an eagle defending its eyrie and its brood. 'But you cannot become Mr Weissbach's secretary. That I forbid.'

'Oh, no,' said Cordelia, looking very sturdy. 'That would not do. But he hopes I will, so he has told me exactly what training to get, and I will be able to use it to get a post with someone else.'

Richard Quin broke into laughter. 'Good old Cordy! I've always told you we needn't worry about old Cordy.'

'I wish you wouldn't call me that,' said Cordelia, 'and stop that hideous guffawing. Mamma, the training should not be so expensive. I just have to study the history of art, it seems that there are classes, and I must get my French and German really good, and start Italian. I will work hard and it will not take long. I will be on my feet before Mary and Rose.'

'How extraordinary!' said my mother. 'Really, how extraordinary!'

'What is extraordinary?' asked Cordelia crossly. Suddenly she looked young and tender, younger than me or even Richard Quin, and it seemed as if she might cry. 'I thought you would be pleased,' she said.

'Why, you silly old Cordy, Mamma is so impressed she can hardly speak,' said Richard Quin.

'Yes, it is wonderful,' said Mamma, 'in the midst of all that – I cannot help thinking of it as cornet-playing, I have always disliked the cornet, it is such a coarse instrument, that woman was so coarse – there you were, quietly making your plans. But, my dear, be sure, I do not want you to rush into anything just for the sake of making a living. There are other things to think of than that. Are you sure you will enjoy it?'

'Quite sure,' said Cordelia. 'I have always loved pictures,' she added dreamily, screwing up her eyes as if she were already looking at one with an expert gaze.

'What a lovely unexpected end to the day,' said Mamma. 'See, it is a good thing after all we went to luncheon with Mr Morpurgo, it has all turned out happily. I thought when we found these chairs free on a Saturday afternoon this could not be such an unlucky day as we had supposed. I wonder when you will know enough for it to be worth while for you to go to Florence. Most of the best pictures are there or in Venice. There are only a few in Rome, which I always thought a great blessing.'

'How can it be that?' I asked.

'Because one never wants to be indoors in Rome,' said Mamma. 'Oh, children, how lovely it is for you to have your lives before you. All the things that you are going to see and do!'

A family of ducks swam up, self-possessed in their smooth and shining close-fitting feather suits, some in brown tweeds,

63

others in a birds' version of men's black and white evening clothes, only with the shirt-front right underneath them, so that their yellow paddling legs stuck out of its whiteness. Then they landed on the strip of grass in front of us and waddled about suddenly grown simpletons, stupid about their balance, not certain where to go. They were myself. Often I felt at ease and then, suddenly, I did not know what to do. I was a fool for all the world to see. Mamma laughed at them tenderly, and wished we had something to give them, and then an old man came up with a paper bag full of bread, and threw them crumbs. He stumbled over the low iron rail that marked the edge of the grass, and Richard Quin just saved him from a fall. He thanked our brother and explained that his sight was bad; and indeed it must have been nearly gone, for his eyes were milky with cataract. After he had given his bread to the ducks he told us the story of his life. He had fought at Omdurman, and that he had been in the Army and had fought in a famous battle was an aspect of his old age, for there were to be no more wars, everybody knew that. Walloh-wah, said the ducks, and went back to the water. The old man bade us goodbye, he told us his name, which was Timothy Clark, of course he had been Nobby Clark in the Army, all Clarks who served their time were Nobby Clarks. We told him our names and he said he had once known someone who was called Rose like me. When he had gone we sat in a happy drowse, the ducks we knew and other ducks inscribed arrowheads on the bright water; the green branches above us sometimes stirred but for the most part kept the pattern of shadow steady as if they were an awning; the people who came and went along the paths on the other side of the lake seemed carefree, as people do when seen from a distance. 'It is beautiful to be at peace again,' sighed Mamma. But presently we heard a clock strike and Mamma said, 'We must go home. Mary and Rosamund, Constance and Kate. . . .' We stood up; and Brown the chauffeur was beside us.

'Are you ready to go home now, madam?' he asked.

'Why, Brown?' exclaimed Mamma. 'Where have you come from?'

'I have been sitting behind you,' he told her. 'You said you only wanted to be here for a little time, so I locked the car and followed you.'

'How kind of you. That was very thoughtful of you,' said Mamma. Her hand sketched a grateful gesture in the air and stopped and changed to a vague blessing. She would have liked to tell him how troubled we had all been, and why we wanted to disinfect ourselves in the park, but that could not be done in time, it must wait for eternity. 'But won't Mr Morpurgo have been wanting you to do something else?'

'He wouldn't want me to do anything as much as he'd want me to look after you, Mrs Aubrey,' said Brown. He took off his cap as if he were insupportably hot, though the day was no more than warm. 'He thinks a lot of you, Mr Morpurgo does. And I'd like to do what pleases him today,' he said wildly, 'for I'm giving him my notice tomorrow.'

My mother wailed, 'Oh, Brown, why are you doing that?'

Brown shook his head and did not answer. He no longer seemed full of blood, but full of tears.

'Think it over carefully,' advised Mamma. 'Mr Morpurgo values you highly. It isn't only that you are a careful driver, though he speaks of that. Heavens, what are our streets going to become! But also he likes you. He enjoys having you near him. I have heard him saying all sorts of pleasant things about you. He is very appreciative of the way you handle Mrs Morpurgo's dogs for her.'

'The poodles!' exclaimed Brown. He was aghast. It was as if he had forgotten them until this moment, though they were among the first things he should have taken into account. 'Yes, I'll have to give up the poodles! Why, it'll be like saying goodbye to my own flesh and blood.'

'Think it over,' my mother urged him, 'think it over.'

To avoid her tender gaze he looked away, and what he saw, the people sitting on the little green chairs or lying on the grass, loose-limbed and Saturday-afternoonish under the network of sunshine and shadow cast by the trees, made him grimace. It was as if he did not like humanity, though that seemed hard to believe of a man built as he was. 'I should have gone long ago,' he said hoarsely, and wrapped his mystery around him and went ahead of us to the car. There seemed no end to the disclosure of pain made by this day in London, the grand London, London north of the river. I was glad to be on my way back to Lovegrove and my practising. Mary had had the run of the piano all day, she should be willing to cede it to me now. In my mind's eye I saw the line of black and white notes, shining and innocent.

III

To MAKE UP FOR the horrid visit to Mrs Morpurgo, my mother took us, either the next day, or a week later, I cannot remember which, to the Dog and Duck at Harplewood. This was a little inn on the Thames which we were learning to like as well as any place except our own home at Lovegrove, though we had come to know it through a tragic event. Among our schoolfellows at the High School there had been a tall and languid girl named Nancy Phillips, whose bright yellow hair contrasted strongly with her pallor and the nullity of her features. There was a faint, sharp sweetness about her, like the taste of raspberries; she wore fussy and frilly clothes and jingling bracelets with an air of surprised distaste, as if she had been put to sleep by a witch and had awoken to find herself in these trappings. She had almost no other characteristics, but I thought of her a great deal. I imagined that her home must be a strange place where she was not at ease, and when Rosamund and I went to a party there I found I was right. It was a large and comfortable villa, which should have been safe and jolly. We were given a splendid tea in a dining-room with embossed red wallpaper and red damask curtains, and silver biscuit-boxes and a tantalus on the mahogany sideboard, and it was no use telling me that it was vulgar, I came from a home where everything was shabby, as nothing was here, and I knew there were more melancholy things than vulgarity. But the drawing-room was frighteningly stupid. It had been furnished by Maples in the Japanese style, not that the family had any oriental connections, but simply because the backwash of the aesthetic movement had by then reached the suburbs. However, the tide had not rolled strongly enough

66

here, and on the pale gold straw walls there hung huge comic pictures of motorists in teddy-bear coats and peaked caps. This place was not safe and jolly, it was sinister. Nancy's Mamma was swarthy and sullen, and rudely went upstairs to lie down, instead of looking after her daughter's guests as other Mammas did. We were left in the charge of her sister, Aunt Lily, and she was nice, though very plain, skimpy and bony and too pink of cheek and golden of hair; but she was not only plain, she looked ill-used, like a doll which has been thrown too often over the side of a pram. It emerged that this was in fact what happened to her in this household, for when she rang for some logs the parlour-maid was rude to her. Then when Nancy's father came home her mother was not glad to see him, and, indeed, though he tried to be nice, he was like a tiresome dog that barks too loud and keeps on jumping up. Though the Laurels had been rich in particularly splendid gas-fittings, chandeliers like brass octopuses and brackets that gesticulated from the walls, all laded with frosted globes engraved with flowers, I remembered it as a dark house, full of shadows.

Very soon after that Nancy's family and her house grew much stranger in our eyes, because they came to be associated with an event which none of us really believe can happen, though we are warned of it from our earliest childhood by the Bible and the fiercer sort of fairy-tale. Nancy's father was murdered by her mother. Nancy and her aunt were left alone at the Laurels, and my father and mother took them in, which was a great sacrifice. It was not that poverty made it difficult to find the extra food and linen needed by our guests, for all Mamma's married life had been spent in performing such conjuring tricks: it was that Aunt Lily talked facetiously and sentimentally and tritely all day long. Until Queenie had met the affectionate and tiresome man who had married her and been poisoned for it, the two sisters had been barmaids, and not at the height of their profession. They had wandered in a defeated continent of the vulgar world, where vulgarity had lost its power and its pride, and had to repeat old jokes because it could no longer invent new ones, and speak of virtues in phrases so worn by use that they gave the same feeling of want as rags. Too often, listening to Aunt Lily's conversation was like having emptied at one's feet a dustbin full of comic songs and jokes from pantomimes, catchwords which had not even that flimsy bond with sense, and protestations about being

67

ready to share one's last crust with a friend and saying what one meant to people's faces instead of behind their backs. Yet if one gave up the idea of direct communication with her, and put what she said with what she did, and let time fit them into a mosaic, the pattern was beautiful. Though what she said when she was at ease was usually inaccurate and humbugging, when there was much at issue she was candid. She knew that falsity destroyed what was of real value. She never ceased to proclaim her belief in her sister's innocence, except in our own home; it was as if she wanted there to be one place where it could be understood that she knew her sister was a murderess but loved her all the same. It might have served her sister's cause if she had pretended the dead man had been a bad husband; but that was not true, so she would not say it, indeed, her Cockney whine changed into something more like a bird-song when she spoke of his gentleness. Through Aunt Lily it dawned on us that murders really were committed, and Grimm's Fairy Tales, which we had all detested as children, were true. But there was, we also learned from Aunt Lily, a way of behaving under the shadow of murder which deflected its evil.

So the woman who had come into our lives clutching at our mother's compassion ended by giving us a sense of safety; and we liked going down to see her at the Thameside inn where she was now working as a barmaid, the Dog and Duck, which was owned by Len Darcy, a retired bookmaker, who had married an old friend of hers named Milly. We enjoyed our visits, especially now that our father had left us, for there there was preserved a splendid memory of him. My parents had always been unable to do many things which quite ordinary people found easy. It was beyond the capacity of my father to give his wife and children a home not constantly threatened by ruin. My mother could not dress conventionally enough, one might almost say tidily enough, to escape unfavourable notice when she went out into the street. But they were able to do things beyond the range of ordinary people. Though my father was by then completely ruined, it was within the compass of his failing powers to save Queenie Phillips from being hanged. He had been so great a pamphleteer that men in authority still felt uneasy when they heard he had been angered by an official act; when he wrote one of his indictments it was as if he had spoken it aloud in every quarter of the town at the same hour. There had been irregularities in Queenie's trial, and he threatened to exploit them. So Queenie was reprieved, and, at the Dog and Duck, my father was looked on as a saint and hero; and also his desertion of us was taken as one of those strange things that ordinary men should not do, but wonderworkers must do from time to time, to restore their magic gifts. 'Mark my words, he'll come back,' Aunt Lily would say to me in a corner, 'in his own time. Some season of the year. I wonder when Michaelmas is? I never can remember.'

We went so often to the Dog and Duck, then and in later years, that I cannot remember what happened on the day that Mamma took us there for the purpose of healing the wounds inflicted by Mrs Morpurgo, my memories run into a continuum. Our visits all began in the same way. We took train on a branch line from Reading and got out at a halt on the water-meadows. We had to be careful that we left no parcels in the carriage, for Mamma enjoyed taking presents to the Darcy household. It gave her an opportunity to follow a tradition she had inherited from her ancestors, who, before they abruptly became musicians, had been Highland farmers, and paid no visits except to remote farmsteads where guests had to help provision themselves. Most of what we brought was commonplace enough: one of Kate's veal and ham pies, made with much grated lemon peel and eggs hard-simmered instead of hard-boiled; green gooseberry jelly, flavoured with elder flowers, in the Irish fashion, which Papa had liked to eat with a spoon, and the new American sweet, fudge, which we had just learned to make. Also there was always one present which bore a strange social significance, and that was a jar of mayonnaise. Uncle Len and Aunt Milly liked it very much, and we gave them their one possible chance of enjoying it. For some reason it was then considered a form of food appropriate only to the upper classes; and though both he and she were able cooks, and eggs and olive oil cost little in those days, they would no more have made it for themselves than they would have dressed for dinner, because it would have made them feel, as they put it, la-di-da. There were also some presents which we were very willing indeed to give, but thought it odd that anybody should want to receive. Uncle Len had had very little schooling, and was always very glad of our schoolbooks when we had grown out of them. It was the arithmetical and mathematical ones he wanted, for he wanted, he said, to find out what all this science was about.

We walked out of the little station straight into the moist wealth of the Thames Valley, taking a footpath across fields shining like wet paint, beside ditches choked with rich uprisings of meadow-sweet and Queen Anne's lace, or peppermint loosestrife. Here and there a fat black crow pecked the grass in unhurried greed; and knots of trees which had never known what it was to be thirsty rose tall and thick-trunked and dense in leaf, giving wide shelter to the negroes in their underclothes. That was what we called the herd of cattle which grazed these pastures. They belonged to a breed which I have never seen anywhere else, with black heads and legs and white bodies. We always paused and surveyed them benignly, for such is the power of words that we came to admire them for their equanimity, as one might reasonably admire people who had had their clothes stolen and kept their tempers. As we went on our way we took in deep breaths, for we liked everything about the Thames Valley, even to the air, and we classed those who called it stuffy with the weaklings for whom cream was too rich.

But Mamma found it tiring. She was not very strong nowadays. When we came to a culvert halfway along the path she would sit down on the low brick parapet and rest, dropping her head and closing her eyes if the sun was strong. I remember one day the rest of us stood by and gossiped about the people we were going to see at the Dog and Duck, Uncle Len and Aunt Milly and Aunt Lily, and the kitchen-maid and the boots and the ostler, all of whom we liked. It struck me as horrible that Nancy was not one of the people we would meet. There was no chance of that, for her dead father's brother had taken her to live with his family at Nottingham, and out of hatred for Queenie would not let his daughter visit Aunt Lily, nor us either, because we were Aunt Lily's friends. Suddenly I was hungry to see Nancy again. I found myself near to tears, I drew away from the others, I went and stood close to Mamma, and said to her, 'What a beast Nancy's Uncle Mat is. It is not Aunt Lily's fault that she is Queenie's sister.'

Mamma said, without opening her eyes, 'You must not judge him too harshly. The gods behave just as badly in the Greek plays and many people read them for pleasure.'

The hot noon hummed round us. We made Mamma get up

and go on; she would be better resting on a deck-chair in the garden. Ahead the course of the river was marked by a line of poplars, the very shape and colour of delicacy. If a waxing or waning moon was a pale fingernail in the heat-blanched sky above them, that was perfect. Beyond the unseen waters the heights of the further bank were soft with woodland. In full summer the rounded hollows between the green treetops were blue-green. When we reached those poplars and the towing-path we always dawdled a little, looking down on the river, the grey-green mystery, the mirror which reflects solid objects so steadily but is not solid, the fugitive which remains. We watched the current and let our eyes run with it, then brought them back to the starting point, so that they could be swept downstream again, until our drunken ecstasy changed to a fear that we were going to feel sick and start squinting. Then we would look across the Thames at the Dog and Duck on its sloping lawns, the tall rockery behind them, the church beside it. The inn was built of plum red brick and sooty black timber, and had been a farmhouse or a forester's lodge three centuries before. Behind it rose the roofs and chimney stacks of a tall extension which had been added to it in Georgian days, when it had been a coaching inn. The church, like many old Thameside churches, sparkled with black flint, and it had a stubborn stone tower. The two buildings, so disparate in form and size and age and kind, were set at such an angle that the eye took them in as one shapely image, and the river washed the mound on which they stood in a wide clean curve, like the arc of a bow. The underlying diagram of the place was good, it was beautiful even in colourless midwinter; not that midwinter was really colourless here, for though the woods were then bronze and the grass greyish the willows leaned orange-red over the waters, and all along the wall dividing the inn-garden from the churchyard there clambered, yellow hand over yellow hand, the winter jasmine. That grew grossly and gloriously, like all plants at the Dog and Duck, where gardening lost the refined character often ascribed to it. 'There's something good in the mere notion of a second helping, no matter what it's of,' I have heard Uncle Len say as he sat at the head of his table; and all the roses and clematis which crowned and garlanded the inn, and the delphiniums and peonies plumply congesting the flower-beds, expressed

71

the same happy feeling that the world had gone too far in its enthusiasm for moderation and the thing had to be stopped.

But this was not a place where life had run to fat and lost its gravity. Uncle Len was burly and red-faced, but when he came out to see who had rung the ferry-bell so early in the day, he wore his bibbed green baize apron with regal dignity, and looked sternly and kindly at the disordered world, as if it were a rebellious subject and he would not forget his duty to give it protection even if it had forgotten its duty to give him allegiance. The women in his care showed how well he had his life in hand. Aunt Milly was a composed little woman with a small puss face under a pile of prematurely silver hair, dressed on the top of her head in an eighteenth-century style, and a habit of clasping her hands at her waist, raising her chin, and looking down her short, upturned nose, as if she were waiting for life to put its cards on the table. Aunt Lily no longer looked like a doll which a child had thrown too often out of her pram. In those days musical comedies exercised the same powers over the imagination of not very imaginative people that the films do today, so Aunt Lily skipped and trilled like one of the chorus at the Gaiety or Daly's; and it was tolerable because her joy was real. She profited greatly from the steady, ruminative cultivation of abundance which was the rule at the Dog and Duck. Uncle Len and Aunt Milly loved her not merely with generosity, but in the several forms she needed as she passed from childhood and maturity, and back to something even simpler. Sometimes they treated her as a sister who was helping them bear the burden of the day, sometimes as if she were their child, and sometimes as if she were a petted cat or dog. They never scolded or teased her for her absurdities, and made no protest when she rushed to greet us, crying, 'All of you with your hair up! All except Cordelia, with her dear little short curls! I can't believe it, when I think what tiny tots you all were when we first met,' though they knew that she had never seen us till we were well-grown school girls. There was no counting the worlds of fantasy she called into being at the beginning of a sentence and let die at its end. But that did no harm, for they were inventions and not falsifications; Len and Milly watched her and smiled as if she had been a child blowing soap-bubbles.

It would have been very wrong indeed to think that the healing power of the Dog and Duck rested on mere geniality,

72

for Uncle Len was so hostile to certain conventional attitudes that strangers might have judged him a hard man. For example, he refused to lose his calm over the Phillips tragedy; and showed impatience if we showed signs of losing ours. He set forth his reasons one wet afternoon, when there were no customers at the inn, and I was helping him to prick out some late seedlings. Two people, working together at that simple task in the gentle stuffiness of a greenhouse, fall into a happy trance as they make the same few movements over and over again, their eyes fixed on the brown earth in the boxes, while the wind slaps the sloping roof above them and sends flurried cascades of raindrops down the glass to say how bad things are outside and make inside seem all the snugger; and it is likely that sooner or later these two people will speak their mind to each other. So in the last half-hour before tea Uncle Len said: 'You may wonder why I keep Lil from losing her hair over her sister in the way people think decent. But I don't hold with it. By my way of thinking, too much has been made of this business. I grant you, Rose, it was hard luck on Harry Phillips that someone poisoned him. A nasty dirty thing poisoning is, and it shouldn't by rights happen to anyone. It nearly always means that the dead man's been done in by somebody he trusted. But a lot of people died that way before Harry Phillips, and a lot more will die that way after him. It's a risk we all take when we get born. Throw away that seedling, love. It's too leggy, it'll never come to anything. Pick one that's got more body to it. Look, they all ought to be like this.'

When he brought his attention back to the Phillips tragedy his reflections ran not so smoothly off his tongue. I gathered that in his judgment Queenie too had had hard luck, and might even be considered as the victim of actual injustice, in being tried as her husband's poisoner. Without actually binding himself, he suggested that there might be some who would hold that if a criminal succeeded in committing a crime without being actually caught in the act, a police force with sound sporting instincts would give him or her best, and let the matter drop. 'But mind you',' he concluded, in a more definite tone, 'Queenie had better luck than she had any right to expect when your Pa got her reprieved. Granted they got her into that court, the black cap was what she was bound to get. And as for what's happened now, it's no picnic for her to be sent to prison, and it's for life, but life means twenty years, and less if she behaves

73

herself, though that I doubt from what Milly says about her temper. But again that's happened to a lot of people before her, and it'll happen to a lot more after her. It's no use,' he said, in tones unshadowed by the least touch of humanitarian melancholy, 'making a song and dance about what's in the general run of things. Now finish up, love, it's tea-time and there's crumpets.'

It puzzled me that a man should be so respectful of social ordinance as to look on mayonnaise as the prerogative of his betters, yet differ so radically from society in his view of murder and justice and imprisonment. But I never fell into the error of supposing him to be hard-hearted, for though he grieved so moderately for Harry and Queenie, his heart ached for Aunt Lily, simply because she was plain. It cannot be exaggerated, the strength of his conviction that there was no place in the universe for women who were not attractive. Once, when we four girls, Cordelia and Mary and Rosamund and myself, got off the ferry and stepped on the landing-stage, I heard Uncle Len say to Richard Quin, 'Well, there's none of this litter needs drowning,' in an undertone, since, strangely enough, litter was then a word never used in the presence of women. This was not quite a joke. Uncle Len was fond of children, and was always sad when there was a burial in the churchyard, and the coffin was small; but had he been assured that the dead child was an ill-favoured girl he would have shaken his head and sighed that for once it was all for the best.

But this was no brutal rejection of what did not please. It was tender concern for what would not be cherished. Once Uncle Len and I were passing by the window of the saloon bar, and we paused to watch Aunt Lily serving the evening spate of customers from the little village which, though it could not be seen from the river, sheltered two or three hundred souls in two streets and some alleys behind the rookery. The gaslight shone on a hairslide Aunt Lily had bought herself on her last shopping expedition to Reading: one of those pieces of jewellery which are made from the wings of tropical butterflies, a strident blue thing which would have put out of key even the pure colouring of a child. She raised her hand to fix it with the gesture of a happy coquette who had never failed to triumph, and the light fell strong on her profile. 'A camel, a ruddy camel!' groaned Uncle Len, going gloomily on his way to the sitting-room. 'Sit down, Rose, love,' he said, and lit his pipe. 'Lil been asking you about Nancy lately?'

'Yes,' I said. 'But of course we haven't seen her. We get letters from her, just as Aunt Lily does, but her uncle never lets her come to stay, though we have asked her again and again.'

He groaned again. 'Lil frets for her all the time. It's Nancy, Nancy, Nancy,' he said. 'It's a shame.' I was conscious that if I had not been there he would have said what kind of shame he thought it. 'If Lil hadn't been born with that 'orrible face on her, and that bag of bones as a figure, she'd have kids of her own and not be eating her heart out for that little perisher. And at least she'd have got a man. We've got no kids, but Milly's got me till I go. God, I hope Lil don't outlive Milly and me.' He pulled at his pipe for a minute or two, staring desolately through the smoke. 'And the little perisher's plain too, ain't she?'

'No,' I said. 'She has lovely golden hair, right down to her waist.'

'But her face is nothing, not to go by her photograph,' said Uncle Len. 'A girl can't get a man if she has to keep her back to him all the time.'

'You're wrong about Nancy,' I said. 'There's something about her.' But I could not explain what it was. That faint, tart sweetness, like the taste of raspberries, that air of being under a hostile spell and dissolving it by irony, I could not then define even to myself. 'She'll get married,' I told him, barely believing it, but feeling that it ought to be true.

'Not if that photograph's telling the truth, she won't,' said Uncle Len, and drew angrily on his pipe. There was not only Aunt Lily to be pitied, there was another plain woman coming along in the person of Nancy. Indeed there was a whole world of plain women who ought never to have been born, who ate their hearts out for other people's children, who would die alone.

Yet that was not the whole of his thought about women. It extended till it overlapped his thoughts about first causes. He had a high regard for my mother, whom most people would have called plain, for she had been made so shabby by misery that her improved fortunes could not restore her; she was an eagle, irrevocably stripped of half its feathers by the storm. He overlooked her plainness because he realised that she had a special value of a rare kind. This he discovered for himself.

Aunt Lily had gathered during her stay with us that Mamma had once been a famous pianist, and she had handed on this information to Uncle Len and Aunt Milly, but the love they bore her did not constrain them to believe everything she said. But on my mother's first visit to the inn, however, they began to wonder whether there was not something in the story, and one afternoon as she walked on the lawn, watching the sun glint on the river, they called Mary and me aside to enquire further into the matter.

'Lil tells a tale,' said Uncle Len, 'that the Shah of Persia sent for your Ma because he'd heard all the top-o'-the-bill pianists in the world play "The Blue Danube", and your Ma left the whole field beaten at the post, so he sent for her to go to his palace, all expenses paid, out in the desert, to play it to him over and over again. I take it, granted that Lil's got everything wrong, that that was the way of it when your Ma was a professional?'

The ratio between Aunt Lily's stories and the facts on which they were founded was constant: she was always suggesting to the Creator that life might have been more dramatic, but never jettisoned His work altogether. We prepared to explain that Mamma had once stayed at the same hotel in Lucerne as the Shah of Persia, and one wet afternoon he had approached her because he had been told that she was a famous pianist, and asked her to play 'The Blue Danube' on the salon piano, and had made her play it over and over again, faster and faster, until by a fortunate chance it stopped raining. But Aunt Milly dismissed her husband's question as unnecessary. 'Oh, you don't have to ask, Len. Look at the way she's walking across the lawn this very minute, not taking one bit of notice of all the teas. Anyone could tell.'

Uncle Len nodded. 'You're right,' he said reverently.

Later I learned what they meant. The sight of my mother, walking as in solitude through the maze of tables on the lawn, her eyes set on the distant wooded hills that lay down together on the horizon, had taken Uncle Len and Aunt Lily back to the race-course, which had been the centre of their lives during their best years, when they had most vividly perceived events. There they had sometimes watched great men as they led their winning horses into the paddock or lowered their field glasses as their horses lost, and the greatest of these had borne themselves as if the multitudes were not there, as if they were alone on the bare downs. Even if they smiled it was to themselves. 'And there was Lord Rosebery, as cool as a cucumber.' My mother's unawareness of her surroundings, which struck the suburb of Lovegrove as ridiculous, linked her in the minds of Uncle Len and Aunt Milly with these great men, and this was a sound perception. Like those great men, she was a public performer. They had made their speeches in Parliament, she had had her concerts. Alike they had had to learn as a first necessary technical trick the art of forgetting the spectators, though these might seem the essential factor of a public performance. Uncle Len and Aunt Lily had detected a discipline, and recognised a special sort of human being that won its place by ordeal.

This perception waked with a myth that lay deeper in their minds. When a woman was great she need not be beautiful, she could be what she pleased, for she had magic powers which were superior to beauty. There were only six pictures on the walls of the Dog and Duck which did not represent horses and jockeys. They were all portraits of the Royal Family. One was of Edward the Seventh, one of the new king, George the Fifth, and one of Queen Mary, and these hung in a vestibule, in simple oak frames, on a wall often obscured in wet weather by hats and coats on a hall-stand. The other three were identical pictures of Queen Victoria, which were very differently treated. They had been given gilded plaster frames and filled the place of honour in the public bar, the saloon bar and the private sitting-room. They were coloured and showed the Queen when she was old and stout, and her face plummy crimson under her crowned white hair. Her eyes looked voluntarily blindish, rejecting all impressions of the outer world as unnecessary to her anointed royal state; her mouth was pursed with something more mystical than mere obstinacy, as if she had just closed it after an oracular pronouncement and would say nothing now that the inspiration had gone from her. The square bale of her bosom was crossed by the sash of the Order of the Garter, which was blue, such a clear blue as should properly have been worn by a young girl. In no way did this icon fulfil the conditions laid down for ordinary women: there was here no concern to please, and no tenderness. That was natural, for this woman did not play her part in ordinary life. She was a ju-ju, she controlled the natural forces which permit us to live and condemn us to die. Uncle Len was no fool, and he knew very well that Queen Victoria had taken little part in the government of England, but he believed that while she was alive and had travelled from Buckingham Palace to Windsor Castle, from Balmoral to Osborne, she had, simply by living, simply by that ritual gyration, conferred peace and prosperity on the British Empire. If he had been told that during her reign the British people had grown taller and lived longer than in the preceding and succeeding reigns, he would have believed it. Well, Mamma was a ju-ju too. She did not need to be excused for lack of tenderness, for she was rich in all feminine attributes except elegance; but for her inelegance she was pardoned only because she was a wonder-working fetish.

We saw the extent of his confidence in her when his pursuit of knowledge brought him face to face with some particularly resistant problem. He knew that Mamma had excercised her mind on little but music and the affairs of her family, yet he expected her, and her alone, to know the answer to anything which struck him as really mysterious, though we, her son and daughters, were bound to have more information of the sort he wanted, since we had just made our way through the schoolbooks, which he was using as a map for the chase. Mr Morpurgo too should have been a help, and he was often at hand. When we were at the Dog and Duck he always drove over from his country-house and sometimes stayed the night. Richard Quin and I had been wrong in our prophecy of a divorce, and I think he found the inn as kind a shelter from the pain of going on living with his wife as we found it from the pain of going on living without our father. But even when he was there it was to my mother that Uncle Len turned for final enlightenment. Thus we learned how it had been in ancient Greece; first you put the troublesome matter to the philosophers and mathematicians, then you went off to consult the Sibyl.

'Now, none of you go away for a minute,' he said one day. 'There's loads of time for you to have a lark on the river before you have your dinner. It'll be late at that. Leg of pork's got to be cooked through. I've known them that met their death for not paying attention to that. Well, there's something I read the other day that I can't understand. It'll be plain sailing for the lot of you, with your schooling and your music as well. It's one of those short bits they put in the newspaper to fill up a column when the article ain't long enough. I always read 'em, and very interesting they are. But I can't get the hang of this one,' he said, softly roaring. 'I got it here.' He took a clipping out of his little notebook. '"Architecture is frozen music." What's it mean, what's it mean?' he asked, each time roaring a little louder.

This time it had to go straight to Mamma. Even Richard Quin and Mr Morpurgo had nothing to say. Mamma said, 'Yes, I've read that before. I can't remember who said it. I should think it was someone who knew nothing about music, probably with the intention of pleasing a musician. Unmusical people often try to please musicians by talking about music just as people who have no children try to please people who have by talking about children, and in each case what they say usually falls wide of the mark. It is very strange and bound to create awkwardness,' said Mamma, looking earnestly into Uncle Len's eyes, anxious to give him the benefit of her experience, since it was information he wanted, 'it is as if there are two great enclosures, and the people inside know they are inside, but the people outside do not know they are outside.'

This was not the kind of information for which Uncle Len had been hoping. He ignored it and repeated heavily, a vein standing out on his forehead, '"Architecture is frozen music." Sure it don't mean anything to you at all?'

'Nothing whatsoever,' said Mamma. 'There is no use not telling you the truth, for truth is what you enjoy. But music is sound, and it is useless to think of it as anything else, and architecture is stone and bricks. A piece of music makes one feel something when one hears it, a building makes one feel something when one looks at it, and there's an end to the connection between them. You must simply remember that whoever said it was trying to be civil to something or someone.'

'But wait a bit, wait a bit,' said Uncle Len. 'You kids can give a bit of help here, I shouldn't wonder? Sound's waves, ain't it? Right! Now suppose you could freeze the waves that make music, would they look like buildings?'

The quicksand of this argument was rising round our knees.

'I hope not,' moaned Mamma, 'it would be a coincidence that proved nothing,' and Richard Quin said, 'I don't think so, I don't see how frozen waves could look like a building with walls and roofs and windows and staircases and cellars.'

'Come to think of it, they couldn't,' said Uncle Len, 'not if they were all going the same way, which I suppose they would be more or less. Grrr,' he exclaimed, and tore up the clipping and threw it away.

'I think it must have been a German who said it,' suggested Mr Morpurgo. He was going on to suggest that it might have been Goethe, when Uncle Len wailed, 'Whadju mean? You're saying that whoever said it might have been a German, when Mrs Aubrey here says that it must have been someone who didn't know nothing about music, when everybody knows that the Germans are more a musical nation than us any day?' Mr Morpurgo opened his mouth, closed it, and made a gesture of despair. 'Oh, it's my fault,' continued Uncle Len, going down on his knees and picking up the bits of clipping, 'it means something all right, and you mean something, but I can't understand it, and anyway I can't see the meaning of the general layout. Here's this thing about music and architecture and here's the lot of you, you kids and your Ma and Mr Morpurgo here, all saying there's no sense to it. Now what'd he say it for, whoever said it, if it don't mean nothing? That's why I want to get my teeth into this science. According to what I understand they keep everything out of it that don't make sense. It's time somebody put the shutters up on this nonsense business. It's all over the place. Granted the man who said this thing is the one to blame, what's this newspaper doing, not letting the thing lie where it dropped, and putting it in at the end of the column where you're bound to read it, if you care for interesting things. Lots I've learned that way. They had a bit last week about how if all the eggs in herring-roes grew up to be herrings you could walk across the North Sea on solid herring. Now they put this thing in about music being frozen architecture that can't be true. You're sure,' he implored us, 'it couldn't mean something?'

It was Mary who found his eye rolling on her. Doing her best, she said, 'I don't think it could, possibly. If architecture's frozen music, then music's thawed architecture, and that doesn't work out.'

'No, my girl, you're wrong there,' said Uncle Len. 'That don't follow. With all the asparagus we've served here, and I thank Heaven every summer for that beautiful bed, though mind you, it's getting old now, I know better than that. Because a thing goes one way and changes into something else it don't mean that it can turn round and go the other direction

80

and end up as what it started. You take melted butter to the table all hot and runny, it don't never cool down to being butter again. Now, why's that, I wonder?' he asked Mamma. She shook her head and held up her hands. His eyes questioned us, Mr Morpurgo, the Thames Valley, the summer sky. 'But, oh, good glory,' he said, plummeting down like a shot pheasant. 'There's the Reading Young Methodist League. Twenty-four of them rowing up so happy, wanting their lunch at an ungodly hour because they rose with the lark, and who the heck asked them to do that, I'd like to know, and an 'orribly frugal meal they been and ordered. Monks I could understand, but they're Dissenters, and why leave the C. of E. if you gain nothing, and anyway not a penny spent in the bar. Well, so long for the moment. Just remember where we got to in this argument, Mrs Aubrey, I'd be obliged.'

'That I will not be able to do,' sighed Mamma as he ran from us up the sloping lawn. 'Oh, Edgar, Richard Quin, will you be able to remember where we left off and help the poor man?'

'No', said Mr Morpurgo, 'I would not have enjoyed what he was saying so much if it had not been too odd to be remembered,' but Richard Quin said, 'I don't think we need remember, it's more a question of being ready to board the bus when it starts again.'

That summed up our duty, and we were always ready to perform it, between fooling about in the dinghy, and bringing people over on the ferry, and feeding the hens, and helping with the lunches and teas. It was never a tedious duty, for Uncle Len's bus travelled by picturesque routes. When he got his first Algebra book (Hall & Knight, of course) Aunt Lily looked over his shoulder and squealed that there weren't just letters and figures, there were a lot of things that were neither, 'orrible things, and he had better get us to explain them thoroughly before we went home. But Uncle Len said, 'If those girls in the laundries can read laundrymarks, I can find out what these mean.' When I asked him why he should find it interesting to read that if all the eggs in herring-roes should turn into herrings the North Sea would be a solid shoal, he answered that, things actually turning out so different, it showed that there was a lot of waste going on in nature, and it seemed funny, because you couldn't keep licensed premises going on that system.

All the same, this careening bus took him a long way towards his destination. Richard Quin had told us that it would, that nobody could be a bookmaker unless he could calculate shifting odds on the course, so Uncle Len should find arithmetic easy and mathematics not impossible, and as horsebreeding was a matter of hereditary strains he ought at least to be interested in biology. It was odd how Richard Quin was aware of all sorts of things the rest of our family, and particularly Mamma, knew nothing about. We had no idea what bookmakers did beyond wearing loud checks and shouting, and not till this matter was raised had we suspected that Kate always had a shilling on the big races and half a crown on the Derby and the Grand National, and that the laundry-man, whom we had imagined to be absorbed in grief over his father-in-law's habit of stealing lead from roofs, took her bets. But when Richard Quin said a thing it was so, it always was; and he was right about Uncle Len's progress, which was rapid, though it never ceased to be bizarre. Presently he read some books on evolution, and when the doctor and the rector made their calls, he used to raise the subject with them, with a conspiratorial air which always puzzled them. You could see them wondering why he had glanced round to make sure that there was only the family present. But since he had only recently heard of the Darwinian controversy, he did not realise that for others the excitement had died down, and he thought of it as a race still pounding its way to a finish which would declare the winner. To talk openly about the origin of species with the doctor and the rector, whom he thought of as connected with rival stables which each had entries in the race, was to him like standing up to watch a trial gallop instead of decently seeking concealment behind a furze-bush. He got many things wrong like this; but he was not making the mistakes of a stupid man, he was guessing like an explorer.

That was how it was for a long time between us. He was an explorer in our territory, and we were hospitable natives, and at the same time we were explorers in his territory, and he was a hospitable chief. Then our relations altered, during a single night, when we were spending a fortnight of our summer holidays at the Dog and Duck. The inn was able to enfold us all. Mamma and Constance shared a bedroom in the old part that overlooked the river, and the rest of us found wilder lodgings in the rooms round the coaching yard which had been added in the eighteenth century. At that time a landowner in the district had joined up two roads and opened a cross-country road from Reading to East Anglia. 'Go straight out of the door,' Uncle Len used to say, 'turn left and keep straight on and you'd fetch up at Norwich. These here motor-cars do it in the day, handy if you want to buy a canary. The best come from Norwich.' But the coaches had not been able to do what motor-cars do for there was a river that kept flooding and a bridge that kept tumbling down, and soon travellers grew shy of this by-road and went back to the old highway; so the Dog and Duck had no need of its extension. A later generation had pulled down part of it, and now the passage in the upper storey ended in a sealed door, with blanched fronds of wisteria thrusting through its hinged side. The remaining rooms, all high and light and handsome, were empty now except for a few pieces of quite elegant furniture, but they were kept scrupulously clean. They had therefore an air of being inhabited by dispossessed and stoical and housewifely ghosts which delighted us. Richard Quin chose to sleep on a straw pallet in a loft, because Letty Lind, the mare which drew Uncle Len's trap, was stabled underneath, and he liked to hear her stirring. It reminded him of the games we used to play in the disused stables of our home in Lovegrove, when we pretended that the ponies and horses which had been there in my father's childhood had never left, and took sugar from our hands by day, and stamped and whinnied in the night. We four girls slept in four beds set in the corners of a square room lined with mirrors, the glass brownish, the frames tarnished, which was divided by folding doors from what was called the Assembly Room, though it was quite small, no larger than the drawing-room in an ordinary house in a Kensington square. This was lit by a large and elaborate crystal chandelier, which must have been brought from some grander place; and when there was a moon we used to open the folding doors and watch, while we undressed, the lustres glittering fire and ice against the moth-soft glow of the walls and the hard black shadows. But one Saturday night when we went up to bed there was no moon, and the electricity suddenly failed. Mary and Cordelia were already in their nightgowns, so Rosamund and I called for Richard Quin and we three felt our way through the darkness to the stairs and went down to get candles and matches.

As we passed through the door which divided the older and the newer parts of the inn, we came on Uncle Len, who said,

'That's another fuse gone, I'll be bound. Many and many a time I've said I was potty to have had the electric light put in that wing, but if you saw the state the Anglers' Club gets into every year when it has its annual banquet in the Assembly Room – funny thing fishing never goes with water – you'd understand why I don't fancy having oil lamps about over there. Wait a minute, chicks, I'll give you the good candlesticks from the sitting-room. Why, whatever?' The bell-box on the wall had broken into a continuous ear-piercing buzz. 'Get the candlesticks yourselves, chicks, they're on the mantelpiece,' he sighed, 'got to go.' He lumbered along the passage towards the public bar, keeping his head down and sideways, like a sad old bull that sees the need for giving battle once again. We followed him, for we knew what the buzz meant. Uncle Len had had an electric bell set in the floor behind the bar so that whoever was serving could keep her foot on it if a customer was giving trouble.

We hated the bar on Saturday night. Then it was crowded with people from the village and from the near-by farms: all men, of course, for in those days no woman ever went into a country pub. The room was full of a disgusting smell. It was a compound made up of the smell of the beer the men were drinking, the smell of their bodies and their clothes (for such people washed far less than they do now and never sent their clothes to the cleaners at all) and the smell of the cheap tobacco they were smoking; and through the windows came the smell of the lavatories in the yard. That every seven days part of the Dog and Duck should be deprived of its puritan cleanliness and turned into a cube of stench revolted us as much as our own periodical need to excrete offensive matter which we would never have chosen to manufacture had we been given the choice; and we thought of both degradations as little as we could. But this time we felt we had to go into the loathsome place because Uncle Len might need our help, and indeed it was apparent that something horrid was happening. All the customers were standing quite still and nobody was saying anything. Their faces were clay-coloured and featureless, yet not stupid; they might have been shrewd turnips. All these blank but not empty faces were looking through the smoke at the bar, where Aunt Milly and Aunt Lily were standing side by side, both with their hands on their hips, and both with a vague, troubled expression on their faces, as if they thought

84

they might be going to be sick but were not sure. Facing them was a whippy little man in a check suit, long in the jacket and tight in the trouser, with a ginger-brown bowler set far back on the close crimps of his blue-black hair. He looked spruce but dirty. It was odd that anybody should take so much trouble over his appearance and yet not think of trying what washing might do for it. 'All I'm asking,' he was saying, 'is my change. It's legal tender, this note is, you can't refuse to take it, the law's the law, and there it is. So you take the money for my drinks and give me my change.' He got a whine into the word 'change' but all the rest was brassy.

'Go on with you,' said Milly, 'a five pound note ain't legal tender, not for a matter of shillings,' and Aunt Lily interrupted as if she were the second voice in a round, 'Go on with you, how could this be legal tender when it ain't legal in the first place? This five pound note's like the cakes we give our teas, Home-made, that's what it is.'

'You dare say that and I'll have the law on you,' said the spruce and dirty man, and then he saw Uncle Len. 'Why, here's the boss. Well, you get your missus to give me my change – she is your missus now, ain't she? Well, you get her to give me my change. Me and my four friends, we had twelve whiskies, and I'm paying for them with a five pound note, and I'm asking you, missus – she is your missus, ain't she – to take the money and give me my change. And let me tell you, my four friends are outside in my motor-car, and they could come back in a jiff if I called 'em.'

'Pick up that note and put down the price of twelve whiskies in the King's silver,' said Uncle Len. 'Six shillings, that is. And when we've spun each coin and heard that there aren't none of them home-made like your note, you can go out and join your four friends in your nasty stinking little motor-car.'

'I got no silver,' said the spruce and dirty man. 'I run clear out of silver, that's why I give your missus this note. And what you got against me, that you won't take my five pound note? You know me well, Len Darcy. You knew me when you couldn't be so choosy.'

'I don't know you so well,' said Uncle Len. 'You was a tictac man when I was one myself, but that's no great link, and anyway it was a long time ago. I think your name's Benny something or other, but I can't rightly call it to mind, and I don't want to. We wasn't friends then, and we ain't that now. What

I can't stand about you is that you're trying to make a fool of me for the third time. You been here twice before in your nasty stinking little motor-car. I'm not for progress, it's the law of nature, but I don't like some of the parties that's travelling in these motor-cars. Some's all right but there's others shouldn't be travelling in anything but the Black Maria, that's the law of nature as it works out with them, and Black Maria it'll be for them again, I'll be bound. Well, you come here in your nasty stinking little motor-car last Whitsun, and my wife changed your five pound note and it was a dud, and this year just after Easter you done the same thing with Miss Lily, and that was a dud too. You ain't going to do that to me again, chum. You pick up that five pound note,' he said gently, 'and you put down your silver, or I'll call the coppers. The station's just round the corner.'

'And how many coppers might you have in your nasty stinking little station?' asked the spruce but dirty man. 'Not as many as I got friends in my motor-car. You ain't got four policemen in your nasty stinking little station. I got four friends in my motor-car.'

'You got four friends with four knuckledusters out in your nasty stinking little car, I don't doubt,' said Uncle Len. 'But you pore ignorant 'eathen, ain't you never heard of insurance? I'm insured with the Pru. I got all the money of the Pru behind me. I'd have the place set right for me even if you smashed it up before I smashed you up, which ain't going to happen, that's against the law of nature, that is. I'd have every penny spent that needs spending without me putting my hand in my pocket if the law of nature lay down on its job. But I tell you it won't. I ain't forgotten how to create a fair masterpiece of a fight.' He looked at himself in the glass behind the bar and smoothed his hair. 'I'm cunning,' he said placidly, 'and unscrupulous. You say you know me better than I know you, and at that you ought to know there's been some people I've taken against who ain't never been the same since. Pick up that note and put down your silver.'

The spruce but dirty man said nothing, but he turned a slow leer on Uncle Len; and Uncle Len lost his smoothness. 'Gawd,' he cried, 'you 'aven't forgotten what I'm like?'

There was a desperate appeal in his voice. The other lost his leer and seemed to be listening to an echo of those words.

'If you knew me so well,' insisted Uncle Len, 'you must

86

remember what I'm like?' The sweat was standing on his forehead.

All the customers stirred and shifted on their feet, and though their faces remained blank and flat, they moved a little closer to the spruce and dirty man. He spun round and faced them, the light flashing from a jewelled pin in his tie and a thick swag of gold watch-chain across his red waistcoat. He stared at these unornamented people and seemed to notice something about them which he had not seen before, and wavered, and spun back to Uncle Len. 'Have it your own bloody silly way then,' he said, 'I suppose you haven't got the change for a fiver in your rotten little till.' He dug slowly in his pockets for the silver and dropped it on the counter.

'Gawd,' sighed Uncle Len, wiping his brow, 'I'm glad you seen reason. Spin 'em girls.' And so Aunt Milly and Aunt Lily did, while the spruce and dirty man leaned over the counter so that the people in the bar could not see, shrugging his shoulders and twirling his moustache and humming. When the last coin had rolled and fallen Uncle Len said, 'Now you can go, Benny.'

But when the dirty man turned about he could not bear all the clay-coloured grins that met him. He jerked back and said, 'Well, goodbye, Len Darcy, and be damned to you for a diddacoy.'

He found he could not leave. He was held by his tie. Uncle Len's right hand had shot out and gripped it by the knot, pressing back and up, against the Adam's apple behind it. At the same time Uncle Len's left hand, acting as if it were on its own, stretched out to the counter, picked up a tumbler by its base, and cracked it on the wood so that the rim was shattered. Then that left hand, holding the broken tumbler, came to rest above his right. The jagged edge of glass must have been touching Benny's throat. The two hands stayed there still as stone. If we could have seen Uncle Len's face we might have known whether he meant to bring the glass that final fraction of an inch nearer. But from the doorway we had only an oblique view of him, we saw only the hunched downland of his shoulders, those still hands, his head slewed away from us. But we could see Benny well enough; and he believed he was going to die. His face had turned into a horse's head, his eyes were rolling and his nostrils snorted, his lips had lifted over long yellow teeth. I felt sure that Uncle Len was doing the right

87

thing, but I hoped that in this instance the right thing was not murder. The silence lasted and I felt faint. I was conscious again of the horrible male smell of the room. I looked towards the two women at the bar, who better than anyone would know whether Uncle Len was going to kill Benny. Astonishingly, Aunt Lily had become a black column, a veiled Eastern woman. She had thrown her skirt over her head. Milly's eyes looked through me; her face meant nothing but that she felt as I did, that whatever Uncle Len did would be right, but that it might be terrible.

Uncle Len dropped his hands. 'Why, Benny, Benny!' he said in tones of gentle reproof. 'You been and wet your trousers. Wet your trousers, and you such a big boy!' The silence endured another second. Then again the clay-coloured faces of all the customers were cleft with grins, grins that widened till the room had the huge clownish look of the Man in the Moon, and there surged out of them rolling laughter like a vulgar sort of thunder. 'Got a cloth handy, Milly?' asked Uncle Len. 'Just throw it over. Now, Benny, get down on your knees and wipe up that puddle at your feet.' The clay-coloured grins gave out their open-mouthed roar again; it pulsed, as if it was shaken out of them by a giant hand. 'That's a good boy, get down to it, right down,' said Uncle Len. As Benny stiffly fell to his knees his ginger-brown bowler tipped off, and Uncle Len caught it, clicking his tongue in indulgent reproach. 'Now, careful, Benny, you don't want everything you got messed up,' he said, and the roar swelled again, it was as if the Man in the Moon had come close to earth, as if he were all that there is to know. A breeze blew in the curtains at the open window, blew in the stench of the lavatories from the yard.

Uncle Len looked down on Benny as he swabbed the floor, and said benevolently, seeming to be unaware of the laughter but speaking loud enough to be heard through it, 'That's right. You can work well enough when you get your orders from a better man.' Presently he laid his hand on Benny's head and kept it there. A shudder ran through the kneeling man and he became a waxwork. 'What you stop working for?' asked Uncle Len, kindly. 'What you stop working for, Benny boy?' Absently he let his hand play with the greasy crimps of blue-black hair, and still Benny was rigid, though one could hear his sobbing breath. Then Uncle Len lifted his hand. 'That's enough now,' he said. 'One more good swab and we'll say the

88

job's done. Right. Now run along, Benny boy. And take that cloth with you and show it to your friends outside in that nasty stinking little motor-car. And remember that something funnier still will happen to you when you're hanged. Better remind your friends outside about that too. And now goodnight, Benny. Goodnight. Goodnight for always.'

As the door closed there was a sudden burst of talk, but Uncle Len held up his left hand. It was still holding the tumbler with the jagged edge. 'Hush,' he said. 'See if they start up the motor-car. They're a silly lot. They might be foolish enough to come back.' He eased the tumbler into the hollow of his palm to get a better grip, and we all listened.

Presently the whirring and the spluttering began, and Uncle Len put down the glass on the bar, saying, 'I thought they'd see reason. And here's asking everybody's pardon. You know this is as well-conducted a house as you can find in the country, and such a thing never happened here before, at least not in my time, and pray God it don't happen again.' He turned towards the bar and said formally, as if Milly and Lily were strangers to him, 'Beg pardon, ladies.' He had discarded his everyday bearing, and was carrying himself with the public dignity of a ringmaster in a circus, which is a real dignity in its way. Then he faced his customers again and cleared his throat. 'My name's Darcy,' he told them, 'and no man alive can call me diddacoy.' There was an instant when it seemed as if his words had struck a blank wall. It might have been that most of the customers had no more idea of what he meant than I had. But there was an approving murmur, and Uncle Len acknowledged it with a bow, then wheeled about. Then he saw us.

He groaned and said to Richard Quin, 'Why did you let the two girls come in here? That there wasn't fit for them to see, it truly wasn't.'

Richard Quin made no answer. His lips turned up at the corners as if he were going to smile, then drooped again. Usually, when life became disagreeable, he found a teasing comment which moved what had happened nearer to what one would have liked to happen. But this time the disliked event could not be changed. Uncle Len's words angered me. There was no difference in courage between men and women, if what had happened wasn't fit for me it wasn't fit for men to see either. But Rosamund spoke sharply for me: 'Why should we not have been here? Aunt Milly and Aunt Lily are here.

89

Anyway we came down for candles and matches. Don't you remember?' she asked harshly, as if she were recalling him to his real duties. 'The electric light has gone in the other part of the house.'

'Why, dearie, so it has,' said Uncle Len. 'But this nasty business put everything else out of my head. Come along to the sitting-room.'

There he handed Rosamund a pair of three-branched candlesticks and gave me another, and lit the candles and sent us on our way, telling Richard Quin to come with him to the stables and he would find him a lantern which would be safer in the loft. But as the door between the two parts of the inn swung behind us I said, 'I think we'd better blow these candles out. Fire, you know.' I had such a sense of general and pervasive danger that I imagined a wind springing up even there, in the heart of the house, and setting our skirts blazing. Had Rosamund been her ordinary self, she would have stammered, 'N-n-no, R-r-rose, if we carry them carefully it will be all right,' but now she instantly bent down and blew on the six lights with an angry mouth. For a minute or two we stood still, breathing hard, as if the darkness were a shelter we had gained by running. But we heard hawking voices from the bar, and a great retch of laughter, and to get further from them we felt our way up the creaking staircase, hanging on to the banister lest we fell at the sharp turn, and once in our room we shut the door, longing to lock it, but the others would have noticed, and Rosamund set the two candlesticks on the chimneypiece and lit them. As the flames swelled and steadied Cordelia and Mary turned over in their beds and blinked at the brightness.

'Oh, have we been terribly long?' I asked, busy with the wicks. Both Rosamund and I were being clumsy with them, our hands were still shaking. 'I am so sorry, we couldn't help it, we really couldn't.'

'What are you talking about?' asked Mary. 'You haven't been more than five minutes, we've been all right.'

Surely it had not happened as quickly as that.

'What's gone wrong?' said Mary, sitting up in bed.

I could not possibly tell her the truth, and Rosamund did not want to. She was taking off her clothes quickly and disdainfully, as if she wanted to be alone with her bare, dissociate body. But though I could not talk candidly about

90

what had happened, I had to talk about it. I was still enclosed in the bar, in the smell and the smoke, in the fear of murder and the loathing of our indecent bodies; my breath insisted on turning into words referring to my imprisonment. I said, 'There has been a hateful scene in the bar. A dreadful man tried to get Aunt Milly and Aunt Lily to change a forged five pound note.'

'Wasn't Uncle Len there?' asked Mary, as though that should have settled everything.

'Yes, he was there,' I said. Rosamund stepped out of the circle of her petticoats, like a cat shaking its paws as it comes out of a puddle. But I could not stop. I sat down on my bed and tried to quiet myself. It was no use. Shuddering, I went on: 'He took charge of all that. He didn't let them give him the money, I mean. But that wasn't the end. He got terribly angry because the man who wanted the note changed called him a bad name. I thought,' I said, the room spinning round me, 'Uncle Len was going to kill him.'

'What was the bad name?' asked Mary. She was not impressed, she simply thought that I was using exaggerated language to convey that Uncle Len had been very angry.

'Why should we want to hear some horrible word used by a man who was passing forged notes?' exclaimed Cordelia, jerking her head up from her pillow.

'How stupid you always are,' said Mary. 'You were born not seeing the point. The reason I asked was that it's so strange for Uncle Len to get really angry because someone called him a bad name, it's as if the Thames overflowed because someone threw a rotten apple into it.'

'It was an odd name,' I said. 'Diddacoy.'

'Diddacoy,' repeated Mary. 'Hm. It's not in Shakespeare.'

Rosamund ripped off her stays, pulled on her nightgown, rolled into bed and lay with her face to the wall. 'I don't believe it's in the Bible either,' I said, wishing I could stay quiet like her and not have to go on and on talking about what I wanted to forget. 'And Uncle Len,' I found myself saying, 'said such a queer thing. He said his name was Darcy and nobody could tell him diddacoy as if they mustn't call him diddacoy because his name was Darcy.'

Without turning her head, Rosamund said, 'Do stop talking about it, Rose.'

'Yes,' said Cordelia, 'you keep on saying this word, and for all you know it may mean something quite disgusting.'

'The trouble is,' said Rosamund, keeping her face to the wall, speaking quite loudly, 'that it can't matter twopence what it means. How can it be of any importance whether a horrid little sneak-thief calls Uncle Len a disgusting name? Yet there was Uncle Len, making a fuss about nothing, as my father does, and—' She checked herself and for an instant drew the edge of her sheet across her mouth. We all know that she had been about to add, 'and as your father did.' But she went on, her voice shaking, her stammer gone and replaced by a fluency that was far more painful, 'I didn't think Uncle Len was like that. I was sure he was different. I thought he would get on with what he was doing and not be like the others and keep on finding out reasons why everything has to be horrible when it might be all right, if only they would keep quiet. Why couldn't Uncle Len have let that man call him a diddacoy and walk out of the bar? He would have gone out and driven off if Uncle Len hadn't stopped him, just because he had to make a fuss.' She rolled over on to her back, stretched up her round white arms, and cried to the ceiling, 'I want everything to be nice. Oh, I hate men,' and let her arms fall, and turned back to the wall.

The naked hatred in her cry appalled me. It had always before been we who were excessive, not her. Who was to moderate us, if she exceeded us? I appealed to her, 'But you like Richard Quin.'

'I love him,' her muffled voice said angrily, 'but it is a shame he has to be a man, he should not have been born a man, what will happen to him in a world where men are so awful?'

'Oh, he'll be all right,' I said, speaking angrily because I was afraid.

Mary, angry too, snapped, 'I am sure that whatever Uncle Len did wasn't wrong.'

'Of course, of course,' I said. But I must have spoken without assurance, for Cordelia then began the performance with which she met all catastrophes, and putting on her white, responsible look, made a claim that she had foreseen all this, and that it would never have happened if anyone had listened to her. She said that after all the Dog and Duck was only a public-house, and though the rest of us had insisted that because it was in the country everything would be different, she had warned Mamma that something disagreeable might

92

happen. This performance was always startling because it was hallucinatory; she had had no doubts concerning the Dog and Duck and she had had no such conversation with Mamma, but her eyes were grave and glassy with sincerity. There was no way of arguing with such nonsense, so we always threw things at her; this time Mary threw a pillow at her, and I just missed her with a copy of the *Strand Magazine*, and we told her that if there was anything wrong with the Dog and Duck it was that she was in it. But Rosamund cried, 'Oh, blow out the candles, blow them out now! My head aches, I must go to sleep.' She spoke as if sleep were a horse that she would mount and ride away the instant darkness fell, and I thought this absurd, if she had a headache like mine. For the useful hysteria of youth, which protects the unformed mind from too much distress, was working on me. I was not thinking of what happened in the bar; it was present to me only as a dimly seen image, as the Man in the Moon leering down on a sodden waste of brown mud, because I was preoccupied by a pervasive pain which made the bones of my face feel tender and my eyes smart, and there were twinges like toothache inside my skull. But Rosamund was right. I sunk my face in the pillow so that if I should sob nobody would hear me, but I had not time to sob before I slept.

Then suddenly I was awake. We were all sitting up in bed because there had been a knock on the folding doors. They slowly opened and Richard Quin said softly, 'Is anybody awake? Can I come in?' He was a narrow shape against a trembling pallor, a haze of light above his head. The curtains had not been drawn in the room behind him, so it was lit by the diffused radiance of the moonless night and the great chandelier glimmered above like beetlewings and cast a vague illumination on his fair hair. We whispered, 'Come in, come in,' but for an instant he paused on the threshold, forgetting us, turning towards the window. Out in the garden a young owl had hooted. 'So like a flute,' he said. Then he came into our darkness. 'Rosamund, Rose, are you all right? Uncle Len was so worried about you. He said you would be 'owling your 'eads off. And that was a beastly thing that happened in the bar. You two others were well out of it.'

There was the little cough of a struck match and its brightness wavered and spread. He stood between my bed and Rosamund's and asked, 'You are all right, you two? You are all

93

right?' I answered, 'Yes, we are quite all right,' but Rosamund said plaintively, 'Oh, it was horrible.' That was something I could never understand. If one was asked, when one had a cut and a bruise, whether it hurt, surely one had to say that it did not. But Rosamund never recognised this obligation though she was at least as brave as I was; if a runaway horse ran up on the pavement or an iron shutter fell from a shop front, Rosamund simply moved away and looked particularly bland. But I had noted that when our doctor said to her, 'Does this hurt?' she opened her large blue-grey eyes very wide and answered, 'Oh, yes, it does,' and it was as if she were making him a present by her confession of pain; and he always behaved gratefully, as if she had given him something nice. Now, as Richard Quin looked down on her, she lay back on her pillows and did not hide her face though it was wet with tears; and he drew in his breath between his teeth, but went on looking down at her as if she were a field of flowers.

He sat down on her bed and said to the rest of us, 'Listen, it's late. But I do want to tell you something extraordinary that Uncle Len's just told me. It's really why this awful thing happened in the bar. Do you know, Uncle Len's a gipsy.'

All of us except Rosamund bounced with astonishment on our beds. 'A gipsy!' It was as if he were no longer in the house but was moving about in the night outside, in this intractable light which could not be subdued by the darkness.

'Yes,' said Richard Quin. He went on hesitantly, as if the story had been told him in a foreign language, and he was not sure how to translate it. 'He says that everybody named Darcy is a gipsy. His mother was a Beckett and one of his grandmothers was a Lee. He said that a bit like someone in Shakespeare talking about nobles. Great Earl of Washford, Waterford and Valence.'

'Lord Talbot of Gordrig and Urchinfield,' I said.

'Lord Strange of Blackmere, Lord Verdun of Alton,' said Mary.

'The thrice victorious Lord of Falconbridge,' said Richard Quin. 'We've left out a line somewhere, but never mind now. Anyway, Uncle Len was born in a caravan on Holmwood Common in Surrey. A lot of the Darcys live there. But he ran away when he was ten years old.'

'Why did he do that?' we wondered. All of us but Rosamund were sitting up now, hugging our knees. 'Wasn't it fun to be a gipsy?' asked Cordelia. I thought it odd that she of all of us should put that question.

'That's exactly what I said,' Richard Quin told us. 'But Uncle Len says that if you are a gipsy and you have to run away, and he had to, you can't run away to other gipsies. It can't be done. But you'll have to hear the whole story. You see, when Uncle Len was ten years old his father and mother died. They went off with a lot of the Darcys and the Becketts to a horse-fair and left Len with the caravans because he had a stomach-ache, and when they got back they all fell ill, one after the other, because there had been something wrong with the water at the pump they used when they were at the fair. Several of them died, and his father and his mother were the first to go. So they sent him away to his mother's sister, and she had married beneath him. That is, her husband had nothing to do with horses. Uncle Len says his father knew more about horses than anybody he's ever met since. But his aunt and her husband lived near High Wycombe and made cane seats for chairs. It didn't sound too bad to me, for they made chairs out in the beechwoods where the felled timber has been left to season, and the gipsies finished them off with the wickerwork there too. But Uncle Len says it was a terrible comedown after the horses, and he felt like an old woman wooding. That's what he said. He says the gipsies always send old women into the woods to gather firewood because even a gamekeeper wouldn't like to stop an old woman getting some sticks to keep herself warm. It would be a mean trick if everybody didn't know about it so that it's really a kind of joke. Well, he couldn't stand it. So he ran away and worked as a stable-lad over at Lambourn. He got on very well there, but the worst thing happened.'

'Oh, what?' we asked.

'He got too big and heavy to be a jockey,' said Richard Quin. 'By the time he was thirteen there wasn't the least hope. But he wanted to stay with the horses, so he went to work for a bookmaker. He had great luck for the bookmaker was very nice and so was his wife, that's her in the enlarged photograph in the silver frame on the sitting-room chimneypiece, wearing a big hat with feathers in it, and all those buttons down her bodice, and a big cameo brooch. They were like a father and mother to him, and they made his fortune. They left the business between him and a cousin in Swansea, and he ran it for her, and when she died he sold his share in it and came here. He says he's been very happy, but it still hasn't been as good as being a jockey. But he says that as it is he wouldn't change places with the King of England, and anyway by now he'd be too old to ride and he'd probably be here anyway. Still, he sometimes wakes up in the night and thinks of what it would have been like to ride a Derby winner. And it worries him a bit that he's not with his own people. That's why he doesn't talk about being a gipsy. But he wouldn't be anything else and he wouldn't deny his father and mother for anything in the world, that's why he wouldn't let that man call him a diddacoy.'

'Is a diddacoy someone who lives in a house?' asked Mary. 'I thought they called them gorgios.' We had all read Borrow.

'Oh, no,' said Richard Quin. 'If it just meant that it wouldn't matter being called one. Gipsies don't mind people who live in houses, they just think they're rather simple, but they know the world couldn't get on without them. Gipsies seem very reasonable people.'

He paused, and my heart ached. He had had a talk with Uncle Len such as I had never had. Richard Quin and Uncle Len; Richard Quin and Mr Morpurgo; Richard Quin and Rosamund; each was an alliance from which I was excluded.

'But a diddacoy,' Richard Quin continued, 'a diddacoy's a sham gipsy. He's someone who's got thrown out of his cottage because he couldn't do his job or because he's been in prison, and so he leaves his village and goes and squats on a common, and he tries to live like a gipsy, but he can't. To begin with, all proper gipsies belong to gipsy families, and they all know who they are. That's why, if you're a gipsy and run away from your family you can't just join another gipsy family. They'd know who you were, they'd have to send you back. And then gipsies can do, really do, all sorts of things. They do all this wickerwork, this basket-weaving, and they're better than any other blacksmiths at some kind of ironwork, and they've this great gift for horses. Uncle Len says nobody understands horses like a gipsy, and that's natural, he says, because a horse and a gipsy have minds that work the same way. A horse gets frightened at what it doesn't understand, and so does a gipsy.'

He fell silent, and laughed to himself. Now again there were several young owls hooting, but further away, down in the woods by the river. 'Why, there's the proof,' he said, 'that Uncle Len really is a gipsy. He thinks that people who are not

96

gipsies aren't frightened by what they don't understand. Well, anyway, gipsies can do some things really well; and there's another thing.'

He paused. Uncle Len had told him something that he was finding it hard to tell us. It could not be a secret, or he would not be repeating it; but when it was spoken of they had been as close as if they had been talking secrets. I said, 'Go on, go on.'

'Gipsies do steal,' he said. 'Uncle Len owned it. They steal.'

'Oh, Richard Quin,' exclaimed Cordelia, 'you didn't ask him if gipsies stole!'

Richard Quin was silent for an instant, then he whistled four bars of music, as if he had gone away from us all into a dream. But they were four bars of music which he specially liked and used as a spell to avert despair. Indeed Cordelia was terrible. We were learning that someone whom we loved nearly as much as Papa and Mamma was quite a different person than we had supposed; but she had felt forced to interrupt, because of her fear that Richard Quin, who never blundered, must be a blunderer, since all our family except herself were always blundering. We all looked at her in puzzled anger, and she looked back at us, puzzled but not angry, simply puzzled because we were puzzled, her eyes wide, her short upper lip raised above her teeth.

He went on, 'It's only natural, you know, that gipsies should steal. Moving round a country you get a notion that the whole place is your own property, and when you find things belonging to people who aren't as good as you are, you can't help believing that you have a right to them. Say there's an awful lout of a farmer, there doesn't seem any harm in taking his chickens and eggs. But of course it's wrong. Uncle Len doesn't remember his father stealing anything at all except once or twice, when there was a reason. But diddacoys are different. They're rubbish from any rathole. They hardly know their own names, lots of them have just nicknames. And they haven't any trades. They can't do basket-work, not properly, they don't know where to find the right willows and if they do they can't cut them, and they can't do ironwork, and if they get hold of a horse now and then it's just scrub stuff. And diddacoys steal because they have to, for a living. It isn't like the way gipsies steal, there really is a big difference, if you think over it. So when a gipsy thinks of a diddacoy it's like looking at yourself in one of those distorting mirrors they have on piers. So, you see, Uncle Len had a right to be angry when that man called him a diddacoy.'

'Oh, yes,' we said. 'Oh, yes,' but Rosamund cried plaintively, still lying back on her pillows, 'Yes, it must have been horrid for him, but why did he have to make all that fuss?'

One of the candles went out, and Richard Quin turned to the chimneypiece and lit it again. As we watched him we saw in the brown depths of the mirror four other girls watching another schoolboy. 'Oh, there was more going on than what we saw,' he said mildly. The candle went out again, and he took a pen-knife out of his pocket and began to cut the wick. 'Uncle Len,' he said slowly as he worked, 'and the man who tried to change the forged note knew each other quite well really. His name was Benny Rossi, and they started level, but he has gone down as Uncle Len has come up. He's supposed to have something to do with bookmaking, but Uncle Len says that's just a blind, and it's better not to know what's behind it. Anyway, he goes about with a gang and one of their dodges is that they pay at pubs with five pound notes, and get the change. Part of the game is that the notes aren't even good forgeries. The publican is supposed to look at them and see that the people who tried to pass it are saying, "This isn't a fiver and you know it, and we know it, but you've got to take it or leave it, and if you don't take it we'll smash up your pub." So you see that what happened tonight was quite something to make a fuss about.'

We were breathless at the thought of such evil threatening our friends. 'But what about the police?' asked Cordelia angrily.

'It seems they aren't much good when this sort of hooligan comes along,' said Richard Quin, absently giving a last twist to the wick he had been mending. As he spoke the calm of the night was suddenly broken by a clamour of birds. They were flying towards the inn from the woods down by the river; and they were shrieking like children in panic. It was so dreadful a sound that we could think of nothing else. 'What is that?' we cried. 'Oh, listen, what is that?'

'What is what?' asked Richard Quin, his back still turned towards us. But now the birds were circling round the eaves, still shrieking, and not even his preoccupation could keep him from hearing them. 'Oh, that. Why, a hawk is raiding a wood, and the poor creatures have wakened up in their nests to find that death was among them, and they are literally flying for their lives.'

A bird bumped against the window and scuffled for a clawhold on the ledge, and was jerked out into space again by the catapult of its terror. We all wailed, and Richard Quin said, 'You must not mind so much, these things often happen.' But he listened with us to the winged lamentation as it shrilled higher and higher above the house and keened into the distance, and the silence fell back into place. 'Rosamund, Rose,' he began again, 'did you tell the others about the tumblers? No, I suppose not. Well, Mary and Cordelia missed something. Uncle Len smashed a tumbler on the bar so that the rim came off and left a jagged edge, and he threatened this Benny Rossi with it as if it were a dagger. Well, it seems it was the only thing he could have done. That's how these gangs fight. If a publican won't change their forged notes, they smash their tumblers, then each has his own weapon and he can cut people down their faces and slash their clothes and afterwards he just throws down the tumbler on a stone floor or on the cobbles outside in the yard and it breaks, and then there's no weapon and no fingerprints for the police to find afterwards. So these hooligans haven't anything to fear, and they just go ahead and make the place a shambles before anybody can even call the police. And though Uncle Len talked about being insured he was bluffing. Insurance is a wonderful thing, he says, but it never pays for all the damage, and if a pub's once been smashed up decent people are apt to go somewhere else, and there's the pub at the other end of the village, the Raven, and Uncle Len says that though it's a wretched place, customers might go there if they were frightened to come here, and he can't blame them. So when a gang comes along, you're sunk, you're absolutely sunk unless you know the trick of breaking tumblers on the counter and fighting with the broken glass, and getting into action as soon as they do. So you see, Uncle Len had to do what he did. He was angry about being called a diddacoy, but also he had to show that he hadn't gone soft and could still fight when he was angry. So he couldn't help it, he really couldn't.'

We all said that indeed we saw, we exclaimed at the dangers that had encompassed Uncle Len, at the courage with which he had annulled them; all except Rosamund, who still lay back on her pillows. She was pressing her thumb against her lower lip, as she often did when she could not make up her mind. She was very babyish in some ways, this was very near sucking her thumb. While Cordelia was saying that all the same she could not understand why the police did not stop this sort of thing, Richard Quin moved to Rosamund's bedside and stretched out his arm and ran his fingers deep through her hair and tumbled her heavy golden curls over her face. But under them it could be seen that she was keeping her thumb pressed against her lower lip.

He sighed as if he were too tired to talk any more, but went on: 'Oh, you know, you have to admit it, Uncle Len is a great man, Wellington would have liked him. You see, he had to take hold of Benny's tie with his right hand and smash the tumbler with his left. He had to do it that way, he couldn't help it, because he was standing with the bar counter on his left; and he says he hadn't the slightest idea whether he could do it or not. He had never tried it with his left hand, why should he? But if he hadn't been able to do it, then Benny could quite easily have reached out and smashed a tumbler himself, for of course the bar was on his right. But Uncle Len had to risk it, just to show he was on top. Oh, he was wonderful.'

Rosamund took her thumb away from her mouth and shook back her curls and sat up in bed, clasping the sheet to her breast with one hand, and looked up at him with great clear eyes. 'Of course,' she said, 'I remember that. Uncle Len broke the tumbler with his left hand.'

'With his left hand,' he repeated, coaching her slowness.

'But that was terrible!' she exclaimed in a sudden fluttering flurry. 'Why, it is as if someone were to tell you, your whole life depends on whether you can thread a needle with your left hand. Oh, poor Uncle Len, poor Uncle Len!'

It was the kind of thing she understood. With her talent for serenity she would have ignored the existence of diddacoys, had she been a gipsy; and she would have avoided the attention of hooligans by the use of her talent for evasion, which was nearly but not quite the same as her talent for serenity. But when a man was asked to do something with his left hand which he was used to doing with his right, that evoked her pity. It was like the crisis in a fairy-tale, where the princess will be changed into a pig or a frog if she cannot fill a basket with wild strawberries in the winter woods; and it was

100

to some such early world as that, more simple than ours and yet more strange, that she belonged. Now that she could sympathise with Uncle Len's plight she was at rest, and she was totally restful, just as she had been totally hurt when Richard Quin had come into the room. They exchanged clear and shining and blank smiles, as if they were a prince and princess in a fairy-tale, looking forward to their featureless and eternal happiness. Richard Quin wanted nothing to spoil the moment of harmony which, though I was excluded from it, I knew to be exquisite. He turned about abruptly and blew out the candles, and said in a voice that trembled a little, 'Goodnight, my silly sisters, goodnight, Rosamund.'

Through the darkness she stuttered, 'Goodnight, Richard Quin. I am sorry I was so stupid.'

'Oh, you were not stupid,' he told her as he went through the door. Though he spoke tenderly the way he said it suggested that he meant either, 'No, you were not exactly stupid, but you were certainly going along in that direction, but it doesn't matter,' or, 'No, considering that you are stupid, I don't think you were being particularly stupid.' Surely that was rude, yet it was not rude between them, and I heard Rosamund settle down again in bed with a contented sigh.

Mary and Cordelia and I chattered for a little about the new Uncle Len that our brother had left painted on the darkness. Mary said that we must be sure to give him a really good birthday present, I wondered when his birthday was, Cordelia said she had it in her birthday book and expressed wonder that the rest of us did not keep up our birthday books, it was such an easy thing to do, and, as the present instance proved, so useful. There grew on me the sense that round my bed was the dark room, round my room was the dark house, round the house was the dark garden, the dark garden lay on the side of a dark hill beside a dark river which protected it like a moat, which was the Thames but also seemed as I sunk down into sleep to be Uncle Len, flowing so strongly from his unsuspected beginnings to his unknown end. As I was taken by my dreams, I no longer recollected what my brother had told us about Uncle Len as a story but rather as a long composition he had played us on the flute, on that second mouth set obliquely to the first which the fingers have to teach to speak. Once I woke up and thought I heard Mary crying, and I sat up and said anxiously, 'What's the matter, you ass?' but it was laughter that was shaking her, and she gasped, 'If it is true that everybody, absolutely everybody who's called D'Arcy is a gipsy, then *Pride and Prejudice* is quite a different book from what we thought.' I laughed back, 'And how Elizabeth would hold it over him!' and we slept again.

Then I woke up in the white light of early morning and lay looking round me with that sense of ease which anoints the young when they do not have to hurry out of bed to school. The rains of the previous winter had soaked in through a gutter and left a couple of stains high on the dado above the two windows. One stain was like the helmeted head of a woman, the other was like a spread hand. Uncle Len had said he would get down to a job on the plaster and mend the guttering outside as soon as the season was over and he had a moment to himself. He was indeed wonderful. He had been born of wild people, his childhood had been ruined and his youth disappointed, and if he had wanted to take revenge on the world he had the strength and cunning to do it, yet he did small things about the house as though he were a tame, weak man good for nothing else. Eager to see him, I got up; and lest I should wake the others I took my clothes in my arms and dressed in the passage, near the sealed door which was pierced on its hinged side by blanched fronds of wisteria. They were growing long and straggling, the last leaves on the spurs were tiny, we had nearly come to the end of this summer which had been happy although Papa had gone away. I went out of the silent part of the house into the small morning noises of the inn. Some horses were clopping their hooves on the cobblestones in the yard, men were calling to them, 'Yup, yup,' as if they were eating soup, and then all at once shouting in priggish warning, like schoolteachers telling one that one is going to knock over something when one is not, 'Oh yo! Oh yo!' Then the horses gave exasperated neighs, saying it was all a fuss and they could get on all right if they were allowed to do things their own way, and then there was a contented orderly scamper out to the road and the hoof-clops became softly resonant and died away. The kitchen door was ajar and I heard Milly and Lily exchanging remarks which were like the cawing of the rooks when they left the elm-trees in the morning or came back to them at night, which meant nothing yet were not meaningless, since they proclaimed loyalty to a routine. The kettle must be full boiling or the tea won't be what you could call tea, yes, indeed, and the pot must be 'ot to the touch. All the people at the Dog and Duck dropped their h's, not invariably but to impart emphasis. Horrible was always 'orrible, and surely 'orrible is much the more impressive of the two words. But I did not hear Uncle Len coming in with his caw and telling them for goodness' sake to get on with it, or he wouldn't get his breakfast before closing time. I went out into the garden and he was not there either. But Rosamund's mother, Constance, was walking on the lawn at the river's edge, a cup and saucer in her hand, and I ran to join her.

Constance was very like her daughter, yet was comic. Rosamund recalled classical sculpture, but Constance was like a statue, not a very good statue, imperfectly Pygmalionised. Her skin was smooth as marble and her calm was like marble too; and it seemed probable that under any sudden catastrophe she would simply keel over, her queenly stance unaltered, and it would then be our duty not to bring her brandy and rub her hands but to call on the officials of some museum who owned the tackle that could restore her to an upright position. But today she was not only comic, she was also exquisitely in harmony with the quiet grey morning, as she walked beside the glassy river, sometimes raising the O of her cup to her bland lips, while her large, perfectly shaped hand held the O of her saucer steadily level, and her wide eyes rolled slowly from side to side. As I called to her she set her cup back on the saucer and pointed to the window of the bedroom she shared with my mother.

'Your Mamma is still sleeping,' she told me when I reached her. 'There is no doubt she is improving.' We took some steps together, and she drank again. 'She is slowly getting over the loss of your father. The first wild grief is gone,' she said, in tones so flat that it seemed as if no such thing as grief could exist, 'but she has to fight against what lasts far longer.'

'What is that?' I asked apprehensively.

'Why, she misses your Papa coming in from his office and telling her what has happened during the day.'

'Surely that can't matter so much!' I exclaimed.

'It matters a great deal,' she stated. 'When a marriage comes to an end, whether through death or some such accident as has happened to your Papa, the wife is always distressed, whether she loved her husband, as your Mamma did, or not.' She paused and thought, but gave no example. 'Because he no

103

longer brings her in the news,' she ended. She raised her cup to her lips again, and seemed to forget that I was there. We strolled downstream, she veiled in her reflections, I remembering that if Mamma had been deserted by her husband, she was fleeing from hers. They would not suffer in vain, for I knew too much ever to have one of my own. The river was dimmed by broken mists drifting along the shining surface in hummocks and wisps, not so fast as the current, more nearly at our pace, and above us a struggling sun was pale as the moon. The summer, we said to each other, was nearly over.

She said suddenly, 'Oh, there is Uncle Len. This morning he found that one of our boats had not been tied up properly and had been swept away, so he and Tom went off to find it.' The two boats had just rounded the bend of the river where dark grey woods, sharp-edged against a pale grey sky, seemed now to meet and form a solid wall. The pot-boy was rowing and could hardly be seen in the fogged distance; his boat was just a dark shape which spurted forward, sped on till it flagged, then spurted on again. Uncle Len was standing in the stern of his boat, rooted to his solid midriff in the mists, which there a shaft of sunlight was touching with yellowish silver. He was backwatering with an oar, bringing his craft along as swiftly as the other, with a trick of the arm as delicate as he was gross, a trick which had the air of being a secret he could not have imparted even had he wished. I had seen him make many such movements. Of course he was a gipsy.

'Run and tell Milly and Lily to start his breakfast,' said Constance. 'I came out to keep watch for them.'

I gave them warning in the kitchen and went down the village street to fetch his *Daily Mail*. Our happiness had slipped into its groove again.

IV

OUR HAPPINESS at the Dog and Duck was so great that it was the first place where Mary and I felt any prolonged twinge of rebellion against our destinies. Usually we accepted the knowledge that we were pianists, not in the sense that we chose to play the piano, for that implied that we could have stopped if we had wished, but because we had been born so, as Hindus are born Brahmins or Untouchables, so we made no fuss about it. But at the Dog and Duck, when we had to sit practising at the piano Mamma had hired from Reading, we often sulked. I would rather have been on a bench in the garden, shelling peas or stringing beans into one of those big china bowls, white inside, dark cream and fluted outside, which are surely among the handsomest of household objects, until the ferry-bell rang and I put down my bowl on the grass and slipped on my padded gloves, and took the punt over, hearing first the lovely gush of the water as the pole parted it and went down to the one right place where it should strike the river-bottom, and then the delicate spit-spit-spit of the drops it scattered as it came up between my twirling hands. That was another grievance. Even in padded gloves, that was all the boating we were allowed to do. Richard Quin and Rosamund were good about taking us out on the river, but that was not quite what we wanted. They often took us into the arcade of some backwater they had discovered, not to be seen from the bank, nosing the boat in slowly so that the green crystal pavement was not shattered more than need be, until we came to the inner reach, which seemed sealed by greenness at each end, and we sat as quietly as if we were in church, nobody knowing that we were there, and the ruffled water settling to

105

crystal again around us. But Mary and I could never be the showmen.

Our resentment really went deeper than that. Mary and I would have liked to have a life together on the river which would have proved us as close companions, sharing as many secrets, as Rosamund and Richard Quin. Also it irritated us that even the restriction on our rowing was not quite our own. Cordelia was infringing our rights in our grievance, by a fantasy which ignored the absolute certainty that she would never be a violinist. The great teacher who had heard her play had dispersed her hopes so brutally that even her iron resolution was convinced and broken, and she never touched her violin now. It was even shut up in one of Mamma's old trunks; we could not think why Mamma did not give it away. But when she was asked if she would like to take out a boat she would assume her white, worried stare, which suggested that she was bearing in mind some important consideration wantonly ignored by everybody else, and she would look down at her hands and shake her red-gold head. This trick afflicted Mary and myself with a sense of panic. Cordelia was trying to live our lives, not because she had no life of her own, because there was concealed in her small, compact, delicate, biddable-looking body a self so gargantuan in its appetite that she wanted to snatch whatever good she saw on the plate of any other self. Music was our food, so she had tried to take it away from us. She had failed because it had ceased to exist as soon as she had laid hold of it. It wasn't hers. But we could not have even the pleasure of feeling forthright indignation at her attempted theft, so impudently persisted in after the nature of things had proved that it was impossible, because we knew that what she was doing had another meaning, which deserved our pity. She had been hurt by her failure to be a violinist in the same way that Mamma had been hurt when Papa had left us. She had been married to something and had been deserted. But again we could not feel sorry for her in comfort, because our musical training by Mamma had left us with the belief that to play an instrument badly was as shameful as any crime short of murder. In our eyes, therefore, Cordelia had been miraculously rescued from mortal sin and ought to be rejoicing at her salvation. It is one of the major disharmonies of life that complicated relationships are not reserved for adults. The wind is not tempered to the lamb, shorn or unshorn.

Indeed a lamb may be delivered over to the blast at its strongest, just because it is a lamb, and subject to some mood peculiar to immaturity. One afternoon, when Mary was practising, I followed the towing-path that ran from the inn-garden through the churchyard and along the foot of the steep woodlands. Presently my eye was caught by a cast branch lying on the ground, the leaves of which were dusty-white on one side and the berries a bright dark crimson. Looking up I saw on the edge of the wood the low tree from which it had been broken, and I tried to break off another branch, the berries were so bright. But the fibre was tough, and to get a better purchase I climbed the rising ground behind the tree. But even then I could not snap it, and I tired of the effort, and looked over my shoulder into the wood and took some steps into its dusk; and although I had left my childhood I was immediately overcome by that sense of the world's strangeness which visits children as intensely as if they were accustomed to be somewhere else. Since the wood was uphill it was very dark. There were some beeches, unaltered by being where they were; they raised against the sky layer after layer of green design, and so much light filtered through and between their leaves that their lower branches were as splendid as the upper. Those trees might have been standing free and clear in an open field. But the firs cut off the light, though they etched only a spare and spiky pattern on the sky, and their underbranches were bare and fretted with sordid shrivelled twigs, and the stunted hollies and hawthorns that grew beside them had the look of broken furniture in an attic. Here and there on the earth between there were deep cushions of emerald moss, but there were more brambles and much coarse, blanched grass, and there was an air of natural want, of vegetable shabbiness. It was odd that there was not a sound to be heard, for the treetops must have been thickly peopled with birds and squirrels, and I knew the ground that I walked on to be the ceiling of galleries and halls where rabbits and stoats and weasels had their homes. I listened to the silence till it became itself a sound loud as a trumpet, and as if it were calling me or some others I ran, either obeying it or fleeing from it, I did not know which, back to the edge of the wood. But my terror was only half-real, and it was pleasant enough to keep me from going right out into the open,

107

so I stayed in the dusk, leaning against the trunk of the low tree with dusty leaves and bright berries, and I looked down on the river and saw it strange as the wood. It flowed with a haste so like an air of purpose that it was hard not to think it a great snake fully aware of what it was on its way to do. In the woods on the other side of the water, opaque with that dull green which is the sediment of summer colour after August has drained off its radiance, I saw a signal. One tree, and no other, had been touched by autumn and was bright gold. It must have been growing in a deep cleft on the hillside, for it was visible only from this spot; I had not seen it as I came along the bank. It was shaped like a blown flame, but that clear gold was the colour of light and not heat. In this childish mood, this retreat into legend and fairy-tale and dream, I saw this as a flag flown by some immensity, not a giant, for that would have been too ordinary, a mere magnification of my own kind, but by a cloud with a will, or the force behind one of the seasons. I clung to the tree-trunk, pretending that I believed that the world was made of the enlaced and breathing bodies of natural things, and that one among them was communicating with me by this tree, while at the same time I was thinking that I must bring the others here after tea. It was then that I saw Richard Quin and Rosamund standing just below me at the water's edge, and heard him say, 'It is a queer thing, colours do not seem as bright to me as they did when Papa was still alive.'

I let go the tree and slid down the bank and ran towards them, crying, 'Papa isn't dead.'

They spun round and faced me with exactly the same movement, straightening themselves and letting their clenched fists fall by their sides, and trying to hide the naked pity in their faces by putting on their blindish, indolent air. It was not, as I sometimes thought, that one was copying the other. They were so alike in nature that it was a wonder they were not the same person.

'I didn't see you, I didn't see you!' groaned Richard Quin. 'Oh, I should have known you might be about, we are so apt to go to the same places.'

'I am glad she heard,' said Rosamund. 'Now he won't have to be the only one of you that knows. It has been so hard on him,' she told me.

The three of us drew together on the path, and I found that

I could only whisper, 'Oh, Richard Quin, you might have shown me the letter.'

'What letter?'

'Didn't he write a letter about it?'

'No, there wasn't a letter. Papa only wrote letters to the papers. Not to us. At first I only guessed. I thought you might have guessed too. You were there when it first came out, that day last spring. Don't you remember? The day we were out in the garden showing Mamma the tulips. The hyacinths hadn't come up, Rosamund didn't plant them. Don't you remember?'

'Yes, of course I do. But what are you talking about? We never mentioned Papa.'

'No,' said Richard Quin. 'But Mr Morpurgo brought Mamma all those flowers. Such a lot of flowers.'

'What are you trying to read into that? He is always bringing us flowers. Far too many flowers. Mamma is always giving them away.'

'He never brought us quite so many before or since,' said Richard Quin. 'Well, people send flowers to funerals.'

'She must sit down,' Rosamund told him, 'there is a tree-trunk over there.'

While they guided me I cried out, as if I were reproaching them, 'I saw that golden tree too. I meant to bring you here after tea.' I sat down behind them and rocked backwards and forwards, my elbows on my knees, my chin on my palms, while their hands stroked my hair and my face and my shoulders, very lightly, as if what I had heard would have bruised my flesh. 'But you must have more to go on than that,' I said, contemptuously.

'I have, but that was almost enough,' he said. 'Think. Mr Morpurgo had been away, and he had come back different, and he said to Mamma that he felt happy because his wife was coming home, and he was ashamed of being happy, he felt as if he were being callous about something terrible that had happened. And he spoke as if he were begging Mamma's pardon, as if she were involved in whatever it was that he thought terrible. What is it that could be terrible both for him and Mamma? Only one thing. I guessed then that he had been abroad to see Papa, and that Papa had died.'

The darkness in the wood behind us, where the starved holly and hawthorn looked like broken chairs and rickety

109

tables, was the real world. 'What, at that place that smelled of oil?' I asked.

He nodded.

'Where was it?'

'In Spain, I think. Those horrible daughters of Mr Morpurgo's had a box of Spanish sweets they said he had brought them. He would always bring back presents, whatever he had gone away to do.'

I thought for a moment of the atlas, but not to any purpose. We had never done Spain at school. 'But Papa need not be dead. In a place like that they probably put people in prison for debt. Papa had been away from us for quite a time, he must have got into debt. Perhaps he is in prison.'

'Nobody ever gives people flowers because someone belonging to them is in prison,' said Richard Quin, 'and if Mr Morpurgo had found Papa in prison he would have paid his debts and got him out.'

'But he said it was a dreadful place,' I persisted. 'Perhaps if one went to prison there, they would not let one out, and one would just have to stay there. Like dying.' I used it as the absurd ultimate, which is only brought in for the sake of argument, which does not really exist. But it existed. Its existence was proved by the faces of Richard Quin and Rosamund, which, now I looked at them, were not the same as they had been before, when there was no question of Papa being dead. The real world was indeed that strange world where a dark wood could feel poor and rivers had business, and nameless forces could set trees alight for a message that had no meaning. For there death could be; but in the ordinary world where one played the piano and did lessons and ate and slept there was no place for this thing that was not an object, nor an action, nor really a thought that one could think, yet surpassed in violence any storm and left a huge hole where something huge had been. There was a pain in my head because the two worlds were meeting there.

'Oh, Rose, my silly sister, Rose,' said Richard Quin. 'Our father has died. But, you know, you must not grieve too much, such things are always happening. I was quite sure that they were happening to us, and of course there isn't any reason why they shouldn't, when we were at Mr Morpurgo's house, and he got so angry with his beastly wife, because she asked Mamma where Papa was. Oh, I know he got angry with her about other things afterwards, but his fury began when she put that question. He could have killed her for it. And don't you see, he'd told her to be specially nice to us about Papa. I don't know if he had told her exactly what it was. I think that though he was so keen on her coming home he didn't trust her, which seems so odd.'

'Why do you say that?' asked Rosamund. 'Your mother loved your father, and she didn't trust him.'

'Yes, so she did,' said Richard Quin, 'but all the same it seems strange. I can't understand it. But anyway, Mr Morpurgo had told his wife something, and he had told her too that she must not let it out. Don't you remember her asking, "What was it that Edgar was telling me about your husband? That he'd gone on a journey?" It was then he went quite white. So I said to make quite sure, "He has gone to Tartary," and then – oh, don't you remember? Mr Morpurgo said, "Yes, he has gone to Tartary".'

His mouth was stopped by what it had said. I repeated, 'Tartary? Tartary? But that's in Asia. It's where Marco Polo went. What's that to do with Papa? When you said that I thought you were making fun of Mrs Morpurgo because she was so rude and stupid, it was like saying, Oh, he has gone to the North Pole.'

'There's another Tartary,' said Richard Quin. 'It's an old word they used to translate Tartarus.'

'Oh, no,' I said, my voice a whisper again. 'Tartarus was Hell. You can't have said that Papa had gone to Hell.'

'No, no, not that Papa had gone to Hell,' he said, 'I didn't say that. But Tartarus — ' He stirred, and pointed at the woodland on the opposite bank as if the place was there. 'Tartarus wasn't Hell. You didn't have to be wicked to go there. The sons of the Titans were in Tartarus. It says so in the sixth book of the *Aeneid*. You did that last year, didn't you? Well, don't you remember? The sons of the Titans hadn't done anything but anger the gods by being nearly as good as they were. A nasty lot, the gods. Anyway, Tartarus was part of the underworld, and one part of the underworld is as bad as another. Oh, how I hate death,' he said, looking across the river, 'how I hate death.'

'If we were to be given life,' stammered Rosamund, 'we should have been given it for ever.' Behind my back I felt his hand find hers.

111

'But Papa had death on as good terms as it can be got,' he told me. 'At the end of that afternoon in Mrs Morpurgo's house, when the rest of you went downstairs and he stayed behind and helped me to put away the books I had been looking at on the window-seat, he said to me, "You need not be too sorry for your father, he did not suffer at all."'

Now it was certain, and tears ran down my face. 'What shall we do?' I said, shivering in my brother's arms.

'Why, go on as we did before,' he answered.

'I want to tear the world to pieces,' I said.

'If you did you still wouldn't find him,' he said, rocking me. 'Papa has gone. He simply is not here. The whole world is the place where he isn't. You'll wake up tomorrow morning and think of that, and you'll wake up the day after tomorrow and you'll think of it again, and morning after morning it will be the first thing to come into your mind. Until it stops, and that itself I won't like. But you must get it over. So now to learn to say to yourself, "It had to happen, he could not have lived for ever," and keep repeating it. Say it, Rose.'

'It had to happen, he could not have lived for ever,' I said. 'It had to happen, he could not live for ever.'

'I would give anything to feel what you two are feeling,' said Rosamund. 'When my father dies, I will be sorry for him, as I would be sorry for anybody who dies. But I won't feel this. You've had things that I've never had.'

'But everything we have is yours,' I said, speaking as generously as if it were not grief that I was offering to share, 'and Papa thought of you as one of us. At the end, when he was getting tired of everybody, he still noticed you and Richard Quin.' It seemed so natural now that as he went down to the underworld he should have turned and looked at these two, who were so very fair.

'All the same,' she stammered, 'he was not my father.'

'But when he liked nothing else, he liked to play chess with you,' I said and stopped, seeing him as he was when he opened the drawing-room door, holding the long pale feather of his quill pen in his stained and wasted hand, and said, in a voice already sounding as if it came from a great distance, that his work was going badly, and he would be glad if Rosamund would give him a game. How thin he had grown, grieving over the world, which had not cared for him at all. I said, 'How did he die?'

112

'I didn't ask,' said Richard Quin.

I stared at him in astonishment. He appeared to be simply watching the river flow by; there was a fork of branches, it must have been half a willow tree, bobbing and canting on the main stream, as if it were choosing its way.

'He's always right,' Rosamund reminded me in an undertone.

'I didn't ask,' he explained, 'because if people tell you things it never comes out right. Think how it always is at school. Something happens, they find some silly stuff written on the blackboard or some lab apparatus broken, and they run about trying to find out who did it. They never get what happens. You're told boys were seen in the schoolroom in the late afternoon when they were really out in the slips, and masters think they left early when they left late, and even when that is tidied up you find that you are being praised or blamed for something you didn't do. The thing is a secret, because every master and every boy is thinking of something that nobody else knows anything about. It always works out the same way, there is a grand pi-jaw, and you stand looking at the bar of sunshine on the floor-boards, and they go on and on, never coming near to what happened. Well, they're always saying that school prepares us for life, and I don't doubt it does. So, you see, if people at that place in Spain told Mr Morpurgo how Papa died, they'd get almost everything wrong, just because they weren't Papa, who alone knew how he died his own, special death. And then if Mr Morpurgo told us what they told him, he would get a lot more things wrong, because he was not Papa, and not these people, either. Something might seem complicated which was quite simple; as simple as if he were lying in bed with a candle, and the wind blew open a window, and put out the light. Or,' he sighed, 'as if he had got tired and stretched out his hand and pinched the wick between his fingers.'

Together we three kept our eyes on the river. There must have been a heavy storm nearer its head waters. We had heard nothing of it here, but the driftwood kept on coming downstream. 'We know all we need know,' he said presently. 'Everything about Papa had come to a stop, and now he has come to a stop too. That's all you can get out of it.'

We were silent again, and then he broke out. 'The awful thing is that I had hated him so! That I do hate him now. I have

113

got myself into Tartarus. Virgil said that got you there. Hic quibus invisi fratres, dum vita manebat, Pulsativus parens. Pulsativus parens. I said to myself that if ever I met him in the street, I would beat him, beat him savagely for leaving us, for taking that packet of jewellery he found in the cupboard over the chimneypiece without making sure that Mamma and you girls had anything to live on when he had gone. I know Mamma did not mind, I know she told us that he was going away because a demon of ruin had got hold of him and he did not want the demon to take us too. But nobody should keep demons if they have a wife and children. That's the last truth, there's nothing behind that one. If I live to be a hundred I shall never find out that that isn't true. So I could have beaten him, when I thought of him I hated him so much that it was like when you are going to be sick and you taste the sickness in your mouth. And the thing is that I was not wrong. Virgil thought so too, he put a lot of people into Tartarus who kept their money to themselves and didn't give their own family what they needed, aut qui divitiis soli incubere repertis Nec partem posuere suis. I'm not wrong, it must be right that I should hate him, yet I wish I did not.'

Just then Rosamund made one of the murmuring sounds by which she sometimes intimated distress, which were not peevish yet made a complaint, like the coo of a dove, and were so brief and faint that one was not quite sure that she had uttered it, and hastened the more to find out whether she, who asked for so little, was actually asking for something now. 'My head aches,' she explained. 'Do you think I might take down my hair?' She spoke timidly, for in those days it was unthinkable that a girl who had put her hair up should ever renounce such a dignity, and to let it flow again would have been Ophelia-ish. 'I shall never,' she said piteously, 'get used to having it up.' She raised her arms to her head, arching her back, so that I thought of a caryatid, and slowly took out the hairpins and shook her heavy golden curls loose, one by one, while my brother watched her and forgot what he had been saying. Though these two had been together since they were children they often regarded each other with pleased curiosity, as if they had just met each other for the first time.

'Now I feel happier,' she breathed. 'You do not mind? We are not likely to meet anybody on the way back. This is a public path, but it is one of our private places.'

'You haven't finished the job,' he said. He was smiling, but he was still not himself, some part of him was glad of a discord. 'You have left two curls pinned up, there, above your left ear, it makes it all look wrong.'

'Oh, I am clumsy,' she owned. 'Isn't it funny, I can sew so well, but I am clumsy. You do it for me.' She knelt down in front of him and bowed her head. At first he did not seem to want to touch her, but he leaned forward and took out the pins, and then ran in his fingers deep into her hair and brought them up to the light, again and again. She raised her face, which was at once brilliant and dim, like the Pleiades. It might have been timidity, or slowness or apprehension, or reserve that veiled it. I think it was reserve, though her smooth forehead and the wide space between her eyes promised a candour more than was required, tending to stupidity. She said to his silence, 'We must go back now.'

'It is so odd that something not metal should be as bright as your hair,' he said.

'We must go back now,' she repeated. 'If we start now Rose will have plenty of time to wash her face and comb her hair before tea. If she scamps it Aunt Clare will see that she has been in a state and will wonder why.'

As I wiped away my tearstains, the implications of what she had blandly said came home to me: Mamma had not been told of Papa's death. I cried out, 'But if you haven't told Mamma we must do that at once. We must, we must. Oh, it is wrong not to!'

When Richard, keeping his eyes on the river, shook his head, and Rosamund, still kneeling, turned on me the blind gaze of a statue, I could not believe it. 'But it's all wrong, it really is,' I said. 'Oh, I know that when we were little we thought that fathers and mothers could not be so much interested in each other as they were in their children because they were not related, but that was only because we were little and didn't understand. That, what they had, being married, must be the strongest link, the strongest link—' I could not find the words, and I thought it extraordinary that I should have to, surely they should see for themselves the point I was trying to make. But neither spoke, and he continued to look on the moving water, and her eyes were still blank. It was as if I were insisting on talking about something forbidden, which indeed I felt I was, and they were waiting in goose-fleshed

115

shame till I had finished my blundering. Though they remained so still I had a sense of a slow pulse hammering through them. 'Oh, however much we love Papa,' I said, shutting my eyes and emptying myself, for the sake of getting to an end, 'this is Mamma's business more than ours.'

There was a moment before they stirred. Then Richard Quin said, 'Yes. But she knows her business. Think how well she knows it. She knew exactly what was going to happen when you and Mary went to play to a really good piano teacher, she knew exactly what was going to happen when poor old Cordy went to play to a really good violin teacher. And I'm sure she knew better still what was going to happen to Papa when he left us, for there's the link, you said so, it must be the strongest link.'

'But if she knows it already,' I said, 'what's the harm in telling her?' But as I said that I knew it was so sensible that it could not be wholly true. 'It's a kind of sacrilege,' I pleaded, trying to get nearer the truth, 'for us to know and her not to.'

'To talk to her about what she knows might be making her read aloud a letter which it had hurt her to read to herself when she first got it,' said Richard Quin.

'Oh, then you do think that he died a horrid death,' I whispered.

'No, truly I don't, considering what he was. He wouldn't be thinking of his death but of what mattered to him. Whatever that was. You know what he was, how he used to go out on the iciest winter day in a thin coat if Mamma or Kate did not stop him, and come back not noticing that he was blue with cold. And you know how Mamma had to make him eat. I think he probably never felt that he was dying. But his death may have looked horrid from the outside.'

I spoiled my face again with tears. 'We guess and guess, and will never know,' I complained. 'The fault about this world is that the people who love each other are separate. It is terrible to care what someone else feels as much as if they were you, and not to know what they feel, because they are they and you are you. It is like being in prison, only the other way round, locked out instead of locked in, not to be Papa, not to be him when he dies, not to die along with him. This is torment, to strain against a barrier that can't be broken and isn't there, that is just separateness.'

'Oh, but you're wrong,' Richard Quin, who was never

awkward, spoke awkwardly. 'You said it was the strongest link. That's evidently what it is. There's nothing like it. People who love each other,' he said, in a sort of agony, 'like that, like our father and mother, they are not separate. They flow together, they are not two people any more.' We were back in our embarrassment, he had to force out the words, I had to force myself to listen to them. 'So you do see, don't you, that if we told Mamma, and she got Mr Morpurgo to tell her everything, we'd be making her look at Papa's death from the outside, when she's already looking at it from the inside.'

That of course was true. 'Yes, yes,' I sighed, and got up, and left him sitting on the tree-trunk, Rosamund kneeling among her spread skirts at his feet, and walked ahead of them back to the Dog and Duck, through a late afternoon already eveningish, we were so close to autumn. The sun had fallen below the crest of the heights above us, and the air was cold, the river nearly white, the reflected woodlands more black than green. I was not unhappy. Young people are uplifted when the scenery around them changes in harmony with what is happening to them; they take it as evidence that life is a work of art and is faithful to some design. I was indeed happier than when I had started out from the inn an hour or two before, in one important respect. After that day I did not weep for my father any more, and I was visited less and less often by the vivid images of him and the sound of his voice. This did not mean that I had become indifferent to him; rather was it that I no longer needed to remember him, because I was never in danger of forgetting him. When I think of what I am I see a high cliff honeycombed with halls and corridors, which are inhabited by children and young girls and women of all ages less than my own, who are my recollected selves, brought back to being every time I knew again the special satisfaction or despair, accomplishment or ignorance, which preserves each from the ruin of time. Since Richard Quin and I talked beside the flowing Thames, Rosamund so quiet at our feet, it has seemed to me that my father lives in these halls and corridors among my selves. We are still separate but we are companions. Yet he was never all I wanted, and I knew it. I have never had any difficulty in understanding how Dante spent his life consumed with love for Beatrice while steadily consuming the domestic affection of his wife, for I practised a like dichotomy. I walked through the dying day, through the summer, aflame with love for my father, but when the night thickened round the Dog and Duck and the fires were lit to keep out the autumn, I was as contented as could be, doing my filial duty by Uncle Len in his office.

Richard Quin and Rosamund and Mr Morpurgo were there too, all at work round the table, with Uncle Len at its head. We were helping prepare his books for Michaelmas Day; and we were just not too snug to keep the figures clear in our heads, what with the warmth of so many bodies in this narrow slit of a room, the wood-fire and the paraffin lamp hanging from the ceiling. For in his office Uncle Len would not have electric light; this was perhaps because he was trying to make it as like as possible to some room he had known in his childhood, perhaps a caravan. He did not often invite us to enter it, and indeed it was nervous work when we did, for much of its space was occupied by an object dear to his heart which was too large for the room. He had inherited it from the bookmaker who had taken him in when he had left the Lambourn stables. This was a square glass box on brass legs, in which two stuffed stoats in white drawers faced each other in a boxing ring, a third in shirt-sleeves standing by as a referee, while behind the ropes mounted three tiers of stoats in evening dress, representing the upper crust of the fancy as it had been fifteen years or so before. Much thought and manual skill had gone to the making of this work of art. It could be seen at a glance that one of the boxers was younger and less experienced than the other, and would never be his equal; something stupid was incised round his snout. Their postures showed to a T, Uncle Len told us, how a pug who knows his business draws an antagonist when he's got a cross-counter in his mind, and he said too that they weren't feathers nor welters but middles, and would stay in that class. The spectators were all portraits, and Uncle Len had identified all but four. Edward Prince of Wales nobody could have missed, if only because he was wearing the Order of the Bath, which Uncle Len admitted was unlikely, though this was supposed to show a slap-up night at the National Sporting Club not long after it had opened. I can still remember Barney Barnato, who had to be represented by a baby stoat, he had been such a very small man; and Sir George Chetwynd, who had faced the unknown artist with the problem of making a stoat look like a man who had looked like a horse. All these patrons of sport were portrayed with the affectionate derision which the poor then felt for the rich. It was as if the rich were pampered animals which the poor kept as pets, partly because they liked the clear eyes and glossy coats which come of pampering, and partly because it created a false assurance of security which, to the insecure, seemed richly comic. Also it was indicated, by a certain pride in the boxers' stance, that they had that which put them above the business of buying and selling, though they were paid, the fee covered nothing but their time.

Though this work of art disclosed new beauties every time we studied it we had no eyes for it this evening. There was real work to be done. Rosamund was comparing invoices with the accounts to be paid or presented on September the twenty-ninth. Richard Quin was checking the catering ledger, I had the wages notebook, Mr Morpurgo was going over the bank-books. Uncle Len himself was writing the letters that would go out with the accounts and the payments, in the large copybook hand he had learned from the bookmaker's wife, who had made him sit down and start his pothooks and hangers when he was turned five foot six and weighed in at eleven stone.

The clock struck seven; the industrious silence spread again. Then Rosamund said tentatively, 'Uncle Len.' When he used his pen he had as grave an air of application as if he were mending a minute and valuable watch; one did not disturb him without due cause or too abruptly. 'Look, Uncle Len,' she went on, 'on this slip from Howlands it says twenty cases of ginger beer, three short, to be made good. But I don't think they were.'

'Good girl,' said Uncle Len. 'I've thought that myself. A cross-eyed driver. It shouldn't mean anything, but it often does.'

His pen scratched on. Presently Mr Morpurgo said, 'Darcy,' and when the pen had stopped he said again, 'Darcy. Do you really want to put so much of your savings by as insurance? Investments would give you more control over your capital.'

'Just let me finish providing for what I want to provide for,' replied Uncle Len, 'and then maybe I'll stand myself a flutter.'

A shadow of pain passed over Mr Morpurgo's face. 'There are investments,' he said, 'that are no more a flutter than insurance.'

'I don't doubt it,' said Uncle Len. 'But there's Milly. If I die soon she'll marry again. She's kept her flesh. Well, the way I've

119

fixed it she don't get a lump sum that a Flash Harry could take off her, she gets an annuity, and if he left her after the honeymoon and she found his luggage full of broken flowerpots she's only got to keep herself till the next quarter. And if he's a good chap it'll come in handy and make him fonder of her. Nobody ever liked a hen less because it lays eggs. You wait till I got Milly seen to, and done a bit for poor old Lil, and I'll try some of your rough stuff in the City.'

Silence fell again. Then Uncle Len laid down his pen and fixed his eyes on Richard Quin, pointed a forefinger at him and said, 'Boy.'

Richard Quin muttered – 'and eleven and fifteen and eighteen, total a hundred and three, three shillings and carry five pound. Yes, Uncle Len.'

'You got your whole life before you,' Uncle Len told him, 'mind you start thinking about insurance the minute you get your first week's wages. You get on to it young and the premiums are next to nothing, and your future's safe. Not a worry in the world, you haven't, if you insure yourself early enough. I wish I'd done it. And Mary and Rose,' he said, his voice weighted with apprehension, 'they ought to insure their 'ands.'

'How does insurance work?' asked Richard Quin.

'Insurance is a precautionary system which comes into being as soon as a society possesses enough statistical records of past experience to be able to make sound assumptions about the future,' said Mr Morpurgo, and Uncle Len cut in, 'There's the Pru and the Pearl and the Sun, and the Norwich and the Union, and the Equitable, and the Scottish Widows. I fancy the Pru myself. Huge great place they got up there on Holborn, they couldn't do no moonlight flitting.' Thus they continued, each surveying the institution from the windows of his private world, till Richard Quin saw it clearly from his own and said, 'I see, it's a sort of game that turns out to be useful. I'll have a go at it as soon as I can,' and went back to his ledger. There was a red silk shade on the lamp above our head; the walls glowed with a rosy dye. We might have felt sad because the summer was coming to an end, but it was impossible for sadness to survive in this room.

V

THE DAY BEFORE Mary and I went to take up our scholarships, she at the Prince Albert College in Kensington and I at the Athenaeum in the Marylebone Road, I went out and bought enough for both of us of the stuff we were allowed to use now we were grown up, *papier poudré* it was called, little books of absorbent tissues that we dabbed on our faces; only fast girls used powder-puffs. When I came back I went into the drawing-room and found Mary sitting at the table in front of a mass of dull sewing, my mother's workbox beside her. She was putting our name-tapes into the things we would have to leave in the cloak-rooms at the colleges, our mackintoshes and shoe-bags, gloves and woolly scarves, and Cordelia was sitting opposite her, watching her with that detached and childish look she assumed when Mary and I were making preparations for our life as music students. She might have been pretending that she was not going with us because she was the youngest, instead of the eldest, and that her time was still to come.

'See,' she said, in a prattling tone, throwing me a snake of white cotton embroidered with red letters, 'don't Mary's new name-tapes look queer? Mary Keith, Mary Keith, Mary Keith.'

'Oh, dear,' I breathed. Mr Kisch had made us do two things we did not much like. He had made us go to different colleges because, as he had hesitantly told me, Mary played better than I did, and I might be discouraged if I were always confronted with her superiority. I had obeyed because, to my astonishment, tears had come into my eyes when he was telling me this, and if I was such a fool as that I had better take warning. Also he had said that it would never do for two concert pianists to come out at the same time with the same surname, we would always be getting mixed up, so I was to keep my name, Rose Aubrey, and Mary was to take Mamma's surname and be Mary Keith. There had seemed no harm in that; but now she was doing it I did not like it. Savages believe in a magic bond between things and their names, and I was savage enough to feel that now Mary and I were no longer both called Aubrey a membrane which had joined us had been torn through. I even imagined that the raw edge protruded uselessly between my shoulder-blades.

Mary stopped sewing. 'I don't like it either,' she said. Two mutilated savages stared at each other, resentful because they had not been fully warned about the initiation rites, but not rebellious, since it was an initiation rite, the one entrance into real life. We knew we had to go through with it.

'It's horrible,' I said.

'What's horrible?' asked Cordelia. I did not answer, and she exclaimed, 'Why, just Mary changing her name? I don't see there's anything so awful about that. She'll have to do it if she marries.'

'But that would be horrible, too,' said Mary.

'Nonsense,' said Cordelia. 'It happens all the time. Hundreds of girls get married every day and change their names. Something that happens every day can't be horrible.'

'You really are an awful ass,' I said. 'People die every day and death is horrible.'

That's not at all the same,' said Cordelia. 'Marriage and death, what could be more different?' Her fingers probed the depths of my mother's workbox, and brought up an old white chiffon scarf. She cast it over her head and her little hands put in a hairpin here and there, and made it a bridal veil. Slowly, as if she were spinning out a pleasure as long as she could, she moved across the room and looked at herself in the square mirror opposite the window. She shifted and swayed until the composition of the picture she saw was quite right; her red-gold curls and small, pure, stubborn face, romanticised by the veil, in the centre of the glass, and as a background the french window festooned round its edge with little white stars of late clematis, and framing the sleepy, misted blue-green distance of the September garden.

I prayed tenderly, 'Oh, God, please let her marry since you would not let her play the violin. Let her be able to fall in love,' I added. Mary and I had frequently remarked to ourselves that we had never met any man with whom we could possibly have fallen in love, though Mary, who was always fair-minded, had pointed out that this might well mean that the men we met felt they could never fall in love with us. But then, in the isolation of a gambler's family, we had met very few men. 'God,' I prayed, 'let her meet some man who is really nice and young enough. What did you think was the good of letting her meet Mr Weissbach?' But as I rebuked the Almighty the savage in me came to life again.

I felt shocked because it was obvious that Cordelia had played this game before the mirror more than once before. She had been able to find the scarf in Mamma's workbox without looking for it, and she had known exactly how to put in the hairpins. But only a minute before she had given away her idea of marriage as a ceremony where one dressed up in order to cast off one's true name, to desert one's family. She had in fact been rehearsing treachery. I had to admit that there was no reason why she should feel full loyalty to us, for I never felt that she was really one of us. That was why I had not wanted to tell her how much I loathed Mary taking another name, it was like letting a stranger into a family secret. This was all wrong, for I was not quite loyal myself. When I had looked at the red name on the white tape, 'Mary Keith, Mary Keith, Mary Keith', I had feared lest Mary had been chosen to assume my mother's name because she had inherited the larger share of my mother's talent. I knew it was not so; it was because Mary Keith and Rose Aubrey sounded better than Mary Aubrey and Rose Keith. But I felt a bitter and idiotic anger, not against Mary but against my poor mother as if she could, had she wished, have gone to her lawyers and seen to it that she handed on her talent to us in equal proportions.

I was to wonder soon if I had not been disinherited altogether. At first I was not greatly drawn to Mr Burney Harper, who was my chief teacher when I went to the Athenaeum. He was seedy with professionalism, looking so much like a musician that he looked like a street musician. His dark red hair sprang from a centre parting in large soft waves, as if a giant handlebar moustache had been transplanted to his scalp. It was in fact a marmalade parody of Paderewski's amber aureole. Too many picturesque touches, including an excessive resort to velveteen, made his suits seem like some kind of native costume. I greatly preferred the appearance of my former teacher, Mr Kisch, who had belonged to that elect tribe, the Jews of Budapest. His eyes were black fire among his finely incised wrinkles, the bones under his yellowing ivory flesh might have been put in by a fan-maker. But I observed very soon that Mr Kisch would have approved of Mr Harper's teaching, which followed the same lines as his own, though it was differently expressed. 'You ignorant little brat,' Mr Harper would say, 'you're not holding that G in the left hand. Don't you see you need it? This is one of the places where Mozart pops in a bit of grand opera into a piano sonata, and your right hand's all right, it's playing as if it were singing an aria with its ribs out to keep all the air in, but what's opera without an orchestra? That G gives the harmonic background, it spreads on the richness, keep it on, on, on, you silly little cuckoo.'

But almost at the same time that I passed Mr Harper as all right, I became aware that he was not prepared to do the same by me. He said nothing comminatory. He was, indeed, very friendly. He told me little things about himself, mentioning quite often how lonely he felt now that his mother was dead. He had lived with her, and he never could get used to going home in the evening and not finding her by the fire. All the same, after each lesson he dismissed me with kind words which were quite spiritless. I did not expect praise, for that is the prerogative of amateurs, who have a limited objective in view. Once one is a professional musician one's goal is set in infinity and one can never be congratulated on getting any nearer to it. All that one can hope from a professional (even if that be oneself) is an admission that one is in a state of motion, and when this admission is respectful it often takes the paradoxical form of a complaint that one is not moving fast enough. This seems inconsistent, but then to be a professional musician one must be schizophrenic, with a split mind, half of which knows it is impossible to play perfectly, while the other half believes that to play perfectly is only a matter of time and devotion. I was fairly certain that had I played to Mamma and Mr Kisch as I was playing to Mr Harper I would have rated the compliment of denunciation, that Mamma would have shrieked, not like an eagle defending its young, but like an eagle doubting if its young were worth defending or even rearing, and Mr Kisch would have shuddered in glittering peevishness. Their scorn would have meant that I was walking with them in the procession that would gloriously never arrive at its destination; but Mr Harper's embarrassed indifference implied that so far as he was concerned I had never joined it. Weakly, I tried to tell myself that he disliked me and was therefore biased; but I knew the suspicion to be absurd. The fantasy of his appearance showed him to be so trustfully fond of people that he dared play at charades without feeling they would mock him; and even had some circumstances forced him to go against the grain and dislike somebody, he still could not have lied about their musical ability. His ear had an honesty his mind could not have overborne.

And indeed he liked me. I learned that suddenly when I was part of the stream of students tumbling out of the Athenaeum into a November dusk, our blood so warm that the slap of the cold air on our faces was like a pleasantry and we laughed as we ran. Girls ran out of school then as they run today, though their skirts were long tubes touching the ground. When I had got outside I halted to look about me, at the gold bar of sunset lying across the Marylebone Road, at the primrose reflection that faced it. The plane-trees were casting their last crumpled maroon and silver leaves on the pewter pavements, the lights of the passing traffic paid out yellow ribbons of reflection on the shining roadway. The haze above was a violet-dun. There was a grip on my arm, and Mr Harper said he knew I walked to Oxford Circus, and he would be glad to keep me company. He went on holding my arm till we got across the road, and that was very pleasant, for the traffic was very disconcerting in those days when it was half motor-cars and half horse-drawn vehicles. Also the beat of the horses' hooves on the cobblestones made a drumming noise, which was quite confusing. When Mr Harper and I got into the canyon of Harley Street an uneasy silence fell between us. He broke the ice by striking an area railing with his stick and saying, 'E, I'd say, or E flat, what would you say?' Without waiting for an answer, he passed on to other matters; and presently I found that he was talking to me as Mr Morpurgo talked to Mamma, in a steady flow of self-revelation, without any attempt to find out whether he was interesting me or whether I would like to make any remarks myself. I listened with pride, for Mamma had told me that this was one of the highest compliments a man could pay a woman.

It was a lovely evening, winter though it was, said Mr Harper; and such evenings always made him think of the days when he was a boy. He had been at Bufton, a famous school in the Midlands, where his father had been music-master, a lovely place, not old, no older than 1860, but built in imitation of the Gothic style by a pupil of Ruskin, and many people considered it as fine as anything done in the Middle Ages. It was very much like Keble College at Oxford, but better, for there was more of it. When November came round he always remembered what it had been like to run out of chapel after carol practice and see the sunset red behind the elms beyond the playing-fields, and scamper round the Big Square (that was what they called the lawn in the middle of the school buildings, though goodness knows why, he said with tender amusement, it couldn't have been more of a circle) and get back to one's house and into one's study, where there'd be a fire going fit to roast an ox, it was astonishing how boys loved a fug, and then eat a huge tea, with crumpets dripping butter and spread with mulberry jam. That was one of the great things at Bufton, the mulberry jam. There was a wonderful mulberry tree in the tuckshop garden, they laid muslin on the grass underneath to catch the fruit as it fell, and made it into the best jam he had ever tasted. It had been a marvellous school, the finest tribute he could pay to the Athenaeum was that it had something of the same spirit as Bufton, and he was proud to say that his father was responsible for a good deal of the Bufton spirit. He had fallen in love with the place as soon as he got there, and his very first year he'd written the famous Bufton School Song, 'Fair are the spires that arise from the plain' – very flat, that part of the Midlands – 'Fair are the dreams of youth in its prime.' And the old man had stayed on forty years after that, though it wasn't easy for the first twenty, because then he'd been under the famous Dr Disney.

I must, Mr Harper told me, have heard of Dr Disney, the Bull they used to call him, oh, a great, great man, he made the school, but he was a devil in lots of ways. But, Mr Harper proudly proclaimed, his father had known how to handle the Bull. One time he got him right down. It was funny, but the two things that the Bull couldn't stand were Hanover and Rockingham. Could I imagine? I gained time by giggling; a German town and a kind of china? But he went on to point out that his poor father couldn't help having to dish them out sometimes, they were the favourites of at least one bishop who sometimes visited them. I recalled that hymn-tunes have pet-names, and that 'O Worship the King' is sung to 'Hanover' and 'When I survey the wondrous Cross' to 'Rockingham'. So, one day after evensong, Mr Harper went on, and I did not mind at all that I had to stand outside Oxford Circus tube station in the biting air until he had finished the story, and that it was not a very good one. This was the first time that any man had ever been in my company not because we had floated together on the current of my family life, but because he had sought me out. It did not matter that he was unattractive. It did not matter that I could not think of any other man I would like to have standing in his place. It was, I vaguely felt, the principle of the thing that mattered.

That night and all the following day I was serene. Henceforward, I thought, I would play better for Mr Harper, and he would be the more ready to see that I was playing better, and it would all be like carol practice at Bufton. But the next lesson went badly. While I rendered Mozart's sonata in C major (the eleventh) he looked up at the corner of the ceiling as if a stain was spreading there, and when I had finished he sighed, 'Oh, leave it, leave it.' There was a small puff of marmalade moustache on his upper lip, so inconspicuous compared to the huge paramoustache which sprang from his scalp that I had hardly noticed it. Through this he blew for a moment or two, then told me that he had thought of me a lot since we had had that stroll together the other evening, and that our chat had told him one thing: that I was a very intelligent girl.

I heard this with surprise. That had been no chat but a monologue, not delivered by me; and though I had found it interesting, especially the bit about the mulberry jam, it had not struck me as a manifestation of intelligence at all.

'So I'm going to be frank with you.' Even after that I was not afraid. He was as cheerful and commonplace as a Christmas card with a robin on it. Nothing was less likely than that he would say anything very terrible. Yet he said, 'You're not doing well, you know. You're not doing well at all.'

I could not speak. A voice within me was saying coldly, 'If you cannot play you are lost. You can do nothing else.' I remembered that when one felt faint one should breathe deeply, and when I came to the surface again I recalled that Mamma thought I could play, and that Mr Kisch thought I could play, and I made myself remember how the Mozart sonata I had just gone through had sounded, and I was sure I could play. I clung to rage as to a spar. I struck the keyboard with both my clenched fists and cried through the discords, 'What do you mean? I am not as bad as all that.'

'Now, now, temper,' said Mr Harper. 'Who said you were bad? If you were bad there'd be no problem, we'd fling you out on your ear, and a nice-looking girl like you would pick herself up, no bones broken, and go home and get married. But you're good, and that's why it makes me sick to see you heading straight for an annual concert at the Wigmore Hall, the Wigmore Hall, mark you, not the Queen's Hall, and sympathetic notices in *The Times* and the *Telegraph*, the sensitive musicality and wide scope of interpretative talent which we have learned to expect from Miss Aubrey, hogwash, hogwash, and more and more of your time spent teaching. There's something horrible, I always think, in women teaching girls. Little gifts of flowers. You couldn't stand that life, indeed you couldn't. Look at the way you answered me back just now. Usually when I say, "You're not doing so well, you know," what I get is, "Oh, Mr Harper, I'm sorry, what am I doing wrong?" Not you. You spit out, "I'm not so bad as all that."'

I weakened. 'Oh, did you mind?' I humbly asked.

'No, I didn't mind,' said Mr Harper, 'but it places you. You mustn't get in with the nice musicianly girls, it's not you. And to get among the others, you've started off on the wrong foot.'

'What do you mean?' I said, getting up from the piano and stamping. 'What am I doing that I shouldn't do?'

He spent some seconds blowing through his little moustache before he answered. 'It's such a pity you were Clare Keith's daughter. She's taught you to play as if you were her, and you're not, by a long chalk. According to what my father used to say, when he was alive, I've lost both my father and my mother, I was telling you about her, your mother was one of those miracles that come into the world part trained. Say Mozart and Liszt came into the world three quarters trained, we can grant her a quarter and to spare. You're not like that, and my father says she was the size of a shrimp, but had such blazing nervous energy that she could get as much out of her instrument as Teresa Carreno, who'd got a couple of carthorse legs instead of arms. You're not like that either.'

I gazed at him as if I had doll's eyes, fixed, of glass. It was the blessing and the curse of my life that I had a genius for my

128

mother. That she had laid her talismanic hands on me was my sole reason for hoping that I in my weakness might survive in this hostile world; it was because I was so inferior to her that I felt I would be only getting my deserts if the world destroyed me. I did not know how he could bear to speak so nakedly of this promise and this threat which tore me apart.

'You can play what music you've heard her play, you can tackle the music you haven't heard her play by thinking musically as she's taught you to think,' he went on, blind to my anguish. 'And now it's gone wrong. . . .' For some time, because music deals with sounds which are not words, words were a maze in which he wandered, never coming close enough to the truth he desired to impart. After several aphorisms had started well and ended in, 'I mean to say,' after he had made several allusions to contemporary pianists which I could not follow, he pursued a line which presently made me aware that he thought Mamma had made a mistake in sending us to Mr Kisch. He did not say this directly; he was so uncomfortable about stating it indirectly that he began to stammer. I told myself, while he felt about for the words he could not tolerate using, that what he said was sure to be biased, for he was like a dog, while Mr Kisch was like a cat, but again I had to concede that his musical honesty could never be deflected, and so I listened, and found he had a case. Mr Kisch had had to give up his career as a pianist because he had caught a cold playing in St Petersburg in winter and it had developed into consumption, and he had had to go into a sanatorium for some years; and when he came out he had, in Mr Harper's opinion, declined from a professional to an amateur.

But Mr Harper could not explain to me exactly what he meant by that. Mr Kisch, he said hesitantly, played as if, as if, as if he were giving a treat to some friends in a room full of flowers. Mr Harper evidently felt that music and friends and flowers ought to be kept apart. And the windows shut, he added. Had I ever seen, he asked, an abominable picture called 'The Kreutzer Sonata', with a pianist and a fiddler going at it hammer and tongs while a lot of people sat round in huddles, looking all woozy, as if there was a gas escape somewhere, though if there had been the pianist and the fiddler couldn't have kept at it. And there was a worse picture called 'Beethoven', with a man and woman sitting looking as if they were full of beer, and it was Beethoven, Beethoven, of all

129

composers, who was supposed to have put them into that state. Music was something you had to do sober as a judge. Hard, you had to be. 'You've got to realise that,' he insisted. 'or it's no use your doing what I'm going to ask you to do. You're a willing girl, you'd do it. But you must understand that it's part of a plan, you've got to start now and get some real technique.'

Now the agony I felt was what a fish must feel when the barbed fly settles in its gill, eeling itself into the wound by its shape. The world was going to destroy me, just as I had always feared. There was nothing before me but to gasp and die. What else had I been doing all my life but 'get technique'? That was why I had had no childhood, why I had seen so much sunlight through window-panes, why tomorrow had always been a day when the hoop I had to jump through would be held a little higher. I felt angrily that I could not have worked any harder, and there I was right. If I had toiled as painfully in a textile mill or in the fields society would have regarded me as its pitiful victim and sent some agent to rescue me. Now this man was killing my hope that I was near to the end of my slavery. Of course I had known that to endure I would have some measure of this drudgery all my life, because a musician's technique keeps in being only through practice, the hand is a lout and keeps on sinking back into ignorance, but surely, surely I had got near the point where work would become almost wholly pleasure and I could give myself up to the meaning of music?

'You listen to me,' Mr Harper went blandly on in his Christmas card way. 'You've got to sit down at the piano and say to yourself, "Now, I've not begun to be a pianist yet, but I'm going to begin today, and it's going to take a long time, but" – Oh, Lord! Oh, Lord! What have I said? You silly little bit of nonsense, you mustn't cry!'

My state was far worse than he perceived. For as I sobbed I was only partly anguished. I also saw a vision of myself walking by the river near the Dog and Duck, as happy as the blessed dead, my mind flowing bright and unconfined and leisured as the Thames I looked on, because I had cast away the burden, so infinitely greater than myself who had to bear it, of my vocation. I would earn a living somehow. I could become a Post Office clerk, and it was snobbish nonsense that one could not work in a shop. Perhaps they would let me help at the Dog and Duck.

'Oh, Lord! Oh, Lord!' wailed Mr Harper, 'I didn't mean to make you unhappy, that's the last thing in the world I'd want to do! Oh, don't, don't look at me like that! You poor little thing, I've been trying you too hard. You are a girl, after all, and you're not Jewish, being Jewish is a great help, these Jewish scholarship kids can go on for ever. You being a girl makes me forget—'

'I've got a scholarship,' I interrupted angrily through my tears.

'Yes, but being a scholarship kid and being a Jewish scholarship kid's not the same thing, somehow. And the important thing is that you're a girl, and maybe you're right in giving up, maybe a woman's happiness doesn't lie in being an artist, maybe you'll do just as well teaching, and anyway you should marry, you're a nice-looking girl, oh, I blame myself —'

His voice broke. By this time we had got over to the window and I had turned my wet face towards the glass and was clinging on to the sash to steady my sobbing body. But at this sign that he was nearly as distressed as I was I whirled about. Yes, his eyes were moist with pity. I realised that he thought me a weaker person than I was, and that it would be pleasant to pretend that he was right, and that it would not be altogether a pretence. I did not trouble to dry my tears, but lifted my face towards his, drinking in his kindness.

'There are things,' said Mr Harper with an air of bravery and revelation, 'just as important as playing the piano, every bit as important, we've got to own it. We live in a beautiful world. Look at that tree down there, it's only a tree in a London back-garden, but with that shaft of sunlight on it, it's really lovely. Though it's bare that bit of light on the trunk makes one think of the spring. Oh, it's a shame to limit oneself but you came to me to learn to play the piano, and I'm here to teach you to play the piano, and I overlooked things I ought to have paid attention to. Playing the piano's become a murderous game. You might say that to play the piano nowadays you've got to turn yourself into a pianola, oh, worse, a barrel-organ, or one of those electric pianos that go on as long as you drop in a penny, churning it out, a machine that can't tire and hasn't a heart. Not that it's wrong, if you can do it. But there's no reason why we should all take the hard way in this life. I've tried to say that in my work, you know. I'm not really a pianist, you see, I'm a composer.'

'Oh, I didn't know,' I said respectfully, wiping my nose.

'Yes, I've written three operas, but you wouldn't have heard of them. I wasn't,' sighed Mr Harper, 'very fortunate in my librettists. But my operas were all about times when life wasn't as hard as it is today, when people paid due regard. One was about the Court of Love in Provence, and another was about Athens before things went wrong, and the last was about Paul and Virginia, but I insisted on having a happy ending. Mind you,' he said with sudden vigour, 'this hardness has its point. How do you think that Rachmaninoff has given us a brand new performance of the last movement of the Chopin E flat minor sonata? Simply because he could get on to all the rhythms that Chopin had in his mind and made us hear them, and how did he do that? Because he's a master of tempo, and he's that because next to Busoni he's got the finest technique of any pianist alive today. Talking of Busoni, it was he who put me on to the thing I was going to ask you to do when you started frightening me. You'll never know how much you upset me when you started to cry. But of course you're right. We'll leave these things to the Busonis and the Rachmaninoffs—'

'But what were you going to ask me to do?' I demanded.

'What does that matter now?' he asked, with what seemed to me a strange and fatuous obstinacy. 'Where human beings are highly strung, you shouldn't put too much on them, it's like thumping out "Les Papillons" with the loud pedal down.'

'Tell me, tell me, what you wanted me to do,' I insisted.

'Would it amuse you to see?' he asked tenderly, and went over to the cupboard in the corner of the room. He angered me by delaying to look over his shoulder and tell me with an apologetic little laugh, 'I'm not tidy, I'm afraid.' I wished he would not go on about himself. 'Ah, here it is. Now tell me, what edition of Mozart's sonatas did your mother give you? I thought so. It's as good as any. Oh, really, it's the best. Well, this is the edition I meant you to work on. Of course you've never heard of it. Nobody ever has. I found it in Switzerland.' He showed for a minute or two a maddening disposition to enlarge on the beauties of Lucerne, and a curiosity as to whether I had ever been there, but I hurried him on. 'I brought it home because not in all my life have I seen such awkward fingering. It wouldn't suit anybody who wasn't an ape. Well,

I make the people who look like going somewhere take this stuff home and break their hearts on it. If I hadn't seen that I was pressing you too hard and realised there wasn't any sense in it, that it was really wrong, you being what you are, I'd have asked you to go home and practise this Eleventh Sonata you've been playing, with this fool's fingering. See what I mean? I'd have told you, go on with this wrong fingering and work and work until you get your legatos as smooth and your allegrettos as fast as you get them now with the right fingering. Ever heard of that one?'

'No,' I said. 'What's the point?'

'The point? Well, then you go back to the right fingering and you find you play it twice as well as before. That's the point of the trick.'

'Does it work?' I asked.

'Of course it does. All Busoni's tricks work.'

I firmly took the volume out of his hands, though they clung to it. 'Yes, yes. I see. Oh, why didn't you tell me at once that this is what you wanted me to do? Of course it will work, and it's going to be fun. I will feel like Liszt playing the Beethoven B flat concerto when he couldn't use his third finger.'

'That's a nice modest comparison, I must say,' he grumbled, following me slowly to the piano.

'Is the eleventh really a good one for this?' I asked happily.

'As good as any.'

After half a page I came on a frightful piece of fingering, did it, and spun round on the stool and laughed up at him. 'How could the ape-handed wonder have thought of that one?'

'Can't think,' he answered absently. I swung the stool from side to side, annoyed because he had liked me quite well a few moments earlier, when I was weeping and rebellious, and now liked me much less, though I was doing what he had wanted me to do. I could not see why he should say so grimly, 'You like that trick, don't you? By next week you'll have broken its back once and for all. You'll go right through this Swiss book, hour by hour, and come out on the other side, like a dog that's been into a river to fetch a stick, and you'll have the facility you were out to get. And it's right that you should. You must do it. It isn't that you're what I'd call ambitious. I don't see you planning a campaign to get your hooks into Sir Henry Wood, or sucking up to the critics. But all the same you wouldn't be happy unless you were at the top. Funny thing, it takes a lot of character, a lot of discipline, to be second-rate. What am I saying? It sounds as if I thought it was better to play badly than well. But what would I mean by "better" if I did think that?' I forbore from starting to play again, because he seemed to be contending with some strong emotion, but I wished he would keep his mind on the lesson. He saw that himself in a moment, for he turned to the window where we had been standing, and made a gesture of dismissal to the winter sunlight and the tree it had turned golden, saying, 'Beautiful day or not,' and was again useful to me.

I was back in my prison cell, my hard labour harder than ever before. Henceforward I engaged in a conflict with every composition I learned which was far below the level of the arts as they are enjoyed and even below the level of human activity; it was animal warfare, such as a mongoose might wage against a snake. Before I performed a composition, in the sense of playing it so that anybody could get any pleasure from listening to it, I went through it over and over again, phrase by phrase, singing each phrase at the tempo in which I intended to play it, then playing it, then singing the next phrase, and so on: I cracked out all passages, even those meant to be legato as oil, in the crispest staccato, to build up the strength of my hand; I practised the skeleton of the composition with my thumbs only, then with each of the other four fingers, and I practised it in octaves. I played it slowly, less slowly, quickly and very quickly, and I chose the pace I found most difficult and repeated it at that over and over again until it came easily. Any passages which I found specially resistant I played in all the twelve keys; and I moved my stool and played the right hand part with my left hand, and moved the stool again and played the left hand part with my right hand. By these and other devices I broke down the composition till its notes had no more relation to art than the blows a boxer rains on a punch-ball; and then I had to put it together again into a work of art.

I sat down at the piano with the music in front of me and sang the whole composition through, strictly observing the time, using a metronome if I found myself hurrying or lagging. After that I put the music away and sang it from memory; and after that I played it through on the surface of the keys making no sound. At this stage I had to hold open the doors of my mind by a conscious effort, and welcome back with a feeling not really different from personal love the part of the composition

I had repudiated and repelled, its meaning. Then at last I began to practise it as a whole, as I would play it to Mr Harper, as I would play it to an audience if ever I got an engagement as a concert pianist, as I was playing it to an invisible audience, the nature of which I cannot define. It could not be called imaginary, for it was real enough to pass the only judgment which I feared. I could conceive that Mr Harper and the concert-goers might be wrong, too kind or too cruel. But this unseen tribunal was always right and was implacable; if I betrayed my composer or my instrument they knew and scourged me. That tribunal was obviously my own judgment. Yet was it? Then why did my judgment so often make me play in a way the tribunal did not approve? But my trade was a mystery. When I had used up all my strength, when I could not go on a moment longer, another strength welled up in me, which seemed to flood me from without, for my will had nothing to do with the making of it, and I had had no inkling it was there. That was glorious.

But the way was not simple. I hardly knew my own mind, that evening in the first winter of my apprenticeship, when I went home and let myself into the house (it was wonderful to have a latchkey, though the fear of losing it was awful) and felt relief because the drawing-room was in darkness. I had dreaded facing Mamma, because of a doubt which was so strong that I would have had to speak of it if I had seen her, and I had forgotten that this was the day of the month when she went on a peculiar errand of mercy. Cordelia had been induced to believe that she had exceptional talent as a violinist by a music-mistress named Miss Beatrice Beevor, a poor silly creature who wore Pre-Raphaelite garments of sage-green or mulberry velveteen, carried white leather bags inscribed in pokerwork with such names as Venezia and Bayreuth, and called herself Bay-ah-tree-chay on the pretext, hardly credible, that she had been given that name in her youth by friends who had been struck by her likeness to Dante's beloved in a Victorian picture representing Dante and Beatrice passing each other in the streets of Florence. Though Miss Beevor's belief in Cordelia's genius had been due as much to besotted affection as to lack of musical discrimination this did not soften my sister's resentment. During the long illness which had followed Cordelia's disillusionment Miss Beevor had sent her fruit and flowers, but Cordelia would never let Mamma leave them in her room, and she tore up the poor thing's letters without reading them. Cordelia could not be blamed for this. She looked as if she were going to be sick when she saw the fruit and flowers, her stony face seemed unaware that her wild fingers were attacking the envelopes addressed in the familiar handwriting. When she and I came face to face with Miss Beevor in Lovegrove High Street my sister crossed the road to avoid her, not out of brutality, but out of pain which made her walk blindly into the thick of the traffic.

Mamma's heart bled for the unhappy music-mistress, though strangers might not have guessed this from her conversation. She rarely referred to her except as 'that poor idiot'. But she often took the opportunity to pay an afternoon call on Miss Beevor in her little Victorian Gothic villa at any time when she could be certain that Cordelia would not return from her classes until after tea. This was one of those days; it was the second Wednesday in the month, and Cordelia would be attending a lecture on the Great Florentine Painters at King's College in Harley Street. So there was no sign of my mother in the drawing-room except the small indentation made by her meagre body on the cushions of her armchair. I knew well what she was doing at this moment, for I had accompanied her on one of these visits. She would be edging her way into what comfort she could find on a sofa piled with tooled leather cushions brought from Italy, keeping her eyes away from the large print of the Victorian picture representing the famous Florentine encounter which hung over the chimneypiece, lest she should break into hysterical laughter; and her foot would be jerking nervously, because she was about to violate her conscience. She could hold out no hope to Miss Beevor that Cordelia would ever forgive her. But she could make some small concessions to the poor woman's depraved musical appetites. Her foot would cease to jerk, her whole body would become tense, she would swallow; and then she would ask Miss Beevor if she had been at a good ballad concert. Her whole musical past would rise up and confront her as soon as she said the words, and she would add, 'But I have just found it out. Very late, I fear.' Or, setting her jaw, she would say that she had heard a Minuet by Madame Guy Chaminade the other day which had been very graceful, and she now understood (and again there would be a confession of a wasted life, of a delayed revelation) why Miss Beevor thought so well of this composer.

While I stood laughing in the empty room, an owlet hooted in the basement, and I knew that at least one of us was down there having tea in the kitchen with Kate because Mamma was out. We liked the sound the owlets made in the woods by the Dog and Duck at night, and we made it our private call. When I went downstairs I found Mary sitting at the table, drinking strong tea, as we had not been allowed to have it till we were grown up, while Kate in her basket-chair read aloud the *Daily Mail* serial.

Mary started to tell me that I would have to pour some hot water into the teapot, there was such a thing after all as tea that was too strong, but I had to put my fear before her at once. 'Mary,' I said, 'I don't believe we're going to find it as easy to be as much of a success as we thought we were. Half the people at the Athenaeum play as well as I do.'

I was so anxious that my voice cracked. But Mary's face remained as bland as cream. 'Yes, I know. Half the people at the Prince Albert play as well as I do. But we needn't worry.'

'Why on earth not?'

'Because nobody except us seems to notice that we don't play particularly well. They don't see through you at the Athenaeum, do they? Nobody's shown any signs of seeing through me yet.'

'But some day they must,' I persisted.

'Well, they've had a term and three-quarters to do it in,' said Mary. 'If they were going to find us out they would have done it by now.'

'But the critics and the conductors?' I asked, and my voice cracked again.

'The chances are they won't either. My teachers are just as much taken in by me as the students. Aren't yours? What about Mr Burney Harper? And maybe we're not really taking them in. Possibly we have a slight advantage over the other students, though I don't know what it is, and I don't believe it amounts to much. Anyway, we'll have got it from Mamma. Do fill up that teapot. I really have over-done it, it tastes like ink.'

My confidence was restored, though it chilled me that she was talking of herself and me, of our teachers and our fellow-students, as if we were all dead and she were reading about us in a book, not a real book but a text-book, a volume of the encyclopaedia. I asked her no more questions and she said, 'Do go on, Kate. Rose, this is a lovely serial. The hero's serving a sentence in Portland Jail instead of his twin brother, at first because there was a mistake and afterwards to save somebody's honour, and now he's escaped and stolen a boat and rowed out to sea, and the warders have taken another boat and are rowing after him. Go on, Kate.'

'That I won't,' said Kate. 'Who would have thought it, it opened so well, but it is nonsense, it is wicked nonsense. While you two have been talking I have looked at the end of the instalment and the Honourable Rodney is rowing straight into Portland Race. I have been reading these stories since I was a kid, I had to read them to my granny because she could not read though she never owned to it, and I know that tomorrow we will be told how he got across Portland Race and made his way to freedom, because the warders dared not follow him into the Race, and wicked rubbish that is. My father always said no craft was ever built that could live in Portland Race, and that stands to reason. Why, to look down on it from the distance is terrible. The sea boils there like the water in that kettle, only it is colder than ice, the current fetches up from the bottom the cold stuff that has never felt the sun, and draws it down before it's warmed, so when the poor man's boat capsizes the waves will worry him like a dog and freeze him to death, and that's a frightful way for a poor man to die who has been sent to prison for no fault, and I won't read of it.'

'But that won't happen,' said Mary. 'You'll see, Kate, the writer won't kill him. You said yourself you knew that he would be saved in the next instalment.'

'He cannot be saved,' said Kate, 'not if he gets caught in Portland Race.'

'But this is only a story,' I said. We were concerned, for though she was speaking quietly she looked as she had done when her eldest brother's ship had been posted overdue for forty-eight hours, and she did not know he had been left ashore sick at Lisbon. 'The convict is not real.'

'Portland Race is real enough,' she answered obstinately.

'Well, it says in the Bible that in the end there shall be no more sea,' said Richard Quin, who was with us in a mud-stained jersey, his cheeks bright with the cold and one of the games he played.

Kate went down on her knees to help him off with his heavy football boots, but would not let him have it his way. 'True enough,' she said, 'but it will be a great pity and nothing gained, for two wrongs do not make a right.'

'Don't worry, it is probably a mistake in the translation, and the right text is that there shall be no more Portland Race, and some half-gales for the sake of excitement, but no whole gales, and just the sea left with all its wickedness taken out,' said Richard Quin, and took the bun that Mary had just put on her plate.

'Pig,' she said, 'I meant that for myself.'

'Yes, I know,' said Richard Quin, 'but he for God only, she for God in him.'

'Don't dare say that beastly impudent line even in fun,' I said.

'It's a nice line really,' said Richard Quin. 'It sounds just like a flowery compliment if you say it in pidgin English.' Bowing, he laid his hands on his chest and narrowed his eyes and squeaked the words, and they did sound good Li Hung Chang. 'But you girls are wrong about Milton. I've meant to speak to you about it for quite a long time. I know he was frightful to his wives, and what I think is just as bad is that he kept on writing his friends poems which showed he didn't care a rap about them, he had nothing to say about them, Lawrence of virtuous father virtuous son, Cyriack whose grandsire on the Royal Bench, Fairfax whose name in Arms through Europe rings, and all that touch; and as for Lycidas, you couldn't write about a real friend's death that way, there isn't any horror of death. But all the same Milton knew all about words, on words he was all right, he really was.'

'Words,' sniffed Mary, 'words,' and I jeered, 'Words, what we like is meaning.'

'Oh, you do, do you, you couple of dotty musicians,' he jeered back, 'what you like is sounds that in that sense don't mean anything at all, not in the way words do when they're used in a newspaper. Poetry is like music, it gets at meaning in another way, you needn't snigger. I know more about it than you do. I'm going to be a writer.'

'Well, write if you like, but don't stick up for Milton,' said Mary, and I said, 'No, because he couldn't have meant anything good, because he was a horrible old hypocrite, keeping his wives just as slaves who could write down his poetry and writing that thing all about freedom called Areowhatever—'

139

'Children, you must not quarrel,' said Kate, 'not even in fun—'

'This isn't fun,' I said. 'Kate, you don't know what a hog Milton was, a perfect hog—'

'You may not have heard both sides,' said Kate.

'But do you really want to be a writer like Papa?' I said doubtfully. It had seemed so contentious and dusty compared to music.

'No, not like Papa,' said Richard Quin, shaking his fair head stiffly, as my father would have shaken his dark head, had he wished to dissociate himself from his father. 'Not politics. Poetry. Yes, I know quite well what I'm going to do. I shall start by getting into Oxford, I can manage that though it's true I haven't worked, and then I shall get the Newdigate Prize for Poetry—'

'This is the first time I've ever heard you say you wanted to get a prize,' said Mary.

'Well, I don't really want the Newdigate,' said Richard Quin, 'not what you'd really call "want", but one must begin somewhere.' He took my cup of tea, and of course I did not mind, though I said I did, and pulled his hair.

'Be quiet, all of you,' said Kate, 'I hear your mother's key in the door. Put on the kettle, one of you. No, fill it with fresh water, that water has been boiled up twice and would do for you but not for your mother. She will need a good cup, too, she always does when she has been to see Miss Beevor. Her maid is a good sensible child from an orphanage, I have talked to her in the fishmonger's, but poor Miss Beevor would not know how to train her. Oh, ma'am,' she said to my mother, 'go upstairs and I will have your tea ready in a minute. You look,' she said censoriously, 'very tired.'

This was not true. She said it only because she thought that my mother's benevolence must be limited like the money in her purse, and that some day she might pay it all out and there would be nothing left. In fact my mother was flushed with happiness. 'I would rather have it down here with the rest of you,' she said. 'How beautiful that fire is, with the coals pressed together like that and glowing. They are just the colour of those pink roses we have by the gate. Do you know, I really like Miss Beevor. I like her very much.'

We all cried out in protest, and Richard Quin said, 'Oh,

140

Mamma, don't go on forgiving everybody as if you were St Francis, we like you better than him.'

'Lots,' said Mary. 'I don't believe the birds liked being preached to.'

'What, did St Francis preach to the birds?' asked Kate. 'Whatever for? If he really liked birds he would have done better to preach to cats.'

'Yes, it has to be admitted that there he chose the easier way,' sighed Mamma. She pondered for a moment, then, overcome by the horror that any public performer must feel at the thought of a completely unresponsive audience, she exclaimed, 'Preach to cats! No, one must not ask the impossible, even of saints.' Her mind, doubtless because she was thinking of what cats do to birds, swept us anxiously. 'You must not be cruel to unfortunate people, particularly when there is no reason for it. Miss Beevor is a generous woman,' she announced, in glowing indifference to our mockery, 'as fast as I say I like the composers she likes, she says she likes the composers I like. I know both of us are lying,' she owned, 'but really no harm is done, the score remains as it would have been if we were both telling the truth, and it is very pleasant of her.'

I broke into laughter at the further joke she did not see. Did Miss Beevor, I wondered, signal that she was about to make concessions to what she considered Mamma's depraved musical tastes, by stilling a jerking foot and swallowing? But nobody asked me why I was laughing, for this was one of the fortunate evenings which every united family enjoys from time to time when its members, returning from the day's occupations, find such amused delight in recognising each other's oddities that strangers might suppose them to be meeting for the first time after years of separation. There was, however, a shadow on my pleasure. I had been disconcerted when Mary had met so calmly my doubt regarding our gifts as pianists. It was as if I had put out my hand and touched her and found that she had been changed to ivory. This was absurd if I had really been seeking from her a reassurance about our futures, for she had given me that. But I had in my heart of hearts been hoping that that was just what she would not do. I would have liked her to answer, 'Yes, it is true, we are not remarkable. It is absurd to think that we can ever make our mark as great concert pianists, though we will do enough for teachers. So we need not work so hard, and it will not be wrong

141

for us to leave time in our lives for other things.' But apparently I had two hearts, for when I imagined her giving that answer I knew that I would have been just as disappointed. It had not merely been the insanity of a moment, that impulse I had had to accept Mr Burney Harper's anxiety about my technique as a final dismissal, that equally strong impulse I felt a minute later to accept any technical discipline that he might impose on me. I was like a sea pulled by two moons. This must mean a boiling of the waters, tides that rushed up and carried away structures meant for living in, and then receded till earth that should be covered lay naked. I wanted to play the piano, and I did not want to be stretched on the rack of that calling. This was my secret, which I did not dare to speak, for fear of undermining life as I knew it.

I had another secret, which I now suppose was part of the other. I wanted to make friends. We had friends, of course, at the Dog and Duck, and we had Mr Morpurgo; but they were not young and they joined us to no others. I wanted, so much that I wept at night, to be part of the general web, to be linked with boys and girls and men and women who were not yet what they would be in the end, and would disclose themselves in plays, and would let me act with them and find out what I was. But nobody wanted very much to be with any of us except Richard Quin, who constantly attached people of all ages to himself by simply meeting them, so that we were surprised, when we went for walks with him through Lovegrove, by the number of grown-ups who nodded and smiled at him, by the number of houses which were not just sealed boxes for him.

'I don't know who the bald-headed old man is, but the other one, the upright old thing with the red face who waved his cane, that's Surgeon-Major O'Brien. He was in the Crimean War, in all that row about Florence Nightingale. He is still angry with her as a meddler. But he is a good old stick.'

'How did you get to know him?'

'Oh, easily. I play the flute sometimes for the vet's wife, who wishes her husband was something literary and thinks of Papa as a sign and a wonder, and has a club for chamber-music and once met the Dolmetsches. They live next door to the Surgeon-Major. They spoke of him and said how funny it was to hear him talk of that Nightingale woman. His cat was ill, so I offered to take along its medicine. I often go in and see him for a minute or two, he's very lonely.'

142

Or it would be, 'I wonder why anybody built a house in the Chinese style right in the middle of an ordinary road.'

'Silly, the Chinese house was here long before the others. They are built on what used to be its grounds. You must come in and see the inside, it is strange too. The people are nice, they would be glad to show it to you, they are proud of the place. Their grandfather was a naval man who built it when he came home from the China station, but their father lost all his money in railway shares, you know there was once a boom and a panic afterwards. So he had to sell the gardens, but could not bear to give up the house. And the grandson who lives there now loves it too, though he is far too poor to live there, really, for the father was like ours, he kept on getting ruined, da capo, da capo.'

'But how did you get to know them?'

'I was curious about the place, so I asked the postman who lived there, and he told me that the owner was the cashier who takes in the money at the Gas Company offices. I got Mamma to let me take along the money one quarter, and made friends with him. I told Rosamund, I forgot to tell you.'

It was not fair, this private golden age which had been given Richard Quin, where there were neither strangers nor trespassers, only friends and open doors. For he did not like people more than we did, he liked most of them less. He was to shock me by his indifferences to the sort of friendliness for which I longed, one night in the following spring, when we went together to a party given in a big dull villa by a girl called Myrtle Robinson, who had been in the same class as Mary and myself: a girl who was quite rich, because her father manufactured the Constantia Robinson brand of jams and jellies and pickles. It was a mark of Richard Quin's power to go in and out of people without heed for the usual boundaries that he was invited, for he was the only person there who was still at school, and this was because some days before he had travelled down from London in the same railway carriage as Myrtle's mother, a heavy, timid woman with white eyelashes, and had carried her parcels for her. But when he got to the house he was as irritably ungrateful as Papa might have been.

'Why, what a waste of an evening this is going to be,' he grumbled to me as we stood in the still congealed crowd of guests among the potted palms in the drawing-room. 'When they are so rich, why can't they have one single picture worth looking at? Nothing but gondoliers and cardinals. That's a good oath. Gondoliers and cardinals, it sounds worse than what Othello said, goats and monkeys! And they haven't any books. And there isn't a pretty girl.'

'Shut up,' I muttered, 'and anyway you're wrong. That girl by the piano has beautiful golden hair.'

'Yes, I've seen her, how dare she, with so plain a face? It is almost the colour of Rosamund's hair.' Rage shook him. He was frenzied because Rosamund was not there, because he had so little of her now that she had gone to her training in the children's hospital in an eastern suburb, hard to reach from Lovegrove.

I said, 'But you did choose to come.'

'I know, I know,' he admitted. 'But all the same, it is a waste of time. There is so little time.'

For a moment he was quiet beside me, swallowing his resentment, and then he set about building a diversion for himself. I knew the signs. A tremor ran through him, as if he were a bird tired of his perch, and then he smoothly crossed the room by doing favours. In those days old people were always complaining of draughts; their years brought the mirage of a blasted heath into every room at every season. Myrtle's grandmother lived with the family, a little bent old woman, whose face, brown and shrivelled like an unpeeled almond, seemed the tinier because the pleated white lawn and trailing black crêpe of her widow's cap were so unusually massive. The corner where she sat in her wheeled chair had suddenly appeared to her as a cave of the winds, and Richard Quin found her a corner which he assured her was peculiar in its peace, and she believed him. Then he knelt and freed a girl's shoe-buckle from the hem of her lace skirt, and when he stood up was brought by a single step to the spot where he wanted to be, where Myrtle's mother shifted from foot to foot with her back to a window, fingering her moonstone necklace and smiling about her with unperturbed surprise, as if there were more guests than she had expected but there was enough in the kitchen for all comers. When she saw Richard Quin she said, 'Oh, it's you!' and her smile became tender, amused and flattered. He must have been charming to her in the train. My brother affected to catch sight of something through a chink in the silver and blue brocade curtains behind her, put his eye to it, and cried out to ask her if she knew what the moon was doing to her garden. He seemed astonished because the moon was so big and yellow, though he and I had watched it rise over the trees at the end of our lawn, before we started for the party. Myrtle's mother, as if pleased to please him, drew back the curtains and let him take them from her hands and open the french windows. The standard rose-trees on the edge of the lawn gleamed as if moonbeams were wet paint; at the foot of a gentle slope a lily-pond was zebra-striped with white light and black glass; a rose pergola behind it seemed cut finely in hard stone.

In those days young people did not stray into gardens during dances, at least not in Lovegrove. To sit out in a conservatory among potted plants that were not usually there, that had been hired for the evening, and listen to the dance-band (which was here the trio which played every afternoon in the tea-room at the Bon Marché in Lovegrove High Street) was considered a sufficient departure from the normal routine to make the situation as heady as it could safely be. But Myrtle's mother, smiling now like a deaf person almost sure that the sound of music is again penetrating a long useless ear, made us free of the night my brother had revealed to her. Between the waltzes, the gallops, the polkas, the barn-dances, the Bostons, the one-steps, we walked in the moonlight, easy with each other as if we were disguised in masks and dominoes. Sometimes my partner and I passed Richard Quin and some girl, and each time I had to note how perfectly he had assumed the adoring and humble voice, now hesitant, now artlessly precipitate, which would reconcile a girl proud of being newly grown up to being paired off with a schoolboy. Then I met him no more, and the perspiring trio from the Bon Marché, Mr Krause, Miss Mackenzie and her sister Flora, ceased their good-natured thumping and supper was served. We took our plates of chicken mousse and our goblets of claret cup out into the garden, and found seats on the rustic benches and on the steps leading to the striped lily-pond, and my brother was with me again.

A thread of sweet sound was spun into the night. My brother had gone home during the last dance and fetched his flute, and was playing it in the summer-house behind the pergola. Above us the sweet hollow voice rose and fell, doubled back on itself and glided forward, ubiquitous, tracing a pattern among the stars and another within us, behind our breast-bones. Myrtle's mother had been lumbering down the steps, breathily asking us if we had everything we wanted. Now she bent over me and sighed, 'When he asked me, I didn't think it would be as good as this.' Moving as if she were a bear, as if her feet were soft rounded pads, and her limbs were thick and hardly jointed, she went down to the lily-pond and stood still beneath my brother's music and the night sky. There was a rounded hedge of hair above her forehead, according to the fashion then set by the Royal Family; the moonlight seemed entangled in it. She looked up at us through the darkness, turning her illuminated face from side to side, as if she wanted to be sure that all of us received the blessing of her smile, which was ecstatic yet tentative, hardly convinced of the fullness of her own gratification.

The young man beside me had ceased to speak or move. He held his goblet an inch or two from his lips and did not drink. His name was Martin Grey, and I had met him several times lately, at dances and at tennis tournaments, and he had always sought me out. He had a sweep of fair hair across his broad forehead and deep grey eyes, and I had found him more interesting when he talked about sailing, which was his hobby, than I would have thought possible. So interesting that now, when my brother played, I knew that if he wanted to marry me I would be content to live with him all my life long and never leave Lovegrove. I would give up everything to serve him, and it would be no sacrifice, for it would be an ordinary life, and that was good enough, there was no need for an exceptional destiny. I did not love him, but I could do so if he would say he wished it. My brother's music was proclaiming that there would be a huge vacuum in the universe, a hole that would swallow all, if we did not fill it with something that the notes defined with a clarity forbidden to words.

But the young man did not speak or move. It was not to be expected that he should. That sort of young man would find his wife among the more prosperous families in Lovegrove, whose daughters stayed at home after they left school. I knew well that that was the supreme attraction. It was no good at all for a girl to be clever, and not much good being pretty; 'staying at home' was what was irresistible. I was better off than some not in that case. Poor Eva Lowson, who had been one of the prettiest girls at our school, was now a cashier at the Bon Marché, because her father had 'failed', as they put it in those stable days when a man went bankrupt, so she had not been invited to the party. But all the same I was at a disadvantage compared to all the other girls sitting beside their partners in the warm moonlight, simply because I was known to be committed to a profession. I was not in the leper class with Eva, but I was, so to speak, wearing a nose-ring. I sat there beside Martin Grey, feeling a little cold and thinking how right the suffragettes were; and then I remembered that his father was the manager of the bank where my father had kept his account. There can have been no such real point of indifference between the Capulets and the Montagus. I burst out laughing and was afraid that Martin might ask me why, but he did not notice.

Down by the lily-pond Myrtle's mother was suddenly abashed. Her fingers went to her moonstone necklace and it could be seen that she was wondering what she was doing out there, in front of everybody, all alone. She moved slowly, as if she thought delay would make her less visible, out of the moonlight into the flanking shadow cast by a knot of trees. Beside me Martin raised his goblet to his lips and began to drink. Till then I had been listening to my brother's flute as if I were one of the strangers to whom he was playing, but now I knew that I was not. I was as much divided from the young men and women, simply because of what I was, as Myrtle's mother was by her stout middle age. So now I listened to Richard Quin with the special knowledge that came of being his sister, and I was astonished by the simplicity of the strangers. They were melting under the influence of a tenderness which they believed to be in his performance, but was not there. They were inventing it because they needed it. The music promised sweetness which was for himself alone. He ached with a desire to be in another place than this, where he would find that sweetness. If he felt concern whether they found the same delight for themselves, it left no trace in the sounds he made. And he felt no such concern; from this and that, over the years, I knew he did not. There was this excuse for his indifference, he had already discharged whatever debt he owed to them. He could speak of what they desired and they could not. Without him they would have been voiceless. With him their need pierced the night like the reply to the ray of a star. Yet surely that was not quite right, surely one never discharges one's full debt to other people. But again that

147

cannot be true, if the payment one makes is large enough. I could not work it out.

I was angry with Richard Quin after the party ended. In the hall Myrtle's mother stood beside her husband, who was as softly and slowly ursine as she was, and they eyed Richard Quin with wonder while they thanked him, as though they found him as prodigious a guest as a unicorn, and hoped that other legends also would come true; and under a rosy lamp they reverently watched him take me down the path. Outside the gate knots of young men and girls and chaperons were saying goodbye beside a line of cabs, and as we passed they cried out their thanks to my brother; and a girl's voice cried out shyly and bravely, 'Rose, because of your brother, we'll never forget tonight.' Our road home was folded round a hill, and below us Lovegrove lay dark as woodland within the yellow pattern drawn by the street-lamps, for our suburb went early to bed. Beyond, the lights of London were reflected on the clouds as a rusty glow. Richard Quin looked down on the landscape as if it were unpeopled space, and said, 'Well, I got myself out of that dreary mess pretty well.' His voice was shocking and beautiful in its coldness, like a glacier stream.

We did not speak again until we had come to our house, which slept like all its neighbours, but was theatrically illuminated by the street-lamp at our gate. The gas-light was not very strong, but the shadows it cast brushed the grooves in the pediment and the shadows under the veranda as if they were black paint laid on canvas, and the creepers might have been cut out of metal. 'The curtain rises on a small Regency house standing in a suburban garden; the time is midnight,' one of us said, I forget which. When we had opened the false-looking door and let ourselves into the creaking and obscure reality behind it, we took off our shoes and crept downstairs into the kitchen and got ourselves some milk from the larder, cool off the slate shelves. We always did this when we had been out with strangers. While we drank it we sat on the kitchen table, swinging our stockinged feet.

Richard Quin said, 'That clock has the loudest tick. I can't think how Kate can stand it.'

'She says it's company when we are out.'

'What horrid company.' He shuddered and went on with his drink. 'I say, they used to make wine-glasses cloudy-white like a tumbler that has had milk in it, did you know? I saw some in the antique shop near the Town Hall. They might do for Mamma's birthday. Not to use. There are only four. But they would look all right on the chimneypiece in the dining-room and they are Mamma's sort of thing. But talking of time and birthdays and all that, you saw that poor old lady, Myrtle's grandmother? Well, she was the original Constantia Robinson. The one the firm's called after,'

'Was she? How very strange.' I added, 'I mean, the widow's cap.'

'What was strange about that? Wasn't it like anybody else's who wears that kind of thing? They're horrid things. I wouldn't like my widow to wear one.'

'Yes, it was like any other, I suppose. What I meant was that last year the firm was fifty years old, they had lots of advertisements about it. And it was she who started it. She made jams and lemon curd and pickles in her kitchen, after her husband had died and left her with three children. Well, fifty years is a long time. She has probably forgotten what her husband looked like. It must be so strange to put on something every day in memory of someone she might not recognise if he came into the room.'

'She will have forgotten him if she didn't love him and she will remember him if she loved him,' said Richard Quin.

He took my empty glass and went into the larder to get more milk for us both. While he was away I had that illusion which comes on one in a sleeping house; I could feel the earth turning on its axis, bearing houses and sleepers through the night towards the day.

When he sat down beside me on the table again he said, 'Now I would like to go for a long walk. Wouldn't you like to be on the top of Purley Downs now, staring the moon in the face?'

We had crept into the house, we could creep out again. I smiled at him, proud of being admitted into his wildness, but I shook my head. 'But if we did we should be no good for work tomorrow.'

'I don't care about that,' he said. 'Oh, I do, really. I am all right, you know. I mean to write, and anyway I will always pay my way somehow. But I needn't bother to tell you that, you're not Cordy. But about that old woman, Myrtle's grandmother, there was one queer thing. I went into the kitchen to borrow the waiter's bicycle so that I could come back here and fetch my flute. I couldn't have borne to talk to one more of those silly girls. Well, the Robinsons' kitchen is a whacking great place. The whole place is absurdly big, of course. What do people like that want with so many rooms? They haven't got lots of beautiful pictures and china and books to house, and you can't imagine they would ever want to give a grander party than the one they gave tonight. I can understand the way Mr Morpurgo lives, and the way they live at the Dog and Duck, and the way we live, and the way Kate and her mother live, but I can't see the sense of what goes on in between being gorgeous and being simple. But anyway the Robinsons have a scullery twice the size of this kitchen, with a double sink, a colossal thing, and a shelf running all round the walls, covered with all the sort of ironmongery we used to want to buy for Mamma's birthday when Papa was here and we had horrible old saucepans. Do you remember, we would see a huge fish-kettle in that shop on the corner, and come back and tell Kate we were going to get it for Mamma, and Kate used to say that a double boiler would be better, big things like that were only for the households of the nobility and gentry. Where did she get that phrase, I wonder?'

'It is on the label of one of the famous sauces,' I said.

'Good for her to pick it out. It makes one think of Shakespearean courtiers. How nice, putting a sauce-bottle to one's eye to get a distant rumour of the Tudors, like putting a shell to one's ear to hear the sea. Well, anyway, under this shelf in the Robinsons' scullery, there were pails, lots and lots of pails, between twenty and thirty of them, and they were all full of eggs, floating on something the servants call water-glass. They say it keeps the eggs fresh for six months at least, a year's more like it. In the pails that had just been filled it's like water, but greyish, the eggs look like the ghosts of eggs. When it's older it goes white and crusty, they might have been laid up by Egyptian priests for the mummies to eat in their tombs. Well, it seems that in the old days people used to put down eggs in summer when the hens lay lots and eat them in the winter when the hens had stopped laying, and in remote places in the country they still do it. But hardly anybody does it now. And nobody in towns, nobody in a place like Lovegrove. But the old lady, Myrtle's grandmother, Constantia Robinson, the original Constantia Robinson, she insists on doing it.

'They did it, of course, on the farm where she was brought up. Just think, that farm was much nearer London than here;

it really wasn't far outside Lambeth, it was in Crockton, near the place where the London road forks and there's a big church standing up between the two roads. That was years ago, if she was a widow half a century ago, she must have been a child back in the fifties. Well, ever since then she's been in the food business, or her sons have, and she's seen food getting cheaper all the time, and nobody having to bother about keeping it, the shops do that for you, you go in and buy it off marble slabs, and eggs particularly you don't worry about, they're cheap enough any time of the year, unless you're deadly poor. Why, even at our worst we've always had eggs, and of course the Robinsons are cracking rich. But the old woman can't bear it if there aren't those pails and pails full of eggs in the scullery. She tries not to interfere with Myrtle's mother over running the house – they're very nice people, you know, you can tell that from the way the servants speak of them. But she will have those eggs put down in water-glass. She knows people think she's being silly, but she can't help it. She gets so worried in case they're not doing it that she gets up at night and hobbles down that staircase, holding on to those awful carved banisters, and goes down into the scullery to make sure. Usually they hear her and go down with her, but twice they haven't, and she fell, and the servants found her in the morning and called down the family. How queer it is to think of all those ordinary people standing in the kitchen in the early morning in their night-clothes, looking down on that tiny creature, that sort of witch, on the floor. It is sad for Myrtle and her mother that they have white lashes, that must be dreadful for a woman. They get terribly worried about their grandmother and want to have someone sleeping in her room, but she won't hear of it. She's a fierce old thing. Afraid of draughts but of nothing else.

'What's so odd is that they don't really think she's being silly. They believe in her. She's something like Mamma, you know, everything seems to come through her, and so of course it does. Everything in the place, Myrtle's father, Myrtle, the villa itself and all the stuff in it, down to the nobility and gentry fish-kettles. I know it was Myrtle's father who turned the business into a big company but she had the idea, she actually made the jam. I wonder how one turns jam into a company. Not that I'd ever want to do it. I want to write. Rose, do you think I could write? But I know I could write. I know I can write. Anyway, I'm for old Constantia, shuffling about the kitchen in the dead of night, making sure that whatever happens there'll be food for her family. I know it's nonsense, the shops are five minutes away. But shops are daylight business, and, don't you feel, what happens at night matters more?'

The quiet house moved on through the night; he let his mind run like the sand falling through an hour-glass; I lost my sense of separateness from him. When I put out my hand and ran my finger along the fine line of his jaw it was as if I touched myself. We were more or less the same person, and since one cannot envy oneself, I did not grudge him that he had got something out of the evening, and I nothing. Indeed, I had come back with an entry on the debit side. I knew that a day I had hoped for would never come. My sisters and I had had some harsh treatment at our school which could not be charged to our own defects. It was of our father's debts that our schoolfellows whispered in corners, throwing us oblique glances which served the double purpose of letting them flatter themselves that they were taking care we did not hear, and leaving us in no doubt at all as to what it was we could not hear. But I was sure that as I grew older I was growing less savage, and I had supposed my schoolfellows also were being civilised by time. So in my mind's ear I had often heard them saying to their mothers, in voices, made delightful by shy contrition, 'But this time we want to ask the Aubreys to our party. Yes, I know, but we were wrong about them, they are really very nice'; and I had foreseen that at their parties their brothers would ask us to dance again and again with a charm that I found it hard to visualise precisely, for the reason that though I had seen these young men since they were little boys they were faceless and figureless in my memory. I did not think it exorbitant to demand so much from young men to whom I had given such perfunctory attention; there had been no reason why we should trouble to imprint each other's images on our minds while we were still children, but now it was different. But it was not different enough. Of course it was something that Myrtle Robinson had asked me to her first grown-up party. But Lovegrove did not want me. Not that that mattered much, I was so happy sitting in the kitchen with my brother, listening to him while the clock ticked, while the stars shifted over our roof.

Part Two

VI

AFTER CORDELIA SUFFERED such cruel disappointment over her failure to become a violinist we felt she ought to be exempt from distress for ever. But we had so little in common with her that she seemed almost abstract: an inorganic burden like a knapsack.

It was not to be believed how suddenly that burden fell from our shoulders.

The news of our enfranchisement came at the end of a summer's day. We should have been practising hard for the end of term concerts which were given by both our musical schools, but we did not go near our pianos – and I can remember no other day in our youth when this was true – because so much was happening. First of all, Aunt Lily had been staying the night with us, because next morning Mr Morpurgo was taking her to see her sister Queenie in the prison to which she had been sent when she had left Aylesbury Jail, and this made an unrestful beginning to the day. She always meant to obey my mother's advice not to wear her best clothes on such journeys, for fear that their elegance would make her sister discontented and the wardresses envious. Nevertheless her appearance always needed some chastening touches, not for the reason Mamma had given, but for poor Mr Morpurgo's sake. This time she had restrained herself sufficiently not to wear her best clothes, which consisted of a navy blue coat and skirt with many brass buttons and an Admiral's tricorn hat, the whole thing inspired by a romantic dream of how the ladies who went yachting with King Edward the Seventh might have been attired. The dress she wore was plain and dark, but it was then the fashion for women to wear at their throats a thing called a jabot, a gentle version of a hunting stock, made of white lawn or fine linen, with two ends hanging loose for three or four inches in front. Aunt Lily's attempt to follow this fashion was not successful but was arresting. Her jabot was made of starched linen and it stuck out at right angles to her flat chest. She might have been a signal rigged up by a company of mariners shipwrecked on a reef, to catch the attention of passing craft. There was an air of gallantry about the composition, but that would not have stopped little boys from laughing at her in the street. So we had to praise the effect in the evening, and in the morning Mamma had to sigh and remind her of the probable effect of such elegance on poor Queenie in her prison dress and the wardresses in their uniforms; and then Aunt Constance, who lived with us now, ran upstairs and came down with her workbox and perhaps a collar from an old dress which she changed for the unfortunate jabot, while we all stood round and said such things as, 'It seems a shame', and 'Of course it doesn't look nearly as nice,' at which Aunt Lily sighed, 'Yes, I know, but of course your Mamma's right. It's too cruel to make them feel what they have to do without.'

These proceedings were particularly delicate that morning, because Aunt Lily was nervous, so nervous that she was shivering, as she had been before and after her last two visits to her sister.

When she had lost her jabot and was no longer an announcement that rescue was imperative, since the crew was running out of water and the cabin boy had broken his leg, she sat down on the chair in the hall grasping her handbag and umbrella and the little exercise book in which she wrote down all the news she thought would interest Queenie, and opening it sometimes to correct an inaccuracy. 'I mustn't tell her that down where we lived Mr Hayter, the grocer, ran away with a barmaid from the Blue Boar. It turns out not to be true. How awful people are. How awful I am, telling her a story that wasn't true. The harm it could have done.' She looked as if she were about to burst into tears, but she was wonderful at catching the ball of her own mood in mid-air. 'What am I saying?' she exclaimed. 'What harm would it do if I told that story to Queenie; who could she repeat it to in that horrible place? And how could it possibly hurt anyone if she did? Nobody would know who the people were, and come to think of it I don't myself, there are two Mr Hayters in that grocery business, which one it was, or wasn't as it turns out, I don't really know, and there are three barmaids at the Blue Boar, and who can tell which it wasn't, even if they found out what district we lived in. Oh, silly me, silly me,' she lamented, smiling round at us with the innocence of Adam and Eve before the invention of guilt. Mamma instantly exclaimed, 'How sensible you are! To attach little if any importance to a fault which miraculously has no practical consequences, which causes no sufferings! What a lesson to all those wretched saints!' But she added, her voice rising in urgency, 'You must remember that it was harmless by a miracle, and you must thank God for intervening between you and yourself.' This admonition received no direct answer, for Lily had already raised her voice in song. 'Can't get away to marry you today, my wife won't let me. But where,' she said, her voice sliding down to speech level, 'is our Mr Morpurgo?' My mother reminded her that Mr Morpurgo was not due for half an hour, and that he had shown his characteristic kindness in working out the exact time when they ought to start for Waterloo, not too soon and not too late, so that she could catch the train without an unnecessay wait on the platform; to which Aunt Lily did not exactly reply yet did not merely remark, 'Yes, but gentlemen do hate ladies to be unpunctual.'

This was typical of all their conversation, which for long periods would seem not to be a true interchange, and travelled on parallel lines that might never meet, had they not suddenly fused on to understanding. A little later Aunt Lily suddenly stopped singing and burst into tears, sobbing into her handkerchief that she didn't want to go to that horrible place, even in summer it seemed so cold that her winter chilblains started up again and what she'd find there and she couldn't bear it, and what she'd like to do would be to go upstairs and throw all her clothes on the floor and get into bed and put her head under the sheets. But soon she gave a brave howl and said that of course she'd go and what a silly she was to think of not going to her sister, her own sister, when she was in a bit of bad luck, and she pronounced herself a rotten job, and no class, and kicked her bony left ankle with her bony right foot.

Mamma then gave her what strangers might have thought rather too scholarly an address, pointing out that throughout the ages great writers had composed plays universally

157

admitted to be the greatest of all plays, called tragedies, which showed great men, kings and conquerors and statesmen, facing just such violent events as Lily herself had had to endure, and in these tragedies the kings and conquerors and statesmen were always represented as bent and broken by the confrontation. Lily had, my mother reminded her, sometimes bent under her cruel experience, but had never been broken, not for one moment, so she had every title to respect in her own eyes and everybody else's. At this Aunt Lily accepted the clean handkerchief my mother had been holding out to her, blew her nose and stopped sniffing, and gazed into a golden distance. 'If anybody does write a play about me, and from what you say it seems very likely, I wonder who they'd get to play me? Edna May, I'd like it to be.' This was an American actress of surpassing beauty who was at that time making a great success in London as the Salvationist heroine of a musical comedy called *The Belle of New York*. 'She's rather me, I think,' said Aunt Lily. 'Yes,' my mother said, but her voice died in her throat. So we all said, 'Yes, we had noticed it.'

All was well. Perfect communion had been established between Mamma and Aunt Lily, they had debated spiritual matters and come to an agreement enabling them to contemplate Creation without fear, at least for the moment, though without resort to conventional patterns of argument. When Mr Morpurgo arrived ten minutes later it was natural enough that he should look round with an air of contentment and say, 'What a happy atmosphere there always is in this house.' He himself was a calm and impressive figure, in the clothes he always wore when he took Aunt Lily to see Queenie: clothes which suggested that he had not made up his mind whether he was going to a funeral or to Ascot. He stayed only long enough to pin on Aunt Lily's chest the orchid he always brought her on these occasions from his Sussex greenhouses, and to give his chauffeur time to leave in the kitchen the usual presents of fruit and vegetables, and then they were off. He always seemed a little uneasy and anxious to be on his way at this stage in the proceedings, I think the reason was that he knew how solemnly Mamma regarded the tragedy of the Phillips family, and was afraid she might be shocked if he knew what pleasure he took in these journeys to prison. There were indeed innocent ingredients in that pleasure: for one thing he liked Aunt Lily, and for another he was surprised and pleased that, although he had been spoiled all his life, he could discharge a disagreeable duty. But he was also the child who stares at the accident, knowing he should not. Either he feared Mamma's disapproval, or he feared the raising of any issue which might prove to him she thought of him as a child.

Even then Mary and I did not get to our pianos. We went down with Mamma to the kitchen, which was very busy, because our Cousin Rosamund was a probationer at a children's hospital in London, and this was her monthly day off, and now that her mother had come to live with us she always spent her days off with us; and she always arrived in a state of hunger, because the hospital meals were so bad. She was even hungrier than the rest of us, who all liked food. This was just what my mother wished, for now that we had sold the family pictures she was able to pay the tradesmen's bills as soon as the envelopes tumbled through the letter-box on to the hall mat, and she took a voluptuous pleasure in the purchase of provisions of even the dullest sorts. She still did not buy extravagantly, as to quantity or exotic quality: when a wolf is driven from a door it leaves its ghost behind. But instead of paying a single and embarrassed visit to the butcher's shop to buy the cheapest cut that could be tricked out with evergreen turnips and carrots, those loathsome dietary cosmetics, she would make two visits in order to buy the best chops for Irish stew on Wednesday and a perfect rose-red silverside for Thursday and Friday, without the phrase 'a bit on account' being uttered and no fear that it ever should be uttered again: and sometimes, when Mary and I brought home some music-students or Richard Quin some schoolfellows, my mother's present happiness coalesced with her past, and she was inspired by memories of the parties her father and mother had given in Edinburgh when she was young. This often led her to a dead end. My grandmother's favourite cookery book not only prescribed that a braised ham *à la parisienne* should be moistened with a glass of brandy and half a bottle of sherry, it explicitly stated that a ham for which this amount of liquid appeared excessive was, quite simply, not worth serving. Mamma drooped over such injunctions as if she had actually taken food out of her friends' mouths in not providing them with such dishes, but she set her targets lower with superb results, and years afterwards musicians who had been at college with us have recalled, with greater enthusiasm than

159

they gave to memories of us, our veal and ham pies, and indeed they were unique. The jelly was an exquisite silvery topaz.

So we had a good enough lunch planned for Rosamund, but now we had to alter it in view of Mr Morpurgo's asparagus, which was the slender, bright green sort, not the white logs the restaurants serve, some really small broad beans, and lots of those tiny unripe gooseberries which still have thin skins and a mild flavour. In the end nothing survived of our original menu except the cold chicken and mayonnaise. We decided to start with hot asparagus with melted butter, and serve the chicken with broad bean salad, and scrap the treacle tart for gooseberry fool. This change of plan meant that Mary and I simply had to help. It was not just laziness and frivolity that was keeping us away from our pianos. Kate had always too much to do, and Aunt Constance had her hands full, for she was ironing a pile of underclothes for Rosamund to take back to the hospital and she had still to finish a new nightgown for her. So Mary and I took the gooseberries and two bowls and two pairs of scissors and a tray for the tops and tails, and with all of them around us we sat on the iron steps that led down to the garden, and sang every now and then 'Clip clip! Clip clip!' as our scissors attacked, till we noticed that we had company. In the grove at the end of the lawn a pair of turtle-doves were hidden somewhere in their high green residence; not brawling, throat-clearing Cockney pigeons, but true turtle-doves, such as still came deep into the London suburbs in those days, cooing tenderly, and meaning every coo.

I am writing all this down in full knowledge that it will not now seem important, for the reason that that is just what marks off that past from our present. Everything was then of importance. Everything enjoyable had an equal value. In life we were not divided. Life itself was not divided. Mamma sleeping upstairs, on a rickety old bed because she would not replace it, partly because she hated to spend money on her own comfort, and partly because old furniture acquires the power of an old dog to make claims; Kate and Constance working in the kitchen, speaking sometimes but not to say anything, just to confirm their companionship like the turtle-doves' cooing; my brother Richard Quin, like a coiled spring, out of sight, down the road at school; Rosamund, out of sight too, but, golden and splendid, sitting in the lumbering tram that was carrying her down through South London, radiating her peculiar unfocused amiability, smiling at everybody, smiling at nobody, and Mary and I sitting here on the steps, getting ready the lovely things to eat; we were all one with the grass and the flowers and the trees and the sunshine. And we were on about something, we were not passive, we were in a plot to maintain for ever the sun, the sky, the delight. At times I come on shreds of this unity still clinging to the earth. Driving through a village on a Sunday afternoon, I pass a cricket match on the green, and the silver gleam of the white flannels under the golden sun, the ball in flight, the monosyllable of the ball on the bat, the flower-bed of the spectators, the Red Dragon on the inn sign, the coasting clouds above – for a second all seems conspiring for an eternal perfection of delight. But now such sights come rarely, and at that period, I do assure you, they were the connective tissue that held the whole of life together.

That morning was both long and short. About noon we heard Rosamund call out as she came into the house, but we stayed where we were as she always spent the hours before lunch alone with her mother, and indeed we had enough to do. After we finished the gooseberries we had to go round the garden and look for the apple mint left by the people who had lived in the house before us to get some sprigs to cook with the broad beans, and then we had to beat cream for the fool in the cool passage; and when we took the finished white whorl in the basin down to the kitchen Kate made us taste things, the mayonnaise, which in our household was faintly flavoured with tomato ketchup, the almond buscuits which Kate doubted now were light enough to eat with the fool; the queen cakes we were to have for tea. Then Mary and I sat down on the steps again and waited, singing a Chopin Nocturne as du Maurier had made Trilby do (we thought he was showing his musical ignorance till we found that Pauline Viardot, Mali-bran's sister, had really done just that at concerts, over and over again, and with Chopin's approval).

There were only five of us for lunch, Mamma, Rosamund, Constance, Mary and me. Cordelia's work at the art gallery and her classes kept her in town till late afternoon, and Richard Quin had his midday meal at school. This was as well, for I think Cordelia could not bear Rosamund's Greek, blind look. She felt as a famous conductor did if an orchestra stonily ignored his baton. For the moment she was wholly ours, and we fused as families do when they are together again after they have been parted, and Rosamund and Mary and I became much more alike than we really were, and Mamma and Constance, who were as different as wine from milk, settled down into a mild resemblance. We sat at the table for a long time, partly because of Rosamund's wolfishness, partly because that was the leisurely pace at which the warm day was passing. Then we cleared the table and one of us broke a plate, but it did not matter. As Mary and I could never help with the washing up, because of our hands, we two went out into the garden with Rosamund and put down some cushions on the lawn under the trees. Rosamund lay on her back, the shadow of leaves on a high branch falling as a changing mask on her face, and we stretched out on our stomachs, our heads at her feet, our elbows on the ground, and watched her and sucked grass. Always, when we saw her again after she had been away, we were specially aware of how unlike anybody else she was.

She murmured praise of the gooseberry fool, and then said, 'But it was different.' She had had gooseberry fool before in our house and it had been all right, oh, more than all right, but not lovely like this, and Mary said yes, she did think it could be fairly classed as a lucent syrop, and I said, but not tinct with cinnamon, that wasn't it, and Rosamund said, no, she realised that, but probably in argosy transferred, and we said, well, no, it was a local product. Someone had said to Kate on a tram that all fruit, and especially gooseberries, tasted better if one dropped a couple of elderflowers into the sugar and water one was cooking them in, just for two minutes, and Kate had been so much impressed that when the time came for elders to flower she looked round for some to pick. But as the Victorians considered elders to be the most vulgar of trees, suitable only for the meanest municipal park (and parks were mean indeed in those days) they were not to be found in our genteel suburb of Lovegrove, except in the gardens of a large and pretentious Victorian villa, somebody's folly and long untenanted, which stood incongruously at the corner of our road of little Regency houses. There the elders had taken over, mobbing the flowering cherries, the apple trees and the laburnums which lined the carriage sweep, and thrusting up their fibrous canes through the gravel in front of the Doulton-tiled Italianate porch; and there it was that Kate went as soon as she saw

162

through the railings that the flat, greenish-white filigree flowers were appearing among the coarse leaves on the flimsy branches. She went by night, for to her cutting a sprig from a tree in the garden of an empty house was not much less criminal than shop-lifting, and she was terrified by the knowledge that there was a police station about a quarter of a mile away, for she believed that policemen had the right to take straight to prison all persons guilty of any offence whatsoever, even as mild as this. Her state was worsened because she was afraid of the dark and of ghosts. The day after this daring theft she had found that there were no gooseberries yet in the shops, so she had tried the recipes on some stewed apples and found that it did in fact give them a special exotic charm. She then formed a great desire to give Rosamund gooseberry fool when she came down for her next day off, and on the night before had made another foray among the elder thickets in the deserted garden. But this had seemed a useless achievement. When the greengrocer left our order he told her there were still no gooseberries, and she seemed to resign herself to making a treacle tart; and deep was her conviction that God was punishing her for theft.

Naturally, in these circumstances Mr Morpurgo's punnets of gooseberries would be received by Kate as a gift not from the gods but from God. There were the little gooseberries like jade beads in the straw basket on the kitchen table, and there was the pilfered elder branch lolling sideways in a high jug by the scullery sink, the flowers still fresh enough to be luminous in the basement shadows, so Kate said quietly but firmly, 'It was meant.' Mary and I knew well that she was not speaking to us but to her conscience, which she saw as worsted. She was bidding it civilly not to bring up again that little matter of trespass and larceny. This made us all laugh hugely, we three girls, lying on the lawn in the sleepy sunshine. It was so like Kate, who wanted to be good and was good but abhorred that excess of emotion which the eighteenth century called enthusiasm. Hardly a muscle of her face had moved during this moral death and reprieve. We laughed too at the tale she had told us of sitting on a tram with a stranger and falling into a discussion about gooseberry fool and elderberries. How had the conversation started and where did it go from that point? The whole thing was odder than it seemed at first, Rosamund pointed out, if you considered that all this must have happened when gooseberries and elderflowers were out of season, no passing sight of market-garden or waste-ground could have brought them to mind, for Kate had had to wait quite a time before she could try out the recipe. We laughed over the mystery and fell asleep.

I was awakened by a flurry of birds in the branches above, but stayed quiet for fear of disturbing Rosamund, until she stirred and said, 'You have so many more flowers in the garden now.' She was leaning on her elbow, a blade of grass between her teeth, and was looking about her at the lupins and the late peonies in the long bed by the wall, the standard roses near the house, the clematis and the jasmine beside the iron staircase. What she said was true. The flowers in our garden were like the cream in our larder, there was enough where there had been almost nothing until my father had gone away. But always when I thought of my father's disappearance and his probable, or, rather, his certain death, such trivial facts faded and left me almost as soon as they came into my mind, and I was overcome by an abstract sense of grief, something like the moan of shingle dragging back to sea between breakers, although I made no sound. I pressed my face down against the grass, while Rosamund yawned that she loved blue flowers, and seemed to sleep again. But presently she spoke, laughing. 'Elderflowers. Imagine them being nice to taste as well as to smell. And the taste is delicate, while the smell's coarse and heavy. But I like that. I like a scent to be heavy. The other day a patient who works at a florist's gave one of the sisters some tuberoses. Just two or three, but you could smell them every time her door opened. And the scent was so heavy one could have weighed it.'

'Nothing heavier for me than lilac,' murmured Mary, and I asked, 'Rosamund, if you like that sort of thing how can you bear the hospital?' It was not so foolish a question as it sounds today. In those times the standard disinfectants were fiercer beasts than they are now, and skinned the inside of one's nostrils, while lying down beside the offensive odours of the place rather than dispersing them.

'Oh, that's different, nursing's my music. Hospitals are my concert-halls.' She plucked a fresh blade of grass and laid it crosswise between her teeth, and closed her smooth bluish lids. 'I want to do nothing but nursing, all my life long.'

'Well, nobody's stopping you,' said Mary, sleepily. 'That's

164

what's so lovely about the way things are going. You're nursing, and we're playing, and nobody is trying to stop us. Though our sister Cordelia, I think, often fears that all this will come to no good.'

We must have slept for some time, for when we woke the shadows were all different, bluer and longer and shifted noticeably to other angles. Rosamund was sitting up, resting on one hand, and looking round her. 'Forgive me if I go on about blue flowers,' she was saying. 'I do so love them. Where was it, that place you went and stayed, where there was an old house high above the sea, and there was a flower-bed built up on the edge of the cliff, so that you looked at blue flowers rising to blue sea, and above that there was blue sky? Somewhere in the West Country.'

Neither Mary nor I answered for a minute. Then Mary said, 'That was Lady Tredinnick's house in Cornwall,' and stopped pulling up daisies to make a chain and laid her face against the grass. I had not known she minded as much as I did.

There was nothing really wrong, nothing that we were forced to recall often. It was only that both of us knew that Lady Tredinnick was going to ask us to stay with her again, and perhaps would so many times, but we knew that she would always ask us at short notice, because she had to wait for a time when her sons were away; and that had a tiresome significance for us. Lady Tredinnick was a patron of music of the dedicated sort that existed in these days; she did not seem to be very rich herself, but she knew many rich people who liked her, and she was always conjuring up scholarships and support for orchestras out of thin air, and she gave up mornings to musical charities to do the accounts and use copying-machines for appeals. We had played for some of her charity concerts and had got to know her quite well, drawn to her because her grey hair was almost as wild as our mother's, though the rest of her was quite different. She had blue eyes shining like sapphires, a skin burned to leather by years in Asia, and a thin body always attired with military neatness. It was as if she could have coped with anything that men could cope with, but long hair, no. She seemed to like us as we liked her, and showed it sometimes in an engaging way by drawing close to us when she was in drawing-rooms full of potted palms or in drill halls (for her sort of concert had to be performed in places less majestic than proper concert-halls) and telling us, without

165

shame at the irrelevance, of some place she had once visited that she had greatly preferred: say, a forest on a foothill of the Himalayas, where on the further side of an impassable mountain stream, roaring over sheer cascades, she had seen, growing high on a deodar, what looked at first like a swarm of huge white butterflies, but which under contemplation showed as an orchid, more beautiful than any she had ever seen, of a species she had not then seen nor ever was to see recorded anywhere, and utterly inaccessible: a sight given to her as a treasure shown to a child, not to be touched. There was sweetness in these flights of hers into the past and there was no malice against the present, they did not discredit, they simply superseded what surrounded us. We were pleased when she asked us to a dance she was giving for a niece, but frightened, and she was so nice that we were able to tell her so; and she said that that would be all right, we must come and if we did not feel at ease after half an hour she would arrange for a carriage to take us home. As it was it went all right. A Bond Street dressmaker for whom our Aunt Constance did embroidery sold us two of last season's models for very little, and we had partners for every dance. But when we went home Lady Tredinnick was standing with two of her sons in an antechamber, saying goodbye to everybody, and she kissed us with her dry lips and said that we had looked beautiful and our dresses were pretty, and held us back for a moment to tell us how nice it was for people of her age to make such friends late in life, and we glowed. We were loving and happy, it was our hour, which we had not paid for with music, but which had come to us just because we were what we were apart from being musicians. But as we went out into the hall, a large mirror showed us Lady Tredinnick turning to her sons, her brown face still brimful of light, and eagerly asking them some question which might have been, 'Don't you like the two little sisters I met at the garden-party?' and even, 'Don't you think they are pretty?' Both the young men had danced with us more than once, and had talked to us with an air of interest. Yet each replied to his mother with an indulgent smile and nod that instantly faded. It was clear that they thought nothing of us.

I do not know why we should have been so profoundly affected by the indifference shown towards us by two young men for whom we ourselves felt nothing more positive than a pale reflection of the friendship we felt for their mother. But I

166

only knew I felt their rejection of myself and my sister so keenly that it came to me not in words but as a sensation of a sword slicing down through my heart. Possibly this was because I had realised during the evening that they and the other partners were the sort of young men whom my father would have liked us to marry, and had even madly expected to his very end that we would marry. But other perceptions added to that distress. There was the realisation that the quite different kinds of young men we worked beside in our music schools did not like us so very much more than these young Tredinnicks, though they would not have dismissed us so finally, because they respected our music; and there was the darker, and bewildering, realisation that men find a special pleasure in rejecting women, and will contrive to do it even to women who have not been offered to them.

Rosamund had rolled away from me into the shadow that had left her, and was lying on her side, her cheek in the cup of her hand. I was too miserable to care if she wanted to fall back into sleep, I said, 'Rosamund, do you go to hospital dances? Do you hate them?'

'No,' she said, without opening her eyes. 'If one is not having a good time oneself one can always watch the people who are.'

'But the young men are so awful. They are all like Mr D'Arcy, but worse.'

For a long time Rosamund said nothing. She was, I saw, when I looked at her under my lids, struggling with a return of the stammer she had suffered from when she was a child. At last her tongue got free and she asked, 'Have any people asked you to marry them yet?'

'No,' said Mary. 'Men do not like us. Oh, except – except – somebody likes Rose – or me – he cannot make up his mind.' We both laughed so much that we could hardly tell Rosamund, and as we got the words out she laughed so much she could hardly hear them – 'he is a vegetarian –'

'And wears suits of tweed that his mother weaves at home –'

'– she seems to know a sheep –'

'– and she tailors the cloth herself –'

'– and he is studying composition so that he can write an opera on *Beowulf* –'

'And he wanted to take the early British harp as his second instrument –'

'– No, the earliest British harp, as it was reconstructed from fragments found in a Wiltshire barrow –'

'– But it had only three strings –'

'– and the Principal lost his temper and said he had never heard such damned nonsense –'

'– and his parents christened him Leofric Canute –'

'– Not christened, registered, they are Druids, the names were a concession to modernity –'

But suddenly something struck me. I stopped laughing and said, 'Rosamund, does somebody want to marry you?'

Pulling another blade of grass and setting it between her teeth, she stammered, her eyes still closed, 'Yes. One of the doctors at the hospital.'

I felt a kind of vertigo. It was as if we had all suddenly found ourselves on ground far higher than we had known before. I felt angrily, 'He will not be good enough. And he will take her away.'

Mary said, 'Do you like him?'

'Like? Oh, yes. I like him.'

'Is he good-looking?'

'Yes. And he is tall enough to dance with me. Lots of men I cannot dance with, but they insist on asking me, if they do not they will have to admit that they are shorter than I am, and they don't like that. And there I have to go round the room, wanting to pick them up in my arms. But Robert is tall. Quite tall.'

'How old is he?'

'Twenty-seven.'

She was taking pleasure in telling us about him, she plainly hoped that we would ask her more questions.

'What's his name?'

'Robert Woodburn.' She repeated it more slowly. 'Robert Woodburn.'

She liked him. This might be the last time, I panicked, that she ever came to see us, tired from the hospital, specially glad because we were the only people that belonged to her.

Mary asked, 'Are you going to marry him?'

She sat bolt upright, her eyes open and grave. 'Oh, no,' she said. 'Oh, no.'

'But why not, if you like him?' I said. I was sure she liked him very much. We must not, I told myself, stand in her way.

168

She stared round her, at the house, at the garden, at the place where she had lived with us, the place where, I think, she most liked to be, as if what she saw would help her to answer. She looked at the bees visiting among the flower-beds, and the drift through the air of the pale green tree-flowers, and the long flights of the birds, and she stared up at the blue void above us, blanched with the great heat. Then her eyes lit up, for she had seen our brother behind us, running down the iron steps from the house. He came with great leaps and bounds across the lawn, a cross between an angel and a clown, crying out, 'Rosamund, I've brought a present for you.'

'Dear Richard Quin,' she said. 'How kind you are.'

'Don't you want to know what it is?'

'Not very much,' she said placidly. 'I know it will be nice.'

'Why didn't you bring it to her?' I reproached him. Life was getting silly. If one liked a man, and he wanted to marry one, I supposed one married him. If somebody is giving somebody else a present, well, it ought to be given.

'Oh, I couldn't bring it out here,' said Richard. 'It comes from a garden, but now it's an indoor thing. Anyway you'll see it in a minute, Kate says tea's ready.'

Miss Beevor was at the tea-table. Only a week before, my mother, standing by the french windows, had raised a pensive finger to her lips and said in tones of melting tenderness, 'Those delphiniums Miss Beevor always admires so much will be out in a few days. I must ask her to tea, the poor, poor idiot.' So there she was.

'Rosamund, your present is on the sideboard done up in a bag ready for you to take back to the hospital,' said Richard, 'but there's almost the same thing on the table. You see,' he explained to us, 'I stopped and looked in at the window of that dairy round the corner from my school, I often do, they have such a specially nice china swan, not coloured, pure white; and I saw they had a pile of honeycombs, and it struck me how like they are to Rosamund. Look at that one on the table, the one we're going to eat. Nobody'll ever do a better portrait of Rosamund than that.'

We all exclaimed, for though honeycombs were then very cheap, costing only a shilling or two, they belonged to the same starred class of objects as certain flowers, such as orchids, which, even in places where they can be had for the plucking, nobody brought up within our imaginative system can regard

169

as suitable for everyday enjoyment; and indeed the honey-combs were like Rosamund. They were golden like her, and her sweetness was private, reserved to itself in cells. She cut up the honeycomb as ceremoniously as she would have cut a birthday cake, standing up to do it and smiling at us. But the honeycomb she cut not in slices but in little squares, and that surely was as well, for now I look back on that afternoon I cannot think how we ate any tea after that mid-day meal. But it is to be said in our excuse that we were always hungry for the very good reason that we were working about as hard as young people could. Rosamund was working ten to twelve hours a day and was ill-fed; and I realise now, on seeing the properly curtailed hours prescribed for modern music students, that Mary and I were taking as much out of ourselves as has ever been demanded from young girls under twenty, except in slavery. And as for Richard Quin, he was awake soon after dawn and out in his own music-room in the old stables, trying out some new thing, either an athletic exercise or a new piece for one or other of the several musical instruments he had learned to play, or perhaps even a new instrument; and he ran through the rest of the day at full speed, learning his lessons and meeting new people as if they were lessons he had to learn, and then suddenly, after darkness fell, hurrying up to his room and falling suddenly asleep, racing into dreams that kept him laughing and muttering. So all our engines had need for stoking, and we stoked them, but with ears cocked to my mother's conversation with Miss Beevor, which was, as always, a remarkable discharge of quixotically accepted obligations.

'Have you thought any more, Mrs Aubrey,' Miss Beevor began, 'about the little outing we planned to have next week?' This was her way of alluding to my mother's suggestion that they should go to a concert together: a suggestion that was little less than saintly, considering the history of their relationship.

'No, I left that until we could talk it over together,' said Mamma. 'Richard Quin, please go and get us *The Times*.' The newspapers were still left in the study after we had had a look at them during breakfast, just as if Papa were still in the house and keeping a journalist's hours, and waking at noon. Also since my father had held a crumpled newspaper to be as disgusting as muddy shoes, we handled them very gingerly over our bacon and eggs, and Richard Quin was smoothing out the rough print-cobbled pages of *The Times* when he brought it to Mamma.

'Well, on Wednesday Max Vogrich plays the Mendelssohn G minor with the Orchestra at the Queen's Hall, 'said Mamma after a moment's study, in a calmly dismissive tone which was lost on Miss Beevor, who said that that would be very nice, adding 'He has such a beautiful touch.' I am not acquainted with the musical affectations of today, and it may still be that to talk of 'touch' was a sign that one was one of the lesser breed without the law, as we used to put it.

But Mamma who was listening only to imagined sounds, had gone further down the column. 'Ah,' she cried, 'the choir are giving the *St Matthew Passion* at the Albert Hall that very same night! Oh, how glorious. I never hear it with less joy than I did the first time I heard it, thirty years ago in Vienna!' She blazed up in ecstatic flame, but almost immediately damped down the fires. 'No,' she said, kindly. 'No. Perhaps a little heavy. But how extraordinary. Here's something else. I did not know she came to London, I thought that when she played at that party she said she would not come to England again she was too busy, so many of the best French musicians won't cross the Channel. They are so insular and nationalist. Not like the Germans. But here it is, Wanda Landowska is giving a concert at the Wigmore Hall on Thursday. And a delightful programme, delightful, Bach and Scarlatti, Rameau and Couperin. A muddle but delightful. And all that harpsichord music is so interesting historically. Oh, Mary, and you too, Rose, you must hear her. After you have heard her play the pieces you have only heard on the piano, you will realise that quite a number of composers have been prophets, they have frequently written compositions which could not be properly performed, could not be fully realised, on the only instruments then existing, they were never truly heard till the piano was invented. Oh, you must hear her, children, we must all hear her—' She had gone up in flames again, but as her burning glance swept the room it fell on Miss Beevor, and again the fires were damped. 'Yes, children,' she went on, 'you must see to it you get to that concert. But I do not think I want to hear her again. You and I, Miss Beevor, will go to the Queen's Hall and hear Max Vogrich.'

But Miss Beevor had become more sensitive to the family atmosphere than my mother imagined. 'I would prefer we did not,' she said sitting up very straight. 'I would like to hear the *St Matthew Passion.*'

'No, no,' said Mamma, 'it is so long, it demands such attention, now that I have to make up my mind about it I see I am too old for such feasts.'

'If it is not to be the *St Matthew Passion,*' said Miss Beevor, implacably, 'let it be this young woman you have been talking about.'

'No, no,' said Mamma, 'do not think of her either. Let us leave such things to the young, we will go to the Queen's Hall.'

'I do not want to go to the Queen's Hall,' said Miss Beevor. 'I have been to the Queen's Hall. On several occasions. I know that I am not a gifted musician. Nor a highly trained one. But surely it need not be taken that I am quite without musical taste.'

'Oh, you are mistaken, Miss Beevor,' sighed Mamma, with an instant adaptation to the needs of the moment so smooth as to be almost to her discredit. 'I may be old, but that isn't any reason why I shouldn't brace myself to have one more evening with genius. So the Albert Hall and the *St Matthew Passion* it must be.' For an instant she looked wildly about her. I have never known anybody who suffered such anguish if she hurt anybody's feelings. She said, 'So we should have a very satisfactory evening before us.'

Because we all wanted to laugh, and were also wrung by our mother's recognition that she had wounded Miss Beevor, we began to clear away the tea-things. Rosamund sat where she was and sighed, 'Oh, dear, tea at St Katherine's isn't like this at all,' and Richard Quin said, 'Have you really had enough?'

She shook her head and laughed, 'Of course not. Is there such a thing as enough?'

'How will you eat your honeycomb at hospital?' asked Mamma. 'Can you have your own things without having to give so many people shares that they're lost to you? I know you would not mind, but I would like you to keep something for yourself.'

'I do put things on the table,' said Rosamund, 'but not this. I wouldn't share what Richard Quin gives me for anything. I'll put the honeycomb in my locker, and draw my cubicle curtains, and eat it with a spoon when the food has been too dreadful, and after I've said my prayers at night.'

'You can eat honeycomb with a spoon?' exclaimed Miss Beevor. 'Isn't it dreadfully rich?'

'Nothing is dreadfully rich to Rosamund and me,' said my brother. 'They're rich, and rich is something right in itself. Rosamund could eat a spoonful now, after all that tea, couldn't you, Rosamund?'

'Oh, surely you couldn't,' exclaimed Mamma. But Rosamund laughed again and said that she could, and Richard Quin carved a spoonful out of the honeycomb and held it to her lips, and she looked up at him and stammered, 'Thank you,' and brought her mouth down to it. But he suddenly drew it back, crying, 'I've thought of something better.' He took up the cream jug with his left hand and poured it over the honey, and held it out to Rosamund, saying, 'Yes, this will be better still.'

'Oh, no, not cream with honey,' our elders objected, 'that will be far too rich. And after all that tea.'

But Rosamund swallowed it down, and threw her head back on her strong throat, and said dreamily, 'That was lovely, the smoothness of the cream, the roughness of the comb, the sweetness of the honey.'

And Richard Quin, who had given himself another such spoonful, stood and looked at it with the same sleepy concentration: for a minute they looked too fair, too strong, too solid and monumental in their pleasure, for this small room, for us. But soon they went out together, taking the tea-things down to Kate, and they stayed away till Constance asked me to go and warn Rosamund that the cab would be coming soon to take her to the station. I found them sitting together in the dark half-way up the basement stairs, which was a place we often used for talking secrets: nobody could hear you upstairs, and somehow it did not matter about dear Kate. The two were not laughing then, and I had an idea that Rosamund might have been telling Richard Quin why she would not marry the doctor, though she liked him. It struck me that it was a pity that Rosamund was older than Richard Quin, they might have got on well if they had been married, and one could imagine the ceremony. For a minute my mind floated off into an area of images which suggested no words: the eyes on peacocks' tails, the grooves in the glassy waters that pile up around the posts of a weir. As I gave my message the two turned their faces towards me and grew less remarkable, and we were together as we always had been.

173

When she was dressed, and Richard had got from Kate the case in which we had packed her clean clothes and the food, she went into the sitting-room, where Mamma and Constance were still talking to Miss Beevor.

'You look a very grown-up young lady,' said Mamma, looking up at her tallness. 'You look more splendid than my girls, you look more like the people I used to play to, in big houses, in palaces. Are you sure you like nursing?'

'I told Mary and Rose,' said Rosamund proudly, 'I nurse as they play.' She tossed her head in parody of her own pride, and then the stammer began to choke her. But she insisted on saying, 'There is one thing.'

'One thing?' said Constance, quickly but still placidly. She knew there was probably something that could be done to right it, whatever it was, provided one did not become excited.

Rosamund forced herself to say: 'I cannot bear it when children die of burns.'

My mother looked away from her, out into the garden, where there was proceeding that liquefaction of colours which deepens and fuses the flowers and leaves and grass on summer evenings, under a sky of green crystal. She might have been calling on buried truth to disinter itself and come to our help. Constance picked up some needlework that she had set down on the table, and said, with calm acidity, 'Ask no questions and you'll be told no unbearable truths.' Richard Quin put his arms round Rosamund's shoulders and rested his head against the bush of her thick hair. She said, 'Oh, well, if everything should stop, should come to an end, you know, one would remember that such things happened and mind less,' and toured the circle of the elders, giving her smooth lips to their pleated cheeks, and was gone.

I went to my piano and made up for lost time by practising till it was quite dark, and then went into the sitting-room and found Mamma sitting there among the shadows, the gas not lit.

'We have all had a lovely day,' I said, and sat down beside her. 'But, oh, Mamma, why you crying?'

'I was awful to Miss Beevor,' she quavered. 'I have lost the knack of dealing with her. I used to give her quite a lot of pleasure when she came here – and goodness knows I have not asked her nearly often enough, I think she is very lonely – by saying when she left, "Goodbye, Bay-ah-tree-chay," but

174

tonight I did not dare. She might have thought I was laughing at her, for she thought that about the *St Matthew Passion*. . . .'

I did not have time to comfort her properly, for suddenly Aunt Lily and Mr Morpurgo were with us, she hungry and tired and disturbed as she always was after such expeditions. He was tired too, and nervous lest Mamma should think he should have taken better care of his charge. On this occasion he had some grounds for anxiety, because this time Aunt Lily was in an unusually poor state. As a rule she returned in a state of garrulous and mendacious optimism, alleging that the head wardress had whispered in her ear telling her to keep her chin up, the King was considering giving Queenie a free pardon after the New Year, or Easter, or August Bank Holiday. But this evening she was squealing with misery, and turning and twisting her little bony body as if she had St Vitus' Dance.

At supper she was silent for a time then put down her knife and fork and told us: 'She's lost her spirit. Queenie's lost her spirit, and I know who's done that. It's a funny thing, but when I see that ginger-haired wardress I always find myself remembering the words "ruptured kidney". I've only heard them once in my life and that was years ago. At the very first place where Queenie and I worked, when we were just girls, bits of the shell on our feathers, a customer made an awkward mistake. He thought one of the other customers wasn't the welterweight champion for Middlesex, but his brother, who wasn't there, he thought, but he was, and the other one who wasn't was dead of the 'flu, but the matter wasn't cleared up till he had asked the one he thought wasn't to go outside to settle a difference, if I make myself clear. "Ruptured kidney" was what the coroner said at the inquest. I never thought of the words since till I saw that ginger-haired wardress. "I'd like to give you something, my lady, that'd leave you with a ruptured kidney." That's what passes through my mind every time I see that little ginger-haired so-and-so.'

'That is only natural,' said Mamma. 'But eat your supper, what you need is to go straight off to bed.'

Lily repeated for the twentieth time, 'She's lost her spirit, her spirit's gone.'

'Oh, Lily dear,' said Mamma, 'are you sure what you notice is not just that your sister is being good and kind again. But if you think that she's being ill-treated Mr Morpurgo will help you. He knows people at the Home Office; they will look into it.'

Not listening, Lily said, 'I tell you, it's all gone, the old Queenie. She sits there like a beaten dog. She never let out at me once the whole time we were there.'

'Oh, my dear, eat and get to bed. When you have had some sleep things will seem different, and you may find you have something to balance against your misfortunes. You are so brave, you'll be glad to see what a relief it will be to your sister if she doesn't feel that she has to rage against you and can take the affection you give her.'

'Who's saying she was ever rude and unkind to me? Nobody ever had a better sister than Queenie's been to me,' wailed Aunt Lily, forgetting that most of the people in the room had at some time or other seen Queenie turn on her a glance remarkable in its inclusive contempt, which had suggested that had she cared to address the company present on her sister's insufficient bust measurement, her slightly projecting teeth, or her unwedded state, she could have gone on for a long time. But Aunt Lily was not for the moment paying much respect to reality. She passed on to a representation of Papa as a Cockney version of a Greek messenger, describing the imprisonment of Queenie in terms of pity and protest which seemed unlikely, considering he had frequently expressed the opinion that she was damned lucky not to have been buried in Holloway Prison instead of being alive in Buckinghamshire. 'Time and time again, I've heard your father say, and bless him wherever he is, and there's many could bear me out, that he didn't think we knew half of what went on inside Aylesbury Jail, I'll swear on my Bible oath, he used to say, that your poor martyred sister's suffering such torments as haven't been heard of since they done them to Maria Monk, and I doubt as if she'll ever get out of that hell-hole alive. And why should we care, asked someone. Someone who happened to be there, trying to be smart, you know, and your father answered quick as a flash, "Because she's one of the finest women that ever lived and—"'

My mother, who had been swaying on her chair with fatigue, was suddenly still, and said, sharply, 'For heaven's sake, Lily, what is really the matter?' I do not know how she knew.

'I'm telling you,' said Aunt Lily, cutting her tongue and lettuce with an air of defiance.

'No, my dear, you are not,' said Mamma. 'Mr Morpurgo, why is Lily in this state?'

'I have no idea,' said Mr Morpurgo, 'but poor Lily has been unhappy, very unhappy, all the way home.'

'Didn't any of them say anything to you?' my mother asked him, and he shook his head sadly. He would be thinking that Mamma was thinking that Papa would have found out what had gone wrong.

There was a moment's silence. Then Aunt Lily threw down her knife and fork and rested her elbows on the table and hid her face in her hands, and raised it to bawl. 'She's asked me to put flowers on his grave.' As nobody said anything she wagged her tear-stained face at us, and pierced our dullness with a full scream. 'His grave. Harry's grave. Her husband's grave. She asked me to put flowers on it, me that knew the minute the coppers came what she'd been up to.'

'Oh, Lily, dear,' begged Mamma, 'do not scream, do not cry, get on with your supper and go off to bed. You are such a brave woman, and you do things no other woman could do, and then you make a fuss about things you really should be able to take as a matter of course.'

'This ain't a matter or course,' protested Lily. 'It's disgusting. Flowers on his grave. It's so unlike her. She done him in. We all know she done him in.'

'Lily, just think. You are so intelligent, but you will not think. Can't you see that if one had happened to kill one's husband, or anybody else, it would be very difficult to find a way of telling him one was sorry except by putting flowers on the poor man's grave? I really cannot think of anything else one could do in such a situation. Now, do be sensible and be glad that your sister is settling down into her real self, and have a good sleep tonight, and we will see about the flowers for poor Harry tomorrow morning.'

'You're too good,' sniffed Aunt Lily, and took up her knife and fork again, saying, 'I know I'm a silly girl. Always was.'

In a low voice, like a child talking to a companion who has come off just well enough but not too well in a family row, Mr Morpurgo said to her, 'Give me time in the morning and I'll drive home and get some flowers, so that they'll be absolutely fresh.' Lily answered with a nod and a watery smile, but then

177

looked doubtful and said, 'Thanks ever so, but, if you don't mind, nothing fancy,' and as he looked puzzled explained, 'I mean, none of your giant South American doodahs. If this were a wedding it would have been a quiet one.'

The meal continued in silence. In other households it might have been supposed that one of the older children had been rude to someone and had been smacked down by authority; and as on such more usual crises the younger members of the party are silently convulsed by laughter. Mary and Richard Quin and I saw that Aunt Lily had been exhausted to a shock, that the part of her which was as serious and venerable as anybody we knew had recoiled from the darkness known as sin, but we also saw that Mamma had been very funny, and that twice over. First, when she paused before uttering the word 'happened' in the sentence beginning 'if one had happened to kill one's husband'. We all were aware that she had been about to say, 'if one had killed one's husband,' but had thought it incumbent to introduce a word suggesting that the fatality might have been, to some degree, accidental in nature; and we were aware too that this was not only to spare Aunt Lily's feelings, it was out of a far-flung politeness to all the killers of the world, of whatever time. She was making things no harder than they need be to Burke and Hare, Charles Peace, Tamberlane and Robespierre. She would have risked her own life to bring them to the scaffold, but she would never have insulted them. Her second absurdity was flattering to us, and all created things. When she said that she could not see any other way that a murderer could show his regret for his crime except by putting flowers on his victim's grave, her glance had swept round the table and rested for a fiery instant on each of our faces. She really had thought that one of us might come up with a valid solution to that insoluble problem. As always, she was expecting more of life than its best friends would have claimed for it; but no look of disappointment, of discontent with the family she had borne and the friends she had gathered, passed over her face, and never had, except when my eldest sister Cordelia played the violin.

That exception came to my mind as I cast my eyes round the room to avoid seeing the repressed amusement that was giving the faces of Mary and Richard Quin an unnatural blandness. So it was that I noticed that the dining-room door was open, and Cordelia was standing in the hall outside, looking in at us all, but not moving. She had not taken off her outdoor things. A small black straw hat with a curved brim and a little veil round the crown was still perched on her red-gold hair and shadowed her perfect little face; and a long coat was fluted round her waist and then fell in pleats, making her sturdiness look as if it were fragility that could easily be snapped across. She had put down her gloves and her handbag, and her hands were crossed on her chest, her long fingers with their nails polished, but not varnished, according to the fashion of the day, intertwining just at the base of her little round neck. I could not see her expression but I assumed that, as she was looking at her family, it would be disagreeable. What are they doing now? she would be asking. What have they been doing while I have been away? How long is it before they will bring down ruin on themselves and on me? But she moved forward into the gas-lit room, and I saw that I could not have been more wrong. She was a gazelle, a lamb, a dove. She was meek. She greeted our guests and refused to take her place at table because she was not hungry, in a barely audible voice, and sat down in a corner of the room, still in her hat and coat. All this was odd, but I felt no curiosity, taking it for granted that this was simply another of her impersonations, which might be abandoned at any moment. But as soon as Mr Morpurgo had driven away and Aunt Lily had been put to bed, and I had gone to the room I shared with Mary and was undressing, Mary came in and said, 'Something is going on. I went into the dining-room because I saw a light and thought Richard Quin hadn't turned the gas off, and there were Mamma and Cordelia, and Cordelia was behaving as if she were telling Mamma the facts of life. She looked at me with infinite patience until I went away.'

'It is too bad, Mamma has had such a long day,' I said, and I was going to put on my dressing-gown and run downstairs and break up whatever silliness was going on, but just at that moment Mamma came into the room and sat down on my bed. She told us in hesitating and incredulous tones that Cordelia had had news which, Mamma said, would make us all happy, and indeed that was true. For some time past Cordelia had been talking a great deal about a girl called Angela Houghton-Bennett who had been a fellow-student in one of her courses at the School of Art, and who had asked her to her home on a number of occasions, though for one reason or another she never brought her back to our house, although Mamma said we must always try and return all hospitality. Now it appeared that Angela had a brother called Alan, and he had proposed to Cordelia, and would be calling tomorrow morning to ask Mamma for her consent.

Mary and I were stunned into silence, but Mary recovered and asked, 'When are they going to get married?'

'Sooner than usual,' answered Mamma. It was then the custom for engagements to last a year or more. 'His father has to return to the East for a long journey in the autumn and the family think it will be much nicer for them to marry before he leaves.' She looked at us sharply and we looked back blankly. But she knew quite well she had spoken with a satisfaction of a kind she would not have wished to feel, and that we had noticed it. She said, gravely, 'Of course I am pleased. Particularly as all this art business couldn't really have led anywhere. So of course I am glad that she is going to marry.'

We asked how old he was and what he did, and she said, 'He is eight years older than Cordelia, which is just right. And he is a civil servant, he is in the Treasury, and your father used to say that was where all the cleverest men went. And it is better still about his father. He was in the Indian Civil Service. Your father always said that that was the greatest service in the world. Oh, there are many reasons why we should be glad.' Again she was putting a problem to us and we could not solve it for her. She was silently telling us 'Reassure me. Tell me that I am not pushing Cordelia out of the house, tell me that I am not determined to get rid of her at the first opportunity. Tell me that I am considering this proposal for her interests and not for ours, that if I think him unsuitable for any reason I will be honest and ask her to hold back and consider the possibilities of happiness all over again.' But we would not help her. We could not help her. We knew that Cordelia hated us, and we were still too young to have lost the child's feeling, inherited from the primitive, that a person who hates can work a spell on whom he hates and destroy him. I remember the agitated, brief, fluttering goodnight kiss Mamma gave us as she left the room, with deep contrition, but still I knew that it was useless for Mary and me to try to give her what she needed.

Once she had gone we lay down on the beds and waved our legs in the air. 'It will be wonderful to have nobody in the house who hates us,' I said, but Mary had a more impersonal attitude to the news. 'Why should anyone want to marry Cordelia? Anybody could see with half an eye she isn't kind. I can understand why anybody should want to marry Rosamund, even if she weren't beautiful. She's kind. But why should a man want to marry a woman who doesn't do anything to people but blame them for things they haven't done? It will be like spending one's whole life being rubbed with moral sandpaper.'

'Yes, I'm sorry for Mr Houghton-Bennett,' I said. 'But I don't know him and I don't care, really, not really, what happens to him so long as we don't have to go on living with somebody who is perpetually cross. But, of course, I agree with you. It's odd that anybody should want to marry Cordelia.'

'And what is odder still is that I somehow don't think people are going to want to marry us.'

'Don't let's bother about that tonight,' I said. But I knew what she meant, people said how wonderful we were but they kept at a distance. But all the same, I was right, it was too late to start thinking about it that night.

When we were dressing in the morning, we heard noises in the drawing-room below, and when we got downstairs we found Cordelia and Kate standing in the middle of the room, which looked quite different, for all the furniture had been moved. Cordelia was saying to Kate, 'Now I think that looks a little better,' and then she turned her white stars on us and asked, 'Are you going to be in this morning?' We said shortly that we would not, we had lessons and went off to have breakfast. Presently she came in and said that she was sorry if she had been rude, and added gravely, as if we were all in church, that she was going to marry somebody called Alan Houghton-Bennett, and he was coming about eleven o'clock to get Mamma's consent, and she had hoped we would meet him. Because we knew that she was lying and was glad that we were going to be out, and because we had ourselves been lying in saying that we had lessons that morning, an atmosphere of false amiability was established. But we were shaking with anger, not only because of her desire to get us out of the house, which was after all as much ours as it was hers, but because of her new manner, which had changed a little, and not for the better, since the previous night. She was still meek, but her meekness was pretentious. Though she was a lamb, it was one which had got itself embroidered on a church banner. There was also a sort of pietistic prudery about her, which we suspected of alluding to a side of life about which we knew little but, in the light of that knowledge, did not greatly approve.

'It's as if she were the Virgin Mary,' I said, 'And as if what she is making a fuss about was not an engagement but an Annunciation.'

'That's putting it rather high,' said Mary. 'She reminds me more of Miss Higgins when she gave that special biology lesson that we couldn't attend unless our parents gave written permission. Don't you remember? Miss Higgins told us with magic lantern slides how a calf was born.'

'Oh, I remember all right,' I said, 'we all agreed it would have been more interesting if the calf had told us with magic lantern slides how Miss Higgins had been born.'

We giggled and ran out into the garden and shouted up to Richard Quin's window and got him down with us to play our private family elaborate form of catch-ball, breaking off to exchange more heartless jests at the expense of our sister. I blush to recall our savagery, but it did not last long, we were so sorry for Alan Houghton-Bennett and so certain of the dire outcome of his resolve to marry our sister. He turned out to be a likeable person, tall and good-looking, with grey eyes and black hair, intelligent in the way Papa had liked, and very polite. He appalled us by his vulnerability indicated by this obvious sincere politeness of his, this real regard for other people's feelings. So far as we could see, he would have no defences against our awful sister.

There were only two grounds for hoping that he could survive. One was that she really loved him, and that seemed possible. Otherwise she could not have changed so completely; she worked on herself as drastically as a mezzo-soprano has to if she finds it necessary to change herself into a coloratura-soprano. That, of course, might not last. The mezzo-sopranos who have successfully converted themselves to the higher range must be very few indeed. But a second factor in the situation was her great enthusiasm for Alan's family and his home, which might well be lasting. Sir George Houghton-Bennett was plump and balding and, except that the Asian sun had burned him as brown as Lady Tredinnick, he was exactly like any other elderly gentleman one did not remember very well, and his daughters Olivia and Angela were exactly like the girls one did not remember very well, and Lady Houghton-Bennett was exactly like millions of people since she was disguised by the hideous and individuality-destroying uniform imposed in those days on the middle-aged and elderly women of the prosperous classes. She had masses of hair done in the teapot style, on which there rested nearly all day long, even at her own table when she was entertaining guests, a large and heavy hat; her skirts were long and weighty and trailed behind her; her bodices were boned till they might as well have been cuirasses; her sleeves were vast from shoulder to elbow and then constricted to the wrist, and out of doors she wore high boots with high heels which made her stoop as she hobbled along. As she went about the day's business, this gear (which was utterly unfeminine, which neither followed the lines of a woman's body nor suggested the distinctive virtues of women) obliged her to bend and balance this way and that, with the result that her face was always distorted by a false peevishness. Moreover, though Lady Houghton-Bennett had a good mind, and used it, having written several useful handbooks for the use of British soldiers' wives in India, teaching them something of the language and the everyday customs of the native population, she was now compelled to waste her time on such insensitive routines as 'leaving cards', which meant that she must spend an afternoon every month or so driving in her carriage to the houses of her friends and acquaintances, not to see them but to leave with the servant who opened the door her own and her husband's visiting cards, which had to be distributed owing to a code of which I can now remember nothing except that it meant that one was going away if one turned up a corner of one's card. The tedium of these rituals, together with the weight of her clothes, caused occasional failures in geniality; but like her husband and her daughters, she was remarkable for her good faith. They would not have gone back on a promise, and to them any contact with another human being, even so little as a 'good morning', constituted a promise, which could not be broken unless the other party to it made a disavowal. Even their concentration on fact, which was absolute and barred them from any understanding of the arts, was a way of keeping faith with the world about them. Of course Cordelia had to love people who had won so long ago and so finally the war against insecurity that we had waged all our lives. This was so particularly because the security attained was not only material but moral. They were as good as Mamma but in quite a different way: and as Cordelia had never been able to emulate Mamma's type of virtue, this gave her a second chance and she was, quite humbly, grateful.

But surely Cordelia did not have to love their awful house. This was a Victorian mansion high on Campden Hill, built of greyish brick; and within its walls Asia had taken its revenge against colonisation. It was full of brass cobras, elephants' feet, teak furniture, Indian silver bowls and ebony and ivory screens; and Cordelia liked it. The first time she took Mary and myself there, and the parlourmaid left us alone in the drawing-room, she looked round at its horrible treasures and said to us solemnly, as if we were all quite little children, 'Do not touch anything.' Mary and I were stilled. We were not little children, but she was a little child, and she would never grow up, and the terrible fears of infancy would always be with her. She was afraid that her beautiful new toy, her marriage, would be taken away from her if her naughty little sisters did not obey the rules the fairy godmother had laid down. Puzzled by what she saw on our faces, she stared first at me and then at Mary. 'What is the matter?' she asked quite pitifully. 'Why are you looking at me like that?' Mercifully, Olivia Houghton-Bennett came into the room at that moment, a little late because she had forgotten the time playing with the darling little kiddies (a word then used by all classes) in the East End Settlement where she worked three times a week.

'She cannot help it,' we found ourselves saying of Cordelia, after that, and we remembered how Richard Quin had been saying the same thing about her for years. It was strange how our brother, who was younger than we were, who was still at school, had been wiser than either of us for quite a long time, though wisdom was not his overt aim. He lived for pleasure, delicate pleasure, the easy exploitation of his body and his mind. Of this Cordelia had always disapproved, yet now she gained by it. Lady Houghton-Bennett and Olivia and Angela had instantly fallen in love with him, and, more than that, he was useful not only to them but their friends because he played excellent tennis, could sing and play and dance, and he grew into a sager kind of Cherubino. Thus it was that he was able to save us from a nightmare threat to the wedding-day. It would have been natural for the Houghton-Bennett girls and Mary and me to be bridesmaids, and indeed we would have enjoyed it, for it would have given us the chance to dress up without the horrors of going to an ordinary party. But Cordelia would be so certain that we were doing the wrong thing at the end of her train that she would be compelled, perhaps at the very climax of the ceremony, even at the moment when Alan was putting the ring on her finger, to turn round and seek us out with her white stare. When we hinted this to Mamma, however, she hinted back that she did not see how we could explain this to Lady Houghton-Bennett without intimating that we had found Cordelia a difficult sister, and Cordelia herself became like a distracted dove, ruffling its feathers, when we expressed our reluctance to follow her down the aisle. I think she feared that the Houghton-Bennetts would be put on the scent of our hopeless undesirability as sisters-in-law if we departed from the routine. It was left to Richard Quin when he was playing tennis with Olivia at Ranelagh to blurt out with apparent tactlessness that Mary and I suffered from agonising stage-fright if we found ourselves the object of public attention anywhere but on the concert platform. It made us feel sick, he said, and added that on one occasion we had actually been sick, and that he doubted whether, try as we might, we would be able to go through with it, and he thought it probable we would baulk at the last moment. He made this tale more convincing by inventing an anecdote about Liszt fainting when officiating as a best man at a friend's wedding (Liszt of all people! But the Houghton-Bennetts would, he rightly supposed, not know about that). We followed on by half-finished sentences and anxious looks next day when our bridesmaid dresses were mentioned; and soon all was well and Cordelia had the look of a general who has altered and improved his disposition of troops.

She was a child. But not, we sometimes thought, a lovable one. We realised that, when she came into our room one night, quite late, when Mamma had gone to bed. She was wearing one of her trousseau dresses, which had just come from the dressmaker, and she said that she wanted our opinion as to whether the sleeves were not set in crooked. They were perfect. We told her that the dress was lovely, and that she would look lovely in it, as she did in all her dresses, and Mary asked, very gently for her, what was worrying her.

Cordelia's voice failed her. She moistened her lips and

whispered, 'Sometimes I am afraid Papa will come back. Before the wedding,' and she added, in a voice sharpened by dread of a threat that would overhang the years that would go on for ever, 'or after.'

We could not answer. This was too pathetic. All of us, even Kate, were counting the days when she should leave the house; and all of us, if we had heard Papa's key in the door again, would have been transported with joy, we might have turned into birds, and flown about.

I said, 'But Cordelia, Papa is dead.'

'How do we know?' said Cordelia, her eyes full on my face.

'We know,' I said and Mary said, 'We know.'

'But we have heard nothing,' said Cordelia, suddenly slipping into her old role of the only sensible person in the house, 'absolutely nothing. It is not that I did not love him, I often thought I loved him more than any of you. Of course I would like him back. But Mamma has told Alan's mother that Papa is dead, and if he turns up, what will they think?'

Mary broke the silence. 'You know as well as we do he is dead.'

'But how do we know?' Cordelia asked, impatiently, angrily.

'Shut up,' I said. 'We know, for one thing, because Mr Morpurgo went away about the time that Papa left us, and he came back utterly wretched, and was especially kind to Mamma, and indeed kind to us all. What could that mean except that Papa was dead.'

Mary's fingers slipped into mine. So neither of us added, 'By his own hand.'

'Well, if you think so, it is all right,' sighed Cordelia. But after a minute she reverted to the role of the most sensible person in the house and said, 'But could not we ask Mr Morpurgo?'

'No,' said Mary. 'He loved him. Do go to bed.'

'I will,' said Cordelia. 'I will be able to sleep now.'

In point of fact, Cordelia need never have given herself away to us, for the Houghton-Bennetts had dealt in their own way with the phenomenon of our Papa and there was no need for her to concern herself with him. Mamma was so obviously irreproachable that it never occurred to them that there could be anything scandalous about Papa. As we learned long afterwards, the Houghton-Bennetts had been misled by Cordelia's reticence about her father, and Mr Morpurgo's references to his long intimacy with him. They concluded that

Papa had been a Jew and that poor Cordelia had been the victim of anti-Semitic teasing at school; and as the Cordelia they knew was vulnerability itself, this increased their protective love for her. They were, indeed, all at sixes and sevens in their estimation of us. It was obvious to us that the Houghton-Bennetts were behaving with extraordinary generosity in welcoming so warmly a daughter-in-law from a family with no social position and no fortune. What we did not realise was that though we had, all the same, something to say for ourselves, they had never grasped this. They knew nothing of music, partly because they were not musical and partly because they had been so long in the Far East; though like practically everybody else in the world at that time, they had heard of Paderewski, that was all they knew of the subject, and the fact that Mamma had once been famous could not enter into their minds, there was no place for it to go. When Olivia and Angela came to our house and we showed them Brahms' signed photograph and boasted that he had given it to Mamma because he thought her the best woman pianist since Clara Schumann, they were unimpressed, though visibly touched at such importance being attached to such a drab souvenir, for the reason that their home on Campden Hill was rich with silver-framed photographs of Royalties and Viceroys and Governors and Rajahs; and they would hardly have credited that Mamma had some of those too, but they were kept in the trunks in the box-room. They thought of our home as humble, in the Biblical sense of the word, and as free from vainglory; and of Cordelia, whose blazing ambition had all but burned down our house, as the humblest of all. They doted on us as Wordsworth doted on his cottagers. Indeed, looking back on them, I think we were a relief to the Houghton-Bennett parents' noblest part; for they looked on their son's marriage as an affirmation of the claim that they owed debts to other than Caesar. It is ironical that at the same time we were feeling towards them like unscrupulous horse-dealers who have sold a dangerous horse to an urban simpleton.

But nobody could have believed that irony played any part at our sister's wedding, it was so beautiful. They were married in St Mary Abbott's which is a church of distances, and all the distances led to masses of flowers – Mr Morpurgo's flowers – and Cordelia's eyes were set on some sacred goal behind those flowers, until she neared the altar, and then her gaze marvelled at the candles and thanked the cross for all this beauty, and for more than that. For when she reached the altar, there could she take the vow of obedience which her whole being craved, since she was framed only to obey. She was submission, she was sacrifice, and nothing else. At the sight of her many people in the congregation were wiping their eyes, and we wept also, but our tears were inspired by the bridegroom, awaiting his bride, not knowing that he might as well await a river of lava.

It was terrible to see them standing side by side in the Houghton-Bennetts' drawing-room, which really did not look so bad now they had taken out the enormous ivory model of the Taj Mahal and the ivory lily (with coral stamens and jade stalk and leaves) embedded in a black velvet panel and supported on a Burmese silver easel. We were exhilarated to see that no matter what the eternal truth of the situation might be, the festivity celebrating it all looked very pretty. The drawing-room and the staircase were crammed with people who were happy as people are at a wedding where the bride and bridegroom are romantic figures; and the air was alive with the curious exhalation of sound which rises from chattering people yet is so much more like a bird-chorus than human speech. It went so well that as soon as the reception line came to its end Sir George and his wife went and sat on a sofa, and whenever they did not have to talk to the guests, spoke to each other in laughing undertones, and it could be seen that they had been much in love, and were still so in their elderly way. We were slightly shocked by Mamma, for though she should have known better than anyone there this marriage would end in misery, she was certainly enjoying herself, and making her own success, for Aunt Constance had made her look quite ordinary by putting her into fancy dress and turning her into an early Victorian, with a coal-scuttle bonnet to hide her wild hair and shade her wild eyes, and a tight-fitting bodice and a full skirt that she could not make untidy. She had met an old lady and gentleman in whose house she had played when they were first married and she was young, and the three were sitting on a window-seat, and all might always have gone smoothly for her ever since they had last met. Rosamund and Richard Quin too, were taking the occasion in a light-minded way with Olivia and Angela and their friends. But, when we took a minute to reflect, outsiders who did not know might have thought we were enjoying ourselves; and that, we suddenly realised, was exactly what we were doing. Only Mr Morpurgo was looking sad, which surprised us, for we thought he had never seen through Cordelia. It was not till some days later that we discovered that his gloom was among the ironies of the occasion. He had not been in the least disconcerted by the marriage since Mamma had approved it and he took it for granted that she was right about everything. But the reception had shocked him by revealing what was in his eyes a world of terrifying poverty. He knew that many people were poor, and that our family had been poor until our father left us, but that was the result of failure: of inability to get to the top. Here, however, was a crowd of people who were all successful, and had for the most part been certified as such by this and that decoration and title, but their wives had not a Paris dress among them, and few of them had carriages or motor-cars, and they seemed undisturbed by finding them-selves in a house where the furniture was ignoble and there was not an Old Master – not even, he pointed out to us afterwards, an Old Master *drawing* – on the walls; and what made it worse was that they owed their success to the exercise of gifts which he knew he lacked and esteemed far above those he possessed. He was so preoccupied by shame at the injustice by which the world had favoured him above his superiors, that I doubt if he had a moment to consider the possible future of Alan and Cordelia; and I have to admit that we forgot our prophetic gloom till it was time to go upstairs to help Cordelia into her going-away dress (which was a coat and skirt of pale amber facecloth in which she looked transparent, about to rise into the skies) and there our vision of them returned to us in full measure. True, she seemed to be changed. Always before, when we had done her up, to use a phrase which long ago lost its meaning, she had put it to us that we were ruining for ever whatever garment it was that we were buttoning or hooking or snapping, through that preternatural clumsiness from which she alone of all the family was exempt; but now she remained still under our fingers and thanked us. Also her goodbye kisses she gave us felt as if she had really been fond of us. But we knew the truth, and were astonished when we saw that Kate, who came down like a hawk on all our faults, wept under that kiss. But it was under Alan's kiss that our eyes filled with tears. The honeymoon was to be spent in Florence, and we imagined him suddenly shocked into woodenness by his first discernment of our sister's real quality, against a background of cypresses and campanili which should have been the framework of happiness.

But we were wrong. We could not have been more wrong. When Cordelia and Alan came back from their honeymoon they settled down in a little white box of a house, in a turning off the Victoria Road, in Kensington, and Mary and I had grimly said to each other that whenever Cordelia saw in the papers that there was going to be a concert at the Albert Hall we were likely to go to, she would ask us to come in for a meal, and it would be dreadful, for she would do it only out of a sense of duty. These invitations came, but soon we found we were eagerly waiting for them, we would have been disappointed if they had not come. Cordelia had not cast off the character she had assumed on the day of her engagement. She still had no will of her own, only a desire to please and find out what gave most pleasure. It might have been said she had no character, had there not been some of her old blacksmith-forge quality in her limitation of herself to amiability. She never ran an eye over us when we went into the house, and convicted us of untidiness and lack of the sense of suitability. She simply asked us our opinion on what she had last done to the house, which was indeed a marvel, not only to our eyes, which had so long looked on only poverty, but to any person looking back on it from this age which is called affluent. Like all young people of moderated means at that time, Alan and Cordelia employed two servants, a cook-general and a house-parlourmaid, and the place shone bright and clean as few households do today. The dining-room faced south, and the sunshine fell full on the table at lunch-time striking prismatic rays from the silver and glass, each piece of which was polished as highly as polish can go. The whole house was full of light, the furniture was rosewood and elegant and in winter the curtains were of padded white chintz with huge flowers on it and in summer of ruffled muslin. There were flowers about, and always nice things to eat. But all that was as nothing to the prevalent good will, the way they welcomed us, the way they liked us to stay as long as we could without running the risk of being late for the concert. They would even come out with us to the garden gate, to be with us as long as possible.

One day, I remember, in the first winter of their marriage, we

190

stayed with them till the last minute. The four of us lingered, looking round the little front garden, and they explained to us that it was still a mystery to them.

'You see,' said Cordelia, 'we don't know what half the trees are,' and Alan said, 'We do know that this is a laburnum, and that's about all,' and then Cordelia said, her intimation so like his in tone that she might have been his sister and not ours, 'And this is a syringa, but this? We don't know.'

'And this we know to be a hawthorn,' Alan went on, 'but what colour? White, red, or pink? And you must allow it makes a great difference to a hawthorn. And to the house. Almost as much to the house as it means for a woman whether she has got fair hair or dark hair or carrots like Cordelia.'

'The old lady next door speaks to me, but she doesn't know what colour it is any more than we do, for she came here only a month before we did so doesn't know any more than we do. The people opposite would know, of course, for the husband's father lived there before them, he bought the house when it was first built, and Thackeray used to come to dinner with them. But how can I go and knock on their door and say, "Please, what colour is the hawthorn in my garden?"'

We did not want to part, they walked with us to the pillar-box. Our enemy had gone away, had not just left our house, but had vanished. Someone whom we did not know was wearing her clothes and her body, someone whom we did not hate, someone whom, it often seemed, we did not love enough. That December this sister-stranger and I were in her drawing-room, which was one of those anti-winter sym-phonies that can be composed by putting together a bright fire in a basket grate under a marble mantelpiece, bowls and trumpet-vases full of bronze and gold chrysanthemums, and cushions and curtains predominantly white. It was an Edwardian formula and it worked. Cordelia was moving round the room, collecting the tea-cups and little plates to make it easier for the parlour-maid when she came in to take out the tea tray; and she shifted into a corner a tiered cake-stand of the kind fashionable in those days, a wedding present from a French friend, an Art Nouveau construction with silver plates in the form of lily-pads. On the top plate there was left one small sugared biscuit. She looked at it, then looked away, and then looked at it again. I knew she wanted to eat that biscuit very much, as one sometimes wants to eat something for which one has no real hunger, simply because a childish and irrational appetite insists and seeks to prove that enough is not as good as a feast. She put out her delicate hand and raised the biscuit to within a millimetre of her lips, and suddenly drew it back and gazed at me with round eyes, saying, 'Would you like it, Rose? Oh, do have it, Rose.' There was a moment when the light of the room swam round me like slowly moving water. I knew Cordelia through and through as one knows a long-feared tyrant; and this complete knowledge told me now that, even had it been not a sugar biscuit in her hand but a great treasure, she would have given it to me. I did not feel abashed. I simply felt astonished at the quiet, prim force of her desire to surrender to me everything and anything which could give me pleasure. My memory was not wiped out. Indeed, as I smiled at her and shook my head, because I could not speak, there flashed before me a picture, as little mitigated as it had ever been, of the years and years during which she was a devouring nuisance, a resident plague in our midst. But all that was now over and done with. The cut end of an ugliness was lying in my mind, it lay loose, it was something to be thrown into the waste paper basket.

The experience was impossible to describe, it was so much more than itself. But when I told Mary that I found Cordelia much nicer and hardly anything of the old punitive terror, it seemed she herself had noticed a change, and found it disconcerting. She said she felt like a keeper at the Zoo who suddenly found that all the animals in the Lion House had been replaced with angels. 'It would be difficult,' she imagined, 'not to approach them with a spiked pole from force of habit.' And she added, 'For goodness' sake we must stop defending ourselves against her.' Richard Quin simply said, 'Of course, of course,' when we talked about the change and hurried off to go skating at Queen's with Olivia and Angela, which was natural enough, for it was Friday evening, and he made a point of spending an hour or two during the weekends in being useful to the Houghton-Bennett family. He listened to Sir George's stories of the Far East; and he took Lady Houghton-Bennett to the wrong concerts, which she so constantly and invariably chose in preference to the right ones; and he took the girls to parties or theatres or skating-rinks, to any other gatherings where an adolescent still at school was acceptable as the male escort then obligatory. This was a real kindness, for there was an ugly paradox in the society of that day. Convention relegated unmarried women to an inferior position, and insisted that they must always be accompanied by men on all social occasions and at places of entertainment. But only rich young women found it easy to get the necessary husbands or escorts. This was very odd because though there were more women than men in Great Britain – something like a hundred and three women to a hundred men – the surplus had no bearing on this phenomenon, since it was due to the longevity of women. There was, in fact, a full force of husbands and dancing-partners available, had they only come forward; and I could not account then, and cannot account now, for their reluctance except by supposing that men do not like women and find pleasure in preventing them from doing what they want to do. What made Richard Quin unique was that he had not a drop of this masculine vinegar in his veins, perhaps because he was so male that he had no reason to be irked by the sexual division. He had a profile as fine as any girl's, but he could not have been taken for a girl, and when he played a girl's part in a school play there was no illusion, and I can remember that when I threw my arms round his shoulders it felt as if he had a delicate armour under his skin. With his maleness, this other element, the difference of every cell in his body from every cell in ours, he was protecting us. Though Cordelia had always bullied him worse than any of us, perpetually complaining that he was spoiled and would come to no good, when I told him how she had changed there came only this: 'Of course, of course,' and it seemed clumsy and inelegant to remember even faintly her past faults. He bore no grudges. And he was working all he could for Cordelia by ingratiating himself with the Houghton-Bennetts, for they would not blame her so much for taking Alan from them since they had had him as their amusing page.

Mamma's reaction was different when I told her that Mary and I had begun to like Cordelia, even to love her, because she had changed. She said, 'Of course she is changing. You have all changed. Mary and you especially. Much of the original brutality has gone.' But what wonder, for the whole world was changing.

VII

MARY AND I made real successes in the few years that followed Cordelia's marriage. We were gold medallists, a great conductor gave us the chance to play with the best provincial orchestras, we were soon at the Proms, we never had to worry about filling the hall for our recitals. The only thing we had to worry about was the danger of getting tired and letting people come between us and our work for the very reason that they admired it. But the charm of our success lay in the fact that it was not unique, it was set in an age of success. Everybody and everything was developing according to some principle which commanded romantic perfection. I remember playing the Mozart Twenty-third Concerto at a Queen's Hall concert one summer night when the intelligence of the audience made their listening a better performance than my playing; it was spiritualism, Mozart was there; and they applauded at the end as if the hall were burning about us and they must say what Mozart meant to them before they were buried in the rubble. Mary and I drove away to a party through a London which was moonlit and transfigured. In all the squares waltzes and one-steps and tangos were exhaled from porticoes wearing striped awnings like masks, and in the gardens dancers walked on the moon-frosted lawns, the moonlight shining with phantom coldness from the young women's bare shoulders and bright gowns, and making breast-plates of the young men's shirt-fronts. It would have been easy for assassins hired to kill these young men to hide behind the sooty trees and aim at those gleaming shirt-fronts, but no human being could be so pitiless towards their youth. At the great house to which we had been invited, we sat in a courtyard where the moonlight sobered an

194

extravagance of flowers, and watched a black stage, and listened to music as different from the music I had played as a Mongolian face is different from a Western face, until yellow limelight shone on the stage and showed us a girl whose face was tragic though she wore the full tarlatan skirts which till then had been the livery of the least serious of the arts, who was light as a feather yet as grave as Hamlet. Then Nijinsky leaped from a window in the darkness behind the stage and halted an instant in mid-moonlight before he dropped into the yellow limelight, uttering with the speed of light a prophecy that he and we were to travel to strange places and often see nature transcending what we had been told were its limits. Every time we left our pianos the age gave us such assurances that there was to be a new and final establishment of pleasure upon earth. True that when we were at our pianos we knew that this was not true. There is something in the great music that we played which told us that that promise will not be kept, though another promise will give us more than that, but in its own time. That we did not believe this assurance which sustained most of our contemporaries added to our loneliness; but we could enjoy their achievements. And let there be no error, their achievements were enjoyable. This faith in the dispensation of pleasure was not a form of guilt, those who held it were not drunken or idle or cruel, and accepted kindness itself as a pleasurable act. Simply the world appeared to be whispering to its peoples that it was about to turn into a rose, into a jewel, into wine, and those who heard often responded by actions that were wholly delightful, though they are now seen to be appropriate.

We should have been perfectly happy, had it not been that Cordelia, instead of valuing Richard Quin for his loyalty to her, was vexed by a perpetual dread lest he was turning out badly. She was nearly her old self when she was moved by this fear. She was looking at Mamma with her old white stare when I came in on her one afternoon, and found her trying to find out what Richard Quin's last school report had been.

'But he will be leaving school in six months, Mamma,' I can remember her saying, 'has he no idea of what he wants to do?'

'Well, he is sitting next month for a scholarship at Oxford,' said Mamma.

'But the headmaster has told you he will never get it, he is

195

not working hard enough,' said Cordelia, savage as she used to be.

'If he fails, then he can take a year and rub up his piano and violin, and he is sure to get into one musical school or another,' said poor Mamma.

There was a silence. We looked at Cordelia, daring her to say he was not good enough, in view of her own violin-playing. But we did not like to defend the plan that he should become a musician, because there was in fact in all his playing the anti-artistic quality of improvisation. He played as a bird sings, which is not the recommendation that the unmusical believe.

'Surely he realises,' said Cordelia desperately, 'that he must earn his living? – that he cannot live on you?'

Again Mary and I were awkwardly silent. Cordelia was doing what she had always done, she was blaming other members of her family for weaknesses which were particularly her own. She was always asking us in front of people whether we had lost things, when it was she and she only who constantly left things in trains. Now she was suggesting that Richard Quin was going to be a burden upon us in a way which would be specially unpleasant in a man; and it was not for her to do that. We had got scholarships for our musical education, and had cost Mamma very little during our training, and now we were making money. But Cordelia's classes in foreign languages and the history of art had been quite expensive, and she had never earned a penny; and on her marriage Mamma had made a little settlement on her. But she went on, and we began to feel miserable, for indeed we were ourselves beginning to be puzzled by Richard's indifference about his future. It seemed that nothing in him was striving to have its way with him, as music had had its way with us.

'Are you worried about him, Mamma?' asked Mary abruptly.

'Not in the least,' replied Mamma.

'That is the worst of this family,' grieved the old Cordelia. 'You take nothing seriously, you don't realise things.'

'No, dear,' said Mamma.

'I wish you could get Richard Quin to come up to town and have a talk with Alan's father,' said Cordelia importantly. 'By the way, where is Richard Quin? It is six o'clock, do you not expect him home for tea?'

196

'I do not really expect him,' said Mamma, growing more and more placid. 'He has so many friends.'

'But a boy of that age should not just roam about, with nobody knowing where he is,' scolded Cordelia. 'He should come home to tea at regular hours, he should settle down to his homework, this is all wrong. I do not know where it will lead. It is the greatest misfortune that he could not be sent to a public school. I would,' she said, with a sincerity which would have touched us had anyone else been speaking, 'far rather that poor Mr Morpurgo had done nothing for me and spent all the money on sending Richard Quin to Harrow or Rugby.' This was a great deal for her to say for Mr Morpurgo had given her her house, which she passionately loved, more than most people love their houses, more as a child loves a doll's house.

It was just then that Richard Quin came in, carrying a teapot. The sight made Cordelia click her tongue against her palate, for it meant that he had been down in the kitchen getting Kate to make him fresh tea, and it was another proof that he was living an unmanly life among a crowd of women. He put down the teapot and kissed Mamma and waved a hand at the rest of us, and said, 'I talked to a man on the bus coming back from school, and asked him what he had in his basket, and it was a pigeon, and he asked me to go home with him and see his pigeons, he had thirty-six. And do you know, there are lots of people in London who think of nothing but pigeons?'

'Were they lovely?' asked Mary.

'Oh, far lovelier than you would think, I could hardly believe it when I held them in my hands,' said Richard Quin, his mouth full of bread and jam. 'And this man and his wife adored their pigeons, they were Seventh Day Adventists, and that means that they cannot drink tea or coffee or beer or wine or whisky, so instead they got drunk on pigeons.'

'Is the coo pleasant when you are quite near them?' asked Mamma.

'Yes, it is,' said Richard Quin, 'and it is so funny to feel it rolling right through their bodies, it takes much more organisation than you would think, they use all of themselves for it. But the wonderful thing is how they fly. The man let me do it. Oh, not the best racing ones. They have to be let out of a loft and handled very carefully. But there were some which did not really matter, and he showed me how to send them off.'

197

He stood up behind the tea-table and the light shone back from him. 'You pick up the pigeon as if it were a ball, and you throw it into the air, and when it is up there it starts flying. It is as if you were bowling and the ball became alive.' He flung out his arm two or three times towards the ceiling, his curved hand quivering with the pleasure it remembered. 'You would like the feeling, Mamma,' he said, sitting down again to eat.

'So I should,' said Mamma, enchanted.

'Well, I will take you along some day,' said Richard Quin.

'Wouldn't he think it odd for someone as old as me to want to do it?' Mamma asked wistfully.

'No, no. You see, I told them a lot about you,' said Richard Quin.

Cordelia asked impatiently, 'And your lessons? What about your lessons? Will you not be late, starting your homework?'

'Oh, that will be all right,' he said.

'Will it?' she asked. 'Have you any hope of getting that scholarship?'

Richard Quin's eyes narrowed, he seemed to bite back a sharp answer.

'Don't you want to go to Oxford?' Cordelia pressed.

His eyes were wide again. 'Yes, very much,' he said. 'I can't tell you what I would feel if I could be sure that I were going to Oxford.'

All of us except Cordelia were surprised by his gravity, for he seemed to take no more thought for the morrow than the lilies in the field, which did not disturb us, since we knew that he was among the lilies and not among the weeds.

'Yes,' Cordelia persisted, her exasperation growing, 'but are you sure you ought to go to Oxford? Would it not be better for you to try a musical career?'

He made a face at her. 'How afraid you are, when you think someone is going to succeed in doing what he wants. A minute ago you were scolding me because I was not working hard enough for an Oxford scholarship, now because I say I want to go you tell me that I shouldn't go to Oxford at all.'

She was disconcerted, for a minute she stared at him as if she at last understood something, but she hastily ran back into her anger, and cried at our amused faces, 'You are all hopeless. It is not fair to the boy. Richard Quin, you must make up your mind about your future. I wish you would give up one of these evenings you are always frittering away playing games and come and spend an evening with Alan's father.'

'That is just what I arranged to do yesterday,' said Richard Quin. 'He has found out how well I can skate, and we are booked to go to Prince's together one evening next week, so that I can give him some tips.'

Cordelia was ruffled by our laughter, and left us. In the hall she said meekly to me, after she had kissed me goodbye, 'Forgive me for being cross with Richard Quin. But I am so worried in case he becomes a burden on you all.' I was coldly silent. It would have been quite possible for Mary and me to borrow enough money to send Richard to Oxford on our existing contracts, and I was enraged, because she was again pretending, as in the days of her unprofitable career as a child violinist, that she was the stay of our household and the rest of us were imprudent and incapable of supporting ourselves. But she passed from my anger into a kind of trance. She stared at me, lifting a tremulous finger to her lips, and murmured, 'And the disgrace,' and went out into the darkness, hurrying back to Alan.

It happened that she did not hear at once that Richard Quin failed to get a scholarship but succeeded in winning an exhibition at New College, and had gone at once to Mr Morpurgo to ask him to lend the money to make up the difference between the exhibition and his probable expenses, so that he need take nothing from Mamma or Mary or me. Neither Mary nor I wrote to tell her, simply because we hardly ever thought of her except when she appeared before us. Mamma did not write either, but that was because she was growing noticeably remote and inactive. She played the piano less and less, and very often let a whole day pass without opening it. We were not sure whether she was ill, or whether what we saw was the result of age, for she had indeed married later than was the custom for women at that period and she was much older than the mothers of our contemporaries. We took her to a Harley Street specialist, but he could find nothing wrong with her, and as she did not seem to be in pain or to be worried about herself, we pushed our sense that she had changed to the back of our minds. But it was a sign of that change when, in spite of her resolution to keep Cordelia in our circle she did not write to her about Richard Quin's success. And Richard Quin did not write himself, because her doubt about his future was the one point on which he was sensitive. We had never seen him downcast before, except about that one misfortune which could still draw tears to the eye of any one of us when we thought of it; the loss of our father. Every event except that had struck Richard Quin as either agreeable, or capable of being made so or nearly so, either by laughter or by his particular innocuous kind of finesse. But when Cordelia said that she did not think that he ought to go to Oxford and showed that she believed him worthless, I saw the light go out of him for an instant. It was almost as if what she thought were true, and she were forcing him to admit guilt which till then he had always falsely denied. So he did not write to her about his exhibition. But he met Rachel Houghton-Bennett by chance the day after it was all settled, and she passed on the news to Cordelia, who was with us by the middle of the afternoon.

We had even fresher news to tell her, but she would not listen to it. We thought this a pity, because it had pleased us all. About noon that day I had been standing in the hall reading a press cutting; we hated letters, we had not enough time for them, and we always kept them on the hall-table and read them when we had a spare moment. Our agents handled all our engagements, and we had had a telephone put in, so it worked quite well. Then I heard someone knocking, and I opened the front door, and found a tall pale girl, about my own age, standing outside. She said in a flat voice, 'I hoped you were still living here,' and I recognised Nancy Phillips.

I pulled her in and called to the others, and Mamma and Mary and Kate all came out, and we were so glad to see her that for a long time we never thought of moving out of the hall. She said she was well, and she would have been good-looking if it had not been for her lack of colour, and a doubtfulness which made not only her movements but even her features tentative and unimpressive. She had not had a very pleasant time since she saw us. It had been a great relief to her, she told us, to read about Mary and me in the papers, because so little had happened in her own life. It turned out that she had not been trained to do anything since she had left school and she had just been at home with Aunt Clara.

It was then Mamma seized her arm and said, 'Take your hat and coat off. And do you want to stay the night? There is a bed for you,' and Kate said, 'There is a lot of food, I have much more now to cook with than I used to have.'

200

It had disturbed Mamma and the rest of us when Nancy was a schoolgirl, her idleness. It was so heartrendering. We were having such fun working, Mamma enjoyed our work as if she were living her youth over again, and if we often forgot to read our press cuttings Kate never did, and she liked it when people gave us flowers. But Nancy had neither work nor anybody about her who worked. She had, indeed, nothing. She knew it, she turned sad eyes on Mamma and said so, and confirmed it by her pallor, her listlessness. When Richard Quin came in for lunch, she marvelled to see how grown-up he was, and when we told her how he was going to Oxford, and she was really glad, and he thanked her for her gladness by kissing her, which pleased her very much, she looked like a child holding a shell to her ear to hear the sound of the sea.

At luncheon and afterwards she told us all about her life in Nottingham. She had not written to us, because her Uncle Mat still felt very bitter against her mother, he had loved her father so much. It had hurt him quite badly that she had insisted on writing to Aunt Lily, and she had never dared to tell him that she would have loved to see her. The trouble was not that she had been afraid of him, though he was a blunt man, indeed he prided himself on his bluntness, he was so blunt that he had not many friends. It was that he and his wife had been so good to her. They had two sons of their own, but both were married and one was in Melbourne and the other in Singapore, and so they had treated Nancy and her brother as their own children. Her eyes were wide with wonder at their kindness, but she did not seem to be remembering any scenes that had been shaped and informed by that kindness. I remembered how Papa had likened Uncle Mat to a bull, and it seemed probable that Nancy had experienced such tedium as might befall a young girl who had been adopted by a benevolent bull and cow. They had given her brother a good education, and he had trained as an accountant and had gone out to Canada, where he was doing well. It was terrible, the centrifugal force exercised by the kindness of this blunt man, which drove its recipients outwards over the continents. So Nancy had been quite alone with her uncle and aunt for the last few years. But they had done everything they could to prevent her feeling lonely, they had given her a wonderful coming-out dance, and had often taken her on holidays to stay at lovely hotels, all over England and Scotland.

201

'I think they hoped that I would get married,' she told us, 'but, of course, I am not very attractive.'

She paused, and I wondered that Richard Quin did not tell her that she was graceful and had lovely hair, for he was clever at reassuring girls about their looks. Olivia Houghton-Bennett was very self-conscious because she was rather tall, and I have heard her murmur to him, as they went into a room, 'Am I looking awful,' to which he answered, with convincing hesitation, 'Yes, you are, rather. But I think it is only because you are stooping and crawling about sideways like a crab, if you would stand up straight you would look ripping.' But he made no attempt to reassure Nancy, and I saw why, when she went on: 'And, of course, everybody knows who I am. Aunt Clara and Uncle Mat thought that nobody guessed, because they made us change our names. I have not been Nancy Phillips since I left this house. They made me call myself Nancy Kingston. There is some sense in it, my father's mother, Uncle Mat's mother, was Nancy Kingston before she married. All the same, it sounds a silly, made-up name. It is not mine.'

She ran her fingers distastefully along the table-edge in front of her, and let them drop in her lap. She was without employment, she had had her own name taken away from her, she had nothing.

'And it was quite useless, too,' she continued. 'Everybody in Nottingham realised who we were as soon as we were brought there, and of course nobody wants to marry me.' It was as well that Richard Quin had not told her that she was pretty, for if he had convinced her of it that would only have made her more certain that people did not want to marry her because she was the daughter of a murderess. 'And I would not care, either, to marry anybody who thought it was nothing that my mother murdered my father.'

'I am so glad that you have grown up a sensible girl,' said Mamma. 'That is quite the right way to look at it.'

'It was an appalling crime,' said Nancy, and yawned, as if she had thought over the quality of her mother's deed so long that it now held nothing for her but tedium.

'Appalling,' agreed Mamma, 'as your mother would be the first to admit.'

'But would she?' asked Nancy. 'I always thought she pretended she had not done it.'

'That was at first,' said Mamma. 'I think we would all have

202

done that at first. But she is completely changed now. Nobody could look down on her as she is today.'

Nancy started, looked at her incredulously, and then was silent. She said, 'So it is all right. I mean, there is a way of thinking about it. At Nottingham we never spoke of it, and it was terrible. You must tell me about this afterwards. I hope you do not mind me talking about this in front of you all, but it has been so hard for me, and you have always seemed able to understand anything.'

We all said she could talk about it all she liked, and Mamma asked if she would like some pudding, and Nancy said, 'Indeed I would, I had this pudding when Aunt Lily and I were staying with you, and I have often told Aunt Clara about it but we could never get a cook to make it.'

This delighted Mamma, for it was a queer pudding you beat raspberry jam into and steamed in an open mould, not covered with a cloth or with a buttered paper, and nobody could get it right except her. Kate never acquired the knack. Then Nancy began talking about how we had all washed our hair and eaten roasted chestnuts by the fire, and all the silly jokes we had made, and as the meal came to the end she said, 'I don't want to rebel against Uncle Mat and Aunt Clara, they're quite elderly now, they were much older than my Papa, and they have been very kind to me. But I said I wanted to come up to London to the theatre with another girl, because I must do something about, about, you know, being who I really am. I must see Aunt Lily again. I really must. But that will hurt Uncle Mat and Aunt Clara very much, for they say she is working as a barmaid in just a common pub, it is not even as if she was employed in a proper hotel.'

'But it is a heavenly place,' said Mary, and we all said how lovely it was and how much we enjoyed going to the Dog and Duck, and how nice Uncle Len and Aunt Millie were.

'So that is all right too,' said Nancy. 'Now what can I do about seeing my mother?'

'I was coming to that,' said Mamma, 'but before we talk of that, let me say now – and you must listen, children. You three, you have had a great deal of success lately, and now you have Nancy back here, but it must not delude you into thinking things will always go easily. But come into the drawing-room, Nancy, and we will tell you where your mother is and we can talk over what would be the best thing to do.'

So we scattered, and Mary went over to practise in the music-room which Mr Morpurgo, at a cost which it is bewildering to remember, it was so small, had built for us as a Christmas present on the further side of the stables, and Richard Quin went up to his room. He still slept in the attic, though he could have had Cordelia's room. He said he had been too happy there to leave it. I went to find Kate, and we were thinking what we would give Nancy if she stayed for supper, when Cordelia came in. I told her about Nancy, but she was not very much interested. She said, 'How nice, dear, but where is Richard Quin?'

'Oh, of course, you haven't seen him since he got the news, you haven't congratulated him,' I said. 'Come upstairs, he is in his room.' I ran up before her, calling, 'Richard Quin, Richard Quin, another sister to flatter you.'

We found him lying on his bed, Mark Twain's *Life on the Mississippi* open before him, and a Jew's harp in the palm of one hand. It amused him to play phrases of real music on that humble instrument, lifting it suddenly to his lips as he read and twanging out the notes, twice or thrice, while he went on with his reading. He had that capacity for doing two things at once which enrages those who have it not. When we came in he did not rise but took up the Jew's harp and welcomed us with the equivalent of a flourish of trumpets, but stopped half-way to free his mouth so that he could say 'How pretty you look, Cordelia, in that black hat.' And so she did, it was one of those silky long-haired beaver hats we wore then, and against it her red-gold hair and peachy complexion were delicious.

'What are you doing lying down in the middle of the day?' she asked. 'You should be out of doors.' She turned away to give herself reassurance by looking at her neat perfection in the mirror, and said vaguely to its depths, 'Out of doors or something.'

Richard Quin's face grew grey. He had expected that at last she would praise him.

'And what is that you were playing? A Jew's harp?'

'I play it a lot,' he told her, raising himself on his elbow and smiling and knitting his brows, as if he were anxious to please her but knew that there was practically no way of doing that.

'What an extraordinary thing to do,' she said, with her crossness. 'They are horrible things, errand-boys play them in the streets. You do not play in the street?'

He fell back into the pillows laughing. 'Only when I find I am passing Doctors' Commons.'

'Or the College of Preceptors,' I suggested. These were all places that had amused us when we heard of them in our childhood.

'Or Negretti & Zambra,' said Richard. 'In fact, I stand outside Negretti & Zambra and give them as much of the "Ruin of Athens" as I can get on a Jew's harp,' said Richard.

'But Negretti doesn't like it and knocks on the window with the curling-tongs he uses to frizz his long black ringlets,' I said.

'Oh, he likes it well enough, but it disturbs Zambra, who is always casting horoscopes,' he said.

'You are too old for this perpetual nonsense,' said Cordelia.

'We do other things as well,' I said. 'Mary and I play the piano a little, and Richard here has won an exhibition at New College.'

'Yes, it is about that I want to talk,' said Cordelia, vehemently.

'Is there anything to say about it except that it is very pleasant?' I asked.

'I will not be an expense to anybody,' said Richard Quin, gently. 'I have arranged with Mr Morpurgo that he will lend me the money for the balance of my fees, and I will pay him back gradually.'

'Gradually,' said Cordelia, and gave a despairing laugh. 'That is what I want to point out to you. It will be a huge debt. It would be disgraceful not to pay it back, after all that Mr Morpurgo has done for us. Do you really feel able to bind yourself to such a heavy responsibility? Do you really want to put your whole future in pawn?'

'If I could raise anything on it, I certainly would,' said Richard Quin. He lifted the Jew's harp to his lips and, rolling his eyes, twanged out the opening phrase of 'Se vuol ballare' in *The Marriage of Figaro*, investing it with an air of low cunning and avarice. 'Me Shylock, me Fagin – I can't think of any other sinister Jews – me shady cousin of Disraeli, he must have had one. But, Cordelia, stop being an ass. I am greedy as Shylock, I grab at Oxford in my sordid, scheming way. But I also am wrong because I do not scheme at all, you are afraid I will go to Oxford and do nothing. I cannot take the wrong turning in two opposite directions. Tell me, what is it you really think is

205

wrong with me? What do you really fear is going to happen to me?'

She raised her clenched hands to her mouth, and swayed, with bowed shoulders, and for a minute she looked, in spite of her youth and her loveliness, as desolate as King Lear wandering on the blasted heath. She recovered herself and said hastily and insincerely that he misunderstood her, that she did not think anything about him was wrong, she was only anxious because we had no father and Mamma had lived so much out of the world and it was so difficult for a boy to find his own way in life, she was moved only by her love for him. But she was so confused with foreboding, she could not finish her sentences. Richard Quin raised himself again on his elbow and watched her. 'I wish you would tell me what you see me doing,' he insisted. Both of us were aware that it was more than foreboding that troubled her, it was clairvoyance. Her eyes rested on a point in space where there was nothing, her breathing was disturbed, her lips were dry. But it perplexes me that he should wish to know what she was seeing, for she was plainly at odds with her gift, neither controlling it not yielding to it. I wondered if he had recognised some flaw in himself which only she among us all had detected, and sought now to see if it would bring him to such ruin as had befallen my father. I prayed that the ruin might fall on me instead, and in the moment of passivity that follows an ardent prayer, like the silence that follows an explosion, I knew that there was no flaw, there would be no ruin.

I went and sat on his bed and said, 'But it is all right,' and took the Jew's harp and twanged a phrase at him, I have forgotten what, which also said, 'But it is all right.' He took it out of my hand and twanged back a phrase at me which I did not recognise and did not understand.

'That horrible noise,' said Cordelia, covering her ears.

He laughed up at her, and asked, 'But tell me, tell me. What do you fear will happen to me?'

'It is all so difficult,' said Cordelia, pitifully. 'Going to Oxford without any preparation, we have all been brought up so badly and at first there was no money, you will never understand, either of you, how awful it has been for me, because I am the eldest. Now there is really too much money, or rather it is coming into the house too easily, with Mary and Rose getting this extraordinary success with hardly any effort. I am so afraid that you will have no sense of proportion, and will get into debt.'

For a second he was silent. Then his bed shook with laughter. 'It's the éclairs the Warden won't be able to stand.'

'The éclairs?' said Cordelia.

'The millions of éclairs. Fresh every morning. Iced with the family crest.'

'Oh, be serious,' she begged.

'The éclairs. Chocolate éclairs. Coffee éclairs. Never with custard inside. Only cream.'

'Well, I should think so,' I said, 'éclairs with custard inside are a fraud.'

'But not cream in the giant one. That's the one I'll get sent down for.'

'What's going to be in that?' I asked.

'A nautch girl. I'm going to have it hauled into the quadrangle on the night of my birthday, and she'll dance naked, while Negretti & Zambra play the triangle and the flute—'

'They won't,' I said. 'They're awfully proper.'

'I'll fool 'em,' said Richard Quin. 'I'll put them with their backs to the giant éclair and stick a cobra in front of them, and you know how they forget everything when they get a chance of snake-charming.'

'Stop this idiocy,' said Cordelia. She rattled the end of his bed and cried out, 'I don't think you should go to Oxford at all.'

'Cordelia,' he begged her, 'please, please be glad that I can go to Oxford. I cannot tell you how much I want to be there. I would give anything to be sure I would be there. In those gardens at New College. On the river.'

'In the gardens. On the river,' she exclaimed bitterly. 'You never think of work. Of being like ordinary people and getting the power to live ordinary lives. You only think of pleasure. Yes, yes,' she told herself, holding her face between her hands, 'that is how it is going to go wrong.'

'How what is going to go wrong?' he asked eagerly, and put out a hand to shake her when she did not answer. Then he looked on the baffled blankness of her face and dropped his hand and rolled back on the bed and began again, 'Eclairs. Eclairs. There will be two giant éclairs. In the second—'

'Be serious,' prayed Cordelia, 'be serious.'

But we heard Mamma's voice calling from downstairs. 'Rose. Is Cordelia up there with you? Bring her down to meet

Nancy,' and we heard Nancy crying, 'Cordelia and Rose. What luck you are here today.'

I said to Cordelia, 'Come on, you must see her, she will be hurt if you don't go at once, she loves being back here.'

We went on to the landing and leaned over the banister, and there was Nancy's face, drowned under the little house's shadows like a flower covered by a flood, looking up at us.

'You look very grand,' she told Cordelia. 'If I had met you in the street I would have known at once that you were a married lady.' There was a pause while Cordelia laughed and preened herself. 'Is your husband nice?' pursued Nancy, with a simplicity that made us all laugh, and Cordelia told her that she must come to tea with her and find out for herself. Nancy wanted to know all about her house, and Cordelia told her until Mamma said, 'Nancy's neck must be breaking, come down and talk to her on the level.'

A cloud came over the kindness of Cordelia's face, she looked back over her shoulder at the open door of Richard Quin's bedroom. 'In a minute, in a minute,' she called, and returned back to complete her self-appointed task. I followed her, meaning to break out and protect him, by telling her that he was as well able as Mary and myself to survive her constant belittlement, and that he would get on at Oxford as well as we had done at the Athenaeum and the Prince Albert.

But in the few minutes we had been away our brother had fallen asleep. He was not shamming. His features were not defensively blank, his body was not deliberately and completely relaxed. His mouth was troubled, his brows were knit, he had let the Jew's harp fall on the quilt, but his fists were doubled. He was lying awkwardly, he had not waited to arrange himself before he fled the waking world. But his face, sunk sideways on his pillow, was delicate and shining like a crescent moon, and his body was as if he were running and winning a race in a world with another dimensional system, where athletes could carry on a contest of speed horizontally and without moving from the same spot. I would have liked to stay with him, but it seemed not to be right. Cordelia made a movement towards the bed. She had always enjoyed waking people who were asleep; and indeed it is as great an alteration to the state of a fellow-creature that we can make short of killing them or giving birth to them. But her hand dropped, and we stood looking down on him in silence. The cold light that fell from the winter sky through the high attic windows made him look very fair. We went out and left him sleeping in his narrow room, between the four sloping walls, hung with his musical instruments, his boxing-gloves and his fencing foils, his rackets and bats.

VIII

WE WERE NOT surprised when the war came, for we had heard our father prophesying it all through our childhood. Because of what he had said we knew also that it would not be short, that, indeed, it would never end in our life-time. That State, he had told us, had taken so much power from individuals that it did not have to consider the moral judgments of ordinary human beings, it could therefore commit crime and was taken over by criminals who saw the opportunity, and who could use it for crime on a national scale, and would kill and rob not people but peoples. We had also been warned by our music. Great music is in a sense serene; it is certain of the values it asserts. But it is also in terror, because those values are threatened, and it is not certain whether they will triumph in this world, and of course music is a missionary effort to colonise earth for imperialistic heaven. So we were not so sorely stricken by August, 1914, as many other people. Indeed we had our consolations. It was proved to us that music was not making a fuss about nothing, and that the faces of our parents had been distorted out of common placidity not by madness but by the genuine spirit of prophecy.

When the war broke out, we had just moved into a house in Norfolk we had been lent for the two holiday months by Sir George Kurz, a Jewish financier with an Austrian wife who had been a violinist and was very friendly to us. It was not their own home, they lived in a great seventeenth century mansion a couple of miles away, this was a small Georgian house on land they owned which they used to entertain those of their friends who, being musicians or painters or writers, would not want the bother of staying in other people's homes. It stood high on the landward side of one of a cluster of hills that lay between a long sandy shore and the East Anglian plain. The air was salt, and when the wind was in the right quarter we could hear the North Sea beat on the sands, but we could not see it. Behind the house the turf rose steeply to a crumbling cliff. Our windows looked down on a bronze bowl of cornland, with one whitewashed village clustering round a grey church-tower where there was a gap in the hills, and the ribbon of the road which flowed across the bowl ran out into the blue distance of the flat farmlands beyond. We had thought we would like to be there, for it was part of our hosts' kindness to leave two servants and that meant that Kate could go on holiday and Mamma did not have to worry about going to register offices. It was strange to find that we were going to suffer there a wound as sharp as that which had been inflicted by the loss of our father. The days of that glorious summer filled the bowl of cornland below us with light which turned the corn from bronze to copper, and filled the house with the darkness of fear. It was not for ourselves we cared; for only Mamma and Mary and I were there. It was for Richard Quin that we were afraid. Had we learned that we were all going to be killed we would not have been frightened, only awed, foreseeing a fiery translation, such as our music often prophesied and as Mamma's being led us to regard as probable. But now one of us had to go forward towards death alone, and that the youngest of us.

He had been camping in Wales, and he was due on the 4th of August to drive across the country to us in the car he had bought with some money he had earned by playing with a dance band, a French sports model of a make that has long since disappeared. We spent the afternoon sitting in the garden, looking down on the ribbon of road which ran across the bowl of cornland. It was hot, and we would have liked to bathe a second time as soon after lunch as was safe, though the bathing was dangerous, as everything seemed to be at that moment, and we had to swim with a tiring caution. But in any case we did not like to leave Mamma. It seemed certain that the Germans were invading Belgium and that England would have to come into the war, though we could get no news later than what the morning papers had brought us. We could not ask the Kurzes, for they were away in Scotland, and we did not yet know any of the neighbours. Mamma would not have been well even if there had not been this extreme uncertainty. She had grown much thinner and had no strength, and she was often racked by storms of quick, shallow breathing. She had one while we were sitting on the lawn, just after we had had tea.

Recovered, her eyes always on the road below, she said, 'I am so useless now. I have lost my sense of how things happen, of how they are done, of what they are. When you girls were down on the sands I walked in the orchard and I found myself looking at the apples and thinking, "What are those round things? Why are they hung on those bits of wood?" And when I turned round and faced the house it would not have seemed unnatural if they had flown away like birds that had settled, though again I would have believed it if I had been told that they were made of paper and had been fixed there with tacks by men in green aprons. My mind is on a train that is going out of the station and leaving my body on the platform.' Suddenly she cried out, 'Look, he is down there on the road.'

His car was an odd sharp violet-grey. The bright dot bumped across the bowl and passed out of sight as it turned up the lane which wound uphill to our house, it rattled and snorted into the carriage sweep. Richard Quin jumped out and we saw he was disturbed as we were. He stayed beside the car and called over the flower-beds an urgent enquiry, which we could not hear.

Mamma struggled to her feet and cried, 'Is it war?' But her voice was too weak to reach him. He jumped a flower-bed and ran to us across the lawn repeating his enquiry. She was trembling so violently that she would have fallen had it not been that Mary and I caught her in our arms. Gently we lowered her into her chair and waited to hear our brother's announcement.

'You cannot,' breathed Mamma, 'really be asking if there is a refrigerator in the house.'

'I jolly well am,' he said. 'You see, Mamma, I started from Wales yesterday afternoon, and I slept last night at Warwick, and this morning I had got so far on my way that I was just three miles off Powerscliffe, and I had always heard that it was a nice old fishing-town, and I was still twenty miles from you, so I went there and had bread and cheese and beer in a pub down by the harbour. It was full of fishermen, and I asked them what the news was about the war, and they didn't know, they didn't seem very much interested, except in the risk there might be orders telling them not to put to sea. They were awfully good chaps. Then other chaps came in, members of an association of bank clerks who were camping out in the district and sailing. They were a bit more worried about the war. They were very nice too. Then two great big chaps came in and started playing darts with the fishermen, and they had a few drinks, and they seemed to get a bit tight, and then they began to bet the fishermen and the bank clerks a hundred to one that they could beat the lot of them at darts standing on their heads, So I knew they were tree-fellers.'

'How did you know they were tree-fellers?' asked Mamma, the war forgotten.

'Once two of them came into the bar at the Dog and Duck and started making bets, and Uncle Len stopped them but let them stay in the bar and do their stuff and gave them drinks on the house,' said Richard Quin. 'You see, tree-fellers are wonderful chaps, they have to be practically acrobats, I've often wished I could take some weeks off and go and learn the elements of the job. When it comes to cutting down the tree-tops they have to do appalling things like lying along a narrow branch on their backs and sawing off the branch above them, and they often have to hang upside down and work, so it's comparatively easy for them to play darts standing on their heads. You get down on your head and steady yourself with one hand and throw with the other, and swing up on to your feet between throws to get your blood back out of your head. The ones at the Dog and Duck showed me how, and I practised. Well, most people don't know that tree-fellers can do this, and if they did nobody can tell a tree-feller from anybody else, so when they're travelling across country from job to job they go into bars and have a few drinks and people think they're tight and when they bet people that they can beat them at darts playing upside down they think it's because they're tight, and they take the bets, and of course the tree-fellers win no end.'

'It isn't fair,' said Mary.

'Nobody's being fair,' said Richard. 'The people who take the bets think they're going to get some money out of a chap who's tight. And anyway tree-fellers have a very tough time, I wouldn't grudge them anything. Their job takes them all over the country and they only settle down for a few weeks at a time, they have the roughest houses and it's hard for them to marry,

213

and when they get old they fall out of trees or get pneumonia and die in the infirmary. I don't see why they shouldn't take some money off people who are usually living much softer lives. So I didn't give away these tree-fellers at first, but later I thought they were taking too much money off these fishermen or these bank clerks, and they kept on putting their own best men up and still getting beaten. Though nobody seemed very much interested in the war we were all drinking much more than we would have in the ordinary way. So I challenged them myself, and they thought I was tight, and they gave me huge odds, and I beat them, I was much younger, and they took me on again and again, and I always won, and then I wouldn't take my winnings. By this time everybody was laughing and shouting, and the landlord kept on saying we couldn't carry on like this in the bar, and they ragged him and when I said I had to go and I still wouldn't take my winnings, then the tree-fellers went out and bought me a lot of lobsters and put them in the car, and it got to be a sort of joke, the fishermen rushed out and got some their wives had been boiling, and the bank clerks bought some, and I drove off, up to the knees in lobsters. So if there isn't a refrigerator here we're rather sunk. We can give some away tomorrow. But I'm too fagged driving to see to it this evening.'

'There is a refrigerator,' said Mamma. 'This house makes its own electricity. The Kurzes are the kindest people.'

'I have never had enough lobster,' said Mary. 'There may not be so many to give away tomorrow.'

'Remember, children,' said Mamma, 'lobster is said to be very indigestible.'

'Up to now,' I claimed, 'none of your children have ever eaten anything they could not digest. The only question is whether there will be any lobsters at all to give away tomorrow.'

But there were about three dozen in the car, and we even had difficulty in finding room for them in the refrigerator. We had a wonderful dinner; and afterwards, when Mamma had happily gone to bed and Mary sat down at the piano, Richard Quin and I walked on the lawn in the soft August darkness.

'I wish women could go into pubs,' I said. 'Uncle Len lets us be in the bar at the Dog and Duck if there are not many people, and I always like it. And it must have been fun at Powerscliffe.'

'It was a good rag,' he said. 'But it was odd, being with all

214

those people, and feeling so damned cold and lonely. Where are the nearest houses I can leave the lobsters tomorrow?'

'At that village where the road takes a bend by a church where the hills start.'

'Oh, that's near enough. I wonder what sort of people live there.'

We halted and looked through the night down into the landscape. Beneath us the bowl of cornland, frosted by the light of the young moon, looking larger than by day; and the indigo sky, not anything, simply a nothingness and a miracle in which the heavy stars were suspended. The village was a clot of brightness, and farmsteads on the high ground which we had not seen by day now shone like the eyes of wild things which thought it safe now to show themselves.

'I can feel everything tonight,' said Richard Quin. 'I can feel how every stalk of corn grows up from those fields. I can feel how the light in that farm over there is heating the glass chimney of the lamp. I can feel how the stones in that church tower are locked together with mortar. I can imagine how the works of the church clock whirr and make a fuss before the hour strikes.' He walked away from me and called his own name into the darkness, six or seven times. Then he came back, saying, 'It's funny, if you repeat your own name it soon begins to sound quite meaningless.' But he called it out once more, straight up to the vault of the sky overhead, and might have again, if he had not broken off to say, 'Rose, Rose, look at Orion. The stars are glorious now. It's such a fat buttery light that drips from them in summer time. I would like to sit up all night and watch the constellations turning and sliding off the sides of the sky beneath the horizon. I've never done that. The trouble is that sleep is good too. Too many things in the world are good. When one enjoys something one is always missing something else. But sleep is very good. Let us sleep now.'

When the papers came at noon the next day and we learned that Great Britain was at war with Germany, we all had a glass of sherry, though we hardly ever drank, and Richard Quin explained to us that now we could settle down and have a good holiday, because he had applied for a commission in a regiment in which poor Mr Morpurgo had served in the South African War, and he thought he would get it, for Mr Morpurgo was helping him, but it would take some time. So we were there together all through that beautiful and horrible August,

215

though not alone. We had invited some guests beforehand, and indeed expected Nancy Phillips to be with us for most of the time, for Cordelia had very adroitly put an end to the prejudice Uncle Mat and Aunt Clara had conceived against our household. She had remembered that Alan had a relative, a Cousin George, living in retirement near Nottingham, who had acquired a title. The Houghton-Bennetts had several titles in the family, and were proud of them, but were embarrassed by this one for it had been earned too easily. The others had come by way of Colonial Governorships or Army Service but Cousin George had been knighted because King Edward had visited the industrial town where he had been a Town Councillor at the time of an influenza epidemic, which had not spared the Mayor or the Deputy Mayor, so it had fallen to him to conduct the royal party round a new hospital. Cordelia and Alan visited this relative and manoeuvred him and his wife to accompany them in a call on Uncle Mat and Aunt Clara, who felt that they had no right to stand between Nancy and such aristocratic friends. So she came to stay with us that summer, and was very happy, and fell a little in love with Richard Quin. We knew it when Rosamund came for the only weekend she was able to manage, as she had her proper holiday earlier in the year, and Nancy followed her and Richard Quin with spaniel eyes and said, without malice but with relief, 'It is a pity they are not the right ages. If he had not been younger than her, they might have made a couple.'

But we were joined by other guests who were unable to make such remarks, who were so unrelated to us that they could never speak of our relationship, who could say nothing to us except what people dancing or weeping in the streets to the tune of history say to each other. Musicians we knew only little or not at all, who had intended to spend the summer in France or Italy or Switzerland, members of the strange army of friends enrolled by Richard Quin, some of the girls who had been at school or college with us, reported themselves to us for one reason or another and were invited, and came to sleep in our house, or in a great barn that stood high on the hill, or in lodgings in the neighbourhood which had been vacated by nervous visitors, as it was bruited about that East Anglia was the probable theatre of German invasion. Kate and her mother were suddenly with us, saying that they could not abide to be separated from us at this time, particularly as all Kate's brothers had gone to sea, and they helped in the house, so the two servants left by the Kurzes were not dismayed, and everything was agreeable about this time of carnival which preceded the Lent that was to endure all our lives.

We were of course never without awe of the future, never without pity for the men who in the first and middle days of that month went out to die and in its latter days died their anticipated deaths. But we were very gay. We did not go to the seaward side of the hill again, for we were not far from the exact spot of the coast where it was supposed that any invading German force would make its landing, and the sands were taken over by the military. But we swam in a river not far away, and as soon as the Kurzes returned from Scotland they made us free of the lake in their part. Also we spilled over the fields, too, and helped with the exuberant harvest and all of us made music in our several ways. There came to stay with the Kurzes a grey-eyed young man named Oliver whom we recognised after a day or two as the composer whose works had been played at the concert in Regent's Park where we heard we had got our scholarships. We were embarrassed at seeing him again, because he had given us inscribed copies of his songs, and we had lost them on the way home, not carelessly but because we were so excited, and we always felt that we ought to own up. With a fervour that was partly a desire to expiate this guilt we took up our flutes again and joined in the performance of a cantata he had written on the subject of Venus rising from the sea at a South Coast resort when the Mayor and the Corporation were opening a new pier and taking down to the depths with her the Town Clerk, who was the tenor. We liked his music, which had a deliberately thin quality which was a search for the economy which had gone from Victorian music and had not been brought back by Elgar. We thought we might have liked him, too, had he not been suddenly drawn from us as Richard Quin was to be drawn a week or so later. It turned out Oliver had liked coming to us much more than we had thought, when he said goodbye to Mamma and thanked her for the times he had been to our house he suddenly could not speak any more, and bent down and kissed her hand. Mamma cried over his bowed head, 'And khaki is such a hideous colour, the old scarlet was far better.'

After Richard Quin had gone the others lingered for only a few days. By the end of the week we were alone. Then we went and stayed with the Kurzes while Kate and her mother helped the two servants to restore the house to order. The Kurzes had beautiful pictures and furniture, but it was as if we were looking at them through deep waters; their two sons were with the British Expeditionary Force. Mercifully the house was requisitioned for a hospital, which gave them something to think about. When we got home we found that all our possessions too were now remote, divided from us by a chill clear barrier; and that here too the part was greater than the whole. The Kurzes' great house had been dwarfed by the rooms their sons had left empty, and our house was nothing more than Richard Quin's attic. Mary and I got on with our lives as well as we could. Our careers for some time continued. The First World War did not suddenly turn on civil life and strangle it as the Second did. Simply we saw a fungoid bloom of ruin slowly creep across the familiar objects among which we had been reared.

For the first twelve months we had to carry out existing contracts, and still went on tour through the provinces. But there was a mournful intimation in the restriction which was at once applied to our elders and betters. The great pianists of those days, Paderewski and Busoni, and Rachmaninov and Pachmann, would go to their favourite among the great London pianoforte makers as they arrived from the Continent to undertake an English tour, and would spend a morning choosing a friendly instrument, and would have it shipped from town to town. That practice was abandoned in the autumn of 1914 and was never to be revived. The rise in the cost of labour and freight after the war made it an extravagance that not even the greatest virtuosos could impose on his impresario. This was, I think, in view of the mystical relationship which develops between a pianist and his instrument, a far greater pity than can be demonstrated on technical grounds. Gradually such signs convinced us that for the moment the world was going to stop its readings from the *Arabian Nights' Entertainment*. Travel became more and more uncomfortable, our fees and our engagements alike grew less.

But we were fortunate in that our misfortunes came at a time when good fortune would have inconvenienced us. Before the war Mary and I could take any engagement away from home and know that Richard Quin would be with Mamma at night. But now that he was in the Army Mary and I had to scan our

218

engagements to see that they did not clash, in case Mamma were left alone. Even when they did not, we eyed them mistrustfully, because they might mean that we would miss one of Richard Quin's leaves. There was not anything we wanted to do but be as much with Richard Quin as we could manage. It happened that he liked the Army and it suited him, and each time he came he was more joyful and more of a man, and more deeply infatuated with some mastered technique. We would save up our meat coupons to buy him a duck, our sugar and eggs and butter and dried fruit and make him a really rich plum duff, and we would open one of the bottles of wine Mr Morpurgo had given us so that we could entertain, and dinner would last a long time, and afterwards we would sit round the fire, and Kate would come in and join us, and he would sit with his glass in his hand, finishing the wine, telling us all about gunnery, and how it was almost as much fun as music or cricket when one had got into the theory of it. Because of his bearing there was nothing lachrymose in our desire not to miss a minute of his leaves, it was a gay greed for pleasure.

We felt, I remember, almost guilty, as if we were doing something improperly light-minded, when we accepted an invitation to play for a war charity in Oxford, one Friday night in the late autumn of 1915, because we were promised by one of the promoters that he would let us stay for the weekend in a lodge on his estate, which was not far from the camp where Richard Quin was stationed. We enjoyed such engagements, though of course a charity concert is not a concert, too many people are there for other than the private reasons which alone should drive one to a concert, for we always played on such occasions the lovely old fountain-spout duets such as Schubert's *Reposez-vous, bon chevalier*, and *Notre amitié est invariable* and *Grand Rondo*, and Schumann's *Ball-Scenen* and *Kinderball*. They soothed our audiences and us by their placid superfluity. Only in a secure community could pairs of people sit down at a piano to spend hours in perfecting performances of an artistic form in which nothing actually very important can be said, in which there is merely reaffirmed the pleasantness of the pleasant. At Oxford we played three such duets, and were then put into an old-fashioned carriage, a phaeton, I believe, and were driven along the moonlit High, all its towers and archways etched in silver and underlined with sooty shadow, into a countryside where the hedges were sharply bright as barbed wire. A turn of the road suddenly showed us the moonlight squandered over a broad river, which I suppose was the Thames, in which black bulrushes appeared to have huge clubbed heads as they stood sharp-cut in the shining water. We left it after a hundred yards or so, with regret, with a sense of guilt, it was so wrong that this beauty should lie so splendidly open to eyes that were not there. Then we followed a great brick wall for a mile or two till we came to high gates and a little polygonal Gothic lodge beside them, with the moon shining back from the panes on one of its sides. A sleepy woman with her hair in curlers opened the door, showed us a queerly shaped room where there were two beds, set at an angle, the shape was so very weird. She said, 'Your brother came here this evening,' and smiled at the recollection, and almost forgot to give us the packet he had left for us. It contained some salmon mayonnaise sandwiches and a note, 'I leave these because you two are always hungry. In the morning walk over towards the camp when it is getting on for noon. It is two miles up the road. I will meet you.'

We woke the next morning to find that there was a light fog which blotted out all the gaunt arms of the trees about us. There was an air of suspended safety very like that period of the war, the arms were so very threatening, but they came no nearer. The woman brought us breakfast in bed, with strong tea and brown eggs and real butter, and told us to eat what we could, here in the country there was plenty. But there were no newspapers. We lay and pretended that a copy of *The Times* would come later in the morning which would tell us that the war was over.

Mary said, 'Oxford looked nice yesterday. If Richard Quin ever goes there he will ask us down to dances.'

'But you hate dances,' I said.

'It would be different with Richard Quin,' said Mary. 'He would have nice friends.'

Noon was a long way off. We lazed until the woman brought in a can of hot water, and first Mary and then I washed in a big china basin, our nightdresses dropped to our waists and tied up by the sleeves. By this time the sun was shining strongly just above the mist, which it changed to the colour of topaz. We were faintly dyed with it, we decided we were Redskins, and Mary begged being Wenonah because she could not bear being Laughing Water, a name we had decided when we were children was what Seidlitz Powders thought of themselves as being called, since there was no reason to suppose that things are not just as conceited as people. We went out of the lodge singing bits of Coleridge Taylor's music, which made us think of the Albert Hall, and talk of the conductors we liked and hated, until the winter landscape captivated and absorbed us. There was this topaz mist, which closed in on us more closely on the left, where it rose in a wall just beyond a hedge whose bare black winter-bones were loaded with deep crimson berries, than on the right, where there was a beechwood, with lucidity stretching into the distance between its silver trunks. In and out of the hedgerow weaved fleets of very small birds, some of them bright yellow. In the wood there were pools of black glassy water, and at their bottom the sodden leaves were visibly rotting, were a soft vegetable paste, yet were distinct in every vein and every indentation. Here and there, high on the tree-trunks, were brackets of pale fungus, delicately fluted, and on the ground were clusters of toadstools, reddish and squat, like details out of the illustrations of comfortable books for children. We did not know that the country was so interesting in winter-time, we had thought of it as being like an opera-house, empty and dark; nor had we heard before such silence. This was an active principle. If we stopped walking it was too silent. We were not frightened, there was obviously nothing to frighten us. Only we feared that Richard Quin might not come to us out of the mist.

We came to a cross-roads, and Mary asked, 'Did he say keep straight on?'

'Yes, but he said nothing about a steep hill,' I answered. The road before us mounted sharply and disappeared into the mist, which here had paled, had grown grey again. It was suddenly wet against our faces. We were standing by a gate that led into a field where there was a conical haystack, sliced in half, distraught straw sticking out of the cut surface, and an agricultural machine lying beside it, showing rusty metal teeth, and on the other side of the road a brick house turned a windowless wall towards us.

'Let us wait here,' said Mary. 'We might miss him, it might all go wrong.'

There was a mist within the mist. Clouds of a grosser fog, quite white, showed through the general grey mass of

221

moisture. Above, the dimmed sun was small and bright, like a new shilling.

'How alone we are,' I said.

'I hear all sorts of things,' said Mary. 'Or is it the blood in my ears?'

'It is the blood in our ears,' I said. 'Yet I am not sure.'

We stood still. A white cloud was driven past and through us. We heard, or did not hear, the lowing of distant cattle.

'Richard Quin will not be long now,' I said. 'He is always very late when it does not matter, and very punctual when it does.'

'He is here,' she smiled.

He had come suddenly out of the mist on the steep fall of the hill, running and leaping, his head bare, his cap held in his hand. He had not seen us, he was shouting a song to himself as he ran, and twirling his cap on his fist to mark the time. We cried out to him, and he saw us, and we ran towards him, and he shouted a welcome. But it was not Richard Quin. We halted, and he cried out, laughing, 'You quite thought I was Richard Quin, didn't you? People often take us for each other, from a distance. But not close to.' That indeed was true. His hair was fair-over-dark, like Richard Quin's, but there was a greenish tinge in the fairness and in the hollow of his temples and round his nostrils, while Richard Quin's hair was true pale gold where it was not dark, and shadows showed a blueness in his skin. This boy's eyes, too, were more grey than blue, while Richard's were more blue than grey; and his features were not so much delicate as finicking. But of course everybody was inferior to Richard Quin, and it was hard on anybody else to look like him and challenge comparison, so we looked on the stranger benevolently.

'I am Gerald de Bourne Conway,' he said, 'I expect your brother has told you all about me. I'm his best friend. I don't know what we could have done without each other, out here among the Philistines.' Already, from these few sentences, we knew that he talked too much. 'As soon as I saw your brother, I said, "There's somebody who speaks my language." You can always tell, can't you? Your father was awfully clever, wasn't he? So is mine. He got a first in Greats and the Locke Prize for Philosophy. And the Newdigate. Of course he's wasted as a country parson. But it was a family living, and he was the youngest and didn't inherit. So what could he do?'

We murmured agreement and gazed on him still more tenderly. Of course Richard Quin had found a cripple to carry on his shoulders, of course he had not abandoned his favourite sport of mercy. At the same moment we heard him singing in the mist, and our hearts contracted at hearing his real voice, and we shouted to him. He too came suddenly out into visibility, running and leaping, but correctly, classically, not like this fragile and flimsy copy of himself.

'Sorry I'm late,' said Richard Quin, after he had taken us in his arms, 'but you know, there's no technique for terminating an interview with the Colonel before the Colonel wishes it. I hoped we'd meet you almost as soon as you'd got started.'

'It didn't matter,' said Mary, 'but we had got becalmed. And in such a dull part of the country.'

'Yes, isn't it dull just here?' said Richard Quin, looking round him. 'There must be a lot of turnips somewhere near. Ah, yes, in that ramp over there. They give it out. But come on up that hill. At the top it's fine weather.'

'Fine weather?' we echoed doubtfully. The mist was like a wet towel, we might have been by the sea.

'Yes, that's the odd thing about the country in winter,' said Richard Quin. 'It packs away the most extraordinary things.'

'The most extraordinary things,' said Gerald de Bourne Conway, emphatically, tugging as it were at Richard Quin's sleeve, and begging to be treated as one of us. Richard looked at him kindly. 'Gerald has told you who he is,' he said. He might have been saying, 'I would not care to tell you that myself. But for the moment I must take charge of him, you must bear with him.' So we pleased Gerald by describing how we had taken him for Richard at first.

It was true what Richard had said, the hill rose to a ridge where there was a blue and silver day, and the sunshine was reflected strongly from the white cloud packs which filled the valleys below. We walked on either side of our brother, Gerald sometimes ahead of us and sometimes at our heels, like a young dog, and it was as if we had all the leisure in the world, and there was no fear.

Richard said, 'I tell you, winter is the time to be in the country. Summer is spread all over the place, you hardly ever come on any pocket of private weather, except a shower here and there. But in winter one hillside will have the full sun on it, and on the next there will be a storm, and sometimes a whole

223

district will stop being England and will look like Scotland and its hills will be mountains. And, look, winter in the country is a blonde, you never thought of that.' He took us through a gate and we walked alongside the road on a patch of downland, and he showed us bare bushes bright as bone, and red leaves clinging to beech saplings, and bright orange willows, and the buds that were everywhere if one looked for them, though it was not yet Christmas. 'And look down in the valleys, there are lots of fields which are being ploughed and got ready, and some with even a green fuzz on them,' he told us. 'Did you know there was such a thing as winter wheat? The truth is there is no winter in the country, there is always something growing.'

'And the air up here is not merely cold,' said Mary. 'In London and Manchester and Liverpool the winter air has just had the warmth taken out of it and the damp put in, or it has been displaced by wind.'

'Wind is just part of the enemy,' I interrupted. The enemy in our household was what made cakes burn when they had been in the oven not nearly so long as the cookery book said they should be, what gave one a cold just before a concert.

'But what we're breathing now,' said Mary, holding her arms out to it, 'is the Hallelujah Chorus.'

We three moved on singing. Gerald murmured in my ear that his sister had a very fine voice, everybody had said that she ought to have it trained, someone awfully good who really knew what he was talking about had said that she ought to sing in opera, but she had married a very good chap, who owned thousands of acres in Yorkshire. After half a mile we came up against barbed wire and went back to the road, which curved and brought us to a dip in the ridge where there was a knot of cottages and a sturdy little church, hardly more than a tower, giving back blackish brilliance to the sun from its flint walls. It was old and had the look of a shepherd in his plaid. But when we went inside we found that somebody had made it new and not at all protective. There were pews of varnished pine, and olive-green rep hassocks and cushions, and only a plain cross on the altar. The walls were distempered drab, it might have been a schoolroom. We stood in the doorway and sighed.

Gerald de Bourne Conway said, 'Ooh, isn't it Protty?'

When he explained that he meant Protestant, I asked him if he wasn't a Protestant, and he told us, tossing his head, that his father went mad if anybody called him that. 'We're Catholics,' he said. 'It's awful cheek of the Romans to talk as if they were the only Catholics.' He took a step into the church, and his nose wrinkled. 'Smell the carbolic soap. I bet nobody's ever swung a censer here. I bet they have Morning and Evening Service too.'

'Why, what do they have in your father's church?' asked Mary.

'He celebrates mass,' he answered cockily. 'I've served for him ever since I was six. You should see me in my cotta. Look, not a crucifix in the place. And not a bit of plate on the altar. And I bet they call it a communion table at that.' Looking scornfully about him, he moved down the aisle. He had held his cap under his arm all the time we walked on the downland, and the wind had ruffled his hair. He looked too young to be a soldier, he might have been a schoolboy and this a class-room and the altar a master's desk. As he went further from us mischief appeared in his movements, he might have been a schoolboy considering what he might do to spoil the class-room while the master was absent from his desk, whether he could pour something that stank into the ink-wells or scrawl with coloured chalks on the blackboard. We felt concern for him. His movements were too simple, it was certain that when the master came back to his desk he would know what offences had been committed and by which offender; and though it was the boy's desire to damage his school, he was a schoolboy, and the proper place for him was school, he would miss the other boys if he were sent away. When his hand twitched towards a pile of hymnbooks, when his strutting brought him to the sanctuary steps, it was as if the master had returned and was a grave presence at his desk. But Richard Quin called softly, 'Gerald, Gerald,' and he tiptoed back to us.

Beyond the village the ridge broadened, and there were sentinels at the great gates of a park where yew-groves stood twisted and black and old on the sage-green winter turf, and in the distance cedars of Lebanon lifted their tiers of shade round a red-brick house with a white colonnade; and the best of the day was over. We had to be with other people after that. It had not mattered having Gerald with us, for he was part of Richard Quin's spiritual uniform, as his Sam Browne belt was part of his military uniform; this was the recipient of pity without whom our brother would not have been complete. But these other people had really nothing to do with us. We were with them only because they too were being whirled to disaster by the turning earth, and they prevented us from concentrating on our brother, whom we desired to learn by heart. But they were kind. The Brigadier's wife held a Pekinese under each arm, and as she had eyes like a Pekinese, and as her bust fell so loosely that the two Pekinese seemed extensions of it, she looked as if she were as curiously made as any tribeswoman that Othello had ever met; but she liked music, and had heard us play, and arranged for us to stay with her or one of the other wives whenever we could get away to see Richard Quin. So we went often, and Cordelia and Alan went down once or twice too, and everybody thought she was very pretty and gentle, but she did not really enjoy it. She paid a special visit to Lovegrove to tell us, not fiercely as she would have done before, but plaintively, and yet so insistently that it was still objectionable, that she thought it a great pity for Richard Quin to make such a friend of Gerald de Bourne Conway. People must think he could not be nice if he had such a terrible friend.

In this she was wrong. The officers and their wives understood that Richard Quin was simply protecting Gerald. They knew he himself was all right, because he was a good soldier. There was much in life that Army people evidently did not understand but about this sort of thing they were good. There was no use telling Cordelia this, for she still thought, though she was trying to be nice about it, that all her family was awful, and if we had convinced her that Army people had a shrewd eye for character she would have felt quite certain that they were doubtful about Richard Quin.

But Rosamund was able to come down to the camp with us twice, and each time it was like a big concert for Mary and me, Richard was so happy, and everybody admired her so much, though it was already obvious that fashion was turning away from her type. The new beauties of that age were fair by deficiency and jerry-built in figure, and cultivated an anxious, sickly rejecting stare and gape. But Rosamund was golden as honey, and abundant, and so strong that she never found it hard to lift any of her patients in hospital, and so good-natured that she could pass the spiritual equivalent of that test of strength when she went into society; and people seemed to be glad of her particular exhibition of the qualities they were condemning in general. Indeed it was hard to give them all the slip at the camp, and get out for a walk by ourselves; and of course we were never without Gerald, but that did not matter, he was just like a dog that was all right if it were checked the minute it barked too much and started jumping up, and Richard Quin always knew the right time to do that, and the right measure of comradeship and derision that would quiet him. So the boy did not spoil our walks at all. The last one we went all together, one February afternoon, took us to the high point of one of those ridges that run to the west of the Oxfordshire plains, where there was a ruined windmill by the side of the road. We rested there, looking down into the depth of the valley, where a long beechwood flowed as if it were a river, still dark with winter, soft as soot but brown, not black. The hillside pastures were greyish and needed spring to freshen them, but on some of the ploughed fields there was the green mist of the new crops. It was one of those days when the air is full of water that chooses to be not mist but glass, and the world is seen through a brightening lens.

'You see, there is no winter in the country,' said Richard Quin. He had his arm about Rosamund's shoulder.

'I say, look at those jolly old starlings,' said Gerald.

The flight came low over us, cutting in between two telegraph poles on the road. We heard the creak of the small wings, then watched them fall below us into the valley, till we looked down on them. A thought suddenly ran through them, spreading from the leftmost bird to a last straggler far to the right, and halted them. They balanced on it, going up and down, like a ball bobbing in the jet of a fountain, then swept back on us, and flew above us across the ridge and down into the unseen valley on the other side. But then another thought pervaded the spread body of the flight, and they repented and whirled about, but got no further than the telegraph poles. There they wrote themselves as music on the wires, as close-pressed demi-semi-quavers, and bickered and fluttered. One starling soared up from his wire, flew some ten yards above the road, turned in mid-air as if to mark a decision and alighted on the top branch of an ash-tree. Other birds whirred after him with a consequential air. There was a faction that went, a greater faction that stayed, on the wires, obstinate, quiet as if their obstinacy would last for ever. Then one bird threw itself from the tree towards the clouds in a straight upward dive, and when the force of its surrender to the motion was spent it glided slantwise downwards through the air, as a diver glides slantwise upwards through the water. All the starlings on the wires and in the trees were instantly convinced, and soared up in the same line as the lone one had ventured when he was a dissident, who was now a leader. But they did not fall back, a sense of triumph lifted them still higher. They swirled down the hillside into the hidden valley and rose again, and banked and turned with an increasing intention over our heads and swirled down into the valley where the beechwood ran like a river, and then came up the hillside at us and were back again over our heads, like a roll of drums made visible. Then peace entered into them, they travelled without haste to a hilltop ahead of us, and drifted down into the bronze cloud of a hangar, as if they knew themselves deserving of rest.

'What did that mean?' asked Richard Quin. His arm tightened round her shoulders and he repeated, 'What did that mean?'

She could not speak, she fluttered her fingers before her mouth, to show that she was choked by her stammer.

She got down once to see him when he was moved to Sussex. It was a pity that she could not get away to be with him for all the forty-eight hours of his embarkation leave, but she was only able to come to us in the evening of the second day.

By then it was late spring. There were only the three of us at home, Mamma and Mary and myself. That Easter Cousin Jock had sent for Constance, saying that he was alone and needed someone to look after him and would try to make amends if she returned, and she had stonily packed her bags and left us. She spent the day with us when she could, but that was not very often; and in the evenings the silence silted up in our house. Indeed, it was never quite dispelled even in the daytime, though there was much coming and going, for Mary and I had been asked by our colleges to do some teaching as their staffs had disintegrated under the demands of the war, and we gave many of our lessons at home. Mamma enjoyed this, for we often asked her in for advice, and though she was now too weak and too passionate to play more than a page at a time, she was able to scold both teachers and pupils with enlightening ferocity. But she was not quite so fierce as of old, at least towards the pupils, for of late she had begun to see young people as materially precious, to a degree that cancelled out

228

their faults. She would frown as she listened to a girl of sixteen playing Beethoven and her hands would twitch on her stick, and then she would look down at the hands on the keyboard to trace the fault, and be taken unaware by the innocent flesh, the pliable fingers, the baby nails, and would simply shake her head and sing the phrase as it should have been played. But towards Mary and myself she showed no mercy, for though we were still young in years we were to her outside of time, she often expected us to remember things that had happened in her youth, it was as if it were now revealed to her that all of us had co-existed in eternity, and she could not understand that our portions of time overlapped like tiles on a roof. Her age alone was not great enough to account for this growing alienation from the arrangements of earth. The real cause was the illness which was day by day planing her body closer and closer to the bone. It had mercifully no other symptoms than this emaciation, and the dwindling of a concern for material conditions which had always been perfunctory. Her wild hair was still dark.

Miss Beevor came in early that afternoon, just after I had brought Mamma back to the drawing-room after she had helped me to convince a girl, who was arrogant in the way a good player ought to be in adolescence, that she was wrong in refusing to play Liszt because a composer who wrote that way today would be no good. Mamma said, 'Richard Quin is coming back tonight on his embarkation leave, Bayahtreechay.'

Miss Beevor said, 'Oh. But it will be all right. You are a lucky family. Look at Mary and Rose, and look at Cordelia's wonderful marriage.' She began suddenly to cry. Cordelia had never forgiven her, Cordelia had never asked her to her home. But she was crying over that only because she did not want to cry over Richard Quin's departure to France.

Mamma said tartly, 'It's not such a wonderful marriage as that.' She was becoming terribly frank, and had more than once lately revealed that Alan bored her. She did not really like the idea of men being civil servants, she thought they should not like so safe a way of life.

Miss Beevor said, 'So long as he's happy,' and sat down, and brought out of her kid bag (it had Athens on it in poker-work, she had been on a Cook's tour) her last piece of fancy-work and asked Mamma what was wrong with it. Mamma held it, and she put her head on one side, and said, 'Come now, it's not so bad as that.'

'No. No. Not nearly so bad,' said Mamma, with grave self-criticism. 'Of course it's not.' Then tea came in, and they gossiped and bickered, and Mary and I went down to the kitchen and helped Kate with the supper. She looked very wooden these days. As we worked we saw in our mind's eye the dark bright circle of water in a bucket filled to the brim and set on a scullery floor. But surely if Kate and her mother had seen that anything dreadful was going to happen to Richard Quin we would see it in her face.

When we went back into the drawing-room Mamma had fallen asleep. Yet there was a smoothness about her sleep, it was as if she were in a trance; and she awoke smoothly when Richard Quin came in and kissed her. She said, 'It is ridiculous, you should be going now to Paris, then over the Alps to Italy.' Sleep lay over our household like a quilt during that forty-eight hours. Richard Quin said he was tired, and we all went to bed early, and woke long after our usual hour. We took Richard Quin's breakfast up to him, sure that he would be ready for it, since he was an early riser; in the summertime he had always lived an unobserved life before the rest of the world was about. But this morning he lay stretched in a deep dream, that made him sigh as we looked at him. We took the tray downstairs again and went to Mamma, who was awake, but drank her tea and turned away from us and slept again. We went quietly about the house and got everything ready for the day. We had put off all our pupils. At eleven he was with us, and we gave him breakfast in the drawing-room, and afterwards he walked round the garden with Mamma. Because we had never been able to afford flowers until Papa left us our patches of columbines and our clematises were always exciting. Then he got his flute and played some of his favourite music, and then he asked Mary and me to go over our duets for him. He loved Schubert's Grand Rondo so much that he made us play it three times, and he said we did it better each time for him. 'It is like fountains and ices and chandeliers and fireworks and diamonds,' he said. 'Oh, the fun of music.' He was leaning on the end of the piano, he shuddered and passed his fingers down his face. 'The Army's really very good,' he said, 'better than you can think. But it's been hard to live without music. It is like having one of one's senses taken away from one. But go on, go on, quick. Play something else.'

We gave him a good luncheon, considering it was wartime. Of course he had excellent food in the Army, but we were able to give him some of the dishes he had always liked from childhood, like onions done in pastry like apple-dumplings, with kidneys inside them, and roly-poly with mincemeat instead of jam. Onions were scarce as they always are in wartime, but Uncle Len kept us supplied with them, and Kate's mincemeat was doled out a little at a time and was keeping well. After luncheon Mamma said that she would rest, and Richard Quin went out to see his old head-master and the man and his wife who had shown him their racing pigeons, they had become great friends of his. He was back for tea, and afterwards he brought down some of his musical instruments, and we meant to play, but three of his friends who had been at school with him and could not go to the war came round to see him. One had been rejected on medical grounds, the two others were engineers. They looked at Richard Quin with wonder and dismay, and one said, 'This is all wrong for you, old man, I can't think of you except as amusing yourself.' We left them and went to sit in the dining-room. On many other evenings we had heard the laughter and voices of our brother and his friends in another room, and we could pretend that this evening was as those. Soon Mamma retreated into the blank and upright slumber which had taken her to itself the night before; but she awoke at the right time to remind us that we should start him off on his way to dinner with Alan and Cordelia and the Houghton-Bennetts. We did not wait up for him, that would have been letting the occasion appear too plainly as what it was. But of course we heard him come in.

'Shall we go down and make tea for him?' I asked.

'No,' said Mary. 'So often he has been up later than us and gone down to the empty kitchen and got something out of the larder, he will want to do it again.'

Later the lock of the french window below our room clicked, and we heard his tread on the iron steps and the gravel path. Without turning on the light we got out of our beds and crept to the window and knelt to look under the raised sash. We saw the red circle of his cigarette passing slowly from his lips to his hand, from his hand to his lips, the moth-glow of his uniform, as he stood under the trees at the end of the lawn.

231

'Not everybody gets killed in a war,' whispered Mary.

'No, not even in this war,' I answered.

We went back to our beds and, as on the night before, fell at once into a dreamless sleep, that ended suddenly, and brought us back into the real night of day as wideawake as if we had had no respite from it. The hours passed then as they had passed the day before, pleasantly and with an infinity of pain. We made music in the morning. Miss Beevor came in at noon, wearing her best terracotta velvet, and bringing a bottle of Madeira, almost the last of her Papa's little cellar, so that we could all drink Richard Quin's health together. We sat in a solemn circle in the sitting-room, and all got a little drunk on a single glass. Kate had been called in to take part in the ceremony, and she said suddenly, 'I will leave the washing-up till late in the afternoon. There's been too many breakages.' And Miss Beevor got quite drunk. Suddenly she looked round at us and said with an air of surprise, 'What a distinguished family. Richard Quin, I know everything will go right for you. How soon can you become a Major?'

He said with an air of concern, 'Not until I have had six horses shot under me.'

She said, shuddering, 'Oh, how cruel. But is that so even when you are not in the cavalry?'

We all laughed at her, and she complained we were dreadful to her, and laughed too, and said she must go home now, and she would walk on air, she felt so happy about us, we were all so wonderful. Mary and I took her out, and in the hall we ran into Mr Morpurgo, who had been asked to luncheon. She bent her great height over his pearshaped plumpness and asked playfully, 'Do you know what?' His large viscid eyes, under which there was now a pouch of equal size, rolled up at her. 'It's going to be all right,' she told him triumphantly. He looked up at her with naked hatred, but she bounded on. In the doorway, however, she burst into tears. While she stood fumbling in the white kid bag from Athens, he came up behind her with the handkerchief which had been projecting in perfect folds from his breast-pocket.

'I'll have it washed and send it back,' she sobbed.

'No, no,' he said. 'Keep it, keep it.'

But as she got to the gate he called, 'No, send it back, it'll be no use to you because of the monogram. But I'll send you a

232

dozen with your monogram.' As he turned back, he murmured to himself, 'Better send two dozen. What is one dozen?'

He presented himself in the sitting-room in the character of an aggrieved man, and Mamma and Richard Quin hastened to comfort him. But his woes were not for us to remedy. His first complaint was the South African War had been his war and nobody thought anything of that nowadays, his second that two of the four men whom he employed to find him orchids in the forests of Asia and South America had been seized by the Allies and interned, one in India, one in the West Indies, because they were Germans. When we expressed interest and astonishment on hearing for the first time that he maintained this delightful embassade, he asked us, in the tones of the ant reproaching the grasshopper, how we thought that greenhouses were kept filled. Suddenly he opened the counting-house door and admitted us to knowledge of the details of his colossal expenditure, which became the more whimsical the further it travelled from the realm of necessity, for the more fantastic the results it sought the more certain it was that they could be achieved only by fantastic characters. What was worrying him about the orchid-hunter now interned at Calcutta was that the authorities might find out that the grim and taciturn botanist in their hands was a polygamist of immense range and persistence, who had wives all over the world, every one of them married to him by the most binding form known to her people. As Mr Morpurgo peevishly returned to the subject again and again, expressing forebodings they might stumble on evidence of the wife in Washington or the wife in Copenhagen or the wife in Malabar, and not understand that this thirst for impossible legitimacy ought to be overlooked in such a great botanist and courageous explorer, all of us lost ourselves in laughter. One of his ancestors must have been the professional storyteller of the bazaar in some town of domes and minarets, and he was turning back through the ages for his help.

But there came a time in the afternoon when there was nothing more to say. We had noticed with some surprise that Mr Morpurgo was wearing a wrist-watch, which was then not usual for a man of his age. He plucked it from his arm and gave it to Richard, saying that one of the things he would find as he went through life was that there was nothing more difficult than to find a reliable timepiece; and he abruptly left us. The watch was exquisite, profligate in its union of precious metal and craftsmanship, and Richard Quin was doubtful whether he ought to take it to France, though he loved it as he loved one of his musical instruments, his face was tender as he bent over it. But Mamma told him to take it, that of course it would get ruined, but that would give Mr Morpurgo pleasure too, he could get another one made, and he had so few pleasures. Richard Quin was glad when it was put like that, and went down to show it to Kate, and Mamma turned to us and said, wild-eyed, 'If only Rosamund would come. She will be late. Can anything have happened to her?' But then Richard Quin called to her to come and see something that Kate had given him and Mary said, 'Rose, will you think me dreadful if I toss you to see who is to go to Victoria with Richard Quin and Rosamund, and who is to stay with Mamma? I can't just say to you, "You can go." I am sorry I can't.'

'Of course,' I said, and took out a sixpence, and we knelt on the carpet and tossed it three times. I was tails and I always won.

'That is all right,' said Mary, rising to her feet. 'Now I shall feel it was all in order that I couldn't go.'

I remained on the floor, looking up at her in amazement. Never before had I realised how often Mary had said, 'You can go,' when only one of us could go to the ballet or to a concert or a drive. It is the measure of the distance at which everybody, even those who were most friendly, kept us, that constantly we received invitations that ran, 'Can Rose or Mary come with me to this or that?' We had no intimates who would feel it always natural to ask one of us, because they were closer to that one. But of these alternate invitations, again and again she had stepped back and given me the chance to enjoy a pleasure that was often great. I told her so, I thanked her, but she cried out vehemently, 'No, no, it is not good of me at all. Usually these invitations mean being with other people, which is always a risk, so I do not want to go. This time it means being with Richard Quin to the last, so I minded. But all the other times, you saved me from something.'

She spoke with such passion that I stared at her as if staring would show me her deep hidden trouble. I said, 'But that isn't all, you like me to have the fun of going. So. . . .' I paused, wanting to say, 'I would like to know the other reason why you step aside.' But she broke out, 'Of course I do, and it is a fair

234

exchange, you are so good to me. There is nothing, nothing in you of Cordelia.'

'Well, I should hope not,' I said. 'But, oh, Mary, how happy we could all have been if it had not been for the war.'

'Not only happy,' said Mary, 'Richard Quin would have been more than happy.'

'Much, much more,' I sighed.

I on my knees, she standing above me, we looked into one another's eyes and shook our heads.

'But not everybody gets killed in a war,' she murmured.

'See what Kate has given me,' said Richard Quin, who came back into the room with one arm out of his tunic. His short sleeve was rolled up, and just below his elbow he was wearing a bracelet, made of a few small blue beads, strung at wide intervals on a braid of two or three twisted horsehairs. The beads were vivid but dull, they might have been cut from turquoise matrix. 'I do not like taking it from her. She told me that I must never take it off, day or night. That means she has never taken it off day or night, herself. She wore it above her elbow, it's just right for me here. It is too good of her to give it to me. I had to take it. It may be awkward wearing it, it looks strange. But she wanted me to have it.'

'It is a strange thing to think of her wearing it all the time and none of us knowing,' said Mary.

Mamma said, 'It looks Egyptian.'

We all stared at it, seeing at the same time the bright dark circle of a bucket filled to the brim with water, standing on a kitchen floor. Mamma and Mary and I were all saying to ourselves, 'She would not have given him her amulet if she and her mother had seen anything dreadful happening in the water. For then there would have been no sense in giving him a thing to keep him safe.' Kate was so very sensible. She would have given him something else instead, like sweets or handkerchiefs, that would have been useful to him for a short time.

Mamma said, 'I think this bracelet is very old. They find poor people wearing them in hospitals, you know. They are handed down through the generations. They don't talk about them.'

'How do you know?' I asked.

'Rosamund was talking about it last time she was here. But I had heard of it before.'

'It is a great honour to have it,' said Richard Quin gravely, and rolled down his sleeve and put on his tunic. 'Now I want to go to my room and look over my things. Shout up to me when Rosamund comes.'

But she did not come. We had expected her before tea, but at half past four she had not arrived. Mary and I went down to the kitchen and found Kate sitting with her elbows on the table and her head in her hands. We put our arms round her and kissed her and played with the pins in her cap, and Mary said, 'Oh, dear, I wish it was all as it used to be, and that we could hear the muffin man's bell ringing, and you could give us sixpences to go and buy some crumpets, as you used to when we were little and things had gone wrong.'

'I wonder who buys the muffins,' said Kate. 'I've always found that, gentle or simple, crumpets are no use to them, now there's no butter in the world.'

'Come now, there's some butter left,' I said.

'Some butter is no butter,' said Kate. 'Like eggs. If you have money you should be able to buy all the eggs and butter you want, or it's just as bad as if there were none. I wonder what has happened to that muffin man.'

'Yes, what can he be doing now that there is a war?' I asked.

'Richard Quin would have gone out and found him wherever he was,' said Mary.

'So would your Papa,' said Kate. 'God rest his poor soul.'

So she too knew that he was dead. We had never been sure of that.

Mary rubbed her face against Kate's shoulder. 'I wish Papa was here now,' she said indistinctly. She rarely said anything so obvious.

'People are where they ought to be,' said Kate, 'where they are sent. Some of my people are at the bottom of the sea, others are on it, and there it is.'

We were silent. Each, as we found out later, restraining herself from asking Kate if she were anxious about her kinsfolk who were at sea, so that we could guess from her answer if she and her mother had been looking in the bucket of water, and guess from that guess if she had looked for Richard Quin's future too. But we knew that we should not traffic with magic, least of all now.

'Miss Rosamund is very late,' said Kate. 'Shall I not serve tea? I think I will, as soon as the scones in the oven are ready.'

'What, are there more scones in the oven?' I asked. For on the table, between the chocolate and cherry cakes we had made out of our saved rations, a pile of scones was cooling on a wire tray.

'Those are not good enough,' said Kate. 'Look at them, no lighter than you could buy in a shop, when I wanted to do them so well. But go and tell Richard Quin that tea will be ready as soon as he comes down.'

I found our brother standing in his room with a racket in each hand. 'Has Rosamund come? No? I will come down in a minute but look, Rose, this is interesting. This is a brute of a racket, it always let me down. This is an angel. It plays the game for you. If I got tired, it never did. But I still don't know what the difference between them is. They're shaped the same, they weigh the same. A mystery, a mystery.'

He came downstairs happily, but after tea we were all distressed, for still Rosamund had not arrived. At last he sighed and said bravely, 'Rose, put on your hat and coat, we must start without her.' Then he kissed Mary, who said, 'Oh, Richard, if only we could go to the war with you,' and he said, 'Yes, my dear, we would hold you up above the trenches and use you as a decoy.' Then he kissed Kate, who said, 'There will be no sense in cooking while you are away,' and he kissed Mamma. She said nothing, but Richard answered her, 'No', he said, 'you do not understand this. Think, if it were you and not me who were going to the front, how you would love it. But I should be appalled in that case. Realise what that means. Honestly, I am looking forward to going to France. You know how I love playing games. Well, I find gunnery quite a game. Mamma, Mamma, you must not be sad about me, because I have to do this and I am ready to do it. I am sure that if you had been told when you were a child about all the things that you were going to have to do, you would have thought you had better die at once, you would not have believed you could ever have the strength to do them. Well, it is like that now for me. You do understand that, don't you? The only thing that would make me miserable would be if you didn't.'

'Yes, yes,' murmured Mamma, 'but do be careful, dear.'

We were all delighted by this injunction to a soldier going forth to fight in a World War, and in a chorus of laughter went out to the hall. As we opened the front door we heard the sound of someone running along the quiet street.

'Dear Rosamund,' said Richard Quin.

It might have been expected that she would be distressed by

having had to miss so much of Richard's last day at home and being so late, but when she met him at the gate and threw herself into his arms she was flushed and joyful. She held her cap in her hand, the pins had dropped from her hair, which was nevertheless not in disorder, for it had fallen into the firm barley sugar curls that had hung on her shoulders when we first knew her. Her cape was swirled about her by a light evening wind, but she was as little discomposed as an actress who has a train to manage on the stage. Her gaiety was rich and complete and unembarrassed by the horrible occasion. It was nearly shocking. Yet it was what he needed. He hugged us both tightly by the arm, one on each side of him, and we ran along to the station, as if Lovegrove were our private garden and we could romp as we liked. Under his breath he sang the aria from *The Marriage of Figaro* which Figaro sings when Cherubino is going to war, and weaved talk through it. There was no difference between the youth of Cherubino and the youth of Richard Quin, and it was delightful to pretend that we were in an opera, that Richard Quin would go to the war again and again for hundreds of years and never get there.

He knew so many people. Though Mary and I have been well-known for some years now, we did not know nearly so many people as he did. On the station platform two young men and a girl came up to him and joyously claimed acquaintanceship. We never found out who they were, but they had met him at a performance of the *Messiah* so we went up to the far end of the platform by the signal-box and sang the Hallelujah Chorus softly until our train came in. Handel thought that the world was all right. The men in the signal-box smiled down on us over the levers, they thought we were convinced the world was all right. Mercifully Richard Quin's friends did not get into our train, they were going to London Bridge while we, of course, were going to Victoria. We did not tell them why we were going to Victoria, and the unapprehensive cheerfulness with which they bade us goodbye was convincing, was comforting. But indeed our journey was so ordinary that nothing extraordinary could possibly lie at its end. There was surely some evidential value in the benevolent, untroubled glances the other passengers turned on us. A man who was a little drunk leaned forward and asked abruptly 'Are they both your sisters or neither?' and everybody laughed and was friendly. Surely there were no real dangers. We chattered as happily as if our fellow-passengers had given us absolute proof of this, until Rosamund asked Richard Quin how it was that he had no baggage with him. He told her that Gerald de Bourne Conway had gone straight from camp to London and was taking his baggage with his own to Victoria; and in speaking of the boy his face grew grey and tired. He went on to tell Rosamund that he had visited the boy's home, and she asked hesitantly what it had been like, as if telling him he need not answer if he did not choose. But he told her. 'What you would expect. A vast damp vicarage, with bottles hidden everywhere, there was even a cache of them in the chest of drawers in my room. And lots of framed family trees.' A silence fell on them. Evidently he had told her things about Gerald I did not know.

We got to Victoria too early, so we went down into the underground and came up again at Westminster, and strolled for a few moments between the Houses of Parliament and the Abbey. A blue river mist made the grey stone look soft as feathers but blurred the details and left only the historic outlines, so they looked evanescent and eternal. We went back to Victoria, and were still too early, and felt a great distaste for this place where we had to wait. The space round the station had become one of those areas which, like cemeteries and the corridors of hospitals, are swinging on a turntable between the worlds. There was the implacable and unadmirable façade of the station, drawing to itself a black jointed stream of taxis and motor-cars, and unconnected myriads of men in uniform, deformed by the weight of the kitbags on their backs, of women and children scurrying by their sides, those also deformed, by the weight of grief and stoicism. Within there was a limbo where these people clung together before the men turned and went stooping towards the gates that led to the platforms and the night. Above a great dimly lit illuminated clock said that this was the hour. The occasion was the annulment of life, for what is life but being able to move according to the will? But all the people who got out of the taxis and cars, all the men bent under their kitbags, were doing what their will would never want them to do, which it would never let them do, were it not in the custody of something outside them not certified to be wise or loyal. The clock said that there was not time to start that argument, but there was time for us three to talk a little longer. We turned back to the underground station and stood for a time unhappily among the crowds hurrying in and out along the hideous rounded corridors, that were like huge tiled intestines. Then we saw a soldier and a girl turn aside from the corridor a few yards ahead and knew they must have found a recess where they could say goodbye. We followed them into a short passage running to a closed iron door, and we stood a few yards from the soldier and the girl, who were silent in each other's arms. There were old posters on the rounded walls, one advertising a concert of mine that had taken place a year ago. The white light shone back from the tiles, we all looked very pale.

Richard said harshly to Rosamund, 'I want to live. Oh, God, how I want to live.'

She answered, speaking bitterly, as I had never heard her speak before, 'No. Not to live. To live happily.'

He nodded. 'No. Not just to live. To live happily. That is something you know very well. Poor Rosamund.' He felt for her hand and raised it to his lips.

'To live,' Rosamund insisted, more gently, knitting her brows and smiling obstinately, 'just as lots of other people have lived, and nobody has said they should not.'

'Just that,' he agreed fiercely.

They were silent while their hands twisted and slid together.

He said, 'I want . . . I want. . . .' He wanted so many noble things, I wondered which he would name now.

He said, 'I want to swim. And lie in the sun.'

'I want to swim and lie in the sun,' she repeated, as hungrily. 'With you. With Mary and Rose. With the Mammas on the beach. And Kate.'

'How lovely it is,' he said hopelessly. He was looking at the walls as if he could see through the tiles and their scruff of old posters to all he desired. 'How lovely.'

'Do you remember the honeycomb you brought home for tea the day Miss Beevor was there?' she asked.

'Yes, we shocked them by eating it with a spoon.'

'Drenched in cream,' she reminded him. They laughed together quietly, greedily.

I watched them in bewilderment. Richard Quin's gaiety was valuable because he was grave in his heart, he pondered such solemn secrets. I had thought he would share some of these with me before he went. But he would only stare into Rosamund's eyes and talk of honeycombs and cream.

He said, 'I am so afraid, Rosamund. You cannot think how afraid I am.'

Rosamund stopped laughing and her blind look came on her. She shook her hand free of his and then grasped it again more hungrily, as if to say that he must press closer on her palm and fingers, must bear down on her flesh to come nearer to the blood and nerves and being. Then her stammer came on her, she opened her mouth and her tongue flickered from side to side. But she was able to force out the words, 'Sweeter than honeycomb.'

A memory or an anticipation ran through Richard Quin like fire through tow, and it burned Rosamund too. When it had died down both turned to me, and by the kindness of their faces I felt protected.

'I will say goodbye to you two here,' he said. 'Dear Rose, look after the Rose of the World. And believe me when I say that I shall be all right. In the same strictly truthful sense that it's true that the two angles at the base of an isosceles triangle are equal. No fancy, no frill. Not symbolically, not mystically. Just all right. Now I must go and find Gerald. What shall I do,' he asked, with sudden fatigue, in an almost childish voice, 'if Gerald is not there. But he will be there. He is sure to be there. Now shut your eyes, Rose, and do not open them to look after me.'

As I stood in darkness his mouth came down on mine; and then he was not there.

IX

IN THE MIDDLE of the night, ten days after Richard Quin had gone to France, Mary and I were awakened by a loud noise from Mamma's bedroom. We ran to her and found the room in darkness and switched on the light. She was standing by the chest-of-drawers, where she kept her underclothes, looking down into an open drawer, an overturned chair beside her. She had shrunken so much during the last year or so that her straight cambric nightdress seemed an empty little tent.

We put our arms round her and said, 'Mamma, what are you looking for? Get into bed and we will find it for you.'

'Don't be tiresome, children,' she said, 'I am pressed for time. And turn off the light. I do not need it.'

'But, Mamma, what are you trying to find?' asked Mary.

'Turn out the light,' she begged. 'I tell you I do not need it.'

'But you overturned the chair,' I said.

'A chair might as well be that way up as any other if nobody wants to sit on it,' she answered crossly, 'and I do not want to sit on it. And turn out the light. It hurts my head.'

We turned it out, and into the darkness there entered the tall figure of Kate, who said, 'It is very late, Ma'am, and you should rest, you will need all your strength. What are you about?'

'I want to be sure that everything is clean and tidy,' said Mamma.

'All is clean and tidy,' said Kate. 'Everything is in its place. You would be better in your bed, Ma'am.'

'I do not like to lie there,' sighed Mamma, 'not knowing how things are.'

'They are well enough,' said Kate, and drew back the window-curtain. 'See, they are well enough.'

Both looked down into the sleeping street as if there were more to be seen there than the pale primrose lamps, the cat that slowly trod the middle of the road, the blind houses. 'Yes,' said Mamma, and turned aside, and Kate let the curtain fall. We heard the bed settle slightly under her tiny weight, and presently her breathing told us that she slept.

The next morning it was as if we had dreamed this. But Mamma stayed in bed for breakfast, which she hardly ever did, even now. Nor did she rise for luncheon. She looked not much frailer than usual, and said that she did not feel ill. The only strange thing about her was that she lay in bed with her arm stretched out so that the palm of her hand rested flat on the wall. I had never seen her do this before and I felt shy about asking her why she was doing it. At three o'clock I opened the front door and took in the telegram telling us that Richard Quin had been killed in action. I gave the boy a shilling and the money for a telegram to Rosamund. Then I went to the top of the basement stairs and called for Kate, and her white face glimmered in the dusk below, and she asked, 'Was that it?'

I said, 'Yes. But I suppose you knew.'

She answered, 'No. My mother and I did nothing, out of respect for your Mamma's wishes. But to be sure there was nobody in this house who did not know he was going further than France.'

I looked down into the darkness of the stairs as if it were the water in a bucket, and her faint face might float and waver and change into a revelation. But all that was good in me knew that it was not lawful for me to have more certainty than the bare news of my brother's death. I turned away and went to the music-room and found Mary practising. On our way back to the house we paused in the garden, our arms about each other's waists, and looked at the grove of trees at the end of the lane, and remembered how we had seen the red circle of our brother's cigarette pass from his lips to his hand, from his hand to his lips, eleven nights before.

When we went into Mamma's room she took her hand away from the wall and asked, 'Was that it?' Then she said, 'Oh, my poor son, the youngest of them all,' and laid her hand on the wall again. It was as if she were listening through her flesh to distant sounds. She cried out violently, 'If only death were death. If we could sleep and sleep and sleep. I do not see why we need to be brave for ever. Think shame that in this war there is no discharge. Yet what is asked of Richard he will give.' She pressed her hand close to the wall, her eyes vast, her mouth gaping. 'If he can go on giving it cannot be too much to ask. You have me there,' she gasped, and her eyelids fell, her lips closed, her hand dropped, and she rolled down among the bedclothes towards the end of the bed.

Kate came forward from the doorway. Her strong arms lifted my mother back to the pillows with a seaman's gesture; so might a drowning man be plucked from the surf. Mamma opened her eyes and bade one of us go at once to break the news to Cordelia, saying that she would be more troubled than any of us. This puzzled Mary and me, for we thought it unlikely to be true, and indeed we felt impatient at being forced at this of all times to remember a relationship which had never seemed quite real and now seemed disagreeably fictitious. To be Richard Quin's sister was to adore him, she had not adored him. I said I would go, but Mary followed me out into the passage and said that we must toss for it, we had tossed up for the right to go with Richard Quin to Victoria, we would take our chance on this too. But she won, I had to go.

I found Cordelia sitting in her neat little Kensington drawing-room, idling, which was very rare. There was some embroidery lying on the table beside her, and a novel from the Times Book Club, and her French and Italian books, but she was leaning back in an armchair by the fireplace, her hands folded, her eyes fixed on the red hawthorn tree by the gate in her front garden.

This inactivity was so unlike her that I said, 'I suppose you know?'

She answered, with a return of the irritability which had been characteristic of her as a child, but which had gone from her since she had become a Houghton-Bennett, 'You suppose I know what?'

But of course she had known. She was merely denying our family heritage. But when she heard me confirm the news, I perceived that our mother had spoken the truth when she had said that Cordelia would be more troubled than any of us. She cried in agony, 'Killed, not missing?'

'No, just killed,' I said. She clung to me, weeping, and I was very sorry for her, and I kissed her, but soon felt doubtful. It was not pure grief that was making her hide her face on my shoulder, that was shaking her with sobs. I thought it probable

244

that she was thinking of some way of regarding our brother's death which would justify her in saying, 'It is worse for me, because I am the eldest.' When she raised her head to say, using a favourite formula of hers, 'I suppose Mamma does not realise it,' thus putting forward a claim that she alone was facing reality, I found myself about to utter the sentence, 'You should be happy in realising that now Richard Quin will never go to Oxford.' But a memory of my brother exorcised the evil spirit in my mouth. For I had been looking past her out of the window, and the red hawthorn caught my eye, and I remembered that day when she had told us three that she did not know the colour the hawthorn tree would be when it bloomed, and we had looked coldly at her, unkind about all that she did, as she had been unkind in our childhood about all we had done, and how afterwards Richard Quin had rebuked us for our unkindness. I told her something of this, trying to leave out the accusatory point, even letting her suppose that perhaps Mary and I had been jealous because she had married first, though this was quite untrue, and trying to recall justly my brother's goodness, to invoke it, so that it might descend on us and end this dreadful alienation. I felt him help us, but he failed to complete the miracle. Though Cordelia and I were easier together, there was still something apprehensive in her sorrow which I could not understand and which she would not explain to me. There soon seemed not much reason why I should stay with her any longer. When I told her that I must go back to Mamma she asked if I had had any luncheon and got me some cold meat, and as I ate it I saw that she was looking at me with that white look which meant that she was frightened.

I laid down my knife and fork and said, 'What is it?'

She answered, irritable again, 'What is what?'

At the gate, standing on a dry red pool of fallen hawthorn petals, we kissed goodbye. When I was fifty yards away I heard her running after me. On her face, as she came nearer, I saw the white look. I thought, 'At last she is going to tell me why she is afraid.'

But all she said was: '*The Times*. There should be an announcement of his death in *The Times*. Shall I get Alan to send it in?'

Disappointed, I agreed, and went on my way quickly back to Lovegrove.

When I got home Mamma seemed to be asleep, though all

245

that day, and each time we went in to look at her during the night, her hand was pressed against the wall. In the morning she sat up and ate breakfast, but said to me across the tray: 'I told you some time ago that my mind had forgotten the connection between a number of things, that when I walked in an orchard I had to tell myself that the round things hanging on the trees were apples. That has got much worse lately, all through spring I have had to remind myself that those green things that kept on appearing on the trees are leaves. But now my body is getting foolish. The various parts of me have forgotten what they have to do. My spine is stupid about supporting my neck, my neck is stupid about supporting my head. I do not believe this is just because of Richard Quin. I think I must be very ill, and to make things right I suppose I ought to see a doctor.'

I telephoned, as I thought, to our doctor, and left a message; but there came a stranger, who told us that our doctor had been called up, heard what we had to say and he examined Mamma, and expressed incredulity. It did not seem possible to him that she had, till two days before, risen each morning for breakfast, helped us to give music-lessons, and had gone shopping and received visitors, for she was showing all the symptoms of some grave disease, in an advanced stage. He was not certain what disease it was; it might be this, or it might be that, but he had no doubt that it had progressed beyond any possibility of cure. The condition of her heart alone would prevent her from surviving more than a few weeks. Then there burst on us one of those horrible things that happen in wartime. The doctor was elderly and had, as he told us, returned to practice from retirement simply out of a sense of duty, and of course he was overworked. He perceived that my mother was a brilliant and beloved person, who in a reasonable universe would never have died. He was, no doubt, sickened, as all of us must be in wartime, by the enormous victories gained by death. To relieve his feelings he turned on Mary and me and told us that he was aware that we were celebrated pianists, and that he was forced to the conclusion that we had been too busy pursuing our careers to notice our mother's sufferings, for it was no use telling him that she had reached this stage of her malady in a couple of days. We wept, but only because we had just lost our only brother, because we were going to lose our mother. We knew that the old fool would see as soon as he went home and looked in the case-book that only a fortnight before we had called in our doctor to see if another visit to the specialist would do Mamma any good, and that he had reported her as well enough. Men were like this, moody, unjust, showing their perturbation at misfortune by adding to it; all men but Richard Quin, who had left us. The doctor asked us what arrangements we could make for nursing her, and told us that nurses were very hard to get. I told him we had a cousin who had nearly finished her hospital training, and he suggested that we should get her to apply for leave on compassionate grounds, since our mother would probably need careful nursing.

He made everything sound infinitely tedious, as if henceforward we would have no time to talk to Mamma and help her to bear things, because of a multiplicity of organisational duties, onerous in themselves, which we would find specially onerous because of our moral and mental deficiencies. He also suggested that though he was going to get a specialist down to see Mamma it would be onerous for him and he would only be able to carry out the project because of his superiority to us, and would find it particularly grievous because, of course, owing to our lack of interest in her welfare, this attention would be fruitless, since it had been left too late.

As soon as he had gone I wrote to Rosamund and to Constance, too, and Mary went out and posted the letters, while I went up to see Mamma. 'I wonder if that doctor is gloomy about anything in particular,' she asked, 'or if it is just the breed, as they say about Labradors. I wish we had not had to have a strange doctor, but do not worry about what you can do for me. It will make no difference, this is the end.' She turned her head aside, sighing, 'My son, my son,' and closed her eyes. But she opened them again to look sharply at me and say, 'All this is no reason why you should neglect your practising.'

We sat beside her bed in a house that had changed for ever. The silence that had been silting up in the rooms ever since Richard Quin went away now filled it as an invisible solid. It was not to be dispersed by any noise. Now Richard Quin was nowhere but he was everywhere. He was standing on the lawn, he was on the pavement outside the gate, he was even lying on his bed in his own room. But always his face turned away from us, he refused to have anything more to do with us. Yet we felt guilty because we were not doing the thing, whatever that might be, which would bring him back to us and let him smile and live again. Nothing was the same, even our music. Now when we played we listened for a statement that was made to us without the intention of the composer, that was made, indeed, even by scales and arpeggios. The sounds affirmed our knowledge that Richard Quin was everywhere, was nowhere, was failing us, had been failed by us; and yet they said that though these things were true there was another truth. But the silence rushed in on the sounds, before we could hear that truth. We listened with idiotic intensity, for it is known that this message is never more explicit than that. But we were asking for news of our mother as well as our brother.

It seemed less natural to us that Mamma should die than Richard Quin. We could all of us remember a time when he had not existed, so we had realised that he was not a permanent part of the world. But Mamma had always been there, it seemed to us that she was as little likely to leave us as the ground under our feet. And we could do nothing for her. She was grieving over the death of Richard Quin, but she knew so much more of what was happening to him that we could not grieve in company with her. She sometimes lifted her thin pleated eyelids and cried out things about him and what he was doing that we could not understand, we could not even remember them, they were so far beyond the frontiers of our experience. We could hardly help her physically. She needed often to be lifted up in bed, for any attitude soon grew painful, and, light though she was, we could not lift her. Her body had become so sensitive that she could endure the touch of others only for a second; and it needed Kate's strength to seize her and shift before she wailed in pain. The doctor never called without remarking that we were indeed unfortunate to be of so little use in what he called the sickroom; for what he had seen in the case-book had not altered his opinion of us at all, he had to medicine himself by dislike of us.

On the second day after we had heard of Richard Quin's death Mr Morpurgo came to see Mamma. We did not tell him that the doctor said that she was dying, for his face was swollen and he talked as if he were in church. When he came down from her room he said sulkily that she was better than he had supposed she would be, then asked for her doctor's telephone number and sighed, 'We must have lots of specialists.' He sat with us for a little time but could not speak. On the doorstep he kissed us both for the first time in our lives, and muttered thickly, 'I have no right to be this age when your brother was so young.' Again we could do nothing. We could help him no more than we could help Mamma. I saw the life of these days as a flagon of grey glass, filled with salt water, with collected tears. The occasion of our grief was classically decorous, our brother had died for his country. But our grief was useless. Salt water, spilled on the ground, does not feed what grows there, but kills it.

We could not master any part of this time and make it kinder. There was always the doctor. He brought down not the specialist my mother had visited often before, but another stranger, who had evidently been told that Mary and I were feckless and selfish, and that Kate was clumsy, and who called Mamma little lady. He took care to rub into us the specialists' verdict, and called often, not so much to help Mamma as to remind us. It was infuriating to think how easily, had it been peacetime, we could have disengaged ourselves from this hearselike and denigrating man; but any war constantly inflicts on the peoples involved variations of the torture practised in the French Revolution by which naked persons unknown to each other were bound together and cast into the river, and we could not get another doctor. Mercifully Mamma could outwit much of her pain. When a sudden thunderstorm hurt her head, she could find relief in wondering why a sound that she had loved all her life should now give her pain. She began to master the sensitiveness of her body by speculating about its causes. She was interested in her emaciation, saying sometimes, 'I have found a new bone.' But suddenly that resource left her. On the fourth morning she asked if the announcement of Richard Quin's death had yet appeared in *The Times*, and we gave her the newspaper, which we had not looked at ourselves, for we could not steel ourselves to it. We had had our names in the newspaper because of pleasant things that had happened to us, it should have been like that for him.

She had got us to put on her spectacles. They fell from her face as she clutched at the newspaper with both of her hands, trying to tear it and as she failed she threw herself back on the pillows, crying in harsh, endless, animal rage. Before we had given her the newspaper, she had not been quite our mother, she had been the wax model of our mother, made on a smaller scale, and coloured more like the sheets than like flesh. Now she was a monkey that had been shot by a hunter.

249

I could not take her in my arms because that would have hurt her. I stood quite still and prayed that we might all die. The newspaper had fallen from her bed on the floor and Mary picked it up.

Mamma sobbed, 'To take his son from him.'

Mary handed me the newspaper, saying, 'You should not have let Cordelia hand in the notice. There is nothing she cannot turn to harm.'

At first I could not find the place in the long list of 'Killed on Active Service'. Then I read it aloud, till I came to the words 'only son of the late—' and then I stopped. Cordelia had omitted the distinctive middle name of our father, which he had always used when he wrote or spoke in public, and she had not mentioned the place where he was born and where he had lived till he was unfortunate. Nobody who read the announcement could guess that Richard Quin was Papa's son.

'Cruel,' wept Mamma, 'cruel.'

'She is coming this afternoon,' Mary said to me.

'What shall we do?' I asked, knowing that there was no answer.

'And listen,' said Mary. 'There is somebody at the front door. It is sure to be that doctor.'

'I will not see him,' wailed Mamma.

'You shall not,' I said, and went to bar him out. But it was not the doctor, it was Rosamund, in her outdoor uniform, without her handsomeness, pale and too stout. She laid her arms about our shoulders, then knelt by Mamma's bed and told her, 'I could not come before.'

'It is not possible that instead of the doctor it should be you,' Mamma sighed. 'I had thought that now everything would go wrong. Ah, my poor bairn.'

'I suppose I should take it better, since we have always known it was going to happen,' said Rosamund, 'but till now I was never quite sure that we were not telling ourselves the story because we wanted it not to happen. But, oh, how all of me knows now that it is true. Not a bit of me, to the fingernails, but knows it.'

'My poor bairn, my poor bairn,' said Mamma, 'it is so wrong for me to trouble you now. But you will be able to lift me, I think, and it hurts me so when people touch me, you must forgive me for being selfish.'

'You are not being selfish at all,' said Rosamund. 'You are

250

saving me. Nursing is my music, I am more than me when I nurse. But I weaken, I told you once, I felt like giving up nursing because of the children who get burned, and Richard Quin being killed is like that. When I heard I wanted to walk out of the hospital. But now I must nurse you, of course I can lift you, and that puts me back in safety.'

'Yes, yes, you can lift me and make it easy for me to go,' said Mamma, 'and you can help Mary and Rose not to think too much of it.' Again she drowsed.

Rosamund went on kneeling by the bed, her cheek on the counterpane, close to Mamma's hand, and she closed her eyes. But presently she sat up and covered her ears as if to shut out a noise, and said softly, 'The house is so quiet now.'

'Yes,' said Mary. 'We thought it quiet when he was away in camp, or when he had first gone to France, but it was not as quiet as this.'

'But everywhere it is the same,' said Rosamund. 'In hospital too, it is so quiet. I have been on night duty and when I have walked along the corridors I have had to stop and stand still, my footsteps rang so loud on the stone. Oh, I am so glad to be here. I cannot bear the hospital just now. It is horrible to go on and on down long corridors knowing that where you are going is right at the end, and that you must keep on till you get there.' She dropped forward on her knees again, and laid her face against Mamma's hands, and said, 'But with her it seems all right. You go and do whatever you have to do. I shall be here.'

'Yes, children,' sighed Mamma, without opening her eyes. 'Get on with your playing.' But when we reached the door she called us back, with more strength than we liked. She said, 'Say nothing to Cordelia when she comes. She cannot help it. But see that I am put in the paper as your Papa's wife. And on the stone too.' She started up in bed, agony flecked her lips. 'Your poor Papa,' she moaned.

'Oh, quiet,' said Rosamund, 'quiet.'

Mamma stopped, but asked indignantly, 'And why should I be quiet?'

'You know quite well why you should be quiet,' said Rosamund. 'To cry and toss yourself about, it lets in the other ones.'

'Yes, yes, I had forgotten,' said Mamma. 'Am I older or younger than you? I forget. But anyway my memory is going. They never came back to your house, did they?'

'No, no, never again after that day you and Rose came to visit

251

us,' said Rosamund. She moved slowly towards the door, stretched herself and yawned, and said lazily, confidently, 'It will be all right. I will go and wash and put on my indoor uniform.' But she did not hurry. Now there was an immense sense of leisure about the house, and an unchanging white light, all day it was as if it was a cold dawn.

I couldn't think what time it was when I came downstairs and saw Cordelia standing in the hall, slowly taking off her gloves. She looked very small and the blood had gone from her face. Was it an hour when I ought to offer her a meal? And, if it were, would it be luncheon or tea? She winced at the sight of me and wavered as if she wanted to run out of the house. I suppose she felt guilty about the announcement of Richard Quin's death, and as our eyes met I said, 'The Times. . . .'

She said placidly, 'I thought it looked quite nice. But how is Mamma? Kate let me in, but she does not seem to realise anything.'

I was carrying a tray, I came down and laid it on the hall-table, I put my arms round the incomprehensible and uncomprehending world of her body. It was stiff with fear. There was no use talking to her about The Times announcement, there never would be any use. I said, 'Mamma is much worse. It is the end. The doctor says that she has only a few days to live.' To my surprise her body relaxed, and her face was flooded with pure and affectionate relief. I thought, 'Does she know more than any of us? Is it true that in dying Mamma will escape from an appalling calamity that is going to break over us?' But Cordelia was always wrong.

She said vaguely, 'I wish I could come down here to stay, it must be dreadful for you with nobody to take the responsibility.'

'Rosamund is here,' I said, and she answered, 'What a pity she has not finished her training,' but she was not seriously disturbed. Her eyes went past me and saw my mother's coach rounding the bend in the road which would take her clear of the lava pouring down from the volcano.

Rosamund leaned over the landing banisters and told her that Mamma had heard her arrive and wanted her to come up at once, because she felt sleepy. I realised that Mamma was exercising that technique to which it was very hard to put a name, as she was also candid. And as she went into the room she told Cordelia in a very faint voice not to kiss her, as she

252

could not bear to be touched. Then she cut into Cordelia's enquiries by saying more strongly, 'That's a pretty coat. Stand away from the bed so that I can see it.'

It was one of those Cossack coats that women wore in the First World War, the very short, full skirt deeply hemmed with fur, and it fanned out round Cordelia's beautiful, slender, strong legs, gleaming in black milanese stockings.

'So pretty,' said Mamma. 'You look like a doll. And the little veiled hat, so pretty too. Dear Cordelia.' Her voice trailed away and she closed her eyes.

'You had better go now,' said Rosamund, and Mamma whispered from the sheets, 'So sorry, goodbye, dear.'

Once outside the room and down the stairs, Cordelia said, 'She is far worse than I thought. You would not think anybody could be so thin and live,' and there was peace in her voice. It was not to be argued with, her persuasion that our mother was being borne into safety. But then she frowned and shook her head, and I knew that she had remembered to see with what special severity the impending danger would afflict her. This was her usual nonsense. Yet the patience and tenderness in my mother's voice when she said, 'You look like a doll,' forbade me to feel anger. Kate brought us tea with hot buttered scones, and we ate them with the tears running down our cheeks and into our mouths. Presently I said, 'Is there anything of Richard Quin's you would like to have?' and she did not answer, but looked at me with eyes that might have been those of a seer, or of a doll. I remembered how hateful she had been about Richard Quin's exhibition at New College, but I also remembered what Richard Quin had been, the mischievous smile Rosamund had given as she leaned over the banisters and heard Cordelia belittling her, the patience and tenderness in my mother's voice, so I went on eating buttered scones. Rosamund looked round the corner of the door at us and went away again; and Cordelia, to whom Rosamund's presence was always a challenge, said in a very grown-up way, 'You should not distress yourself by handling his things now, when you have so much else weighing on you.' But her nostrils were dilating again, she was afraid, again she was holding back something terrible she thought she knew.

Rosamund was again at the door. 'I told your Mamma that you were eating hot buttered scones, and she said something about bread and butter and being carried on a shutter. She is worried because she can't remember the verse.'

I ran up and knelt by the bed. Mamma was laughing. 'After all the times I have heard your Papa repeat that I can't remember how it goes. How my mind is going. Has gone.' I recited:

'Werther had a love for Charlotte
　Such as words could never utter,
Would you like to know how first he met her?
　She was cutting bread and butter.

Charlotte was a married lady,
　And a moral man was Werther,
And, for all the wealth of Indies,
　Would do nothing for to hurt her.

So he sighed and pined and ogled,
　And his passion boiled and bubbled,
Till he blew his silly brains out,
　And no more by it was troubled.

Charlotte, having seen his body,
　Borne before her on a shutter,
Like a well-conducted person,
　Went on cutting bread and butter.'

We laughed and laughed silently, as if this were a secret between us, until laughter hurt her too much, and she began to sob, and I wept into the quilt. I felt her fingers on my hair, very lightly and reluctantly, for it was now as painful for her to touch as to be touched, and softly, as if this too were a secret, she said, 'It is so foolish, I keep on thinking that I wish I could die rather than give you all this trouble.' She raised her hand with difficulty, and laid the palm against the wall, as she had done so often just after we heard that Richard Quin had been killed; and a listening look came into her eyes. 'And it will be worse before the end,' she said. 'I cannot go easily. You must forgive me. It seems to be quite an iron rule that it should happen like this. Go downstairs, now, dear.'

But at the door I turned and came back to her; and indeed she needed comforting. 'But to cause trouble. You will need to forgive me. And when it is too bad do not let the children see me.'

'What children?' I asked, cautiously. I was wondering if she had forgotten that we were all grown-up.

254

She slept all that afternoon and all that evening. At ten o'clock that night, when Rosamund was going up to bed and Mary and I were settling down in our chairs on each side of Mamma, there was a ring at the door. I went down and found Constance on the doorstep, the arrows of a rainstorm striking down through the night behind her. In the hall, we were speaking of Mamma's state, when she lifted her fair face, solemn and glazed with raindrops, and held up her hand to hush me. Then from the room above, thinly wailed, we heard my father's Christian name. We were to hear it many times during the next three days and nights. Mamma had suddenly changed into a demented skeleton, who jerked about and cried my father's Christian name with as fierce an anguish as if it were he and not Richard Quin who had just been killed. She cried it so loud that it could be heard in the street, she cried it wolfishly, there was no love left in her. She did not speak of Richard Quin any more, she did not recognise Mary or me. Constance and Rosamund and Kate she knew, only to the degree of knowing that these were the ones who were strong enough to lift her. No drug alleviated the pain of either her flesh or her spirit. They gave her injections, but though she sometimes slept it was not after she had had them, but at unpredictable times, when her anguish became confused and expostulatory. It was as if she retreated into sleep to carry on an argument more forcibly, and when she awoke again it was her anguish that had been refreshed, not her.

But her sleep gave us refreshment, which we desperately needed. I had often wondered why doctors and keepers sought to soothe lunatics who were violent, why their families were so distressed, why they did not shut them in padded cells and let them indulge in what they had chosen as their pleasure. But now, watching my mother, who had become as hideous as a cankered and distorted tree on a windswept marsh, shaken by a demon that lived in each branch, I understood. As she screamed and writhed, the room became dangerous. Had it not been for Constance and Rosamund and Kate, who bent over her, like priestesses and athletes, cunningly bending their knees and getting the right grip to bind without inflicting pain, my mother's anguish might have got loose, not to be made captive again, at least by us. They were injured, these strong women, though Mamma was so frail. The sweat ran down them, their breath was quick and shallow, when we took them

255

food they ate it as if they had been starved for days, the one who was off duty slept as if she would never wake again.

There was a great deal to do. Miss Beevor called on the first morning of this phase to see what she could do for us, and suddenly there broke into our conversation, screeched three times, my father's Christian name. Her poor innocent eyes stared up at the landing. The name was screeched again. The white kid bag, with Athens in poker-work on it, dropped at my feet, and Miss Beevor ran out of the house and down the steps. I caught her up with the bag three houses along the street, and she quavered, 'My own Papa and Mamma passed away so peacefully, I did not think it would be like this, and I remembered too late what my mother had said about not letting the children see her when it was too bad. I sent telegrams to Aunt Lily and Nancy Phillips, who had both said they wanted to come and see Mamma when they had heard about Richard Quin, and told them not to come until we sent for them; and I rang up Mr Morpurgo and told him to cease his daily visits, as Mamma needed complete quiet. I heard a sigh, and the click of a replaced receiver. I told Cordelia too, though I was not sure if that were right. This took time; and we had also to do the cooking, we got the charwomen out of the house as soon as possible.

There were also the policemen to deal with, for Cousin Jock had disappeared. He had been disturbed at the news that Richard Quin had been killed, but he had not let Constance come and help Rosamund. We never heard by what devices he had kept her from doing what she so much desired to do, and indeed we were unaware of the exact nature of the drama he had improvised for the enchainment of his family, in his dingy and narrow house, out of his peculiar resources. Mamma knew, though we did not. But Constance had been helpless until at supper-time she had found his broken flute lying between his knife and fork, and heard from the servant that an hour before he had told her that he was going out and would not be back. 'Did he not say that he would be out till supper?' Constance had asked, and the girl had answered, 'No, he had just said that he would not be back.' Constance had then packed a bag and started out through the rain, calling at the local police-station, where she stolidly reported the disappearance of her husband, in the face of an incredulity which was not to last.

256

Rosamund let Mary and me help her to feed Mamma, even when she was at her worst. There was a wild pleasure in going the whole way with her, though that way was horrible. Then one day, when Mary and I had gone out into the garden and were standing among the incongruously lovely trees, among the late lilac and the early May, breathing in the scents as if they were anaesthetics and might send us to sleep, Rosamund threw up a window-sash and cried, 'Mary, Rose, come at once and see your mother.' We found the room empty of what had filled it for three days and nights. The light was pure, and in a smooth bed Mamma lay quietly. We thought joyously, 'She is going to live.' But she said, 'Rosamund has put me into a clean nightdress, and it did not hurt me at all,' and her happiness was not an emotion but a distillate of emotion, and we knew that she was at the point of death. Her body and her soul were at last disentangled, and they were resting together before they parted company.

'Dear Mamma, how lovely that you are better,' said Mary.

'I am not so much better as all that,' she answered, rather crossly; and indeed Rosamund sitting at the head of her bed was still tense. 'Sit down, children, and stay with me, you need not bother about your playing this one day. It is strange I cannot see you. I am not blind, there is something before my eyes, but I cannot put it all together. Still, I know you are good-looking, I have no need to worry. You are all good-looking, so much better looking than I was. That has been a great pleasure. You get your looks from your Papa.' She sighed deeply, and slipped away from us for a time. Then she said, 'You must give away all Richard Quin's rackets and bats and boxing-gloves and things. But not his musical instruments. Keep them till all of us have gone. I wonder if he would ever have played any instrument really well if he had worked at it. But what a sensible boy he was. How wisely he laid out his time, knowing that he had to go.'

'It was like a man making his fortune quickly in the City,' said Rosamund, 'a fortune for other people.'

'Yes,' Mamma cried out, 'a fortune for other people. And with that he did enough, he should be allowed to rest.' She trembled and looked hideous again.

'Hush, hush,' said Rosamund, 'do not give us over to the power of that again.'

'Forgive me, I keep on forgetting,' said Mamma. 'But it is not just, why should he have to go on and on?'

'He has the strength to do it,' said Rosamund.

'Yes, he has the strength, but that does not mean that he will not suffer and be afraid and feel this terrible exhaustion. They should let him rest.'

'But he was so kind. He could not rest if there was still something he could do.'

'Yes, and that is taking advantage of him,' blazed Mamma, 'and what about me? I have no strength left. I want to come to an end, I want to be utterly consumed by worms, I want to be digested by the earth. For him and for myself I want that peace. Surely we have some rights.'

'Please, please,' said Rosamund. 'I often get so frightened when I think how hard it is to be. Do not make me more of a coward than I am, do not stop helping me, as you have always helped me. Now it seems to you that we are all of the same age. But to me it does not, I am still wholly here, so I see you as older, I cling on to you. I cannot help it, and I cannot help asking you to make it easier for me because I am younger. Forgive me, we are still caught in this extraordinary life.'

'Yes, I must allow for this extraordinary life,' murmured Mamma. Then she cried out in panic, 'How do we know that it will not all be extraordinary?'

'Richard Quin promised us that,' said Rosamund. 'He was a promise that it will not always be hard.' She began to stammer and Mamma cut her short with her agreement. 'Yes, yes,' she said. 'You must pardon me, I go on from blunder to blunder. Ask Kate and Constance to come, they are such examples to me always. And, Rose, I would not mind seeing the children now. But not at once. I am so tired, I must rest a little. Tell them to come this evening.'

When Mr Morpurgo heard my voice, he said slowly, 'I suppose you are ringing me up to tell me that she is dead.' The darkness that surrounds people who are telephoning was full of finesse. He was inspired by the hope we all have that if we name an event we fear, it cannot happen; and the next step in his dream had been that I would say, 'It has all been a mistake, the doctors have been quite wrong from the start, all that was wrong with Mamma was a fever that has passed completely, the doctor has seen her and he says that she is all right.' When I did not say that, he began to touch wood in a different way and confess what he had hoped, but I cut through the web and said that Mamma wished to see him that evening, and asked him to get messages to Aunt Lily and Nancy. He promised like a sad djinn that it should be done. The baker came and I gave him a note to take along to Miss Beevor. Then I rang up Cordelia's house and was answered by Alan. I asked him how it happened that he was at home in the afternoon and he gave me the unexpected news that it was Sunday. When I repeated my message he was sympathetic, but told me that he had put Cordelia to bed, she was so worn out worrying over Mamma's illness, and, unless I thought her presence absolutely necessary, his mother would drive her down in the morning. I said I was sure that would do. Then my conscience pricked me and I asked him to hold the line until I heard what Mamma said.

Constance was sitting by her, in a white overall that looked like a toga, holding on her lap a basin full of lotion that Kate made; she had gone off for two hours one day to pick some herbs that grew on a part of Clapham Common that her mother knew about. 'Wipe my brow,' said Mamma, and when Constance put back the gauze pad in the basin she said, 'Yes, that will do. Send her my love and tell her how much I am looking forward to seeing her tomorrow morning. And think well of her. Promise to think well of her, or I will have to see her tonight, so that you shall be sure how well I think of her.'

She seemed to sleep. I think we all drowsed, though Constance still sat upright. Then Mamma made an exclamation of mild distaste. 'I am listening to someone playing,' she said. 'Is it Mary? Is it Rose? No, it would not be either of them. Whoever it is, is taking the third movement of the Beethoven Sonata in G minor far too quickly. But it is myself, of course, who is playing. I never managed that movement well. Let me go on listening. Let me have all the music I can before I go.' For a long time she lay quite still, sometimes crying out in pleasure, sometimes clicking her tongue in reproof. Her self-reproaches were numerous, and she asked timidly, 'Did I play well, at all?'

'Yes,' said Mary and I together, and Mary added, 'You were among the great ones. Brahms would not have said it, if it had not been true.'

'That is so,' faintly agreed Mamma. 'Mozart and Chopin, they might have lied, but not Brahms. Yet they were so much greater.' She listened for a little longer, but wearied of it, and turned and twisted, and exclaimed, 'How beautifully you play, Mary and Rose! I have provided for you well. But poor

Cordelia! I wonder if there was not some musical instrument she could have played. But it is a mercy she did not sing. There are so many bad songs she would have liked. Oh, poor Cordelia.' She astonished us by sitting up, but fell back at once. 'I cannot bear it any more, my pain has come back, I cannot listen, I am face to face with what I cannot hear.'

Constance took the gauze pad out of the lotion, drained it carefully on the side of the basin, and laid it on Mamma's forehead, but she struck it away. 'I cannot bear it. Oh, Mary, oh, Rose, Papa knew all those years that those jewels were hidden behind the panel over the chimneypiece and he did not tell me; and I knew all those years that the portraits over your beds were not copies, and I did not tell him. Yet we loved each other. If I had told him that those were the original pictures and let him sell them, that might have been the mad gift that softened his heart. But I could not tell him, because I had you children to think of, and he could not tell me about the jewels because there was something, it was ruin, of course, which he had to keep faith with. Our love was useless. My love for Cordelia was useless too. Yet what is useful except love?'

Rosamund said, 'Richard Quin knew that love was not useless. He did all that you and I have to do, and he was debonair. Here is your medicine.'

'It makes me able to listen to music, I will take it,' said Mamma. 'Oh, Mary, oh, Rose, how music keeps one safe. But outside music is this fact, that for me love was useless. I loved your father, I love your father. He did not tell me about those jewels, even when he knew I was distracted because I did not know where your next meal was coming from. And I kept the truth about those pictures from him, though in that awful time when he passed me in the street as if I were a stranger I saw that the reason for his misery was his feeling that he had nothing, the feeling that he had had even when he was rich, he felt,' she wheezed, 'that he had less than nothing, there was a huge debt that ate up everything that came to him. If I had given him the pictures it might have been that he would have felt that he had something.'

Her breath wheezed as if there were an actual crack in her body. 'But perhaps it would not,' she said. Looking from one to another of us, she complained, 'I see something, blocks of colours, but not you. All, all is passing, except my love. I have done nothing for you two with my life, had I not given you my

260

music. I could do nothing at all for Cordelia, I could do nothing at all for your father.'

'But I tell you there was Richard Quin,' said Rosamund.

'Yes, but I do not think Richard Quin was able to do anything for his poor Papa,' said Mamma. 'I want Papa raised from the dead, I want him to shed that cloud of darkness, I want him not to be muttering in that cell out in the centre of the iceberg. He was the dearest of all created things. But as I am getting sleepy with that medicine, I can hear the music again. You need not bother about me for a little.'

About six o'clock Mr Morpurgo came into the house and rolled his pouched eyes about him with his connoisseur gaze, because it had become something extraordinary and intricate, and mysterious like a deeply chased jewel of unknown provenance, now that my mother was dying in it. I put him in the drawing-room and told him he must wait till I saw if she were ready for him. He held me back by my sleeve, and muttered: 'All my life I have been frightened of something that was going to happen to me, and I never knew what it was. It is this.' He turned away from me and went to the window and looked out into the twilight, drawing on the glass with his plump forefinger. Before I could get upstairs Miss Beevor was at the door, but she went down to the kitchen, in case she could help Kate, saying , 'I do not want to see her. Your Mamma and I have come to know each other so well that one more glimpse of her is neither here nor there. But I would like to be here while she goes.' Upstairs Mamma was still listening to music and took no notice of me, but asked Constance for another drink. I went down and told Mr Morpurgo that she was not yet ready. He was still drawing on the window-pane and said, without turning round, 'It does not matter, I am quite happy here.'

Leaving him, I became aware that my feet were burning and swollen; and indeed Mary and I had gone up and down stairs times without number during the last few days. Also I was faint with hunger. I went down to the kitchen, which was ritually clean. The china and glass winked brightness from the dresser shelves, and on a table scrubbed white Kate and Miss Beevor were preparing some dish for supper. But I said I could not wait, and Kate, chiding me and the others for having refused to eat the things she had sent up with tea an hour or two before, cut me a plateful of bread and butter with brown sugar on it, to take upstairs. She said to Miss Beevor, 'I used to

261

give them a lot of this when they were children. It did not make their hands sticky, you see, and their Papa could not bear stickiness, nobody likes it, of course, but he would nearly faint away if he put his hand on a sticky doorknob, so we got them to like this.' Behind me the past was darker than I had known it, not only irrecoverable, but unexplored, unexplorable. My father had been disgusted by something we children did, and Mamma and Kate had devised a way to prevent us from disgusting him, and we had never known of it. All three had not told us, they had protected our pride, the past had been more tender than I thought.

Up in Mamma's bedroom everyone was glad to eat. Rosamund, who was very white, muttered, 'She is much worse,' and took the sweet slices wolfishly. From the bed a toneless voice squeaked, 'You are all eating. What are you eating?'

'Bread and butter and brown sugar.'

'Why, are you little again? But why are you eating bread and butter and brown sugar in the middle of the night? And who gave it to you? You must be careful about taking things from strangers.'

'It is all right, Kate gave it to us.'

'But why is Kate up in the middle of the night and giving you bread and butter and brown sugar? Oh, dear. She would not do such a thing. It cannot be the middle of the night.'

'It is dusk,' we said, 'the light is failing, your eyes are bad, you are very tired, that is why you have made the mistake.'

'No, I should be able to tell the difference between night and day. Now I must see the children. Soon it will be too late.'

'They are not all here yet. Aunt Lily and Nancy have not arrived. But shall Mr Morpurgo and Miss Beevor come up?'

'No. Not yet. Let me rest a little. It is going to be hard. I must hide from them that I would let them burn in hell forever, I would let them be blotted out and never have existed, if it could help your Papa.'

'Then do not see them. They love you and they would not want to be a burden to you.'

'No. That is the kind of thing your father would never pardon. And I will enjoy it. I love them, though I love him better. Rosamund, Rosamund, if there is anything you can do to make the pain better, I need it now. Go away, dears.'

We left the room, and not long after a car drew up, and it was the one that they always hired at the Dog and Duck, and Aunt

Lily and Nancy got out. When we went out Aunt Lily was telling the driver: 'Round the corner to the left, past the turning, there's another that's even better, the Nag's Head, and they'll give you some cold beef and pickles in the bar. But so will the Bull. Then come back here. They'll find a corner for you to wait. Ta-ta for now and thanks ever so.' Then she greeted us. 'I got to know all the pubs round here when I stayed here during Queenie's trouble, running out to have a nip when I couldn't bear it, and sucking peppermints after it to try to deceive your Papa and Mamma, though they would not have demeaned themselves to notice such a sprat's tail of a thing. Oh, my poor kiddies, what shall we do without her?'

'It is so strange that the house looks just the same,' said Nancy, who was very pale.

Though there were only two of them, they straggled, it was difficult to get them up to the front door. I took them down into the kitchen and Kate gave them tea, and they would not sit down. Aunt Lily wandered about, red-eyed, with her cup and saucer. Nancy leaned against the dresser. They were dogs who see the removal vans at the door and fear that they may be left behind. Mary and I would have been like that if Mamma had not made us musicians. Aunt Lily left us to go up and speak to Mr Morpurgo, and Miss Beevor went to lay the dining-room table for the supper which we would assuredly not eat.

Nancy said, 'I suppose you do not believe in people going on?'

'Why do you suppose that?' asked Kate.

'Well, you are all so clever here, and more and more clever people do not believe in God or anything,' said Nancy.

'Everybody in this house believes,' said Kate.

'Then do you really think that your brother and your Mamma are going on?' Nancy asked. She sounded faintly quarrelsome.

'We know it,' said Mary.

'We are quite sure,' I said.

'Then you cannot really be sad,' said Nancy argumentatively.

This is what the death of a father or mother means. The limelight shifts from them to you, and you have to do what you have seen them do. We found ourselves obliged to take over Mamma's occupation and temper the wind to the shorn lamb. With an exultation we believed to be false, I said, 'She is going to Richard Quin,' and Mary added, 'They will go on doing what they did here.'

'Yet you do not seem quite happy,' said Nancy.

'Why, they are tired,' said Kate, 'and dying, even for the chosen, is as painful a business as being born. They do not like to see their Mamma suffer. But all of us in this house know that she is going to Richard Quin.'

We watched Nancy take comfort from the cause of our mother's monumental agony; and presently Kate lifted her head, listened, and reminded us that time was passing and we had better see whether Mamma was ready for her visitors. So once again I climbed the stairs and found that the end had nearly been accomplished. Rosamund and Constance were very pale, and their tall bodies moved as if they were in a trance. From the heap of bones that raised the sheets so little came a hollow straw of speech: 'No, it is no use giving me water, I am eaten up with thirst, but it is not thirst and water will not help. My body is turning me out, and it will stop at nothing. Is that Rose or Mary? Send up the children one by one. I cannot leave it longer. I will see them only for a few minutes. More would be too much for them.'

I brought up Mr Morpurgo first, and as he softly padded towards my mother's bed I noticed that the window-curtains had not been closely drawn. This was a negligence that always annoyed her, so I went over and pulled them till they met. As I closed the gap I looked through it, down on the street. I paused for the moment and tugged the curtains till they overlapped and stood for a second staring as if I could see through the stuff. I turned to Mr Morpurgo, but he was now a dark mass, like a stranded whale, beside Mamma's bed, and her hand was jerking its way across the quilt till it found his shining black head. I left them and went into the next room where Rosamund and Constance were sitting, spent and visionary. I felt under no obligation to tell them that I had just seen a man leaning against the lamp-post by our gate, his face raised towards Mamma's window. He was slender, he was ageless, there was a flash of fairness answering the gaslight, there was an indefinite lewdness about his stance, he was eccentrically dressed, his trousers were too short; though there was a kind of elegance about him. Surely it was Cousin Jock. But I saw no purpose in telling Rosamund and Constance, for we had enough to do with Mamma, and also I was not certain whether he was alive or dead. It might be that the way he stood was shocking because he was not standing at all, but hanging from the lamp-post, with his feet just touching the ground. I was not even certain, whether standing or hanging, he was physically there at all. After spending the last few days on this drag-tide between the world, I was in a state when it seemed quite possible that what I had seen was a phantom. In any case his appearance was a response to my mother's death, and there was no reason for us to carry on the argument any further by noting it. If he were living, she would soon be beyond his reach; if he were dead, he had no power to hurt her. The shape of his body, whether it were solid or a shadow, was an ideograph meaning defeat. Existence was about to split into two, and Mamma was to be one side of an abyss and the rest of us on the other. At this moment he had found that he could not hold his own against her, and the long contention between them had ended in her victory.

We heard Mr Morpurgo come out of her bedroom, tread slowly and softly down the stairs, and close the front door. I took up Aunt Lily next, and then Nancy. Aunt Lily sobbed as she went upstairs, 'What shall we do without her, we shall be all lost kiddies,' and Nancy said, tight-lipped, 'Why do they make such a fuss about murder when ordinary death is so terrible?' But they came out of the room like flowers that had been cut a long time before and had now been put in water. Miss Beevor only went up because Mamma asked for her. To the last she said that she did not want to trouble Mamma, and as I brought her into the room she cried out harshly, 'I wanted to stay away from you because I knew I should have to bother you with a question. But you are the only person I have ever told about that horrible thing I once did. Is it fair for me to go on being friends with Mary and Rose without telling them?'

Mamma cried out sharply, 'Do not tell them.'

'But they might not like me any more if they knew,' said poor Miss Beevor.

'Do not start being stupid now,' squeaked Mamma. 'They will like you for ever. Must you always be a fool? Oh, forgive me, how rude I have always been, so rude to you. But let that thing die. Come close, my dear, I want to thank you for everything. My dear Bayahtreechay.'

They all left us. The night closed in on the house, the clocks ticked away. Kate came up from the kitchen, she had not changed into her black afternoon dress, she wore a clean print and a clean cap and apron, and with Rosamund's uniform and Constance's overall the room was full of stiff white linen, that spoke when they moved; and on the white sheets lay our dark and withered mother. The future was a desert except for music. But even so it was astonishing there was so wild an anguish in us. She had married late, she was now old, we had known her to be ill for a long time, all people die, yet we felt as if she were the first person to die, and we the first people to suffer a beloved's death. But suddenly Rosamund smiled, and we knew it was a sign of wonder.

Mamma spoke faintly, 'I wish my body would spit me out of its mouth.'

'Tell us what to do with your body,' said Rosamund.

'It is dreadful that I am lying down. I feel as if I were falling through the bed but cannot fall.'

'You would like to sit up?'

'Yes. But of course I cannot. It would hurt too much.'

'No. Kate and I can do it.'

'God, help me to do this,' said Kate, and put her hands under Mamma's body with the extremest gentleness, and Rosamund took the pillows and sat where they had been, swivelling herself round so that Mamma could lie back and lean her body against her breast. Now our cousin was not white and tired any more, she was beautiful and golden and content, and against her broad fairness Mamma rested like a twisted branch. It might have been that Rosamund had been walking on a beach and had picked up a piece of driftwood that was in the shape of something sacred, and she was showing it to us. 'This is heavenly, this is joy,' murmured Mamma. 'Mary, Rose, move away a little further, I might be able to see you. No, a little nearer. No, it is no use. Never mind.' But a little later she whimpered, 'My hands are cold, they are so cold they ache.' Constance and Kate knelt on each side of the bed and gently warmed her hands with theirs, and she was quiet. But suddenly there was no gratitude coming from her, neither towards Rosamund nor to the two who had been warming her hands, and she was not thinking of us. It seemed that she was dead, though her eyes still seemed to see. Then she scourged the whole room with one of her flashing looks and cried, 'Yes, yes, it is not so yet, but it should be so,' and she sped from us like an arrow. Kate and Constance started to their feet and threw up their hands in wonder, and Rosamund, smiling, clasped the relic closer to her breast.